EXODUS: EMPIRES AT WAR

BOOK 1

A Tale of Interstellar Warfare

by

Doug Dandridge

The ship rocked again and Lt Commander Maurice von Rittersdorf cursed under his breath. The tactical display showed that the two functional privateers were ranging to either side of him. *Smart*, he thought, since the *HIMS Johann Peterson* (DD 26575) was weak on one side's shields thanks to a couple of lucky hits in the early stages of the battle. So the ships were attacking from opposite sides, forcing him to absorb the attack of one of the one hundred twenty thousand ton ships on the weak side instead of rolling the ship to face them with strength.

"We might still be able to outrun them," chimed in the exec, Lt. SG Katherine Schuler, from the CIC.

"We've lost too much to guarantee that," said the Captain, looking at the schematic representation flashing red with damage. Including two of the stern impeller units, the spatial grabbers that propelled every Imperial vessel. She'd had a good seventy gee advantage coming into the fight, which was how she had run them down in the first place when they had broken away from the tramp freighter they were in the process of taking as a prize. "And we would have to run away with our stern to their fire for a good hour if they decided to pursue."

The one bit of good news to this fiasco was the third enemy vessel that was floating dead in space. The old *Johann Peterson's* gunnery had been good enough to take her out of the equation with one good volley of all three laser rings, followed by a pair of hundred megaton warheads to the hull.

"Ship A is firing," yelled the tactical officer, and the screen colored in the invisible beams of photons converging on the two hundred thousand ton destroyer. The vessel's computer adjusted the electromag field and its cold plasma matrix to intercept as best as possible. One of the incoming beams hit the field at the perfect angle, was bent around the destroyer, and radiated in the opposite direction, nearly striking Ship B. The other hit dead center. Some was stopped by plasma that superheated under the beam. The light that made it through the plasma was spread from a fifty centimeter pinpoint to a ten meter diameter spotlight. Heat was pumped into the hull, some armor boiled away, but much of the beam was reflected back by the nanoparticle skin which shifted to the proper alignment for that particular wavelength.

If only Fredrickson were here, thought the Commander of the warship. But her consort destroyer had made for the nearest military system with a malfunctioning hyperdrive generator, only able to creep along in Hyper III. And von Ritterdorf, as senior commander of the pair, had decided to continue the patrol on his own, against common sense. And then the encounter with three privateers. At that point there was no choice, as the protection of civilian shipping was the primary rational for this kind of patrol, even to the point of sacrificing his ship and crew.

"Returning fire," yelled Ensign Lasardo, the tactical officer, as two strong beams from the A and B rings struck out at the ship. The double hundred megawatt beams, slightly less in the B ring which had sustained some damage, struck the pirate perfectly along its engineering section. Superheated alloy and atmosphere gushed from the enemy's hull, followed by a bright secondary explosion as energies were released within the vessel.

"Missiles," yelled the Captain "and bring all lasers to fire on Ship B."

Cast of Characters

The Exodus III

Admiral Quong Lee: Commander of the Exodus III
Lt. Commander Deborah Blake: com officer
Admiral Molotov: Commander of covering force
Lieutenant Krishnamurta: helm
High Captain Mrrashatana Zzrathrasensi: Commander of Ca'cada pursuit force
Admiral Chang Lee: Fourth grandson of Quong
Chief Engineer Sandra Stoops-Lee: Chang's wife
Science Officer *Horace Mgumba*
Chief of Security, *Jamal Streeter*
Head Councilwoman *Elizabeth Hampton*

The Capital

Emperor Augustine Ogden Lee Romanov I: 31st ruler of the Empire of New Terra. Born Year 933 (67 years old). Crowned in Year 994, after the death of the Emperor Justinian I.
Empress Annastasia Romanov: Wife of Augustine.
Crown Prince Dimetre Ogden Lee Romanov
Princess Amanda: wife of Dimetre
Prime Minister Count Mejoris Jeraviki: Leader of the Lords and Opposition to the Emperor.
Roberto Espano:, deep conditioning programmer.
Archduke Frederich Mgana: political affiliate of PM
Grand High Admiral Gabriel Len Lenkowski: the Chief of Naval Operations
Field Marshal Betty Parker: Commandant of the Imperial Marine Corps
Grand Marshal Mishori Yamakuri: Army Chief of Staff.
Prince Henry: The Spare.

HIMS *Duke Roger Sergiov II (BB 1458)*

Chief Petty Officer First Jana Gorbachev: Chief of Laser Ring B.

Petty Officer Martinez

Lt SG "Count" Jasper Bettencourt: Son of a count and friends with Sean.

Lt. Constance Salvatore

Ensign Connie Caldwell

Lt. Commander Bryson Popodopolous

Captain Sebastian Ngano: Captain of the *Sergiov.*

Lieutenant SG Prince Sean Ogden Lee Romanov: Born Year 971 (29 years old). Fifth child and the third son of the Emperor Augustine Romanov, serving as a weapons officer on HIMS Duke Roger Sergiov II (BB 1458)

HIMS *Joan de Arc (HBC 2984)*

Captain Dame Mye Lei: Commander of HIMS Joan de Arc (HBC 2984). Member Fourth Fleet Scout Force. Born Year 936 (64 years old).

Commander Xavier Jackson: XO.

HIMS *Johann Peterson (DD 26575)/Dot McArthur, DDF 63587*

Lt Commander Maurice von Rittersdorf: Commander HIMS Johann Peterson (DD 26575). Born Year 962 (38 years old).   then Commander H VII Destroyer *Dot MacArthur.*

Lt. SG Katherine Schuler: XO, then commander, *Johann Peterson.*

Ensign Lasardo: tactical officer

HIMS *Seastag (Stealth/Attack 421)*

Commander Bryce Suttler: Commander HIMS Seastag (Stealth Attack 421). One of new generation of wormhole sink stealth attacks. Born Year 955 (45 years old).

Lieutenant SG Walter Ngovic. Tactical

The Donut

Doctor Lucille Yu, PhD: Assistant Chief Scientist and engineer of the *Donut* Project. Born Year 928 (72 years old).

Dr. Rafael Gomez: Negative Matter Engineer.

Dr. Baxter: Chief of Administration.

Sestius IV, F2 Star

Cornelius Walborski: New settler and farmer to frontier world Sestius VI, and member of the local militia. Born Year 973 (27 years old)., *from New Detroit, now Neu Romney*

Katlyn Walborski: Cornelius' wife.

Sergeant McFadden: his squad leader

Doctor Jennifer Conway: Physician and fiancé' of Captain Glen McKinnon.

Captain Glen McKinnon: Captain Imperial Marine Corps.

Senior Sergeant Hogan: Imperial Marine Corps NCO.

Commodore Chung: the system commander

Colonel Klein (brigadier): Commander of Imperial Army Garrison Sestius at Willoughby (the capital).

Lt. Colonel Samantha Thomas: commander of the independent medium infantry battalion

Captain Laura Montenegro: Battle Fort commander

Corporal Sheila McMurty: militia

Montano Montero: Steadholder

Conundrum III: Sector Four HQ.

Grand Fleet Admiral Duke Taelis Mgonda: Admiral in command of 4th Naval District. Born Year 863 (137 years old).

Field Marshal Maxwell: Sector Four Ground Force Commander.

Captain Henninman (Hen): Adjutant.

Commander Nagaya: Intelligence Officer.

Massadara III: Fleet Base, Port Massadara

Vice Admiral The Countess Esmeralda Gonzalez: System commander.

Major General McKenzie Zhukov: System Army Commander.

Captain Jessica Frazier: Senior system flight officer.

HIMS Archduchess Constance Leonardo

Admiral Sir Gunter Heinrich: Commander Task Group 4.9.

Beria: Admiral Heinrich's Steward.

Captain Maria Steinman: CO of Leonardo.

Captain Myra Lamborgini: Flag Captain Task Group 4.9.

Janaikasa

Major Samuel Baggett: Executive Officer, First of the 789th Infantry (Light), 988th Infantry Division. Born Year 941 (59 years old). (Colonel at Sestius, Frederick defense).

Lieutenant Kreiger: Weapons Officer Under Baggett.

Brigadier General Alphonso Marquett: Interim Commander 789th Infantry.

Sergeant Major Terry Zacharias: Senior NCO in Baggett's battalion, and on Sestius.

Ca'cadasans

Great Admiral Miierrowanasa M'tinisasitow: Ca'cadasan conquest fleet commander. Born 2843 AD (1,418 years old).

Fraggaraata Zre'ghattasa IX: Emperor of the Ca'cadasan Empire. Born 1940 AD (2,321 years old). Son of the sitting Emperor at the time of human contact, older brother to the Prince killed in human contact.

Pod Leader Klesshakendriakka

Low Admiral Hrisshammartanama

Pod Leader Llillissarada'ing

Elysium

Archduke Horatio Alexanderopolis: His Imperial Majesty's Ambassador to the Court of the Elysium Empire. Born Year 821 (179 years old).

High Lord Grarakakak, Brakakak: High Lord of Elysium Empire.

HICS (His Imperial Czar's Ship) Ekaterina

Lt. Commander Kathomas Hubbard: Commander.

Others

Ahmadhi-ghasta Mallakan: Grand High Bishop of Lasharan Jakarja Lashana (Church of the Gods Vengeful). Born Year 915 (85 years old).

Ensign Mark O'Brien: copilot fighter Heraklion III

Timeline

2151 AD: Hiro Yamamoto discovers subspace portal generator. Opens subspace dimension to transport of human colonists.

2160 AD: Alpha Centauri B4 colony established.

2173 AD: Tau Ceti III colony established.

2208 AD: Humanity has spread to eight inhabitable systems within 20 light years of Sol.

2250 AD: 12 million humans living outside of the solar system.

2254 AD: First contact with Ca'cadasans on Epsilon Iridani V. Human colony destroyed without warning or trace. Incoming ship discovers colony destroyed and runs back to human space with news.

2256 AD: Human colony at Altair V attacked and destroyed.

2257 AD: United Solar System Fleet established to fight alien threat.

2260 AD: Battle of Tau Ceti, humans meet Ca'cadasans with a five to one advantage in mass and are handily defeated.

2261 AD: Construction started on the six Exodus ships to allow some of humanity to make it to safety outside of human space.

2264 AD: Ca'cadasans, having destroyed all of humanity's colonies, attack the solar system in force. Five completed Exodus ships attempt to leave the system under heavy escort. Two are destroyed before they can make it into subspace. Two enter subspace with pursuit, while Exodus III makes a clean breakaway into subspace.

2264 - 3260 AD: The Long Voyage. With several

fueling stops and explorations, Exodus III travels along the galactic rim and toward the core, traversing 9,760 light years from Sol.

3261 AD: Supersystem discovered, along with remains of ancient civilization that had once owned it.   First human colony founded on Jewel.   Year 1 of New Human Empire.

3268 AD (Year 8):   Humans make contact with traveling merchant ship from Elysium Empire. Discover thriving civilizations that sprung from the ancient civilization that used to inhabit the Supersystem.

3361 AD (Year 100):   Population 2,000,000+. Establishment of the Fleet.

3460 AD (Year 199):   Beginning of Terraforming projects around super system.

3573 to 3579 AD (Year 312 to 318): First Gardasian War, human victory.

3589 to 3592 AD (Year 328 to 331): Second Gardasian War, human victory, Gardasian race absorbed into human empire.

3619 to 3621 AD (Year 358 to 361): First Markanan War, human victory.

3669 to 3676 AD (Year 408 to 415): Second Markanan War, human victory, Markanans absorbed into human empire.

3696 to 3698 AD (Year 435 to 437): Kiniman War, Kiniman race absorbed into the human empire.

3724 to 3733 AD (Year 463 to 472): First Crakastan War, human victory.

3744 to 3762 AD (Year 483 to 501): First Lasharan War, human victory.

3772 to 3784 AD (Year 511 to 523): Second Lasharan War, human victory.

3797 to 3801 AD (Year 536 to 540): First Margravi War, human victory.

3803 to 3808 AD (Year 542 to 547): War of Revolt, Imperial Victory, 150 million humans leave Empire to found Republic of Mankind.

3809 to 3814 AD (Year 548 to 553): Civil War, Constance the Great triumphs over Cassius the Terrible (II).

3815 AD (Year 554): New Constitution establishes Constitutional Monarchy. (Bill of Freedoms added in Year 607).

3841 to 3846 AD (Year 585 to 590). Machine Revolt. Human built autonomous robots rebel against humanity. Billions die before revolt stopped, Man in the Loop Law enacted.

3848 to 3853 AD (Year 587 to 592). Second Crakastan War, human victory.

3873 to 3876 AD (Year 612 to 615): Third Cracastan War, human victory.

3892 to 3897 AD (Year 631 to 635): Second Margravi War, human victory, ends with alliance of Margravi and Klashak with human empire.

3913 to 3936 AD (Year 652 to 673): First Galactic War (against Lashar, Crakasta and Fenri).

3984 AD (Year 723): *Donut* Project approved and construction planning begins.

3984 to 4000 AD (Year 723 to 739): Elysium War, marginal human victory.

4007 to 4008 AD (Year 746 to 747): War of Man, humanity (Imperium) against humanity (Republic). Political pressures bring an end to short, sharp war.

4009 to 4114 AD (Year 748 to 853): The Century of Peace. Empire involved in no extra empire or border hostilities.

4065 AD (Year 804):   Dissidents from New Terra Republic found the Grand Duchy of New Moscow.

4114 to 4131 AD (Year 853 to 870): Second Galactic War, Elysium, Lashar and Fenri against Empire, New Terra and Margrave/Klashak, human victory.

4167 to 4180 AD (Year 906 to 921): Third Galactic War, humanity's victory.

4206 to 4216 AD (Year 945 to 955): Klang Consortium attacks New Moscow. Empire of Terra and Republic of New Terra come in on New Moscow's side.

4256 AD (Year 985):   *Donut* Generates first working wormhole gate.

4261 AD (Year 1000): Empire celebrates 1000 years of existence and growth.

Prologue

Admiral Quong Lee looked into the bridge viewer while he wiped a tear from his eye. The mushroom clouds of the kinetic strikes rose over his beloved homeland. The China of the Ming, Chin and Han would never again exist. Firestorms were raging over the Asian Continent, as well as the rest of the world of his birth. Never again would the beautiful globe of Earth be the harbor of the life it had taken four billion years to evolve. Of course this was all four hours in the past, the time it took light to span the distance to the far outer system from the inner. In a way that made it worse, as Lee imagined how much greater the devastation was in real time.

"Sir," said the com officer, Lt. Commander Deborah Blake, grasping tight the arms of her couch in front of her console, looking over at the grieving commander of the mission to save humanity. "Admiral Molotov wishes to speak with you."

Time for grief later, thought the graying Chinese officer. Now he had to focus all of his attention on the *Exodus III,* and the precious cargo she held. Two of the *Exodus* craft had already been destroyed attempting to get into subspace. Another had been chased by Ca'cadasan ships through the dimensional rift, and so could be counted as gone. The other might have made it, but he couldn't be sure. So as far as he knew he had the last of the seed of humanity in the thirty megaton vessel that pulsed beneath this control room, flying toward the point where she could disappear from normal space.

"Admiral," said Lee, looking at the heavy set

Russian on the right side of the viewer. A tactical display took up the left side, showing the battleship, two cruisers and half dozen destroyers of the other Admiral's command. And the vector arrows of the fifteen Ca'cadasan ships that out massed the Earth force by more than ten times.

"You must enter subspace as soon as feasible," replied the large man in accented English. "There is at least one subspace capable ship in the approaching force."

Lee nodded and checked the display near his command chair. Seventy eight seconds before they could make the jump. And the enemy ships would be close by that time. Very close. Only one of the enemy ships' vector arrows had the hash marks of a subspace drive over it. All of the enemy ships of course would use hyperspace, allowing them to get from here to there in the universe much faster than the more primitive subspace drive the humans were capable of producing. But several in the enemy fleet had been outfitted with an auxiliary subspace drive to allow them to track and destroy human vessels that tried to escape through the lower dimension. Like this ship.

"Do your best, Admiral," said Lee, looking his old friend in the eye.

"Do your best to get the race to safety," said the other man, looking over his shoulder for a second as a quick frown crossed his face. He looked back at the man whose vessel his were to sacrifice themselves for. "We'll keep them off you long enough. But get your ass out of this space and free and clear. And may your ancestors avenge us when the day comes. Molotov out."

"May the Gods bless you," whispered Lee as he

watched the vector arrows head for his ship, impossible acceleration figures in the multiple hundreds of gravities glaring under the points. The forward viewer shifted to a magnified view of the approaching enemy. The view shifted back, and *Bismark* was centered in the human formation waiting for the closing death.

One of the human destroyers flared with white hot vapor when incoming lasers struck the hull. The ship tried to intercept the beams with its electromag field projected out into a compact shield. The light bending field attenuated the lasers slightly, spreading them from ravening pinpoints to larger circles meters in diameter. But they were still too much for the smaller and weaker vessel, which continued to gout vapor while internal explosions ripped through the ship. And then it was gone in a flare of fire when the fusion reactor exploded. Dozens of other flares erupted through the spreading wreckage as the warheads it had carried detonated in sympathetic fury.

"They're too much for us," cried Lieutenant Krishnamurta from the helm, his wide eyes looking over his shoulder at the Admiral.

Lee nodded his head even as he shot the officer a furious glare for voicing the obvious. The aliens were many centuries ahead of the humans in technology, if not millennium. It was as if a tribe of Zulus were attacking a division of twentieth century European armor. And the result was just as forgone.

The human fleet rippled off a spread of missiles, followed by another, hundred megaton warheads streaking at a hundred gravities toward the approaching enemy fleet. Within seconds half of the several hundred missiles flared and died as their warheads were overloaded with the heat of defensive lasers. Counter missiles, leaping out at thousands of gravities of acceleration, took out the remaining weapons.

"Fifty seconds to translation," called out the nervous voice of Lieutenant Krishnamurta. Two more destroyers died on the screen as the words left the helmsman's mouth.

Hold them, thought Lee while he watched the battle on the viewer through narrowed eyes, his hands shaking on the arm rests of his couch. *Less than a minute now. Hold them.*

But he knew that even if they held that the enemy battleship, a monster that must have massed over twenty million tons, would translate after them and blow them out of subspace. That ship was the threat, and if it wasn't stopped mankind would be stopped in its tracks, forgotten for eternity.

*   *   *

High Captain Mrrashatana Zzrathrasensi stared into the viewer as his ships bore down on the human force. Several of the human ships flickered and died when his warships blasted through their pathetic electromagnetic screens, while his vessels' much more powerful shields of the same nature bent and attenuated their pitiful attacks.

"How long until we are within range of the cattle ship," he said in a deep rumble, flexing the muscles of his upper true limbs while stretching his middle limbs.

"Within five twelves of seconds, my lord" answered the weapons officer, showing his tusks in a smile.

"Doesn't matter," said the senior centurion, standing his three meter height behind the captain's chair. "We will go into the lower dimension to follow them if need be, and then they will be grata fodder.

And their race will have paid for it deception and temerity."

"I would prefer to keep them from getting there," growled the Captain, looking at the tactical plot that was thrown up by his chair mounted viewer. "The Emperor wants none of these to escape. And none to survive, less the few thousand we bring from the planet back to the throne as trophies."

The poor beasts knew not what they were about, thought the Captain, watching as two more of the smaller enemy vessels died in antimatter explosions when powerful missiles struck them. In the thousands of years that his people had walked the path of Empire, conquering and subjugating hundreds of races, only twelve had been marked for the total destruction of their civilization. But the cowardly attack by the members of the first system taken from the humans, the detonation of a nuclear warhead under the lander that carried a son of the Emperor, when they had already surrendered. That was too much. That had doomed their race. It had even doomed their planet. Destroying planets was something the race normally didn't engage in, seeing living worlds as sacred. But it was decided that nothing of their gene pool would survive, not the slightest trace of DNA from their world's bacteria. And soon he would render their last forlorn hope a dying memory in the glorious history of his race.

"The enemy refugee vessel is generating heat at a prodigious rate," said the tactical officer.

"They must be preparing to jump," stated the centurion. "I wonder why they have not already gone into the lower dimension?"

"They are relatively new to interstellar travel,"

stated the tactical officer. "They probably are still working with unsophisticated equipment."

"And they won't get any more sophisticated," snarled the Captain, watching the distance close. "Such is the decree of the Emperor."

Warrior officers growled in agreement, and the scales on the Captain's head rose up in response to the anger pheromones filling the air of the bridge.

*   *   *

"We're being pounded, sir," called the chief engineer over the com system. Molotov rocked in the command chair as another gigaton warhead detonated near the ship. *Bismark* was a tough ship, as heavily armored a vessel as man had ever built. But the enemy was of a higher class, and his weapons were tearing the ship apart.

"The bridge is gone," called an unknown officer over the com. "The Captain's dead."

"Route all controls through the flag bridge," ordered the Admiral. He looked at a smaller repeater where a senior officer awaited his orders. "Keep your ship in front of *Exodus III*," ordered Molotov to the shaken officer. "We don't matter. *Exodus* does."

The officer nodded, then threw a quick salute as the image jerked from impact. *Not that a heavy cruiser will last long,* thought the Admiral, shaking his head as the ship shuddered again. *But hopefully they won't need all that long.*

The ship jerked hard as another warhead struck the hardened nanocarbon armor. Molotov felt his consciousness fade for a moment when his head flew back into the neck cushion. He shook his head with the smell of blood in his nostrils and the feeling of grogginess that comes with a concussion. The relative darkness of the emergency lights greeted his sight.

"Weapons and shields are down sir," called the chief engineer over a circuit loaded with static.

"Do we have maneuvering?" asked the Admiral through the fog in his head. He could smell the burning insulation of circuitry, adding to the nausea that threatened to spill the contents of his stomach to the floor.

"Yes sir," agreed the engineer. "I have full power to the engines."

"Shift total control to my console," ordered the Admiral. "And get everyone off this ship. You have thirty to get off the ship or die."

The flag bridge crew looked over at the Admiral through the smoky atmosphere, several shaking their heads.

"I know it's not enough time," said the Admiral, punching commands into the control system. "But it's all I've got to give you."

"We'll stay then, sir," said the Flag Lieutenant, nodding at the rest of the staff. "Might as well see the whole show through."

"Thank you ladies and gentlemen," said the Admiral, tears flowing from his eyes as he set the last command and hit the commit key, setting the timer in motion. "It was a pleasure serving with you. May the first one to hell get them ready for the rest that will follow."

*   *   *

"*Bismark* is dead in space, Admiral," called the tactical officer, Lt. Commander Wilhelm looking over white faced from her station.

"Fifteen seconds to translation," said Krisnamurta in a shaking voice. "We're not going to make it."

We have to make it, thought Admiral Lee, looking at the tactical plot.   One heavy cruiser was still running interference, while a pair of destroyers continued to fire from the fringe.   But all of the enemy ships were gaining, and their fire was coming in fast and heavy.

"All shield power focused to the stern," he cried out, realizing that the tactical officer had already done it.   But he had to do something, even to make him feel like he was doing something of worth.   *Please, dear Gods, get us through this,* he prayed silently to Gods who hadn't seemed to listen to any of humanity's recent entreaties.

*   *   *

"We have them," cried High Captain Zzrathrasensi, watching as the largest human warship started spouting life pods.   *Not that it will do him any good,* he thought, watching as lasers destroyed most of those pods.   "Cease fire on the life pods," he ordered, scowling at his tactical officer.   "Remember, we need some trophies to present to the Emperor."

"Be kinder to blow them out of space," said the tactical officer in a soft voice.

The Admiral inclined his head in the affirmative. It would indeed be kinder.   But kindness was not the order of the day.

"Prepare to open fire on the refugee ship."   The human battleship was coasting dead in space on its last vector, toward the Ca'cadasan force, but with enough side vector to miss handily.   They could come back for it at their leisure.

"Sir," cried the tactical officer, a look of surprise on his face.   "The battleship is generating a large quantity of energy.   Their fusion plants are running full out."

"What," said the Captain, looking over at the side

screen that displayed the battleship. Just in time to see it turn into a streak heading straight for his ship.

* * *

Human inertial compensators were primitive as compared to those of the Ca'cada. At most they could absorb about ten gravities worth of energy, allowing the ships to accelerate much faster than otherwise, though still laughably slow compared to the more advanced race. But human reactionless drive, the grabbers of the fabric of space, could still generate as much acceleration as the energy available to them.

Every bit of energy from *Bismark's* four, one hundred gigawatt fusion plants were fed into the grabbers, along with all of the energy held by the subatomic battery packs. The ship lurched forward at three hundred gravities, two point nine four kilometers per second per second. Every living being on the ship was mashed to jelly against the bulkheads, but the computer brain of the ship kept it on the last programmed course. A quartet of hundred megaton fusion warheads rocketed ahead of the ship at four hundred gravities, detonating as they cleared ten kilometers in front of the vessel. Four more followed, then four more, followed by the remaining three, creating a screen of nuclear fury between the plunging ship and the enemy vessels.

Nine hundred thousand tons of battleship flew toward the largest alien vessel. Within seconds it was hit by lasers. Missiles locked on. As the first missiles approached the fusion plants of the ship went hypercritical, detonating with gigatons of explosive power and blasting the front section of the ship forward. The ship broke up into pieces under the combined assault of alien weapons and its own overloading fusion explosion. But the pieces, including one large section of almost a hundred thousand tons, flew into the alien flagship at a closing speed of over a thousand kilometers a second.

The alien ship was made of alloys and composites much stronger than those of the human ship. It massed over twenty times that of the intact battleship. And it acted much as a man wearing body armor hit by a blast of fast traveling fletchets would act. Holes appeared in the heavy outer armor, and some of the pieces penetrated into the interior. The majority of the damage was done to the outer hull, including the projectors of the subspace drive above the armor.

Several of the escorting enemy were also hit, incurring minor damage, and in one case heavy damage from the shotgun blast. The flag was temporarily out of the fight, but the remainder could still fire. And they unleashed a storm of missiles, accelerating at over a thousand gravities toward the fleeing human colony ship.

*   *   *

Cheers erupted on the bridge of the *Exodus III* as the viewers brought the image of the remains of *Bismark* impacting the only alien ship in range that could follow them into subspace. Lee allowed himself to join in the cheer even as he thought that he had witnessed the death of his old friend and hundreds of Terran Naval personnel.

"They're firing at us," yelled the tactical officer as hundreds of vector arrows appeared on the display, tracking the messengers of death released by the opponent. "Impact in twelve seconds."

"Time to safe entry to subspace," yelled Lee.

The helmsman gave a quick check to his readout

and looked up with a wide eyed stare.

"Sixteen seconds," he said in a hushed voice.

"Translate now," yelled the Admiral. "Don't think about it. Just do it."

"Aye sir," said the helmsman, punching in the override buttons to start the process.

"Eight, seven, six," tolled the tactical officer as the helmsman worked furiously. "Five, four, three."

"Translation now," yelled the helmsman as he punched the final commit. Bridge lights dimmed as the subspace gravitational projectors sucked all available energy into their systems.

Outside of the ship the projectors sent out a wave of gravitons that ripped open the fabric of space. The opening appeared in front of the moving ship, revealing the reddish backdrop of the lower dimension which allowed faster travel between the stars. The huge vessel slid into the other dimension with a slight shudder, the hole in space revealing the bright flecked blackness of the normal universe behind.

"Two, one," continued the tactical officer as the hole behind the ship closed in the faces of the incoming missiles, which continued on into the outer reaches of the Ort Cloud, their lock on the target permanently lost.

"I knew that safety margin was too conservative," said the now smiling helmsman, wiping the sweat off of his brow. Lee smiled back, knowing that they had escaped death. And knowing that they would be long gone and untraceable in the maelstrom of subspace before the enemy could get anything else into the chase. Humankind now had a chance of survival, if they could get enough distance between them and the enemy, find a home, and rebuild.

* * *

Exodus III and her sisters were the largest starships ever built by humanity to that point.   Her inertial compensators could handle five gees of acceleration, allowing her to maintain six gees while the crew was comfortable at a subjective one gravity field.   But Admiral Lee was not one to take chances, and *Exodus III*, thirty million tons of ship, accelerated at eight gees for a week, crushing the three hundred crew in a subjective three gravity field.   And allowing the ship to add two hundred eighty-two kilometers per second to its velocity every hour.   Or forty-seven thousand kilometers per second (.158 c) during the week.   After which the ship throttled back down to six gees for several months of acceleration.

The speed of light was still the limiting factor in subspace, and objects traveling near the speed of light had to move through the wave of radiation that was the subjectively fast traveling particles the ship encountered, further limiting its maximum velocity. But subspace corresponded to real space in a ratio of one to twelve, meaning that traveling one light year in subspace would put the ship twelve light years from its starting point in normal space.   With its material and electromagnetic field shielding, *Exodus* could sustain point nine two c, or a normal space correspondence of about eleven light years every year.

And we're all there is, thought Lee, planning the future voyage in his head.   Three hundred crew.   Fifty thousand refugees in cryo-stasis, with an average age of twenty-six years and an average IQ of 138.   Doctors, scientists, farmers, warriors, the cream of the human race representing all major races and most ethnic groups.   Another fifty thousand mind downloads along with the genetic material to clone those from whom the downloads came. A sperm bank along with three million eggs. The genetic material of all known life forms on the eight living worlds that humanity had explored.

The ship's computers held the sum total knowledge of the human race. Not just every scientific discovery or engineering schematic. But all of the literature from the smallest underground comic to the classic plays of the Greeks. Hundreds of millions of hours of video and audio. All of the great works of art and architecture. As well as several thousand original paintings and sculptures scattered around the ship.

Enough to make a new start for the human race without turning our backs on the past, thought the Admiral. *If we can get far enough away from those who would destroy us.*

"A century should get us a thousand light years away," said Krishnamurta, the helmsman. "Surely that will be enough."

"I don't think so," said Marcus Streeter, the chief engineer. "They'll find us in no time. And we will need time to build our population and our strength before we meet again."

"A thousand years," said Lee in a tone that invited no discussion, looking at the schematic of a captured Ca'cadasan inertial compensator on the viewer in front of him. One of many devices humanity would need to reverse engineer in order to meet the aliens on more equal ground. The aliens didn't seem to progress at the same speed as mankind. Probably the result of the stagnation of a long term Imperia, and the lack of challenging opponents. *Hopefully that will allow us to catch up before they find us*, thought Lee, resigning himself and the awake crew to death aboard the starship.

"Excuse me sir," said Krishnamurta, raising an

eyebrow. "A millennium?"

"Yes," said Lee, nodding his head. "Ten thousand light years. That should give us five hundred years of development and consolidation to get ready to greet our friends."

"But, we'll all be dead by then," cried the helmsman, his face turning pale.

"Our lives are not important," said Streeter, and most of the other heads around the conference table nodded in agreement. "What is important is that the race survive. That the life that our mother world produced survives."

"That is how it will be," said Lee, meeting each of the officers' eyes in sequence. "Anyone who does not want to put the race first can elect to be let off at the first habitable world we pass, in a shuttle, with their share of supplies."

There were no takers to that last offer, and Lee had known there would not be.

*   *   *

Admiral Chang Lee, the great to the fourth grandson of Admiral Quong Lee, sat at the briefing table while the holographic representation of the system slowly rotated in the holo tank.

"It's beautiful," said the Admiral's wife, Chief Engineer Sandra Stoops-Lee, her eyes wide with wonder. "More than six habitable planets, and a dozen or so more that could be terraformed."

"And all orbiting a great black hole," said the science officer, Horace Mgumba, with a frown. "That could be hazardous."

"Or a great resource," said Lee, looking at the visual of seven stars in stable orbit around the black hole.

"Protocol dictates that we awaken the governing council before a decision is reached," said the Chief of Security, Jamal Streeter. "Unless you want to move as we have spoken."

"Take the crown, my husband," urged Sandra, as those assembled about the table nodded agreement. "Why should we have suffered this long voyage, to have seen our grandparents and parents die in space, just so those who passed the years in comfort could rule us."

"Yes, my lord," said Streeter, slapping his side arm with a large hand. "We who have sacrificed should rule."

"Agreed," said the Admiral with a nod of his head, standing up to signify that the meeting was at an end. "We will settle on one of these planets. Wake the head councilwoman that we might make the new order known."

*   *   *

Head Councilwoman Elizabeth Hampton opened her eyes to the glaring lamps of the resurrection room, drawing a deep breath into her awakening lungs and reveling in the stiffness that indicated she was alive. *We made it*, she thought. She had wondered when she went under if she would die in cold storage, either blasted to atoms by their enemies with the ship around her, or ending her existence in a system malfunction.

Hampton closed her eyes, opened them, and turned her gaze on the middle aged Chinese man who stood above her. *He has a passing resemblance to his ancestor*, she thought, recalling Admiral Quong Lee.

"How long," she croaked, coughing the remainder of the freezing liquid that had helped to preserve her cells from her lungs.

"A thousand years, Ms. Hampton," said the man in a deep voice. "We are at our new home, ten thousand light years from Earth."

"Our new home?," she said in a confused tone. She shook her head. "That is for us to decide, Captain," said the woman, attempting to raise herself from the table. "Wake the other councilors, and give us access to your databases."

"I'm sorry, Ms. Hampton," said the man, shaking his head as his cold eyes looked into her's. "Things have changed since you went under. There is a new government, and I am it."

Chapter 1

When mankind discovered Subspace we thought we had found the ultimate solution to interstellar travel. The dimension corresponded to what we consider normal space on a 12.1 to 1 ratio, meaning for every kilometer traveled in that strange space, we traversed 12.1 kilometers in our space. It seemed to be empty of anything we would consider matter. We later found out that matter as we know it could not exist in that space, that energy needed to be expended to protect ships traveling the dimension. Anything not so protected was ejected from that space, in a manner that we considered violent at the time, which was to prove in no way as violent as the next discovery. Mankind voyaged to other worlds and planted colonies, which even communicated with each other through couriers at faster than light. It still took months to years for messages to get from sender to receiver, depending on the distance. But not the many years it would have otherwise. Yes, in those days mankind thought they had found the ultimate means of travel, just as they had thought such of the Clipper, the railroad, the airplane, and then the fusion drive spaceship. And again they were wrong. Hyperspace lay around the corner. Unfortunately it was already in the hands of a power that wanted to subjugate us.

Lecture at the Imperial Naval Academy, Peal Island, Jewel, Year 945.

"Nine hundred and fifty billion beings," said the Emperor Augustine Ogden Lee Romanov, thirty first ruler of the Empire of New Terra, placing his glass on the table in front of him. "I rule nine hundred and fifty billion beings, over seven hundred billion of them human. And all in deadly danger that those fools in the Lords won't recognize."

"You really believe the Ca'cadasans are still a threat?" said the red haired young woman sitting in the lounger to his right, swirling her drink as she watched the holographic fireworks over the skies of Capitulum.

"Of course he does, my dear wife," answered the younger image of the Emperor sitting across the table, his long black hair blowing in the night breeze. "We've talked about this before. It's only a matter of time before they find us."

Most of the three billion citizens of the capital city of the Empire are simply enjoying the celebration, thought the Emperor, watching a kilometers wide dragon chasing another through the sky. *A thousand years of human civilization, unparalleled growth and advancement. And the average citizen in the street thinks the ancient enemy the boogie man. A legend to scare children in their night beds. While there are enough real alien threats in the space that borders their own systems to command their attention.*

"You really think they will be a threat to the Empire, father?" asked the Crown Prince Dimetre Ogden Lee Romanov, his piercing blue eyes looking out of his classic Eurasian face. "After all of these years? Surely they have forgotten all about us by now."

"No," cried the Emperor, slamming his glass down on the table, splashing expensive Imperial Brandy on the surface. The security agents all flinched, their eyes automatically scanning the surrounding gardens of the Prince's palace. "No." The Emperor shook his head as he stared into space for a moment, then turned his gaze onto his eldest son.

"I thought I had taught you better, boy," he growled, watching the Prince's face fall at the rebuke. "As my father before me, and his father before him, I have sworn an oath to never forget that the destruction of the human race lies just over the horizon."

Augustine I looked out over the multitude of lights that shone in the night, the magnificent capital of his Empire. Streams of bright beads danced in the sky as air-cars carried people to gatherings all through the city on this night of celebration. Looking to the south he spied the strobes of a shuttle coming down from space to the final approach on Constance the Great Spaceport. One of thousands a week that landed at the capital, carrying travelers and tourists and the goods that kept the overpopulated world alive. Above the lights and fireworks was the glory of the many nearby nebula, signs of supernova that had occurred within a hundred light years over the last thousands to hundreds of thousands of years.

Closing his eyes he could visualize this city in a different light, as the white hot flares of kinetic weapons struck from the sky, toppling megascrapers from their foundations. Terawatt lasers shone through the dust and smoke as they vaporized screaming mothers and children.

"But surely the fleet will be up to stopping them if they do show up," said the Princess Amanda, laying a soft hand on her father-in-law's shoulder.

"The Fleet has never lost a war," echoed the Prince. "At least to a nonhuman opponent," he continued with a smile. "Depends on whether you consider Constance's fleet or the fleet of Cassius II the Fleet."

"I know," said the Emperor, watching as holographic starbursts brightened the sky, backlit by the pinpoint flares of nuclear demolitions set off by the fleet in space. "We have won over twenty wars. Several over the alien races that are now in the Empire. The Elysa, the Crakista, the Lashara, the Muxxar. All have fallen before us. Even our staunch allies the Klashak and the Margravi have felt our fury in the past.

"But the Ca'cadasans were thousands of years our superiors when last we met, two thousand years ago. They have had two thousand years to advance technologically, and they have surely expanded. While we have been an advancing civilization for only a thousand of those years."

"But the technologies of the ancients," said the Princess, looking out over the megalopolis that was her home.

"They have advanced us, through the technology that we have found," agreed the Emperor. "As they advanced the Elysians that came after them. And all of the then primitive species that are now at the heart of the greatest concentration of space faring civilizations known."

He stared for a moment at the sky, as the terraformed moon Arial crested the horizon to join Jewel's twin planet New Terra as spectators to the spectacle.

"The Ca'cadasans have been in the Empire business almost as long as the ancients," he said with a grimace. "For all of the wealth and power of our Empire. For all of the strength of our neighbors. They will have wealth and resources way beyond us."

"You're still beating that horse, my dear," came a voice from the interior of the house. Augustine allowed a slight smile to cross his face. A smile which broadened of its own accord as the slender figure of his Empress, Anastasia Romanov, flowed into the garden.

"The night is so beautiful," said the young looking woman and mother of five. "The night roses are in bloom," she said, grasping the blossom of the native analogue to the earth flower and inhaling the fragrance.

"I know it's a night of celebration," answered the Emperor, his smile turning into a scowl.

"Then celebrate, my love," said the Empress, coming over to Augustine and sitting gently on his lap, planting a soft kiss on his forehead. "Beat the horse again tomorrow when Parliament is listening."

"Besides, father," interjected the Crown Prince, "you have nothing to worry about. Sean is with the fleet. And the addition of his Imperial Prince to the mix will assuredly double the effectiveness of the navy."

Augustine laughed at the thought of his youngest son serving with the Imperial Navy. *He was raised in a tradition of service*, thought the father. He remembered his own days in the Navy as a serving officer. No slack was cut to the then Ensign The Prince Romanov. Oh, they wouldn't hand his ship a suicide mission. But he was expected to pull his weight, and was not given any special consideration because of his birth.

"You're right as usual, my dear," he said to his wife, a smile crossing his face. "There is nothing I can do to change the minds of those idiots in the Lords tonight. So I might as well enjoy myself this evening."

"And you have a solid majority in the Scholars," said Dimetre, waving his empty glass to catch the attention of an alert servant. "And a solid core in the Commons. Maybe enough to overrule the Lords."

"Maybe," said the Emperor, swirling his own

refilled glass. "But I'll not let it trouble me anymore tonight."

The Emperor raised his glass into the air in the ancient sign of a salutation.

"A toast," he said, looking around at his gathered family. "To the Empire, to the Fleet that guards it, and to the officers, men and woman who man it. And especially one particular officer. Lieutenant SG Sean Ogden Lee Romanov."

"To the Fleet and Grand Admiral Sean," said the Crown Prince as glasses clinked. "And may God protect him."

*   *   *

While the rest of the Empire celebrated the thousand year history of transplanted human civilization, the guardians of that civilization toiled on. With enemies real and imagined on all sides the Imperial Army, Navy and Marines must be constantly ready. Which meant that all of their systems must be up and ready, no matter the day of the Imperial (Old Earth) Calendar.

Chief Petty Officer First Jana Gorbachev was on her third ten year enlistment in the Imperial Navy, twenty of them aboard *HIMS Duke Roger Sergiov II* (BB 1458). And never in all of her years had she seen such a fucked up weapons system. Not that it was their fault, or the fault of the young officer in charge of the B Laser Ring.

"The diagnostics show that everything should be working," cried the Lieutenant at the top of his lungs. "Fucking bitch should be working. But it isn't fucking working. What the fuck is wrong with the fucking bitch."

Gorbachev shook her head as she gave the young

officer an exasperated look. He was a more than competent officer, and she had seen a lot, the good and the bad. A little young for his rank, with the chip on his shoulder that came from trying to prove that promotion came from ability and not birth. *And someday, if things work out badly for his brother, he may be the ruler of the Empire. The one we swear allegiance to in our oath of service.*

"We reconfigured the bitch all of last night," he continued. "You'd think a complete rebuild of the power feeds and microcircuits would result in what for all intents and purposes is a new unit. What the hell is wrong with those damned nanorepairbots?"

"Petty Officer Martinez supervised the entire procedure," said the chief, running a hand through her short blond hair. "I checked his logs, and everything went according to specs."

She could feel the sweat running down her armpits under the regulation protective armor all crew wore outside of the three protective living cylinders of the battleship. She would have preferred to be in those living cylinders right now, in the comfort of regular shipboard clothing. But unfortunately she was a weapons chief, and for some strange reason all weapons on ship were situated to the exterior, where they could actually fire on an enemy.

"And don't even mention using the bots on automatic," she continued, seeing the Prince about to open his mouth. "The Captain will ream you a new one if you even suggest such a flagrant violation of the Man in the Loop Accords. You know he had ancestors on Alderon when the machines took over."

"But we know how to build them better," said the Prince, looking at the schematics of the photon generator that was not working, no matter what the diagnostics displayed.

"Tell it to the citizens, sir," said the chief, pointing her finger at one of the able spacemen who stared at his officer with a look of horror across his broad face. "They still tell stories on the frontier worlds of robot intelligences hiding out in the great dark, waiting to come and kill them."

"Well," said the officer, a slight smile on his face, "I won't argue the point right now. But what and the hell are we going to do with this generator. The other seven on the ring work perfectly. Power feeds, capacitors, nanocrystaline ring focus."

"So we ask the Captain to have the yards pull the damn thing and replace it with another," said the chief, looking over his shoulder at the schematic. *That still gives us 1.4 terawatts on the ring, minus the two hundred gigs on the kaputz generator. And the A ring covers the same arc of fire to the front and sides, though not quite as much to the stern. C and D rings cover that area quite well.*

"We're scheduled to deploy for border patrol in a week," said the Lieutenant, shaking his head. "That will go over real well."

"Look at reality for a second, sir," argued the exasperated chief. "I heard they're having major problems on the antimatter warhead feed in missile mag four. There are over five thousand crew on this fifteen megaton warship, spacers and marines. Five thousand just to keep it working. Our ring can still put out a single 1.4 tera beam of focused or wide beamed energy. Or it can simultaneously put out fifty small beams for point defense. And all configurations in between. I've seen ships go on deploy with much worse."

"So what do you suggest, chief?" asked the officer

as he massaged his temples.

"I suggest that you get some sleep, since you've been going over twenty-four without," said the woman, pointing her finger at the imperial child. "I suggest you let the petty officers and techs under your command continue to work on the system while you rest. The system will be as the system will be when we deploy. We will report status to the Captain when it is time to report status, and he will decide what to do at that time."

"OK," agreed the officer, getting up from his chair and heading toward the lift door that would take him from the number twenty-five photon generator maintenance deck to the central core shaft, and thence to the forward central capsule where his quarters were located. He pushed the lift button and stood there for a second after the door opened. Turning back to the chief the officer pointed a finger in her direction.

"Thanks for the suggestions, chief," he said, looking her straight in the eye and leveling a finger in her direction. "Now I have an order for you. Get the people set on their assignments. That should take you half an hour. Then head your ass to your quarters where you can get out of this torture chamber they call protective armor, take a shower, and get eight hours. Then meet me back here after you get some food. Is that understood?"

"Yes, sir," agreed the chief with a smile and a nod. "I'm always glad to follow the directions of a superior when they result in my being able to be a lazy fuck off."

Sean smiled back and entered the lift. The doors closed behind him and the lift fell down to the center of the ship.

Chief Gorbachev let a short laugh escape from her

mouth as she looked at the closed lift door. It had been her job for almost two decades to take the young men and women who graduated from one of the many Naval Academies that served the Fleet, and turn them into serving officers. This was the first time she had been called upon to take a serving officer and prepare him to become the potential ruler of the Empire. *And I'll give it my best shot*, she thought, knowing that there could be worse young men in charge of the Empire.

*   *   *

Captain Dame Mye Lei looked out from the viewport of the IP pinnace as her new command expanded into view. She had been in at the commissioning and the working up, and knew the crew as well as could be through the six months she had spent with them. But they had not experienced each other on a real deployment, where decisions and actions could mean life or death.

Well, she thought, looking over the elongated diamond shape of two and a third kilometers of hyper VII capable battle cruiser, *at least we'll have legs if the shit hits the fan.*

HIMS Joan de Arc (HBC 2984) still looked wrong to her critical eye, not like the standard hyper VI ships of the fleet. The elongated octagons of the hyperspatial generators top and bottom were too large for her form. The eight etheral space grabbers on bow and stern were too thick, too long, giving the ship an unbalanced look.

And giving her fifty gees more acceleration in space, both normal and hyper, as well as entrance into the Hyper VII Dimension, she thought, watching the ship against the backdrop of the twin world Jewel, then looping around the ship to see her silhouetted against New Terra. *That will give her, with the maximum safe velocity of point nine five C, the equivalent of 35,448 lights. Four times the pseudovelocity of a Hyper VI ship.*

But like every tradeoff it came at a price. The eight million ton ship lost twenty percent of her weapons and armor in order to carry the larger hyper-generators, inertial compensators, and real space reactionless drives. That translated into smaller missile magazines, though her laser batteries were just as powerful as a standard battle cruiser's.

We're not made to fight, she thought as she vectored the pinnace toward the open bay of the port sternward hanger. *We're made to get in, recon the area, and get out with the information. With enough firepower to fight our way out if necessary.* And as a member of the Fourth Fleet Scout Force, they would be doing just that.

The pinnace moved slowly through the cold plasma field that kept vacuum and air separated, and the autopilot took control and brought the small vessel gently down into a landing lock. Mye reached overhead and began switching off the ship's systems while her copilot typed in the voyage log.

"Thanks for mother henning me, Scotty," said the Captain to the Lieutenant SG who commanded the battle cruiser's small flight of recon fighters.

"Pleasure, ma'am," replied the officer to his superior in the slow drawl of one of the frontier worlds.

The Captain hit her belt release and stood up, walking from the cockpit to the passenger/cargo hold, where the outer hatch opened at her approach. A Marine honor guard in full battle armor awaited her on one side of her path to the lift, snapping their rifles to a present arms salute. A line of officers in full dress uniform stood to the other side of the path, rendering hand salutes.

Dropping to the deck in a jump, the Captain looked up at the towering men and women from her five foot height and returned the salute. A smile crossed her face as she looked over her command team.

"At ease," she ordered. The marines behind her snapped precisely to order arms while the naval officers relaxed. "No need for such formality. It's not like I haven't been here before."

"Just welcoming the God of the ship back aboard, ma'am," said the tall, ebony skinned Commander, holding out a large hand.

"The deity accepts your worship," she replied with a laugh, grabbing the hand. "Now get your scurvy asses to your stations before I order a keelhauling. We have orders to sail."

"We're to be deployed?" asked the exec, leading the way to the lift while excited conversation broke out behind them.

"Scout Force, Fourth Fleet," she replied as they walked into the lift. "Bridge," she ordered as the doors closed behind them.

"But," stammered the exec, his face going slack. "That's the..."

"Ass end of nowhere," she finished as the lift started moving into the ship for the two hundred meter journey to the umbilical core. "In toward Galactic North. Nowhere near the exciting borders with the Elysium, the Crakista, or the Lashara. Nowhere near the glory we all seek."

"Something like that," admitted the exec with a grunt. There was a slight shudder as the lift capsule reached the core and turned forward on its eight hundred meter run to the bridge area. "Of course we always have the possible thrill of Klang privateers."

The Captain looked out the lift viewport as they entered the MAM Capsule. One of the four heavily armored inner sections of all Imperial warships, the others being the three crew and control compartments, it held the massive twin energy generators of the vessel, as well as much of the antimatter stored aboard the ship. A marvel and a danger all in one, and one of the reasons warships such as her were not allowed in close orbit around a core world.

"You forget the provincials of the Republic, or maybe even New Moscow," she said with a smile.

"They might bore us to death," he admitted as they exited the MAM Capsule and continued toward the bow. "I never could figure why the Emperor Cassius ever wanted to hold onto them."

They entered the four hundred meter long Central Capsule that contained the bridge, quarters for half the thirty-five hundred crew and marines, and their mess and recreation areas. The bridge was located directly in the center of this armored area, the best protected region of the ship.

"Why Commander Xavier Jackson," said the Captain with a surprised expression. "I have never in my sixty four years of life heard such a scandalous tirade against the divine memory of the Imperial family. Though I admit there is no love lost on the likes of that crazy idiot."

The doors of the lift opened onto a long hallway, and passing crewmen stiffened to attention as they saw the identity of its passenger.

"Now behave yourself," she whispered with a short chuckle. "Before I have to call the marines in and have you put in the brig. Or possibly spaced."

"Yes, your Godship," said the laughing officer.

They strode thirty meters down the hall and stopped in front of the marine guards. The guards checked the DNA patterns on their scanners and waved them in with a salute. *Another little thing to change around here*, she thought as the bridge doors slid open and she and her exec strode into their domain. She couldn't stand that kind of formality when she was a junior officer. Now that she was in charge she could finally do something about it.

"Captain on the bridge," called out the com officer, the first to see her at the door.

"At ease," she ordered as she walked to her chair and sat. "Com, get Naval Yards Traffic Control on the line."

"Aye aye, ma'am," said the com officer, turning to her board and setting up the signal.

Captain Mye Lei looked to the front viewer, where the thousands of shining dots of ships, warehouses and spacedocks glinted in reflected sunlight, while to the left was the shadowed disk of Jewel, the broad swath of enormous cities making her live up to her nickname, the *Jewel in the Crown*.

"Central Naval Yards Traffic Control on the com, ma'am."

"Traffic Control," said the Captain into the com link. "His Imperial Majesty's Ship *Joan de Arc* requesting permission to leave the area of the dock. By orders of the Admiralty to deploy to the Fleet."

"Permission granted, *Jean de Arc*," came the contralto voice of the yard Commander over the circuit. "You may leave when ready."

"Helm," ordered the Captain. "All ahead at ten gravities. When we are clear of the yards take us to two hundred gees. Then shortest path out of the gravity well and jump space."

"Aye aye, ma'am," said the helmsman, punching the commands into his console. The image on the viewer shifted as the great vessel began to gather way and maneuver away from the docks.

"All department heads meet me in the conference room," she ordered, getting up from her chair and heading for the door. "We have some things to discuss."

* * *

The ship rocked again and Lt Commander Maurice von Rittersdorf cursed under his breath. The tactical display showed that the two functional privateers were ranging to either side of him. *Smart*, he thought, since the *HIMS Johann Peterson* (DD 26575) was weak on one side's shields thanks to a couple of lucky hits in the early stages of the battle. So the ships were attacking from opposite sides, forcing him to absorb the attack of one of the one hundred twenty thousand ton ships on the weak side instead of rolling the ship to face them with strength.

"We might still be able to outrun them," chimed in the exec, Lt. SG Katherine Schuler, from the CIC.

"We've lost too much to guarantee that," said the Captain, looking at the schematic representation flashing red with damage. Including two of the stern impeller units, the spatial grabbers that propelled every Imperial vessel. She'd had a good seventy gee advantage coming into the fight, which was how she had run them down in the first place when they had broken away from the tramp freighter they were in the process of taking as a prize. "And we would have to run away with our stern to their fire for a good hour if they decided to pursue."

The one bit of good news to this fiasco was the third enemy vessel that was floating dead in space. The old *Johann Peterson's* gunnery had been good enough to take her out of the equation with one good volley of all three laser rings, followed by a pair of hundred megaton warheads to the hull.

"Ship A is firing," yelled the tactical officer, and the screen colored in the invisible beams of photons converging on the two hundred thousand ton destroyer. The vessel's computer adjusted the electromag field and its cold plasma matrix to intercept as best as possible. One of the incoming beams hit the field at the perfect angle, was bent around the destroyer, and radiated in the opposite direction, nearly striking Ship B. The other hit dead center. Some was stopped by plasma that superheated under the beam. The light that made it through the plasma was spread from a fifty centimeter pinpoint to a ten meter diameter spotlight. Heat was pumped into the hull, some armor boiled away, but much of the beam was reflected back by the nanoparticle skin which shifted to the proper alignment for that particular wavelength.

If only Fredrickson were here, thought the commander of the warship. But her consort destroyer had made for the nearest military system with a malfunctioning hyperdrive generator, only able to creep along in Hyper III. And von Ritterdorf, as senior commander of the pair, had decided to continue the patrol on his own, against common sense. And then the encounter with three privateers. At that point there was no choice, as the protection of civilian shipping was the primary rationale for this kind of patrol, even to the point of sacrificing his ship and crew.

"Returning fire," yelled Ensign Lasardo, the tactical

officer, as two strong beams from the A and B rings struck out at the ship. The double hundred megawatt beams, slightly less in the B ring which had sustained some damage, struck the pirate perfectly along its engineering section. Superheated alloy and atmosphere gushed from the enemy's hull, followed by a bright secondary explosion as energies were released within the vessel.

"Missiles," yelled the Captain "and bring all lasers to fire on Ship B."

"Aye, sir," called the tactical officer, sending the commands to the firing batteries. The three side tubes facing the enemy belched hundred megaton missiles that accelerated at five thousand gravities toward the enemy, followed in three seconds by another trio. The enemy launched counter missiles and a salvo of her own offensive weapons. Just after the enemy missiles left their tubes the human warheads arrived. One was taken out by the enemy counter missiles, winning the duel of electronics against a single Imperial weapon. Point defense took out another, but the third struck dead onto the damaged engineering section and detonated, sending waves of lethal heat and radiation into the enemy ship. A couple of small secondaries followed, then a titanic detonation of the enemy vessel's power plant that turned half the mass of the ship into plasma and sent the rest out in pieces large and small at a significant velocity. The twin enemy missiles were intercepted several thousand kilometers out in bright points of nuclear fire.

"At least their missile and counter missile batteries are not to modern standard," said the exec over the com. "Probably the best the Lasharans could get on the black market to equip with probable deniability."

"Their lasers are good enough," said von Ritterdorf, as Ship B let loose with another blast of beams, and the destroyer rotated her hull and her strong shields in the way. But shields do not normally stop light amp weapons, only attenuate their effect. And enough energetic photons made it through in their trillions, superheating the cold plasma layer, to pump heat into the hull.

"Emitters seven and eight on ring B are down," said the damage control officer. "Heavy casualties on weapons deck 34B."

"Hit them with everything we've got," yelled the Captain, slamming his fist on the seat's arm, the armored gauntlet pushing deep into the pad. The lights dimmed for a moment as the ship complied with the order and funneled all available power to weapons.

Peterson's three laser rings opened with a pulsing power as the starboard missile tubes flushed a trio, then a second trio of hundred meg warheads. Particle beams followed suit with the lasers, sending charged particles (in this case antimatter) and uncharged normal matter into the shields of the enemy at near light speed. The antimatter was stopped for the most part while sapping some of the shield strength, especially the thin layer of cold plasma on the inner section. The uncharged particles slid through the field as if it didn't exist, which it essentially didn't to them, and struck a heavy blow to the armor girding the enemy vessel.

The destroyer pivoted at it fired, bringing its forward tubes to bear as the C Laser ring lost lock. The two forward tubes spat a pair of fifty meg warheads, and then the forward plasma torpedo fired as it bore. A quarter ton of superheated plasma, wrapped in the strong magnetic fields of the follower capsule, headed at point one C toward the enemy vessel. A close in weapon in the best of times due to slow speed and quick dispersion, they were still retained on Imperial ships for situations such as this. When maximum firepower was needed at close range in minimum time.

Half of the missiles made it through to the target, exploding in waves of radiation near the hull, in two cases directly impacting the armor. The hundred twenty thousand ton bulk of the vessel shuddered from the impact as pieces of armor and laser ring broke off and ejected into space. Great gaps opened in the hull and atmosphere spewed out.

Warships, even the patchwork ships used by privateers, were tough beasts with redundant systems. While critically injured, the ship may still have survived the massive assault. Until the lumbering plasma torpedo struck and splashed on the damaged hull. Plasma plunged through the rents of armor and into the interior of the ship as its magnetic fields released and the superheated gas expanded. In an instant the heart of a sun lived for a brief moment in the center of the ship. And the ship died a fiery death.

As the containment systems failed on antimatter storage and missile warheads, they interacted with matter and detonated, blasting the ship apart into pieces, none of which weighed over a hundred tons. The destroyer moved away as the computer interpreted the threat. Laser and point defense projectile weapons swept space near the ship clear of threats.

"Casualty figures are tabulated, sir," said the exec in a hushed voice over the com. "Thirty one killed and another forty-six wounded."

Out of three hundred and eighty naval and marine personnel, thought the Captain, visualizing the faces he would no longer see through the hallways of the ship.

"We're down to six of the fifty meg warheads," continued the exec with a huffing breath, obviously ready to move away from the subject of casualties. "Maximum accel is about one hundred thirty gees, but we can still use Hyper VI to get home."

"And we will have prisoners to interrogate," interjected the tactical officer, nodding toward the screen and the remaining enemy vessel floating dead in space. A small dot that suddenly expanded into a brilliant flare.

"I guess they didn't take much to the possibility of interrogation," said the exec. "Or didn't fancy giving away their point of origin."

"Navigator," ordered the Captain, shrugging his shoulders, knowing there was nothing he could do to prevent an enemy from suiciding. "Plot a course back to the nearest military yard. Maximum speed."

"You noticed the date now," said the exec over the personal com as the Captain rubbed his temples in his chair.

"Goddam," said the Captain. "I've forgotten."

"Well happy thirty-eighth birthday anyway sir," said the exec. "Hell of a way to celebrate it though I must say."

*   *   *

"We have the final production figures, Dr. Yu," said the tech over the com, a smile stretching his face.

"Thanks Jamie," said the tall, blond woman with the slight Asian cast to her eyes. "I'll give them a look." She sent a thought at the computer console on her desk and frowned at the graph thus revealed.

Damn, she thought, chewing on the multistylus she stuck in her mouth. *Plenty of antimatter. Well on the way to becoming the largest producer in the Empire. But the negative matter figures are still horrible. And without negative matter there are no wormholes.*

"There has to be an answer," she whispered while she checked through the schematic of the station. The *Donut* was fully operational, though they had a long way to go as concerned all of the amenities, quarters and offices, for the corporations that would eventually call the huge ribbon around the black hole home. The culmination of three centuries of conceptualization, planning and construction, the largest civil engineering project in the history of humanity, and one of the pieces of the puzzle was still missing.

"Put Doctor Gomez on the com," ordered Lucille Yu to her personal AI. She waited impatiently for several minutes for the engineer in charge of the negative matter production project to come on the line. *Doesn't he know it's not good to keep the Assistant Chief of Project waiting?*

"Lucille," came the liquid voice of the man when his olive skinned face appeared on the screen. His smooth skin did not betray his hundred years of existence.

And he's twenty-eight years older than me, she thought, remembering the small wrinkles that had appeared recently around her green eyes. *How does he do it? Maybe I need to start jogging.*

"I have been looking over the production figures for negative matter, and they don't look good."

There was a few second delay, and Lucille wondered if the man was trying to come up with an excuse, before she realized he was probably well up along the side of the twenty-five million kilometer circumference ribbon that orbited the central black hole of the capital Supersystem. At least a million kilometers from her location.

"I would guess the shipping concerns will not be totally unhappy," said the other scientist, raising an eyebrow, a tight smile on his face. "The complete idiots."

"They're just tradition bound," said Yu, after waiting a couple of seconds to be sure that the other scientist was finished. "Not uncommon in the human animal. And they don't realize that whomever jumps on board this thing early will make a fortune. It isn't like we're going to make interstellar freighters obsolete.

"But we need negative matter to hold those wormhole gates open, Rafael," she continued, "or it won't matter how many wormholes we can open using the hole as a generator."

"We have enough to open a number of passenger and light cargo gates," said the other scientist, frowning, "and we're producing sufficient mini-wormholes for our military contracts."

"But the ship gates," hissed Yu, her eyes burning into the screen. "The military wants to move ships from sector to sector at an instant." Her eyes narrowed as she looked at the screen. "The Emperor wants those gates operating. And with all of the energy of eighty thousand one thousand cubic kilometer generators tapping the gravitation force of a spinning black hole, the greatest power plant in the known Universe, we still can't produce enough negative matter to take advantage of the potential. So what the hell is wrong?"

"You know as well as I do, Lucille," said the other scientist in a low voice, staring into the link, "that according to every theory, and all of our calculations, we should be getting twelve times the yield of negative matter we are actually producing. Some of the youngsters on my team believe that it has something to do with the gravitational swirls of the hole. My team members have suggested farming out the negative matter production to other facilities, such as the solar rings antimatter production generators, while we just concentrate on antimatter and actual wormhole production."

"I don't think the Emperor would like that," said Yu shaking her head. "It was always envisioned that we would be able to produce everything needed for the project right here. In one central location."

"Then inform his majesty that it is not possible to do so," said the older man, shaking his head. "Or build twelve times as many negative matter producers on the *Donut*, and make what is required right here."

"I will get with the Emperor," said Lucille, nodding her head with a grimace. "I will tell him what you said. And I expect for you to tell him what you just told me as well, when the Imperial Family comes here for the dedication tour."

The Director of the Negative Matter Project grimaced but nodded his head, taking responsibility for his part of the problem.

"And I will get with the Station Director and let him know about our problems," she continued, "and let him know that you and your team are doing everything humanly possible to find a way around it."

The man gave a slight smile as he nodded his head. "Thank you for that."

"Yu out," she said, cutting the connection, while thoughts swirled through her head. *The damned thing was being planned over a century before I was born after all*, she thought. *Another decade or so without ship gates surely won't make or break the Empire.*

Chapter 2

We may get blown out of space. But one thing I can guarantee you. These bastards will know they have been in a fight. And those who survive will not be looking forward to another against humanity.

Pre-battle speech to crew by Admiral Sheila Terbourg, just before the battle of the Cat Nebula, Year 124 of Empire.

"That makes forty capital ships so far," whispered Lieutenant SG Walter Ngovic from his tactical station.

"I don't think they'll hear us through the hull and vacuum," replied the Captain of the vessel, Commander Bryce Suttler, winking at his officer, then wiping the sweat off of his dripping face.

"Sorry, sir," said the grinning officer. "Just being this close to an enemy force makes me want to be quiet."

"We're not at war with the Lasharans," admonished the Captain with a wagging finger. "Though I'm sure that would not stop them from blowing us out of space if they knew we were here. So far the new system is working up to specs though."

The Captain hated this kind of duty, even though his vessel was specifically built for it. Better the stalk of a merchant ship, or the destruction of an escort, than this creeping through enemy systems without even the authorization to defend themselves. And it was still damned hot in the ship, though much cooler than the older classes of stealth/attack.

"Two more coming out of hyper," said the tactical

officer.

"Keep a close eye on them then," said the Captain, wiping more sweat from his broad, brown skinned face. "We don't want them to get within detection range, now do we?"

Even though they would have to get within five million kilometers to even have a chance of sniffing us out, he thought. They were on silent running, secondary fusion plants at minimum with just enough energy being generated for life support, passive sensors and stealth field. Oh, she had enough energy stored in the crystal matrix to power up to full and use all systems while the MAM reactors came online. But if they had to do that so quickly they were most probably dead.

"Three more translating," said the tactical officer, looking over his shoulder at the Captain.

"Wait till they move off fifty million kilometers and then creep out of here," ordered Suttler to the helms woman, leaning forward and putting a hand on her shoulder. "I think we've stayed our welcome just right. It's time we get this information to Fleet while they can still do something with it."

The woman nodded an acknowledgment to the Captain. He leaned back and looked over the synopsis of what they had found so far on his repeater screen. It was always a bad sign when the fanatical aliens gathered a large force near the border. And over fifty capital ships in one system was a large force by any consideration.

But now we have the means to keep track of the bastards, thought the Captain with a smile. The old stealth/attacks were good, with their chameleon field and radiation reflecting/absorbing skin, as well as very efficient insulating armor. But the problem with stealth was that though a ship could be invisible to active sensors and visible sight, it would still radiate in the electromagnetic spectrum like a small star. Especially in the infrared.

The older stealth ships generated a continuous subspace opening that they used to dump the great majority of their radiation. The problem with that system was it needed energy generated by the ship to keep the field open, compounding the radiation production. And the subspace gate, though not needing to be tuned as well as a gate used for passing a material object, still had a limit as to how much of a gravity field it could handle. Limiting the ship to stealth operations in the outer portion of a system, away from the really interesting civilization artifacts that a system might possess.

HIMS *Seastag* (Stealth/Attack 421) was one of the new generation of wormhole sink Stealth/Attacks, using a wormhole generated by the *Donut* project to dump its radiation surplus. Without the need for additional energy generation, and able to be used despite the intensity of the local gravity field.

But still too damned hot, thought the Captain while the ship drifted in space. *The system is not perfect and never will be, so we get to stew in our own juices.*

* * *

It's always the heat, thought Cornelius Walborski, looking up into the bright ball of the F2 star, Sestius. Wiping the sweat from his brow yet again with the sodden cloth, he swore at the robotic planter/harvester that could not seem to work as advertised.

Nothing is as advertised, he thought, pulling the burned out circuit board from the opening and looking it over. *If I had more robots I could scrap this one. But I'm already at my limit of three.* Because of the man in the loop law no one could have more robots operating than they could ride close herd on. But he had three thousand acres of terraformed farmland to prepare for planting, if he were ever able to proclaim his land producing and so claim the homestead for himself.

Walborksi put the circuit board in his side bag and strode back toward the temporary house trailer that he and his bride had constructed, right next to the foundation and already excavated cellar of the erecting permanent structure. The construction robot was working on putting the floor beams in place, soon to be followed by the floor. *At least it's working well,* he thought. The only one of the three that was. So they would soon have a weather proof and animal proof shelter. Then he would just have to get the farm to work.

Cornelius took long, lanky steps with his two meter tall frame, reveling in the point eight eight standard gee field of the planet. The days were three hours longer than his native New Detroit, making them more tiring despite the lower gravity. But it also lacked the four and a half billion citizens of the core world. With hard work he could rise to a position of wealth on this world, unlike a core world where he could at most be a skilled laborer.

Two of the dogs came running up and started jumping around him. One barked, a sound that was echoed out in the fields and was soon followed by the other two dogs. Cornelius smiled at the hounds for a moment and ruffled the head of the closest one. *I can have as many of them as I want,* he thought, watching as the dogs cavorted for a moment more, then ran off to the far reaches of the field. *But they can't plow, plant and harvest.* He had to admit that despite that they were damned useful as patrollers, alarm systems, and defenders of the livestock.

As he thought about the dogs one of the kittens they had acquired came jumping from cover and grabbed a native insect analogue from the air. With a crunch the bug was dead, and the kitten proudly carried it back into the shadows for a leisurely meal. *They're good hunters,* he thought of the trio of felines they had gotten from a neighbor. And unlike the native life, they were able to digest and survive on things they had never been meant to eat, just like the human colonists. Bionanites gave all the Earth life the ability to convert Sestius plant and animal proteins and carbs into edible mass. Maybe not the best tasting, but in the case of the felines it made them efficient hunters of vermin on this world.

The sound of construction took his focus from the felines for a moment. He looked over at the house

"Did you find the problem," said his wife, Katlyn, pulling her long blond hair back into a wrap while her green eyes roamed over him. *This is why I came,* he thought basking in her beauty. *For her, and the family to come.*

Both were almost still children, he twenty-seven, her twenty-eight, just out of adolescence. But the government wanted expansion on the frontier, and were willing to fund the establishment of new families on these worlds.

"It's another circuit board that we don't have a spare for," said Cornelius, giving her a quick kiss. "I'll have to go on the net and see if I can get another one delivered out here."

"Have you looked at the north fence yet?" she

asked, handing him a fresh sweat cloth. "We don't want to lose any more of the cattle. And it would be a disaster if any Narn Beasts got into the fields."

Cornelius shook his head at the thought of one of the forty ton native animals tramping through the fields. They were inoffensive herbivores who would starve to death on Earth vegetation, though that wouldn't stop the dumb animals from eating their fill, or stomping crops and machinery that got in their way.

"OK," he said, handing her the circuit board. "You see what you can find on the net, and I'll go repair the fence. Maybe I can get the damned machine to plowing by tomorrow."

"Don't forget you have militia drill tomorrow," said Katlyn, shaking her head. "It's the third Saturday of the month after all."

Shit, thought the farmer, imagining the hell that was militia training, something he didn't have to worry about on the core world. *And I still can't get used to this different calendar.* New Detroit had a much longer year, while Sestius had one closer to the standard Imperial Calendar. Still, the months of this world were longer than the imperial calendar, and that continued to throw him off.

"Fat lot of good it does if someone gets past the orbital defenses," he said with a scowl, coming up with another reason to hate drill. "We'll just be ants under foot to be stomped on."

"When the new Fleet base comes here then you won't have to worry," she said with a smile, standing on her toes to give him a quick kiss on the cheek.

He shook his head and turned away, walking quickly across the field to the broken fences. Part of the price of being a new settler was that his farm was on the fringe, and therefore subject to the attack of wildlife. But just the thought of being one among a hundred and ninety thousand settlers, versus being the small fry among over four billion, brought a smile to his face. *And,* he thought, *the new archduke is to be installed next weekend. The drink and food will flow endlessly for the period of the investiture.* And Cornelius Walborski was still young enough to enjoy a good party, no matter how long and hard the work days.

*   *   *

"I could sure do with a little bit of a party right now," murmured Major Samuel Baggett under his breath while mortar rounds began falling around his position. Earlier in the week the planet Janaikasa had seemed so quiet. The native Lasharans were still their obnoxiously fanatical religious worst, hurling curses on the human invaders to their world while calling on the Gods of their people to return them to the Theocracy of their birth. But shooting and bombing incidents had fallen off significantly.

Until the beginning of the Imperial Millennial Celebration, when all hell broke loose on all twelve of the planets occupied after the last Lasharan War. Then the hidden weapons had come out and the bombs had been planted. And this morning his command, Team A (Companies B and C) the First of the 789th Light Infantry (988th Infantry Division) had been called out to relieve another light infantry battalion that had gotten it caught in a crack.

"They really need to send the heavy infantry in, sir," said Lieutenant Kreiger, the weapons platoon leader for the rump battalion which Major Baggett was commander by dint of being the battalion exec. Lt. Colonel Lefaye, the battalion commander, was leading the other three line companies on an attack along another vector of approach.

"The heavies and the armor are all engaged around the capital," said Baggett, looking over the wall. His visor systems peered through smoke and magnified the image of the rebel Lasharans, three meters of skinny scaly humanoid, manning a barricade. His helmet clanged from a hit as a projectile bounced off.

"Watch it sir," said a Sergeant, sending a stream of hypervelocity pellets towards the enemy. "They got some modern weapons in there. We've taken casualties despite our armor."

"The heavies can take it," said the Lieutenant, shrugging his shoulders. "The least they could do would be to upgrade us to medium suits, if they want us to fight in this urban shit. But the heavies we have can definitely handle this shit."

That they can, thought the major, turning a baleful brown eye on the younger man. *Maybe I should see if I can get into them*. Their own armor could handle a bit of firepower, and gave them the strength of two men, as well as protection from chemical, biological or nuclear weapons. The medium infantry could handle more, and was stronger. But the heavy infantry were true brutes, protected against all but the most powerful infantry weapons, and able to deal out a rifle squad's worth of damage.

"They've too much cover for mortar fire," said the Lieutenant, gesturing toward the plumes of smoke rising from the buildings. "Construction is too heavy for our organic firepower. Maybe some hyper-v missiles might open up the barricade."

"I'm not sacrificing any more men to take out some slope heads," said the major. "See if you can get some real firepower on that."

A wave of small arms fire passed overhead, along with the warbling yells of the fanatics trying their best to kill Imperial soldiers. Troopers returned fire and were rewarded with an occasional scream or yelp as fast moving particles hit flesh. One nearby trooper cursed and pulled back a gauntleted hand that was missing a finger, the glove staunching the blood. Still instinct brought his other hand over to cradle the injured member as he dropped his rifle.

Nothing that won't grow back, thought the major, shooting a glance at his weapon's officer.

"Got some on the way," said the officer. "As soon as they can line up to get the shot."

"What did you get?" asked the major, just before the heavens opened up and streaks of light joined the sky and the earth. The ground rumbled underneath and the city to their front flared brilliant white while rubble jumped into the air.

"Heavy cruiser *Jakarta*," said the weapons platoon officer with a grin. "In low orbit. Took them a moment to boost into position for a volley."

I know I should have joined the navy, thought the major, covering his head and crawling low to get closer to the hopefully knocked out enemy positions.

A flight of ground support sting ships came rocketing in while the last of the rubble was falling back to the ground. The small ships rippled volleys of rockets and swarms of hypervelocity machine gun rounds over the smoking rubble, then rushed forward to drop thermetic bombs before climbing away to the heights and returning to their watch over the battlefield.

"You sure do know how to bring it, Lieutenant," said the major to the smiling officer. "I think you'll go far in this human's army. If you survive this cluster fuck, that is."

*　　*　　*

The lights dimmed for a moment, then strengthened as power fed back into the mundane systems detailed to maintaining comfort aboard the liner. Doctor Jennifer Conway wished that her own system would recover as swiftly as that of the passenger ship. Instead, she kneeled in front of the toilet in her cabin's bathroom and ejected everything she had eaten the last day. It would eventually go to the ship's recycling system, where nanites would break it down into useable substances. That thought made her sick yet again, and her stomach convulsed to send the last bit of thin liquid that resided in her gut out into the open.

Why do I have to react like this? thought the physician, pushing herself up from the floor and leaning over the sink, where she splashed cold water on her face. *Why me, and not someone more deserving, like that damned fiancé of mine.*

But no, Captain Glen McKinnon of His Majesty's Imperial Marines had the kind of constitution that people who travelled between the stars should have. He only suffered the few seconds of nausea that most people experienced when a ship went in or out of hyper. Jennifer was one of the one tenth of a percent who reacted violently to the transition. And no amount of drugs or conditioning seemed to help.

And I feel like a camp follower picking up and moving whenever my boy toy gets a new posting. It's been what? Three times in the last four years. This time she had been promised he would be in place for at least the next five years, and possibly ten. And thinking about being in his arms once again brought a smile to her face despite the fading nausea. *At least he won't be on a damned warship, like the majority of the marines, like he was on his last posting.*

After a shot of anti-nausea the doctor felt much better. Good enough to go find something to replace the contents of her evacuated stomach. She checked the time in her head and saw that it was only an hour away from dinner, and she had a permanent invitation to the captain's table by dint of her social position. Physicians were not all that rare out on the frontier. But they were fulfilling a need out here. They were a convenience on the core and developing worlds, unless there was an uncommon disaster. Disasters happened all the time on the frontier worlds, and a doctor's services were always in demand.

A half hour later Conway found herself seated at the captain's table with several other passengers and the ship's engineer. The Captain was not attending this dinner, which she found surprising, as the rotund little man seemed to never miss a meal.

"Did everyone have a good translation?" asked the engineer in his brogue. Commander Scott was nicknamed Scotty, just like all of the Scottish descent engineers that Jennifer had ever read about.

"Mine was fine, as usual," answered Dermet Tagalag, who Jennifer knew as an Imperial Administrator (read that high level flunky) being posted to Sestius. "The wife had a rough time of it. But then again, she always does."

And you left her in the cabin while you came here yourself to stuff your face, thought Jennifer, keeping her face void of emotion.

"And you, ma'am?" asked the engineer in a tone that let Jennifer know he was asking for the second time.

"Oh," she said, setting her wine glass on the table. "The same old. Violent nausea, sick to my stomach. Something I dread facing."

"And how long will you be out here?" asked Tagalag, his dark eyes looking into hers in the manner of a man who is looking for companionship.

"My fiancé is expected to post out here for at least five years," she said, refusing to return the man's look. "So at least for that long."

"So you won't have to worry about translation sickness for at least that long," said Scotty, nodding his head.

"And maybe they'll come up with something by then," said Tagalag with a smile.

"They've only been working on the problem for the last nine hundred years," said Jennifer with a frown. "I really don't expect for them to come up with anything in the next five."

"They," said Tagalag, in the tone that conveyed that he knew who they were and looked down upon them, "couldn't find their ass with both hands, if you pardon the expression."

"That might be a little harsh," said Jackie Smythe, a mining engineer who Jennifer had learned at a meal earlier on would be looking at opening up some rich sources of radioactives in the wilderness. "After all, there doesn't seem to be a way to determine what causes the susceptibility. Isn't that right, Dr. Conway?"

"Completely correct, Dr. Smythe," agreed Jennifer with a smile. "There doesn't seem to be a genetic component, or a phenotypical structure that correlates with the sickness. And drug trials have been, well basically, random attempts in futility."

"All well and good," said Tagalag, again adopting that tone that Jennifer hated. The one that said government functionaries were superior to people of learning. He looked over at the engineer. "How long till we make orbit? I for one can't wait to get my feet on solid ground."

"At best speed we'll be in orbit in five days," said the engineer with a smile. "Two and a half days of accel, then an equal amount of decel."

"And you can't do better than that?" asked the administrator in a whiny voice.

"I'm afraid not," said the engineer. "The *Queen of the Rings* is not a warship or message carrier. Two hundred gees is the best we can do."

"Could have been worse," interjected Smythe with a smile. "At least she's hyper six. We could have taken another month to get here in a hyper five."

"More like two months," said the engineer, after taking a sip from his wine. He put the glass on the table and leaned toward the mining engineer. "You have experience tramping around on hyper fives?"

"In my younger days," said the still young looking woman. "I did some prospecting over in in sector twelve, the other rim. Most of the ships we used were fives. Seemed like we were cooped up in them forever."

"I think it's a shame that it takes so long to go across a damned solar system," complained Tagalag in his grating voice. "They ought to do something about it."

Whoever they are that can change the laws of physics, thought Jennifer, a scowl on her face as she looked at the man, hoping she would not have too many dealings with him on the planet. *With over a hundred and fifty*

thousand people what would be the odds I would run into him?
She did the math in her head and didn't like the answer.
It was too damned likely.

"Ah, here comes our food," said Tagalag.

The human servers that were the prerogative of the
captain's table brought the covered platters. Jennifer
smiled at the man who laid a platter in front of her, all
the time wondering about the six hundred or so second
and third class passengers who were eating in cafeterias
across the hundred thousand ton liner. The server
raised the top of the platter and revealed a rare steak
and a lobster tail, along a mass of fresh vegetables and a
baked potato. *I earned this, after all*, she thought,
dismissing the other passengers, who weren't after all
suffering, from her mind. *And in five more days I'll see my
baby. And all will be well.*

"No worries about coming out this way?" asked
Smythe after they had set to their dinner for some bites.

"You mean to this sector?" asked Jennifer, looking
up from her steak. "Not really."

"No concern that the ancient enemy might show
up on the doorstep?" asked the mining engineer.

"You don't mean that old tale of the boogie man
coming from the outer reaches to get us, do you?" said
Tagalag in his whine. "My dear. That civilization has
long since fallen."

"Then what about the probes that have been sent
that way?" said Smythe, her voice rising a bit. "For five
hundred years nothing sent beyond New Moscow has
come back. Even New Moscow won't send patrols a
hundred light years beyond their own space."

"Space is still dangerous beyond civilized borders,"
said Tagalag in a tone that told he was lecturing.
"That's why it's best to stay in the Empire."

"My fiancé thinks the Ca'cadasans are real, and still out there," said Jennifer, nodding at Smythe. "But as he says, we have grown up, and maybe they have realized that it is best to avoid us as well."

"Nice philosophy," said Smythe, cutting into her steak. "Not sure I believe it. But nice philosophy."

"So why did you sign on to this sector if you're so worried about alien nightmares coming out of the deeps?" asked Tagalag.

"The money," said Smythe, hesitating for a moment with a piece of steak on her fork. "I want to retire someplace nice, and this job pays well. Much better than I would get in any other sector, save that fronting Lasharan space."

"So why is the money so good for this sector?" asked Jennifer, reaching for her wine glass, which the servers had kept topped off.

"Don't know," said Smythe after she swallowed her bite. "You tell me. But people don't pay over scale for no reason. I've learned enough in my time to know that."

The rest of the trip was very uneventful, as most such trips are. Space travel was too advanced for there to be much in the way of hardship or excitement. Objects were either well plotted, or seen far enough ahead of time to avoid. There were still pirates to worry about in some sectors of space, but not in an Imperial system with its own watchdogs patrolling the lanes.

Jennifer stood on one of the observation decks at the end of those five days as the vessel inserted into orbit. The planet below was a blue and white jewel, a natural life bearing planet that humankind was making its own. From orbit it was breathtaking. She had read about the native life, some kinds of supersized mammalian dominant forms, like a cross between dinosaurs and Pleistocene mammals. *They just had the bad luck for us to be around and want their world*, she thought, then dismissed that path. There were laws in place to protect the wildlife of any world. One half of the biosphere would be preserved for the native species. One half forever as a preserve. Unless people found something they needed more than the native life. Then they would take it, no matter the cost to that life.

She was aware of the other ships in orbit through her link with the *Queen of the Rings'* computer. There were two dozen ships, from a couple of small search and rescue vessels to a lone super freighter, thirty million tons of carrier and cargo. She couldn't see much of them from the deck, only the strobes of a couple and the schematic representations plotted onto the orbital area presented by the computer. Then she noticed something closer, and queried the computer as to the identity. She opened a visual box in her optical center and looked closely at fifteen million tons of battleship, one of the monsters of the Imperial Fleet. She wondered for a moment what it was doing here, knowing better than to send out a query about it. *Probably just a stopover on patrol*, she thought.

"We have docked with the Sestius primary station," came a voice over the intercom, coinciding with a notice through her implant. "All passengers prepare to disembark in the assigned order."

Not long now, she thought, walking from the deck and heading for her cabin. She was already packed and ready, and most of her luggage was in the porter's storage, ready to go. She only had to grab her ready bags and go, and her new life would open up to her.

*   *   *

Captain Glen McKinnon, Imperial Marines, stood by the terminal window and watched the shuttle carrying his life and love touchdown on the field. It was a first class shuttle, coming in on grabber units, able to come to a hover and touch down softly on the tarmac. Other shuttles were landing on the longer runway, these fusion drive ships that subjected their passengers to various bumps and possible bruises. Such would not even be in service on most of the core worlds. The frontier worlds extended the life of old technology, and they were still seen as useful out here.

The first class shuttle came to a halt, and when the ground crew drove out to the ship there was finally a sense of scale. The shuttle was over forty meters in length, and when the cabin hatch slid open there was an orderly exodus of almost a hundred passengers. Meanwhile the robots, under the guidance of the ground crew, popped open the cargo hatches and started to unload the effects of said passengers.

"Well sir," said the Senior Sergeant who had accompanied him as driver this day. "Don't be a total idiot. Run out there and greet her."

McKinnon scowled at the man for a moment, and received a look of pure innocence in return. "You're correct of course, you insubordinate bastard," he told Senior Sergeant Hogan, who was really too high a rank to be driving a mere captain around. But then again, the Colonel had given him the week off, even while the battalion was as busy as a one legged man in a martial arts tournament, because Glen had been long separated from his own love. Jennifer had not been able to leave with the transport that carried the unit and its dependents, having to come along later. And the

Colonel had told his junior officer he didn't think he would be of much use until he got her settled in. Hence the air-car and experienced NCO.

"I'll make sure her luggage gets aboard," said the Sergeant to Glen's back.

Then the officer was too busy navigating the stairs at high speed to worry about such mundane matters.

The security guard waved the officer through the doors, and Glen thought that it was damned fine that the uniform opened doors so quickly. The passengers were starting toward the terminal. In a couple of months the mating walkways would be ready, and passengers would be able to walk in air conditioned comfort to the receiving lounge. But even though there had been people on the planet for over ten years, it was still a frontier world, and improvements sometimes came at a snail's pace. Nonmilitary improvements the officer reminded himself. This sector was receiving disproportionate reinforcements, and he wasn't quite sure he believed the official explanation.

And then he only had eyes and thoughts for the vision in front of him. He had met Jennifer ten years before, when she was a civilian doctor at a fleet base. It had been love at first sight, at least for him. She had taken a little more convincing to sign on with a possible career Marine officer. But her following him on this assignment had proven her commitment to them.

"Jennifer," he yelled, holding his arms open to receive the running form of the red haired, blue eyes beauty that he knew was his superior in everything but physical strength. She dropped her bags to the ground just before she flung her arms around him, or as far around as she could on his muscular bulk. Then their lips met, and they were simply two lovers meeting again.

"You all need to move on," said one of the security people, standing near with a smile on her face.

Glen nodded, picked up Jennifer's bags, and offered her an arm.

"It's so damn hot out here," she said, wiping a drop of sweat from her brow with her sleeve.

"F2 star," said Glen, looking up at the bright white point in the sky. "Heavier gravity than you're used to as well."

"They ran us at this gravity all the way out," said Jennifer, smiling. "I'm almost used to it."

"Well, I've got us some good quarters near the barracks. And only six blocks from the hospital."

"And how are the facilities here?" asked Jennifer, looking at the terminal that was done in early colonial ferrocrete.

"Pretty good for a colony world," said Glen, moving them along toward the terminal. "Of course this is the capital, so it's better off than most of the more rural areas."

"Where I'll be doing most of my work," said Jennifer with a frown.

"You still insist on being a travelling doctor?" said Glen, stopping for a moment and looking down at her.

"That's where I'm needed," she said, nodding. "And that's what I put in for. But don't worry, I can take care of myself."

"And we'll just have to make sure you're even more prepared," said Glen with a smile. "I've got some equipment for you that I want to get you trained up on this week, before I let you go flying out over the bush."

"Yes sir," said Jennifer with a laugh, throwing a salute with her free hand.

A trumpeting sound turned them both around, and Glen smiled at the dozen forty ton herbivores that were being led along the tarmac to a large shuttle. The animals, which he knew were sedated, were still nervously looking around, and he hoped the handlers were prepared.

"What are those?"

"One of the things you need to look out for when you're in the bush," Said Glen, gesturing at the beasts as if he had commanded them to appear. "And there are carnivores out there that hunt them. They'll hunt you too, though you won't give them any nourishment."

"And where are those going?" asked Jennifer, her eyes wide with wonder as she watched the dinosaur sized mammals with their sparse fur over scaly skin shuffle toward the shuttle.

"Some zoological garden somewhere," said the officer. "Maybe even Capitulum."

"I would love to see that zoo someday," said Jennifer, imagining the huge capital of the Empire.

"Well, when we have a free decade maybe we can do the complete Imperial Zoo tour," said Glen with a laugh. He gestured to an air-car which was dropping toward the tarmac in front of them, its official registration getting it into the landing field. "And here comes our ride. Please excuse the insubordinate fool that's driving," he continued as the Sergeant climbed out of the car. "He has a modicum of skill. Which is the only reason he's not a private."

"I love you too, sir," said the Sergeant with a smile, holding out his hand to Jennifer. "I am honored to meet the Captain's lady, ma'am. I hope he was worth the trip."

Jennifer looked up at Glen with a smile on her

face. "Oh, I'm sure he will be Sergeant," she said in a laughing voice. "If not, there will be hell to pay."

Glen laughed back as he handed her into the car, knowing that she spoke the truth. And knowing that he would do anything to make sure she was happy here, or anywhere else they happened to be.

Chapter 3

We have never found physical evidence of a soul. We have looked for centuries for this elusive object. We have weighed bodies after death and found no missing mass except for that excreted from the body with the relaxation of sphincter muscles as the result of death. We have subjected humans to every kind of scan, looking to the atomic level. And still we cannot find a vital force that makes a human a human. We can make life, or brings things to life that were devoid of living processes. Does that mean the soul is not synonymous with life? And does this make myself, a scientist, believe that there is no such thing as a soul, just because we cannot find physical evidence of such? No, it does not. In fact it gives me more reason to believe in the existence of this non-material construct. Remember, the lack of evidence is not the evidence of lack. And something is missing in the humans who are nurtured in an artificial womb, or brought to life as clones, or brought back to life after a certain period of decay. What is lacking? That is not the question. It is certainly something that we cannot measure, but its absence is real. And that is why I believe in a soul.

Lecture by Dr. Natusi Kenyata at the Imperial Medical College, Capitulum, Year 612 of Empire.

"And what kind of creatures have you brought me today, Group Commander?" said Great Admiral Miierrowanasa M'tinisasitow from his chair at the end of the audience chamber. The officer in question had communicated that he had some new aliens they had contacted that he wanted to present to the Conquest Fleet Commander. But he had not been prepared for the strangeness of the aliens.

"They are called Klang," said the commander of a battle group within the fleet, speaking clear and not through the translator, so the aliens would feel discomforted not knowing what was being said. "They run a small Empire to coreward of us," he continued. "Not more than a couple of hundred inhabited systems, and maybe a dozen subservient races."

"I see," rumbled the Admiral, looking over the two aliens standing next to his subordinate. They were almost as big as a Ca'cada, he noted, about two and a half meters of solid muscled biped, one with reddish brown fur covering from head to foot, the other a yellow blond coloration. They were blunt clawed, with large curving horns rising another half meter above their scalps. When one opened his mouth to speak, the Admiral noted the flat grinding teeth of a herbivore.

A dominant herd animal, thought the Admiral, looking over the pair standing next to the six limbed, three meter tall, green furred officer of his people. While not completely unheard of, they were rare intelligences, as herd animals that rose to sapience tended to be even more violent than the vast majority of carnivores and omnivores. Their heritage was normally one of violent fights for herd dominance among the males, and relative docility among the females. Advancing tech normally meant an end to the race as they carried their instinctual drives to a logical conclusion, and the species ended.

The Admiral gave them a smile that revealed his canines and tusks, marking him as an omnivore. He looked at the gaudy and primitive fur and leather panoply that covered torso and groin, leaving arms and legs bare except for the knee length boots. Ca'cadasans tended toward the more practical ship wear, favoring jumpsuits colored coded for rank and function.

"I assume you had a good reason for bringing them before me?" said the Admiral, turning a fierce look at his Group Commander. *I've been with this fleet for over a thousand years*, thought the Admiral, *half of them in some kind of command capacity, and most contacts tend to be more violent.*

"They were scoping out one of my scouts," said the Group Commander, looking over at the alien *guests*. "I believe they were about to attack the scout, which they outmassed by double, probably about a million tons. But they caught sight of one of my battleships before they could let loose a volley."

"And twenty-five million tons of warship made them decide to act civilized," laughed the Admiral, looking down at the aliens who met his gaze with unwavering stares. *Brave enough*, he thought, noting their erect carriage. *But not completely foolish either.*

"That, and a couple of cruisers cutting off their escape," agreed the Group Commander. "We examined their vessel. Not as advanced as ours, but not that far behind either. Then they told me they gained much of their technology from another race. They themselves were still quarreling on their native pastures five hundred years ago, marching to war on foot to besiege walled towns."

"And who would be foolish enough to equip them with advanced technology, with such a recent barbaric past?" asked the Admiral with a raising of eyebrows. His race would only enslave such an easy prey, not raise them up to be a competitor. His left multihand reached out for a glass of cool hallaso wine that a short, simian race servant brought. Another servant brought a glass to the Group Commander, while the guests went without. *No use making them think they are equals*, thought the Admiral, continuing to stare down his nose at the motionless herbivores.

"Their Captain here," said the lesser Ca'cadasi with a gesture to the red furred alien, "said they were a smaller biped race. A race with little fur except for that growing from the tops of their heads, and sometimes from their faces."

Great Admiral Miierrowanasa M'tinisasitow narrowed his eyes as he looked at the aliens, his hands tensing on the chair arms and the glass he held.

"Did they have a name, this race?" asked the Admiral softly.

"He said they called themselves humans," said the Group Commander with a triumphant smile.

The Admiral jumped to his feet, glass cracking in his hand as he roared a loud bellow. The lesser races in the long audience chamber turned with fear on their faces, some looking for whatever hiding place they could find. The marine guards moved forward, lowering rifles, or pulling vibroblades while they leveled shields. The Klang looked alarmed for a second, but hunched down and made ready to meet the treacherous attack they thought was come.

The Admiral laughed for a moment, a deep bass rumble that purred from his chest.

"Thank the gods," he roared, flinging his braided hair as he looked upward. "Thank the gods, but we have found the treacherous abbata spawn."

He looked down to where the marines were closing in on the Klang officers and raised a hand signifying halt.

"Leave them be," he ordered the guards in a loud voice. "They are friends, who have brought wonderful news this day. The Emperor has waited for news such as this for two thousand years. But now we have found them. The race that killed the crown prince those many years ago, in a villainous act of cowardliness, when they blew up the ship come to accept their bondage."

The Admiral walked down the steps from his chair and clapped a large hand on the shoulder of the Klang Captain, shaking the alien with hearty strength. He hadn't even been born of subintelligent mother when the deed had been done. But he had lived for fourteen hundred years, half a lifetime for his race, to be here to avenge that deed.

"These are our friends," said the Admiral, engaging the translator circuit so the aliens would understand. "They are to be treated as Ca'cada, their every need and desire granted. For they have brought the news the race has waited these many years. And my fleet will have the opportunity to obey the decree of the Emperor, and slaughter this race as they should have been slaughtered millennia ago.

*   *   *

"The ruling council will see you now, my Lord," said the smooth voice of the Sergeant of Arms of the Elysium Empire, gesturing toward the now open doorway.

And a large doorway it is, thought the Archduke Horatio Alexanderopolis, looking at the ornately decorated monstrosity that beckoned. At least by human standards it was monstrous, though to the inheritors of the Empire of the Ancients it may have appeared very different.

The white haired human nodded to the tall and slender avian who had addressed him. He got up from his seat and started walking down the hall to the door, his boots sounding off the marble floor of the governing palace. The walk and the high ceilings were intended to intimidate or awe those who approached the governing council. But over a hundred years of government service, seventy-five of ambassadorial duty in one form or another, made the one hundred and seventy-five year old man difficult to awe, and almost impossible to intimidate.

We are the dominate civilization in this sector, he thought as he walked, glancing at the guards of various species who lined the walls in shining ceremonial armor. *We have taken our own science, added what we could learn from these people, and advanced beyond them. Now they come to study in our Universities, and wonder at the magnificent structures we raise on the planets of nearby suns.*

Horatio nodded again at the Sergeant of Arms before walking into the room where sat the governing council. There were five very different beings representing the four most numerous species of the Empire, as well as a token council being from one of the seventeen other species that made up the polity.

And Fermi was correct, thought the ambassador when he bowed toward the seated monarchs. *There were only a few races in the Galaxy in his time capable of transmitting messages to other stars. Even fewer able to travel interstellar distances. The extinct Elysians were the most altruistic of the bunch, raising all of these other, more primitive species, off their planets, and saving them from the destruction that comes to most sentient beings when they discover science. Unfortunately for us the other known advanced race was not burdened with altruism.*

"I greet you in the name of my Emperor," said the

elder statesman to the council. "Augustine I sends his well wishes to our magnificent neighbors."

That statement was greeted by chitering and tweeting and growling as the beings talked among themselves for a moment. He recognized the baring of fangs on the *Lopernian* as a smile, and the open mouth of the reptilian *Nockernan* as anything but. His translation program was blocked by three of the beings, but two were on an open circuit to him.

Wish I didn't have such good olfactory faculties, he thought while waiting for a reply. *The Lopernian's fur smells like sour milk, and I bet the Jranok hasn't had a bath in forever.* But he had to admit that the avian *Brakakak* exuded a sweet perfume that masked much of the odor and went well with the brightly colored plumage of that noble creature, the leading race of the Empire.

"We greet our respected human guest from our brother Empire," said High Lord Grararakakak in his twittering rendition of perfectly understandable Terran English, the official lingua fracas of the human worlds. "We are happy that you are in good health, and will continue to serve as the mouth of your ruler."

"I hope to serve for at least another couple of decades," announced Alexanderopolis in the twittering tongue of the avian race, something that had taken decades of practice to perfect, at least as much as humanly possible. "If not at this exalted post, then at least some other small job that it may please my Emperor to give me."

The Nockernan hissed something to the High Lord, turning a baleful eye on the human while his large purple tongue ran over leathery lips.

You wouldn't like the taste, Boyo, thought the human, knowing that his proteins would not be digestible to that race of carnivores. Just as his Empire's fleets would not be digestible to Elysium's military.

"The Lord Lisssiliss has said that we need to get to business," said the avian with as much of a smile as he could accomplish with a short beak. "We have questions to ask as to the intentions of Terra."

And I'm sure your representatives on Jewel will be asking the same questions, thought the ambassador. *And then you'll compare notes to see if you can catch us in a lie.*

"Ask what you would, Lord," he said with a bow, feeling a bit of the strain in his old back from the courtly mannerism. "I will answer as I can."

"We would expect no secrets from you, Archduke," said the High Lord, with a returning bow that showed as much grace as the most agile human dancer could have produced. "But the truth as you are allowed to speak it."

Horatio nodded his head with a smile. The High Lord was a smooth devil, wise in the ways of diplomacy.

"I will answer as well as I can."

The reptilian hissed again, and the ambassador wished again that he was allowed to translate through his own implant, but the Nockernan continued to block access to his speech.

"We have heard disturbing reports that your Emperor is to ask your Parliament for the funds to expand your military capabilities," said the High Lord, staring with red eyes into the blue eyes of the human. "We wonder what this portends, as you already possess the most efficient and deadly military in this region of the Galaxy. You have won every war in which that military fought. And you have the other two human kingdoms as friends, who seem to be made up of equally competent warriors and scientists."

For now, thought the ambassador, gazing back at the High Lord, then sweeping his glance around at the other four members of the council. *That could change any minute, and we would be their enemies again.*

"You know the story of how we came here," said the ambassador, noting from the rapt expressions that all of the council was listening to his translated words. "We were on the run and defeated by another Empire. One which did not have the altruistic code of our beneficent neighbors, the Elysians. They destroyed our home world and our people, except for the less than hundred thousand or so that escaped to find our way here."

"But that was thousands of years ago," croaked the amphibian Crocodilos. "Surely they have perished in that time, as such violent species are wont to do."

"We believe that they had been expanding for over five thousand years when they encountered us," said the ambassador, looking at the amphibian as he walked over to face the creature. "By our calculations they should be getting close to us, if they are expanding still. And the Emperor wishes us to be ready for them if they show. He is not willing to abandon another home and set sail to far stars to escape the menace."

"It makes some of us nervous," said the High Lord, gesturing to the other council members, "to see a neighbor's arm to an unprecedented degree with the express purpose of facing an enemy that none of us have ever seen. We begin to think of conquest. Not by an unseen enemy, but by the great power in our midst."

"You know we are not conquerors," said the ambassador with a look of disgust on his face. "We expanded through the first half millennium by necessity, and those that were absorbed into our Empire enjoy all the rights of citizens. But we are not conquerors. We have fought against your Empire in the past, and defeated it. I say this not to shame you, but to set the record straight. We did not take your stars from you, any that you had already settled. Because we want strong friends around us, and not angry enemies."

"But you took a dozen populated stars from the Lasharans," said the Lord Lisssiliss, his speech now coming clear through the translator. "And you have kept them now for ten years."

"We could have taken more," said the ambassador, looking over at the councilman with exasperation. He had been over this point many times, and the damned Nockernan just couldn't leave it alone. The human turned away and walked the floor for a moment, feeling the many eyes on him.

"We could have taken the whole damned kingdom of fanatics if we wanted to," said the human, looking back at the council. "If we had wanted to kill a hundred billion of the damned fanatics and lose hundreds of millions of our own in return. We took what we needed to straighten out the borders and assure our security from an enemy we know will attack again in the future. Our allies, the Margravi, who were attacked by the Lasharans at the start of the war, wanted us to lay waste to Lasharan worlds and make a desert of the stars on approach to our allied kingdoms. But we refused, and levied stiff penalties on the aliens who are still our friends, because they value our friendship. Because they had committed genocide on several Lasharan worlds on their border.

"So no, my Lord," said the ambassador, turning his

gaze toward the Nockernon. "We do not apologize for the way we prosecuted that war. Nor for the actions we took afterwards."

That sparked a round of arguing among the councilmen. Alexanderopolis still wasn't tapped into the translation, but he had studied all of these species enough to know their body languages. And he could tell that it was three against two for his side of the argument. Which, while not ideal, was good enough for government work. After fifteen minutes of debate the meeting broke up, with the Nockerman and Jranok storming from the hall, while the others stayed to talk to the human in more intimate conversation.

Later the ambassador had a private meeting in the magnificent chambers of the High Lord of the Council, Grarakakak. The avian ruler sat in his species specific chair swirling a whiskey on the rocks, while the human sat on a chair that had been installed especially for his anatomy, taking an appreciative sip of the same liquid.

"I wish you had been a bit easier on my fellow rulers," said the High Lord, taking a swallow from his own glass. "Ah. We need to keep you as friends so you will continue to trade us this nectar of the gods."

"Deal," said the ambassador, looking at a small sweet cake made with Elysium Honey. "As long as we get your wonderful products in return."

"So what is the deal with the military?" asked the High Lord, looking over his glass. "Will you expand?"

"I don't think so," said the ambassador, shaking his head. "I support the Emperor in most areas, but I really think this expansion will scare too many of our neighbors. And he just doesn't have the support in Parliament for it. Too many of the Lords will vote their pocketbooks, I'm afraid."

"I am not sorry to hear that," said the avian, shaking his own head in a very human gesture. "I like your Empire, and the Emperor as a man. But I am comforted by the fact that the fleet that scares the seven hells out of its neighbors is not going to expand."

"And it comforts me to know that it scares our neighbors," said the ambassador to the being he had come to think of as a friend in the twenty odd years he had dealt with him. "I know we're not going to use it for offensive operations. And the fear factor keeps the peace for all of us." *And forces the rest of you to keep your militaries strong, for when we might need them.*

"Except for the Lasharans," said the High Lord with a twitter that served his race as a chuckle. "Nothing frightens those bonehead fanatics. I'm surprised you didn't transport those from the worlds you took back to their home stars."

"The High Command wanted to," admitted the human, breathing in the scent of fine whiskey along with the beautiful aroma of the alien. "But some bleeding hearts in the Parliament thought it was wrong to uproot the poor souls we had just defeated. So they were allowed to stay, if they wanted."

"And they wanted to, of course," said the alien with another twitter. "So they could keep close and painful contact with the human race."

"You know both of our races so well, Lord Grarakakak," said the human with a laugh.

"And what about this great project of yours?" asked the avian, his eyes narrowing.

"Like most things we build, a little behind schedule and over budget," said the ambassador. "But it appears to work, and we are very hopeful of being able to put up gates throughout the Empire. A real breakthrough in travel and commerce, that we will be glad to share with our friends."

"And that sharing will not be without its benefits to the Terran Empire, of course," said the shrewd alien.

"When it comes to trade, what benefits us benefits our major trade partner," said the ambassador, leaning toward his friend. "And I'll tell you something that is not being given much talk in the news."

The alien leaned in so he could catch what he knew was coming.

"You can always blow a gate up, or just turn it off, if something's coming through you don't like."

*   *   *

Sean was exhausted, as tired as he had felt since coming aboard the *Sergiov.* He thought he had found the problem with the troublesome emitter, something to do with the electromagnetic field that powered the nanites. They had spent twelve hours straight going over those systems, checking all the hardware, then injecting new nanites into the system. And it still didn't work properly. It was supposed to be a ten hour duty shift, which would have left him with sufficient time to relax and sleep before the next shift, fourteen hours later. Now he would have to come in two hours early, with the rest of his command, and work another long day, probably fourteen hours or more. *And that bastard of a weapons officer just doesn't understand*, thought the Prince as he walked past his quarters and headed for the nearest recreation center, one designated for officers.

Duty shifts on the *Sergiov* normally ran ten hours, which provided overlap throughout the twenty-four hour ship days. He wondered how men had survived in the old wet navy days, when they stood four hour watches with eight off, but still got caught up in regular duty days and were lucky if they actually got four hours of sleep in twenty-four. Of course alerts and other duties could play hell with the schedule, but that was part of being in Fleet.

The door slid open as Sean approached, giving him a good look into the crowded room. It was crowded mostly because it wasn't very large. So the thirty officers and warrants in the room took up half the seating, and all of the pool tables. The lounge was called Ten-Forward for some obscure reason that no one seemed to know. Every ship had a Ten-Forward, even though rooms on a ship weren't numbered in that way. Just some obscure tradition that dated back forever, as far as he could tell.

"Your majesty," yelled out a voice that caused Sean to flinch. He had learned early on that the other officers would rib him about his social position, and the best thing to do was to go along with it. Otherwise the lack of maturity of people trying to escape the heavy burdens duty laid upon them would make it worse for him.

"What's going on, Count," replied Sean, waving at the other young Lieutenant who ran the A ring. Jasper Bettencourt was not really a count. Simply the eldest son of a count who would probably live another century and a half. He might get the title someday, in fact he probably would. But nothing was guaranteed over that span of time.

Jasper gave him a laugh and a smile and motioned to a seat next to him at the table, where two female officers already sat.

Maybe I might get lucky tonight, thought Sean, sliding into the seat and smiling at the young blond ensign that occupied the next chair.

"This is Ensign Connie Caldwell," said the other officer, motioning to the small blond woman. "And this is Lt. Constance Salvatore," he said, putting his hand on the top of the female officer's hand. She blushed prettily at the touch, her red cheeks contrasting beautifully with her fair skin and raven black hair. "And would you like a drink?"

"Of course," said Sean, waving at the part time bartender who was working the club on his off hours. "Rum and coke," he called to the man.

"How can you drink that crap," said Bettencourt, a smirk on his face. "When are you going to drink a real beverage?"

"Like that damned Scotch," said Sean, making a face. He had never liked the taste of that drink, so loved by the gentry and wealthy businessmen.

"I love rum and coke" said the blond Ensign.

"Commoner," said Bettencourt with a frown.

The Ensign stuck her tongue out at the young noble, eliciting a laugh from Sean and Salvatore.

"What is this Fleet coming to," said Jasper, holding his hand over his heart. "When people can show such disrespect to their betters."

"What betters," said the Ensign, glaring at the senior officer. "I have twenty IQ points on you."

That's what I like about the Fleet, thought Sean, laughing with the rest while picking up his drink. *No social strictures beyond rank. And even there they are not hard and fast.* Sean thought back for a moment on his upbringing, so different than even those of the son of a count that shared his table. It was always everything under the cautious eyes of bodyguards, not even allowed to be a kid most of the time. And when he did play it was a lonely play, with the sons and daughters of gentry, children he didn't always like. Not able to make his own friends. Sure, the vacation spots were spectacular, skiing and diving and hiking in places that the common folk were not even allowed to see pictures of, lest some idiot use them to plot assassination.

"Intellectual snob," said Jasper in his mocking voice. "Leave it to such as you and you will have all the wealth, and leave us poor nobles, well, poor."

The Ensign stuck her tongue out yet again, then turned toward Sean, looking at him with lovely blue eyes. "Is it true that you're an Imperial Prince?"

"It's true, my dear," said Jasper, clapping a hand on Sean's forearm. "You are sitting with a man who might someday be Emperor of this whole shooting match."

"That is very unlikely," said Sean, feeling a blush steal across his face. "I'm third in line."

"You never know what's going to happen," said Jasper with a laugh. "My younger brother is always telling me I'm going to die out here on the frontier. But I think that's just wishful thinking and all. So what say we get roaring drunk?"

"What say," said Sean, waving for the bartender again. "You know," he said, looking back at Jasper, "in the old navy days, I mean the wet navy, drunkenness was not allowed aboard a warship."

"Why ever not, old boy," said Jasper, his words slightly slurred.

"Because a drunk crew was fairly useless if the shit hit," said Connie with a smile. "We learned that in history class at the university."

"You didn't attend the academy?" asked Sean, looking over at the small beauty. She shook her head. "Not even one of the satellite academies."

"I was a science nerd," she said, looking into his

eyes and sending a thrill up his spine. "My father wanted me to study for a career in physics. But ROTC was something I couldn't pass up, and the chance to work on MAM reactors."

"So you're an engineer?" asked Sean, looking at the woman with a new respect. Engineering officers were known as the nerds of the Fleet. But they also pursued a very physical and dangerous job. A MAM reactor could be ejected to save a ship. Sometimes the engineering duty crew rode them to oblivion.

"I am," she said, pride in her voice. "But I'd really like to hear about you. What was it like growing up in the Imperial First Family?"

She put a hand on Sean's forearm as she said this. *Lucky indeed*, thought the Prince, looking into those big blue eyes.

*   *   *

The twin suns were rising over the low hills as a dawn breeze blew over the assembled masses. The large orange globe of the yellow sun and the smaller globe of its white dwarf consort looked down on a gathering of the faithful such as they had not witnessed in many a year. Half a million beings knelt on prayer mats on the valley floor, while hundreds of thousands of others sat waiting on the low hillsides. The chanting voices of millions of others reached over the hills.

Ahmadhi-ghasta (Grand High Bishop) Mallakan stood on the high platform of the Grand Temple of Jakarja Lashana (Church of the Gods Vengeful) and looked out over the faithful, knowing that his message would reach not just these, but the billions of other worshipers on the planet. And the message would be relayed throughout the Lasharan Hegemony that was his personal fiefdom.

The religious leader took a moment to scan the crowd, recognizing faces here and there at the front, those who had followed him through his bloody rise in the church hierarchy. There were the robes of clerics, the functional work suits of factory workers, intermingled with the uniforms of military personnel. All were thin humanoids of over two and a half meters height, twin macro eyes and quad motion eyes focused on the high platform. There was a smattering of shorter and squatter heavy planet dwellers among the predominantly home world natives. The light of the rising suns glinted from shiny red skins the toughness of leather.

Mallakan winced as the pain shot up his sandaled foot to his right hip. He prayed quickly to the God of Destruction, *Marrala,* that he would live long enough to see the humans vanquished, adding a quick addendum that he would be happy to set that vanquishing in motion. But at eighty-five years he was sure he had no more than a decade left, given the strictures of the church against the life prolonging sciences of the infidels.

"My brethren," he began, hidden speakers amplifying his voice over the hills and valleys of the sacred ground, where the first prophet had heard the word of the gods and started the faith. "We meet here today that I may speak the will of the gods to you."

The chanting rose as he lifted his seven digit hands into the sky, motioning for quiet. Millions of hands were raised in the air in supplication to the gods as the voices died to a murmur and then cut off.

"The humans," began again, looking over the crowd, "with their false gods and heretical ways."

The gathering roared, many shaking fists at the sky,

while a few thousand jumped into the air and spun in ecstasy.

"And their heretical ways," he continued, his voice rising above the din. "A race that does not even worship the same gods as their fellows. Who cannot agree on that which is holy. A race that deserves death, destruction and to fade into the history of the Galaxy as an abject lesson to those who would be apostate."

The roar of the crowd rose to a fever pitch. *Many will be the martyrs to the faith,* thought the Ahmadhighasta. *And they will take many of the infidels with them to the twelve hells, where they will rise again to the heavens, while the infidels burn forever.*

"Some will say that the infidels are too strong in the ways of science and engineering for us to defeat."

"No," shouted the crowd. "No. No."

"But compared to the gods, what is the power of science and engineering? Compared to the will of the faithful, what is the discipline of our enemies?"

The discipline I wish I could instill in the faithful, he thought with a grimace as the valley shook to the multitude of voices. *Their discipline is what wins battle after battle. War after war. The faithful are brave. The faithful are willing to die for the faith. But the faithful do not have the patience to follow orders, or follow a plan.*

"The infidels play dangerous games with our brethren on the worlds they hold," he said as the crowd hushed. "The faithless curs who hold the children of the faithful hostage to the guns of their soldiers and their warships. They brainwash the children in the faith of their false gods. They damn the souls of the children of the faith to eternal perdition."

The crowd roared in anger and fists were waved in the air. Some blaclava blades were unsheathed and waved in the sky, threatening the health and welfare of their wielders' neighbors

"Will we allow this to happen to the souls of our brethren?" he roared, raising both fists to the sky.

"No," screamed the multitude. "No."

"No more," roared the cleric. "No more."

"No more," screamed the crowd. "No more. No more."

Mallakan felt a smile broaden his face as he exposed his carnivore teeth and raised his hands into a prayer.

"May the gods be by our sides, my brothers, sisters and neuters," he invoked, while he looked over the future martyrs to the cause, their blood up and baying for the prey they would run down and destroy.

Soon, he thought, images of dead humans in his head. *Soon.*

*   *   *

The armed transport circled over the mission, door gunners scanning the tree line despite the assurance of the ground forces that they were no enemy in the area. Grabbers on the hull powered down as the lift fans whined, taking over the job of keeping the twelve meter hull in the air. A half dozen similar transports dropped to the ground in the mission landing field while four of the smaller sting ships rotated in pairs along the perimeter, looking for victims.

Flights of transports moved to the north, homing in on the plumes of smoke that marked where artillery was chasing the survivors of the enemy raiding party into the thick equatorial jungle. A ball of flame rose into the air under a sting ship that was keeping the pressure on the guerillas.

Major Samuel Baggett looked from the control

screen in front of his station on the command transport, following the suit cam of one of his officers as he moved through the thick jungle in pursuit of the enemy. Intuiting that everything was in hand on the moving front he turned his attention to the landing field below where the six transports were disgorging the two platoons of light infantry. From the signs of the fight that had ensued before their arrival, the platoon that had held the mission had done a good job of holding the fort. There were the bodies of black pajama clad Lasharans stacked up near the fence, scores of them, next to the two dozen bodies of armored troopers who had been surprised by the assault. Surprised or not the Imperial Infantry had fought according to the traditions of the service, and had kept the enemy at bay until reinforcements had arrived.

And those were not us, he thought, even though this mission had been within the 988th Infantry Division's area of responsibility. Men from an independent battalion had been tasked with defending these structures, and his unit had been tasked with the area reaction force. He looked down on the mission from his side window to note the half dozen larger suits that bounced into the clearing, three of them each pulling a couple of more dead guerillas with them.

Unfortunately for our tall red brothers, a company of heavy infantry was on maneuvers out here in the sticks, he thought, watching the many tons of battle armored troopers gliding across the ground on suit grabbers. *That's where I need to be. The guerillas had nothing that could even harm one of them through that armor.*

But they had the weapons on that ambush they pulled last week, he thought soberly, remembering the op the guerillas had sprung that had killed a half platoon of the well armored and heavily armed troops. *Maybe medium suits are the way to go*, he thought, imagining the half ton suits that were still superior to the three hundred pounds of equipment his own men interfaced with. *Shit, if they really want to get you they will, no matter how much armor you put on.*

"Put us down on the field," he ordered the pilot, and then tapped into the command link to the ground troops. "I'd like to speak with the commander of the heavy infantry when I land," he said over the com while the bird landed with a light thump on the ground.

Baggett slid the door open and jumped from the transport, his eyes scanning the area with the practice of an experienced infantryman. The ground shook under his feet and he looked to the south where a trio of medium tanks, five hundred tons of alloy and heavy weapons each, moved across the roadway.

"Captain Miersham reporting, sir," said a female voice when the large suit landed in front of the major. Baggett looked up at the robotic looking creature. Built in weapons on the shoulders and wrists of the three and a half meter tall construction drew his eyes. The wrist weapons of a command suit were heavier than his own heavy weapons troopers carried, and the armor skin could handle an impact that would spread him and his lighter armor over the landscape.

"Thanks for coming to the rescue these people," said Baggett, returning the brief salute. "Bad luck for the reds though."

"Yes sir," laughed the officer over the com circuit. "About two hundred of them hit the perimeter this morning at sunrise," said the officer, going into report mode. "Launched mortars at the mission while they opened fire from the tree line. Lucky for us one of the sentries was a heavy weapons gunner and planted a laser beam across the field that took out twenty or so of the enemy. We found their dismembered bodies out there in the fields, along with forty or fifty more that the directional mines got."

"And you came in and cleaned up the rest," said Baggett. "Before we could get a response team here."

"Actually a good thing, sir," said the officer, swiveling the suit head to look over the field where further heavy infantry suits were carrying more of the guerilla dead in. "They had antiaircraft set up, lying in wait for your birds to come in. I lost two troopers to their heavy weapons and launchers before we took them out."

"I'm sorry about your casualties," said the major, thinking of all the men and women his battalion had lost in the last two weeks. "And I'm happy you took those bastards out for us. Did the missionary survive?"

"Yes sir," said the Captain, pointing at the large, plasticrete structure. "He took cover with his parishioners in the church. The construction was heavy enough to stop small arms and light mortars, and the enemy never got anything heavier within line of sight to hit it."

"I guess I need to talk with him or her if I'm going to file a complete incident report on this slaughter," said the major, turning away and starting to walk toward the mission church. "Good job, Captain. I'll send a favorable report to your commander."

"Thank you, sir," said the other officer, bounding into the air to jump back to her troops.

A medium sized man of about a hundred and twenty walked out of the church while the major was headed toward it. The man wore work clothes and a clerical collar, sweat beading off his brow in the late morning sun.

Suit environmental systems are working well, thought Baggett as he stopped in front of the man. He felt very comfortable in the equatorial climate thanks to the technology of his light battle armor.

"Are you the officer in charge of this herd?" said the minister, glaring up at the major.

"Yes sir," said the infantryman, raising the visor on his helmet. "Major Samuel Baggett, First of the 789th Infantry."

"I'm Father Michael O'Rourk," said the man, wiping the sweat from his reddened brow with a cloth. "Imperial Catholic Church. And I want to file a report with your superiors on the horrible job of protection you have been doing here. I lost nine parishioners to this attack. What do you have to say to that, Major?"

"These men were not in my unit," said Bagget, looking at the bodies of the soldiers lying forty meters away. "Still, they lost twenty-five men and women from the platoon that was tasked with safeguarding this mission," said the major, keeping his temper bottled up. "And the heavy infantry that came to your rescue lost people as well."

"Yes, well," said the priest, wiping his brow again as the first of the parishioners left the church. Baggett looked at the tall, red skinned beings with their two large orbs and four pinpoint eyes looking around the courtyard.

"You're soldiers," continued the priest. "You're paid to take these risks. I'm also paid to take risks. I put my faith in God and do the work I am called to do. If I live or die, it is in the hands of God. But my parishioners aren't. I think I'm finally getting to them, and driving the faith of hatred from their minds. But they need your protection to survive, so they can grow in the faith."

"I understand, father," said the officer. "But we're spread thin on the ground out here. A platoon per mission is all we can afford, if we're to keep enough back for reaction forces and operations."

"I know, my son," said the priest, looking back as his flock wandered the courtyard or stood looking at the bodies. "It's just hard to see the light of God appear in the eyes of the heathen. And then see that same child dead and mutilated outside the mission, where all of the others find them. After I have told all of them that they will be protected."

"We'll get another platoon out here as soon as possible," said Baggett, feeling some sweat beading on his own forehead without the visor providing environmental relief. "And I'll try to round up some more perimeter sensors and mines. Whatever I can get to strengthen your position. And I'll bring back whatever report you want to file to my superiors."

"No need for a report, my son," said the priest, his eyes roaming to take in the bodies of the Imperial infantry who had died protecting his church. "I will ask God's blessing on those who gave their lives for us. And pray for those mistaken souls that killed them. Would you like my blessing too, my son?"

"Of course, father," said the officer, dropping to one knee. "If you can see fit to give your blessing to a member of the Reorganized Episcopal Church."

"No problem, major," said the priest with a smile, raising his hands for the blessing. "We all make mistakes in our lives. Perhaps one day you will join the true faith. Until then, as a follower of our Lord, may he bless and keep you, now and forever."

Now and forever, thought Baggett, looking up at the F4 sun while pulling his visor down to shield his eyes. *But hopefully not on this baked ball. Unless I can count some of my time here as served in hell.*

Chapter 4

Politicians and diapers should be changed frequently and all for the same reason.

José Maria de Eça de Queiroz

"Damn them to hell," growled the Emperor Augustine I, throwing himself in the air-car seat while the Empress Anastasia climbed more ladylike into her own. The Parliamentary Guards gently closed their doors and the driver engaged the grabbers. A couple of air-cars to the front rose into the night sky, strobes flashing as they warned all other traffic from the area. The Emperor looked up through the ceiling ports to see a pair of sting ships loop overhead, pilots on alert for anything out of the ordinary that might mean a threat to the Imperial Couple. Further up in the atmosphere he knew a flight of planetary fighters looked down on the same scene.

"You knew it was coming," said the Empress, as the car rose into the air to follow the two leaders. Augustine looked to the rear as another two air-cars, each filled with a contingent of six Imperial Secret Service Agents, rose into the sky. There were other cars out there as well. Air-cars and vans with the remainder of the security detachment, looking for trouble.

I almost wish someone would shoot us down, thought the Emperor, pinching his nose and rubbing his temples. *But that wouldn't be fair to Dimetre. This mess requires that I take care of it, and not dump it on an unprepared prince.*

"You still got approval for the continuation of the

Bolthole project," she said, giving him a smile.

"After agreeing to finance the damned thing from personal resources," snarled the Emperor, looking down over the city lights while the procession moved the two hundred and fifty kilometers to the palace complex at a businesslike four hundred kilometers an hour. Over a hundred megascrapers were in view on the megalopolis' skyline, with hundreds of lesser skyscrapers bowing at their feet. *All of those people, living their lives in the secure knowledge that their government will protect them. And it's all a lie.*

"Ten trillion Imperials of our family fortune," said the Emperor, putting his face in his hands as he groaned. "Over half of our liquidable assets just to get it started. And they wouldn't let me mortgage the Imperial lands as well."

"The lands belong to the dynasty," said the Empress, putting her hand on her husband's shoulder. "You knew they wouldn't approve their risk. And besides," she said, giving him a kiss on the cheek, "now they don't have to have oversight on the project. Which means they don't have to know where it is, or what it's about."

Augustine turned on the viewer to his front and set it for an image of the House of Parliament. The large building, a legacy to the Greco-Roman style of old Earth, shone under its external floodlights, while the air-cars of the ministers rose into the night like a swarm of fireflies. The building was the permanent home of the House of Lords, the governing nobles of the Empire, four hundred and fifty nobles from hereditary seats, another four hundred and thirty-six elected from the majority of remaining nobles, and seventy-five from the major religions, sat in that building.

Only tonight, at the Emperor's request, they had met in a joint session of all members of Parliament. The House of Scholars, four hundred members elected from the ranks of scientists and professors, had come from their meeting house on the University planet of Avalon.   And the House of Commons, twenty-six hundred and forty-seven members meeting on the industrial world of Forge, had come as well for the joint session.

The great majority of the Lords had voted according to the wishes of their leader, the Prime Minister Count Mejoris Jeraviki. The Scholars had, for the most part, voted their consciences and sided with the Emperor. And the Commons, the swing vote, had split, with just a little over half voting with Jeraviki, and defeating the Emperor's initiative for military expansion.

"I still didn't get it through their thick skulls that we are at risk of annihilation," said Augustine, looking over at his wife. *I truly love you my dear*, he thought. *But even you think I'm somewhat paranoid.*

"They see the facts as they know them," said his wife, rubbing his shoulders. "We have not seen the Ca'cadasans for almost two thousand years. We are the dominant military power in the known Galaxy. And a military expansion will scare the hell out of our neighbors, and maybe spark an arms buildup no one can afford."

"A buildup that will be needed to stop the damned murderers in their tracks," growled the Emperor.

"But you don't know they are anywhere near to entering our space," said the Empress, throwing her hands in the air. "You have no evidence."

"What about the Special Branch data?" said

Augustine, looking into her eyes. "What about the rumors we have heard of aliens on the move, planets devoid of intelligent life that had until recently been flourishing worlds?"

"Rumors," she said in exasperation. "About planets that are beyond our sphere of influence, or even our realm of knowledge. Circumstantial evidence. Why hasn't anyone seen the damned aliens if they're on our doorstep?"

"I don't know," said the Emperor. "Most of the ships we sent that way have not returned. Maybe only the ones that haven't contacted them directly have been allowed to return. I don't know. But one thing I do know."

He looked out over the city again for a moment as he thought, then turned back to his wife.

"If I'm wrong I may go down in history as Augustine the Mad. We may raise taxes a bit and build a few thousand unneeded ships."

He paused for a second and looked out at the pair of sting ships to his right.

"But if I'm right, and of course I think I am, there will be hell to pay when the enemy does appear at the gates."

*   *   *

Roberto Espanol wasn't sure why the aliens wanted him to program the young officer on the psychotronic couch. But the money was good and he would not have to do any more jobs after this one. He could retire in luxury, and no longer have to ply the dark avenues of his trade.

"You will remember nothing of this," he said in his silky smooth voice to the young flight Ensign. The young man sat perfectly still, staring out into space, listening to the instructions.

"Until the signal is given, and the pathways in your mind connect, you will have no recollection of these events. Even your subconscious will be unaware. The instructions will not exist within you until it is time."

The young man closed his eyes and a peaceful smile appeared over his freckled face. His breathing became regular and he fell into a deep sleep.

"Take him back to his quarters," he told the two men in Imperial Fleet uniform standing by. "Make sure it looks good."

"We'll take the drunken sot back to his quarters," said one of the men in the uniform of a Lieutenant Commander of Aviation. "Looks like he had a little too much to drink on his birthday."

Espanol smiled at the man, who he knew to be a real Fleet officer who was also in his employ. One who was not a part of the Imperial Security Squadron, and not subject to the monthly brain scans of those so selected. And a man whose life would be ended by contract soon after he accomplished his last mission for Roberto Espanol.

After the men had left Espanol set the equipment for self-destruct. The nanites that normally kept everything clean and in repair would disassemble the machinery and office furnishings molecule by molecule. And the molecules would be flushed through the building's recycling system until the last nanite crawled in. It would take several days, but there would be nothing to attract the attention of law enforcement before then. There would be no evidence of this operation.

An hour later, as Roberto Espanol, player in the shadows of crime and espionage, approached his home by air-car, he smiled at the thought of no longer having to play the game. The smile turned to a frown when warning lights came on all through the console of the car. The frown turned to a scream as the car tilted downward and plowed into a mountainside at three hundred kilometers an hour. And of course the fail safe restraint system was neither fail safed, nor did it function to restrain as Espanol's body attempted to push through the carbon alloy of the air-car dashboard.

*   *   *

"The operation is set," came the voice over the link.

Prime Minister Count Mejoris Jeraviki nodded his head as he listened to the voice, then realized how silly that gesture was when the being on the other end couldn't see him.

"I understand," said the Count, a nervous thrill running up his spine. His dreams were within reach, to become the power behind the throne. But his greatest nightmare was also reaching for him. This was treason, plain and simple. And the penalty for treason was clear. Death, death, death. Not even the mind wipe, personality death, that most serious crimes called for. This was Regicide, and the penalty would be the end of him.

"What about the other?" he asked, wishing he hadn't as the words left his lips.

"You don't need to know," said the voice that was different over the com. "It will be taken care of. That is all you need to know." He didn't know who the man was, or if it was a man or woman. Jeraviki was merely the middleman, taking orders from above and making sure they were carried out by the operators he had hired. Operators he didn't know, and he guessed that he wasn't supposed to know. What he didn't know he couldn't tell.

The link went dead. Jeraviki checked the status of the com through his link and was not surprised to discover that there was no record in the link of that call. And none of anything that had been said. *These people are truly professionals*, he thought. He still wasn't sure what they were, only that they had approached him with a scheme that seemed to offer him everything he had ever wanted. He had actually met one of them personally, that had been necessary for him to have any trust in them. But he still didn't know who that man was, and was sure the agent wouldn't talk no matter what.

"Would the Count want anything from the kitchen," came the voice of the major domo of the estate, a man who had been with the Count throughout his life.

"No thank you, Robert," said the Count, looking up from his chair, then glancing at the flames that burned in the ornate fireplace. He looked back at the old man, who was approaching two hundred and thirty years of age, and had been with the estate well before the Count's birth. He wondered for a moment what it must be like to have to work for someone. To have to obey orders. The man was well past retirement age, and could have lived in leisure on a small holding of his own. But he decided he wanted to keep working for the estate, so he would as long as he wanted.

"Bring one of the girls up to my room in a couple of minutes," said the Count after taking a sip from his good scotch on rocks. "The newest one, if you would."

"Yes, my lord," said the old man, his face expressionless.

You don't like acting like a pimp," thought the Count with a smile. *But your loyalty to the family is such that you will keep every secret. Especially since your great grandchildren are so well taken care of.*

The Count took another sip of his drink, his link turning on the trivee over the fireplace. The news came on, his favorite station among the thousands that served the Imperial capital city. They were talking about the vote, and he smiled as he thought again of his victory over the Imperial House. A small victory to be sure. And soon would come a greater victory.

The Count didn't care for more wealth. He was already among the hundred wealthiest men of the Empire, which made him a hundred times richer than any of the despots of history. No, what he wanted was power over his fellow man. Unlimited power. Father had instilled that desire in him as he abused his son into adulthood. He never wanted to feel that powerless again, and the only way to ensure that was to rise to the top. He didn't care that he might have sold his soul to the devil to get it. Soon it would be his, and he would then repay his benefactors for their service to him by making sure they disappeared beyond the grave, so he wouldn't have to worry about their betraying his secret.

He checked the time on his implant, shut down the trivee, and got up from his chair, thinking of the beautiful young girl he had bought on the underground slave market. He would enjoy her while she was fresh, then sell her to someone less discriminating when he was tired of her. He smiled at both thoughts as he climbed the stairs to the master's chambers.

*   *   *

"All is in motion," said the man over his link to his employers. The com went through a net that was not part of the Imperial Planet link, something they didn't even suspect existed. He didn't know who had installed it. And he didn't really care. They paid well for his services, and that bought his loyalty.

"And the Prime Minister?" came the voice he knew must be disguised.

"He will play his part," said the operative, who wasn't even known to his employer as more than a voice and a reputation. "And when his part is done, so will he be."

*   *   *

Walborski cursed under his breath and looked up at the bright pinpoint of the star Sestius. It was very hot today, even by the standards of this hot world. His helmet readout displayed a temperature of over forty centigrade. Add to that an infantryman's skinsuit, strap on armor and torso plates, and a battle helmet, all without the cooling systems enjoyed by the regular military, and it added up to a sweating hell.

The farmer pulled his drinking tube into place and sucked in the cold water held by his camel pack. *At least they got that part right*, he thought, while he looked up at the sun again and tried to will it lower in the sky.

He jumped in his skin when the alert signal went off in his ear, warbling, and grimaced as he watched the heads up display on his visor flash that he had been hit by the opfor.

"God Dammit," he yelled, rolling over on his back. The nearby troopers shot him sympathetic glances.

"You're dead again, Walborski," screamed the First Sergeant as he walked quickly across the hillside to where the platoon had been trying to get into position for an ambush. "What damned demon put you in my God damned company?"

"I'm sorry, Top," said the weekend private, looking at some simulated mortar rounds bursting in holographic glory over the hillside. More troopers' casualty signals flared as they were registered as dead or wounded.

"Keep that damned fool head down," yelled the NCO, looking the farmer as if he were a bug. "There's no time for sky watching on an op."

"If they gave us chameleon suits instead of this low tech camo," whined Walborski, looking at his sweat soaked uniform.

"Don't blame the equipment, troop," warned the middle aged NCO, who during the week ran a bar and grill in the village of Neu Romney. "Special ops don't have much better, since they can't afford to send out an electronic signature. And neither can we."

Just because you were a damned buck sergeant in the damned Imperial Marines, forty years ago, thought the farmer, looking down and struggling up to his feet. *That doesn't make you Field Marshal Rommel for God's sake.*

"You know what to do, private," said the First Sergeant, turning his back to look over the field where half the platoon had crawled out of the indirect fire zone, leaving the other half as casualties. Those men were on their feet, starting their runs down the side of the hill, rifles overhead. "Up and back until I tell you to stop."

"Yes, First Sergeant," said Walborski as he started jogging down the hill, holding his rifle up over his head.

"And don't let me catch you slacking, troop," called the NCO over his shoulder.

Walborski shuffled down the hillside, trying to ignore the stares of the platoon members he had gotten *killed* by his ill-advised move.

"Way to go, dickhead," yelled one of the other men, his face red and sweating.

What's the fucking use, thought Cornelius, glancing again at the sun, figuring he had about another two hours of this shit to put up with. *We'll get ground to shit from orbit before we ever get a chance to sneak up on the bad guys.*

A couple of hours later Cornelius put his armor, helmet and weapons on their racks in the platoon's bunker. The skinsuit had to go home to be cleaned, but the nanites in the bunker would clean and service the tech stuff for them. The farmer looked out at the garage section as he left the armory, envy in his face while he looked at the several light tanks and scout vehicles that shared the bunker with his platoon.

At least they get to ride around in comfort before they get ground to shit from orbit, he thought, wishing he had been assigned to them. But that equipment had gone to older men who had served a ten year hitch in the Imperial Army. Not to someone just out of childhood, with no clue how to use them.

Hope Katlyn got that robot running today, he thought, watching some of the other men walking up the stairs, heading for one of the village bars to drink out the dust that coated their throats. Not for him the camaraderie of the militia platoon. He was the fuckup, the one that they all despised, and the one they all blamed for their misery. *Well fuck them. I have beer at home. And a beautiful sexy wife who has, hopefully, prepared a wonderful dinner for her starving husband.*

Walborski reached the top of the stairs himself, avoiding the eyes of his platoon leader as he exited the bunker. Tomorrow would be another day as he tried to learn to be a farmer. To bring in his crops on a brutal world whose wildlife had other ideas.

It's hard enough doing what I need to do to survive, he thought, walking over to his ground cycle, pulling on his helmet and getting into the seat. *Why the hell do we have to play at army? We've got better things to do. And it's not as if the Empire doesn't have professionals to handle that job.*

Cornelius started the cycle, checked for traffic that wasn't there, a habit from growing up on a crowded core world, and pulled into the street. He moved smoothly down the road until he hit the outskirts of the village, then rocketed ahead at a hundred forty kilometers an hour, letting the flow of the air wash the tension from him as he headed for the farm.

The large moon was rising over the horizon, sending beams of light that illuminated the landscape and the road that cut through it. The great majority of the trees were of Terran origin, with a smattering of the prettiest of the native foliage. This was well within the terraformed area, and Cornelius didn't worry too much about native beasts wandering onto the roadway and into the path of his cycle. Minutes later and twenty kilometers down the hardtop he was approaching his farm, which meant that he was getting near the edge of the Terran area, and though the end of the road was fenced in with gates to let Terran vehicles in and out, there had been cases of fifty ton beasts getting into this area. Something he didn't want to run into while riding a cycle. He breathed a sigh of relief as he pulled into the dirt track leading to his own farm. He stopped for a moment at his own gate and looked out over the fields, and the half completed house that would soon be the home he had always dreamed of. They shone in the moonlight, beautiful in the silver glow.

Cornelius breathed in and let the fragrance of

flowers, native and Terran, tantalize his nostrils. *This is what makes it all worthwhile*, he thought, looking at the land that was his. *The land that will be mine if I get it to produce*, he told himself, a reminder of all the work he still needed to do. *Nothing for it but to do it*, he thought, smiling as he watched the dogs come running out to the gate that was opening as he wheeled the cycle toward it. The gate finished opening and the dogs whined and whimpered as they cavorted around him. He gave one a quick pat on the head, then started the cycle moving into his property, looking back as the gate closed behind him, two of the hounds making it in by the barest margins.

"Katlyn," he called, walking to the temporary house from the storage shed. "What's for dinner?"

"Rations," said Katlyn, turning as Cornelius walked into the house.

Walborski wished that she had been kidding, but he could smell the heat tray on the table where Katlyn had just pulled the tabs. The same kind of meal he had grown sick of back on New Detroit. He was about to say something to Katlyn, to let her know of his displeasure. But the downcast look in her eyes, and the splotch of grease on her face held his tongue.

"I am so sorry," she said, shrugging her shoulders. "The robot took longer than I thought, and I didn't have time to do anything else."

"Is, is it working?" he asked, almost afraid of the answer.

"It works," said Katlyn, nodding her head. "It took all day. I'm exhausted."

"I know, honey," said Cornelius, feeling his own fatigue wash over him, making him almost too tired to eat. He realized that he needed the calories, and pulled open the top of the ration pack. "We'll make it. And ration packs aren't that bad."

"Now I know you're lying," said Katlyn with a laugh, getting up from her seat and walking over to plop down in her husband's lap.

"What do you mean?" asked Walborski as Katlyn put her arms around him.

"Rations really suck," she said with a laugh. She kissed him, her soft lips caressing his. "What did you think I meant?" she asked as she leaned back. "And I've got something much better than rations, if you're up to it." She patted the front of his pants as she stood up, then smiled down at him.

"The hell with ration packs," said Cornelius, feeling new energy while he looked at his wife, as pretty as the day he met her, grease spot and all. He smiled while he stood up, taking her hand and leading her into the sleeping area of the one room shelter. *There'll be hell to pay tomorrow*, he thought, pulling off his shirt. *But that's tomorrow.*

* * *

Sean tossed and turned in his bed, his brain a turmoil of images. The dream had started off very pleasantly, with his making love to the senior CPO under him. And she was under him, bucking in pleasure. The Prince had always had very vivid and lucid dreams, the sex in them as good as any he experienced in real life. And screwing an enlisted woman in his chain of command could only be a dream, never reality. And then the dream changed to something much less pleasant.

Some ships he couldn't recognize were standing off the night side of a planet which displayed the ropy lights of massive urbanization. He could recognize the pattern of lights and the outline of continents and large islands. *Cimmeria*, he thought in the dream, one of the core worlds. Home to billions. He wondered for a moment where the orbital forts were. There should have been several in sight, as all core worlds were heavily defended. *It's just a dream*, he reminded himself. A very lucid and detailed dream, but nonetheless not reality.

A bright pinpoint, blindingly brilliant, appeared on the surface among the lights of cities. The pinpoint spread out rapidly, until it covered several of the cities. More pinpoints bloomed and grew, until a third of the land mass of the hemisphere was blotted out. And then Sean understood the ominous portent of the dream. A core world was being attacked by an alien force. Pummeled with kinetic rounds from orbit, the population being erased before his eyes. And there was nothing he could do about it.

Sean sat up in bed with a yell. He could feel the sweat dripping from his face, and the wet sheets sticking to his body. *It's only a dream*, he thought in a moment of relief. Relief left swiftly when he realized what kind of a dream it was.

The curse, he thought, placing his head in his hands. *The bane of the family.*

He had been told that it was very strong in him, not so much in his brothers. But the legends said it was only strong in one destined to rule. *Well, that's not me*, he thought, calling up the time in his link. *3:37 AM*, he thought. *Dammit. Well, I guess I won't get much more sleep tonight, with wakeup call at five*. With that thought Sean climbed out of his bed and headed to the shared living room that was all his for the moment, his suite mate pulling third watch. He ordered coffee through his link while he sat on the couch and connected into the news net. He felt relieved to find that nothing had happened overnight that might have correlated with the dream. *Nothing we know about yet*, he thought, looking up as the kitchen bot came rolling up with a steaming cup.

That's the problem with a large Empire, he thought, taking the cup and sipping carefully at the hot liquid. *It takes too long to actually get the news from all over. It might as well be a transmitted history lesson. Even with the hyperwave relay system.*

Sean sat there digesting the news. Rumors of something unknown, strange sightings, the normal political wrangling with Parliament trying to cut back on defense while the Emperor attempted to increase it. *Was what I saw real?* thought the Prince, playing the dream back in his mind. Unknown ships taking out a core world. A heavily defended planet with industries vital to the Empire. If the dream was true prophecy, a so called gift of the curse, this was a dreadful prophecy. That something had gotten to the center of the Empire and initiated an attack on the heart of their civilization.

I might need to talk to father about this, thought the Prince as he took another sip of coffee. The Emperor had the gift, though it had seemed stronger in Sean. He had dreamed things in the past that had come true. But nothing before of such dark content. *Or maybe I should talk to someone here, aboard Sergiov.* Sean linked into the medical center and looked at the possibilities, then chose an appointment slot. *It might not mean anything, but I'll feel a damned sight better talking about it.*

Sean finished his coffee and ordered another, then got up and headed for his private bathroom. *Maybe a shower will clear things a bit*, he thought, looking forward to another day of duty aboard the battleship.

*   *   *

Major Samuel Baggett stood next to the Colonel commanding the relief troops and watched the new light infantry regiment parade down the middle of the road, heading into the military compound that would be their new home.   His own men had left the night before, having packed up the unit and sending their equipment to the landing field.   Theirs was to be the first regiment of the division off planet.   The new regiment would get acclimated, and would assume their duties, and the next regiment of Baggett's division would be rotated out as its replacement came in.

"Your men look smart, Colonel," said the Major, glancing over at the man with great mustaches on his face.

"We have a proud tradition," said the Colonel with a smile.

Below the stand the first platoon turned their faces to the officers, the guide on rose and the platoon leader and sergeant rendered a formal salute.   Further up the road bagpipes sent their haunting melody into the air and the color guard followed.   The men were all in dress uniforms, with kilts and sporrans, ceremonial rifles on their shoulders.   Their armor and weapons were already in the compound, and Baggett knew from experience that the men would be spending days getting everything squared away.

"Any combat experience?" asked the Major while the next platoon came into line with the stand.

"A wee bit," said the Colonel in his brogue.   "Most of the men have only served on New Edinburgh, which is not a combat zone by any means.   But most of the officers and senior NCOs were with the unit when we fought the Lasharans back in 988.   I expect them to give the men the wisdom of their experience."

That's what I thought too, the Major told himself. *But I found out different after we came under fire, and the new recruits made the same stupid mistakes new men always make. And didn't learn until they had seen enough of their peers die to know what they shouldn't do.*

"So your lads will be transferring to a frontier world?" said the Colonel, looking over at Baggett.

"Yes, sir," said the Major with a smile. "Someplace nice and quiet. Supposed to be a new military hub out in Sector Four. They're building up the capabilities to make it a well-defended system. Or at least that's what we're being told."

"Don't always believe what you're told, lad," said the Colonel, giving Samuel a knowing look. "Wait till you get there and make up your own mind."

Later, in the air-car to the landing field, Baggett thought over what the older man had said. *He's right. It's best to not believe everything you're told. That seems to be a quiet sector, but they're moving a lot in there. More than I would expect for routine system defense.* He resolved to find out what was going on in that sector when he got situated on the transport. Or at least as much as was being released on the common net.

Chapter 5

All of us who are concerned for peace and triumph of reason and justice must be keenly aware how small an influence reason and honest good will exert upon events in the political field.

Albert Einstein

Prime Minister Majoris Jeraviki sat in the comfortable lounger and took a pull from the expensive cigar in one hand, while he swirled the costly cognac in the snifter held in the other. A night breeze blew over the Capitulum Hills and the appropriately named Mansion District. The sweet odors of native neomums and Terran roses wafted from the gardens below the portico.

Jeraviki sighed as he took in the scents under the light of full New Terra and looked at its glow on the exquisite original sculpture of the fifth century Imperial Donatello. Motion caught his eye and he swiveled to look to the south, where, a hundred and seventy five kilometers away a large shuttle, glowing from the heat of reentry, dropped onto Constance the Great Spaceport.

The one thing I won't achieve in this life, he thought, looking across the dense cityscape to the east, *is the naming of a public structure in this, the Imperial City*. That was reserved for members of the Imperial Family and war heroes, neither of which covered him.

The Prime Minister looked to the east and down the hills to the Imperial Compound, twenty-five hundred square kilometers of palaces, galleries, gardens and barracks, the seat of power of the Imperial family. It had been built when that area was on the edge of the city, and was now surrounded by hundreds of kilometers of urban and suburban growth reaching to the Manson District and beyond.

"How appropriate that you look down on it," said a cultured voice entering the portico. The Prime Minister looked over to where the Archduke Frederich Mgana was approaching with a catlike gait. Jeraviki smiled at his noble superior and political inferior as the ebony skinned man slid into another chair.

"You mean the city?" asked the Prime Minister as a servant brought the Archduke another glass of cognac and the Prime Minister held open a humidor for the noble to select a cigar. The Archduke cut the tip of the cigar with a knife from the humidor, closed the box, and lit the tobacco into life.

"No," said Mgana, nodding at the palace complex. "You have won a great victory today over the family."

"We kept the status quo," he said to the other minister, one who had a hereditary seat as the scion of a Supersystem world. A man who owned most of an entire world, and the titular fealty of the billions who lived on it. Unlike the two million square kilometers that Jeraviki held on Transylvania, and the loyalty of a hundred million or so. And Transylvania, with its predominantly Slavic population, was a core world, with over three billion inhabitants and industrial power to match. But still only a core world, not to be compared to the prestige of one of the original habitations of humanity in this region of space.

Which makes me a low class hick to the Archduke, he thought, looking out over the beautiful landscape of the capital. The Supersystem, sixteen habitable worlds and four habitable moons orbiting the eight stars that circled the black hole, was the true heart of the Empire. Its ninety three billion citizens considered themselves the cream of the Empire, the guardians of the true Imperial Civilization. And it seemed like those citizens would never let an opportunity go by to look down their noses at those they considered less than they were.

But the core worlds that he represented, ninety-eight inhabited worlds in ninety-one systems, with three hundred and thirty-two billion citizens, were the true industrial strength and spirit of innovation of the Empire. *And I'll be damned if we let the super worlds boss us around.*

"The status quo is enough," said the Archduke. "We can't pass laws over his veto. And he can't pass laws. So we are at an impasse. And the power stays in the hands of the nobility. Where it belongs."

You pompous ass, thought the Prime Minister, glaring at the man who looked into the night, unaware of Jeraviki's feelings. *I have an agenda we need to move forward with, that has nothing to do with your damned status quo.*

"Was that a new dinosauroid I saw in the trophy room on the way in?" asked the Archduke with a smile. "Or at least the fucking big head of one."

"That is a Megatyranodon," said the Count with a smile. "Thirty-five tons of predator I bagged on one of the frontier worlds last year."

"Biggest predator I've ever seen," said Mgana, standing up and walking to the balustrade.

But not the most dangerous, thought the Prime Minister, looking at the back of the Archduke. *That would be reserved for our own species.*

*　　*　　*

"So," said the kindly looking woman who sat

across the small room from him in a comfortable looking chair. "Tell me about these dreams."

Sean thought the woman sounded competent, her tone of voice excellent. But then she was a trained psychologist, in her fifties and still a young woman, though over two decades his senior.

"I have had certain dreams all my life that have had the property of prophecy," said the Prince, wondering how much the woman knew about his line and this trait. *She has to know about it*, thought the Prince. While not a common topic of conversation, he was sure it was something that was discussed in the medical and psychological community.

"And these dreams come true?" asked the woman, leaning forward, her eyes widening in interest.

"More or less," said the Prince, nodding his head. "Not completely, because having the dream allows me to act on it before it happens, so things almost always turn out a bit differently."

"So you are not locked into a course of action by the dreams?"

"They wouldn't really be of much use then, would they?" said Sean with a smile. "They would only torment myself and my family. But sometimes trying to stop the dream from coming to pass will make the situation worse."

"Sounds like a two edged sword," said the counselor, who had introduced herself as Dr. Irma Rodriguez. Her uniform had the insignia rank of a Lt. Commander, but she was not in any chain of command on the ship.

"Definitely," said the Prince, looking at the holographic picture of a serene countryside that occupied one wall. Sean looked back at the woman who was patiently waiting for him to go on. "But that is not the worst part," said Sean. "It only seems to manifest itself in a future ruler of the Empire. And I am third in line for the throne, with a healthy father sitting as Emperor, who should rule for another century or more."

"And those ahead of you?"

"My two older brothers," said Sean, picturing their faces in his mind. "Dimetre and Henry. Dimetre is the direct heir, and he's about fifteen years older than I am, with a wife and child. He's the one being groomed to be the eventual monarch. Henry is the spare, but I really don't see him becoming Emperor. Not that he's a bad person, just not of the right temperament."

"And are you of the, right temperament?" asked the ship's psychologist, her eyes narrowing a bit.

"I don't think so," said Sean with a chuckle. "I know for a fact I don't want the job. It seems to consume my father. I would rather have a lesser but suitable appointment, maybe an ambassadorship."

"And just because every other member of your family with this, gift, has ascended to rule, doesn't mean it will happen to you as well," said the psychologist, looking at a flat comp pad she had pulled from the side of the chair. "You are not the only line to have proven precognitive abilities. And no one from any of those families has ascended to rule the Empire."

"So you believe the dreams are premonitions?" asked Sean, leaning forward to try and get a look at the comp. He was frustrated by the screen, which would only reveal its information to a straight on view.

"Oh yes," said the woman as she punched something in on the comp. "Precognition, telepathy, even some cases of low level telekinesis have been verified. Scientific findings in controlled situations. We still don't have a clue how they work, just that they do."

"And my dreams?"

"May just be dreams," said the psychologist, looking him in the eye. "Even if you have the gift of precognition, that doesn't mean that all of your dreams are connected to that ability. You have regular dreams, don't you?"

"Yes," said Sean, feeling a bit of embarrassment as he thought back to an inappropriate dream he had processed recently. Jana Gorbechev would not have been amused that he had a dream of making love to her. Despite her being older, she was a very attractive woman. She was one of the few on board he could actually talk to. And she was in his chain of command, and so totally off limits.

"You don't have to give me the details if it is something you are uncomfortable with," said the psychologist, giving him a sympathetic look. "I don't think it would shock me though. And it would most likely be something I have heard in the past."

No doubt, thought Sean, feeling the heat in his face. *But still not something I want to talk about.*

"Now about this pattern of people with the gift becoming rulers," continued the psychologist, looking again at her pad. "Your great great grandfather had the gift, or I think you called it the curse. And he didn't rise to rule until he was a very old man."

"And that means?"

"It means that you could still fulfill the pattern," said the psychologist with a smile. "If it really is more than coincidence, without something dreadful happening to your family. Your brother could ascend to the throne after your father dies of old age, then you might also get there after he dies of natural causes. You might be Emperor for a short period, something I'm sure even you could stand."

"You forget one thing, doc," said the Prince after a moment's thought. Her eyes looked a question back at him. "As soon as my brother ascends the throne I am no longer third in line for the succession. His oldest daughter becomes the heir, and there are sure to be others coming along."

"And that means?" asked the doctor, raising her eyebrows.

"That something catastrophic would have to happen to the family for the throne to come to me. Just like happened with my great great grandfather."

*   *   *

Twenty-five hundred years after he formulated the theory Einstein was still proven to be correct. The speed of light was the limiting factor for velocity in space. In normal space. But space is made up of other dimensions than those we experience with our senses. Dimensions that correspond to real space in a number of ratios. The speed of a photon is still the limiting factor here as well. But a photon will cover a much greater distance in a given time period in any of these dimensions.

The major problem with travel in the other dimensions is that they reject the matter of our space. They do not like it and don't want to deal with it. They try to actively eject the matter from normal space back to normal space, with extreme violence. It takes enormous energies to open the portals to the other dimensions of space. And it takes not quite as large but still great energies to keep an object in that space so it can travel from point to point at speeds that translate into faster than light in normal space.

Humankind actually discovered subspace early in the twenty-third century AD. Subspace had a normal correspondence of twelve to one with normal space, meaning a photon traveling through subspace for a year and dropping back into normal space would have traversed twelve light years. This allowed mankind to travel to the nearer stars and no further.

The hyperspace dimensions lay on a different geometry from subspace, and took more energy to enter and traverse. Hyper I, with a correspondence of 9.11 to 1 to normal space, was actually a step backwards from subspace. But it opened the door to the higher levels of hyperspace. Hyper II had a 40.9:1 correspondence, Hyper III a 163.55:1. The hyper dimensions seemed to run up to VIII, with a 167,467.38:1 correspondence, but only photons could, so far, be made to travel in that rarefied space.

Ships could travel hyper in the same manner as normal space once they got there. Inertia still existed, and objects still had to accelerate and decelerate in order to build velocity. And normal matter disturbed hyperspace and sent the disturbance out into normal space, allowing objects in hyper to be tracked in normal space, to a degree.

* * *

"We're tracking an object moving in Hyper VII," said the voice of the sensor tech over the com.

"Do you have a heading?" asked the captain, Lieutenant SG Marcus Iltrene, looking at the tactical display on the bridge. The object was blinking on the normal space projection at thirty degrees Galactic North of HMS *Garvanan*'s position. They were out here a hundred light years from the frontiers of New

Moscow, looking for smugglers that might be attempting to run the corner route around the barrier to Klang space. Out here, powered down and listening with powerful passive sensors to the sounds of the Universe.

"Not yet, sir," said the tech. "We haven't got enough signal to determine a heading. Give us a couple of minutes for some differential."

Two more signals blinked onto the display, followed a moment later by a third.

"Four objects on the sensors now, Captain," said the tech. "Initial reading is heading Galactic South by West thirty-five degrees."

"Into Klang space," said the exec from her console.

"But to my knowledge the Klang do not have any Hyper VII capable ships," said the Captain, looking over at a viewer that was scrolling information on Klang.

"Unless it's some human smugglers coming to call on the Klang in fast ships," said the exec.

"If so," said the helmsman, "the Czar's council will want to know who they are."

"Computer has preliminary figures on those ships based on energy signatures," said the tech over the link. "Estimating four capital ships of unknown origin."

"Unknown origin," echoed the exec. "With hyper VII capabilities. Maybe we should let someone at home know what we've found before we get too close."

"Launch a drone toward home," ordered the Captain. "Set it for hyper I until it gets a day away, then up the scale to VII over another day's travel. Put everything we know about these intruders on it, then warm up another and continue downloading onto it."

"Yes sir," said the helm, setting the probe for launch. "Probe away. Translating into hyper."

"Sir," called out the sensor tech. "They have changed course. They're heading right down our throats."

"They made us," said the exec.

"How?" asked the Captain, looking around the bridge. "They shouldn't have been able to detect a hyper I translation from that distance."

"We couldn't," agreed the exec. "Which might mean that they have capabilities beyond ours."

"I'm picking up a translation signal," said the tech, tension in his voice. "They've moved down into VI or below. They've dropped off the plot."

"Wish we were somewhere else?" asked the exec, sweat beading on her forehead. "With some friends as backup."

"Like home," agreed the Captain. "Or at least in the border boundary region with an alliance battle fleet at hand."

"How fast can we be somewhere we could hide?" asked the Captain of the helmsman. "And get us there as inconspicuously as possible."

"Picking up a plot on Hyper IV," said the tech as two blinking icons appeared on the plot. "Cruiser size. Same emission bands as the others."

"Heading?"

"Give me a second sir," answered the tech.

"Get us out of here, helm," said the Captain, looking over at the plot. "Nice and quiet. No more than twenty gees. And get that other probe out there. Move it quickly away and then warp it out at a million kilometers."

The harried helm looked over his shoulder, trying

to do two things at once.

"Exec," ordered the Captain. "Take care of the probe for him. Five hundred thirty gees on heading two eighty by forty five by one ninety. Ten minutes. Have her warp hot on overload to Hyper VIII at nine hundred thousand kilometers."

"That will take her out of existence," said the exec as she programed the probe."

"And hopefully make them think a destroyer sized object just bugged out of town," said the Captain as the *Garvanan* moved onto her new heading and started moving away from the point where she had launched the first probe.

The triangular grabbers pulled at the fabric of space, moving the ship at twenty gees while the vessel bled off inertia as heat. A heat signature that could be traced back to the ship, as long as it was moving.

"Translation to Hyper II," said the sensor tech, his voice thick with tension. "Two cruiser sized objects, approximately three billion kilometers. ETA eleven minutes."

Come on babies, thought the Captain, looking over the plot as the red vector arrows reached for his position. The probe moved toward the vector arrows, radiating as much inertia converted heat as the destroyer.

Iltrene sweated out the minutes as the arrows drew closer. The probe reached its programmed coordinates and translated into hyperspace, a burst of energy that moved it into hyper VIII for an instant before it converted to pure energy. An energy burst that registered throughout the dimensions as the translation of a much larger object.

"One of the cruisers is translating up to Hyper

VII," said the tech.   "Moving away.   The other is continuing toward us."

"All stop and power down," ordered the Captain. "Everything but atmosphere and passive sensors."

"Ship continuing on approach," said the voice of the tech.   "Range five hundred million kilometers."

"We're quiet as a mouse," said the Captain, looking at the tactical as he felt the cold sweat on his face. "Nothing to see here."

"Translation," called the tech, "one hundred and ten million kilometers."

"We have her on scopes," said the helm, as the viewer switched from tactical to a computer enhanced image of the alien warship.   An oblong construction about a kilometer in length.   The cameras examined her for about five minutes as the ship cruised through normal space, accelerating away from the *Garvanan*. The passive sensors registered the sweep of radar and lidar beams as the ship probed nearby space.   But the stealthy destroyer sat dead in space, and only a directed probe would have found her.

After another five minutes, as the ship moved away, it translated back up into hyper VII.   The viewer switched back to tactical and showed the vector arrow moving away.

It began to get very cold in the ship as another hour crept by and the vector arrow disappeared off the screens, the disturbance of its passage through hyperspace moving out of range.

"Bring the rest of life support back online," said the Captain.   "Helm, move us toward home at twenty gees for one hour, then move her up to two hundred gees.   When we're good and clear we'll hyper out and make a run for the nearest naval base."

"I've never been so scared in my life," said the exec, wiping her forehead. "Who were they?"

"I don't know," said the Captain. "But I don't think we've seen the last of them."

"Well," agreed the exec, throwing a smile at her leader. "Just another day in service to the Czar."

*   *   *

What's a celebration without a military parade, thought Augustine I as he returned the salute of the marching unit passing before the reviewing stand. The parade stretched for kilometers in either direction. Dozens of bands and a hundred regiments of infantry had already passed. The present unit's own small band, twenty bagpipe playing Scotsmen in kilts, led the regiment.

And it sounds like cats fighting to me, thought the Emperor, holding his salute as the light infantry, in full battle armor, held their weapons at present arms and looked unflinchingly up at the reviewing stands where stood their Emperor, the members of the Lords seated below his stand.

The Imperial Army was based on the old British Imperial Army, where recruits entered a regiment and moved up the ranks within that unit, until and unless they reached a rank beyond the level of the regiment. And on the ethnic planets created by the Emperor Cassius Ogden, also known as Cassius the Mad, back in the early fifth century of the Empire, the units followed the historical precedents brought in records from old Earth and planted on the worlds by that Emperor. Some people to this day called him Cassius the Mad because of his insistence on making the human race ethnically and culturally diverse based on the histories.

At least he didn't do any harm to the race, thought Augustine as he looked at the ranks of the passing

Scotts from Nova Scotia, and beyond them to the next unit in line, ebony faces under helmets denoting them as being from one of the many ethnic black planets. He could see some Caucasian and Asian faces in among them, since after all even the ethnic planets had members of other races and cultures on their surfaces. *Some say he even strengthened the race by not allowing us to meld into a homogeneous mass. Who knows. He might have been correct.*

His thoughts interrupted by a noise from the sky, the Emperor looked up to where a cloud of close ground support stingships and transports flew over Imperial Square in their thousands. A thousand feet above them flew swarms of neatly arrayed atmospheric fighters, larger than the ground support ships and capable of a much greater turn of speed through the air. Above them the sun glinted on the fuselages of hundreds of space fighters and attack craft, really small warships in their own right.

"They must have sent every military aircraft on the planet," said the Empress, standing to the right of the Emperor.

"Not really," said Augustine, looking back up as the front of the groups of aircraft left the square. The entering swarms behind them seemed endless. "Most of these are from off planet, brought here for the parade. And the space capable are from the training base on the island, and the complements of a couple of fleet carriers."

The stand shook slightly from the noisy passage of aircraft. Augustine felt the ground shudder from another source and looked toward the edge of the square, kilometers away, where a line of large vehicles entered view. He kept glancing over at them as the last four regiments, two of them ceremonial and mounted on horses, walked by.

And then they were in front of the stand, the massive vehicles that caught the attention of the millions of watchers and held them captive. Twelve meters in width, thirty-one in length, with the tops of their turrets reaching ten meters into the air, the twelve hundred ton beasts rumbled past. The eighteen meter barrel of the thirty centimeter rail gun pointed at a thirty degree angle to the sky. The laser crosses on the turret, similar to the laser rings on warships, were cold and powered down. Commanders and gunners stood in their hatches and saluted the stand.

"The new Tyrannosaur IV," yelled the Field Marshal standing just below the Emperor on the stand. Augustine smiled down at his military advisor while trying to remember what he had been told about the latest heavy tank to join Imperial service. The middle aged Asian smiled back and glanced at the line of tanks passing at walking pace. "They're a hundred in a brigade, as well as support and scout vehicles, and a supporting infantry battalion."

"Are they based here?" asked the Empress, her eyes opened wide in awe at the gargantuan machines to her front.

"No ma'am," said Nguyen, with a bow. "The brigade was brought in from Nova Brandenburg," said the Marshal, his eyes gleaming. "The Germans still make the best Panzertruppen for some reason."

"Cassius the Mad's magic," agreed the Emperor. "Are those grabbers on the barrel?" He gestured at the machine directly to his front, where the right triangle shapes at the end of the barrel were suggestive of the reactionless drives of most space vessels.

"Yes, your Majesty," said the Marshal, his smile widening at the chance to instruct his ruler on matters military. "The rail gun can take on ships in high orbit, though they're not really shore defense weapons. The grabbers grip on the fabric of space takes up some of the recoil that ultra-high velocity rounds produce."

"Amazing," said the Emperor, snapping a salute to the commander to his front. "The ingenuity of our species when it comes to making war is amazing."

Hours later the parade ended, as vehicles almost as large as the heavy tanks passed in review. These were the portable ground defense batteries that guarded the surfaces of planets that did not have emplaced artillery.

And we have too many of those, thought the Emperor as he gave the last salute of the day. *And opening up more all the time.*

* * *

"Our new friends have been a wealth of information and intelligence," said the young staff officer, handing a data chip to his superior.

Great Admiral Miierrowanasa M'tinisasitow took the offered piece of ceramic and plugged it into his desk comp. The logo of the Empire appeared on the screen, along with a warning of the secret nature of the information. The logo soon disappeared and was replaced by the image of a mostly hairless light skinned biped. A shock of dark hair on his head and a thatch of hair around the copulating organ contrasted with the smooth skin. The outline of a Ca'cada gave scale to the smaller sentient.

"They are definitely what we are looking for, my lord," said the young officer, viewing his own hand held display. "Humans. Divided into three distinct groupings according to our friends."

"And how did our friends come upon the humans?" asked the Admiral, scrolling through image after image of what must be different sexes and subspecies of the hated, and until now missing, race.

"It seems that merchants from the smallest of the human kingdoms sold technologies to the somewhat primitive Klang," said the young officer, looking up from his own display. "It allowed them to go on a rampage that surprised their benefactors and eventually almost overwhelmed them. Before the other, larger human kingdoms stepped in to intervene."

"And why would they do that for another kingdom?" asked the Admiral, scratching his head.

"According to the Klang, the humans make alliances with other races. As well as their own. Attack one of the human kingdoms and you will have the others come to the defense. Especially if you threaten the existence of large numbers of them."

"And how are these kingdoms organized?"

"The original kingdom, the Empire, was founded by the refugees that escaped from their home planet. It is the largest of the kingdoms, with over a trillion sentients, mostly humans."

"And that would be the strongest militarily?" asked the Admiral as he looked at the schematic of a capital ship on his display. The elongated diamond was set against one of his own capital ships, and was a bit smaller than the three kilometer long Ca'cadasan battleship. *But size is not everything,* thought the Admiral, looking at the unfamiliar surface features of the vessel and wondering what they portended.

"The Klang estimate over ten thousand of the large capital ships, with maybe another ten thousand slightly smaller scout capital ships."

"Scout capital ships?"

"An unfamiliar term I am sure, Lord," said the officer. "Just think of a very large cruiser capable of fighting its way out of a difficult situation to bring back its information."

"Total fleet strength?"

"Between one and two hundred thousand vessels."

"Much more than we have in our conquest fleet," said the Admiral, nodding his head. "We may have to send for a second fleet to clean up the fleeing remains."

"They may not flee, my lord," said the officer. "They have never lost a war, this Empire. And they have been involved in many conflicts, including a civil war between their own forces."

"Someone must have lost that one," said the Admiral with a grin. "Or are they still fighting it?"

"The rebel fleet, which was made up of regular units, eventually beat the government that was then in power and deposed the Emperor."

"Barbarians," grunted the Admiral, giving the image of a figure in battle armor a look of disgust. "To war against their lawful lord."

"They believe that all of the people have some rights," said the staff officer, his own brow wrinkled in thought . "If a ruler misuses his power they believe it in their right to depose them, if they have the power."

"As I said. Barbarians," said the Admiral, looking at the screen that revealed a heavily armed atmospheric craft. "So what about these other kingdoms?"

"The second is a republic that broke away from the Empire four or five centuries ago. They are not nearly as large, maybe two hundred fifty billion or so, with about a quarter of the military strength of the Empire."

"And the third? The one that brought our new

friends out of barbarism, so to speak?"

"It seems that some of the new kingdom's people missed the old ways," said the officer. "They broke away, moved away, and started a new Empire. They are actually the small fry of the human kingdoms. About sixty billion, and a smaller but still competent navy."

"This is all very fascinating," said the Admiral, looking at the star maps with the warning of *accuracy not verified* written across the bottom. "But what can you tell me about their technology? How advanced are they? And how much of a struggle can we expect?"

"Well," said the officer, looking down at his display. "The Klang are about a hundred years behind us. And they estimate that the humans are about a half century ahead of them."

"That far advanced," said the Admiral with a frown, looking again at the display of the capital ship. "How did they come so far? We were a millennium advanced of them when last we met."

"They are an innovative species, my lord," said the officer. "Remember, they had only been out of their system a century or so when we first encountered them. And they ran into other space faring species out here. Some friendly, and others not so. Lots of wars lead to lots of advancement in war making ability."

"How many other species?" asked the Admiral, looking at several new sentient races on the screen.

"The Klang were not really sure," said the staff officer. "We estimate over fifty of them. This was once the home of a thriving Empire that civilized and advanced the many races."

"Civilized," said the Admiral with a growling laugh. "Advanced. What a stupid and silly people they must have been. There is only one thing to do with inferior species. Enslave them, use them, subjugate them. Or totally and completely destroy them."

The Admiral showed his omnivore teeth in a feral smile that grew into a laugh that the staff officer joined. The lesser species who were the servants to the lord Admiral tried to hide in the shadows and escape the notice of the superiors who could have them executed on a whim.

Chapter 6

War does not determine who is right - only who is left

Bertrand Russell

"We're ready to translate out of hyper," called the helm from his station. Von Rittersdorf looked up at the view screen that showed the red tinted space of the hyper dimension. Black dots, the gravity wells of stars, peppered the space in all directions. Ahead was a large black globe, the gravity well of the system they were approaching.   The red triangles of hyper-beacons blinked on the edges of the system.

"Three other ships are tracking us in hyper," said Ensign Lasardo, tapping his tactical board. "One heavy cruiser and two destroyers, verified as Imperial vessels."

"We've sent recognition codes to the pickets," interjected the com tech from her station to the rear of the Captain. "Return codes verify HIMS *Gorki*. Our signals are accepted, and we are welcomed to the system."

"Translate on the mark," ordered the Captain, double checking the receipt of the welcome. Things had been known to happen when approaching a major military system. And he didn't want someone firing on him by accident when he came into normal space.

"On mark," replied the helm, checking his board. The ship throbbed as the MAM reactors throttled up to full power. "Five, four, three, two, mark."

The lights dimmed for a moment as all available energy was pulled into the hyper-translators on the top and bottom of the ship. Space directly ahead rippled slightly, then rippled again. The ripple opened in the center and a small window formed into normal space. The bright point of a near star was centered in the opening. Space around the hole rippled again. The hole expanded until a kilometer wide gateway looked into the universe of normal space.

Johann Peterson moved through the hole at point two c. Von Ritterdorf felt his stomach flip and slight nausea take hold as the laws of normal space took over. The bright star shown in the viewer for a moment. The view switched to the sternward, where the opening was collapsing upon itself until all that was left was a small red pinpoint. Space rippled and the pinpoint disappeared, leaving a view of the bright star field of the local spiral arm.

"Perfect translation," called out Ensign Lasardo.

Any translation you can walk away from, thought the Captain. *And it sure beats the hell out of an explosive expulsion.* After all, it was abnormal for normal matter to exist in hyper. Only through the use of energy to match resonances could matter even survive the passage of higher dimensions. Without that resonance matching hyperspace would expel normal matter from its domain, back into normal space. Sometimes the ship even survived. Sometimes so did the crew.

"Astrogation computers verify Alderzion ahead," called the helm.

"Set course for Alderzion IV," ordered the Captain. "ETA?"

"Including decel time. Forty-two hours."

"We have a corvette signaling us," said the tactical officer. "About twelve light seconds off the starboard at twenty-seven degrees."

The viewer switched to a telescopic view of the small interplanetary patrol vessel. The thirty k-ton vessel lacked the hyper-translators of interstellar vessels. Because of that it could accelerate faster and maneuver much more nimbly than interstellar ships. And the MAM missiles she carried could hit as hard as any that the destroyer carried.

"Vessel identified as CV-AS27985X," said Lasardo. "Part of the system normal space picket."

"Transmission coming in," said the com tech. "Putting on the viewer."

A slender young woman with ebony skin appeared on the screen, a small bridge behind her.

"Lt. JG Ngonasha calling *Johann Peterson*," said the woman in a contralto that sent a thrill up Maurice von Rittersdorf's spine. "Just a little warning that a convoy is getting ready to translate into the system. Please stay clear."

"Coordinates coming in, sir," said the com tech, taping her board.

The main viewer shifted to sternward, where a quintet of ripples were appearing in space. The viewer made the opening portals seem close, but the figures at the bottom of the screen showed them to be a good fifteen light seconds from the destroyer. The ripples opened to reddish holes in space. And through the holes came giants.

"Two super freighters," said Lasardo, while the viewer closed in on one of the enormous globes of the cargo vessels. "Twenty-four hundred meters diameter. Fifteen megaton dry weight with a twenty megaton cargo capacity."

"What about the three smaller ships?" asked von Rittersdorf.

"A four hundred kiloton antimatter hauler and two escorts," said the tactical officer. "A destroyer and a frigate."

The viewer switched back to the scene on the corvette's bridge.

"Thank you Commander," said the Captain, using the honorific of the CO of a small warship. "We would have hated to get in the way of one of those monsters."

"You're welcome, Captain," said the corvette's commander after a twenty-two second break as the light speed transmissions moved from ship to ship and back. "You look like you've taken some damage yourself. Would you like an escort into the system?"

"We've got it under control," said von Rittersdorf. "We had a little bit of a run in with a trio of pirates. My crew and the repair systems have everything back in order, with the exception of a grabber and some of our armor."

As long as we have the mass to fabricate repairs, thought the Captain as the message moved across normal space to the smaller ship, *we can fix just about anything. Between the larger repair robots and the nanobots the ship can damn near repair itself. If not for the man in the loop regulations. Funny what a half dozen worlds destroyed by run amok machines could do to a civilization. Even four centuries later.*

"Well, good luck Captain," said the beautiful Lieutenant. "I tried to get us back in-system."

"See you around, Commander," said von Rittersdorf, snapping a quick salute.

"I look forward to it, Captain," said Ngonasha. The viewer blanked, replaced by a view of the stars.

Two hours later the Captain was sitting in the comparative luxury of his main cabin when the private com circuit buzzed. He broke his link with the computer and the masses of after patrol busy work and activated the com.

"We've got the final casualty figures, skipper," said the exec, Lieutenant SG Katherine Schuler, her green eyes staring from the viewer.

"Good news?"

"Some," she admitted. "The autodocs were able to resurrect three of the dead before they passed the point of no return, and four more are stable enough to turn over to the yards."

"And the rest are still total losses," said the Captain, rubbing his eyes.

"The problems with space battles," said the exec, a grimace on her face. "The ones that are incinerated, or blown out into space and just plain blown apart."

"What about the wounded?"

"Twenty-two returned to duty," said the exec. "Three died and put in stasis. They should eventually return. Twenty-one will require more extensive repairs than we can give them on board."

"Thanks, Kathy," said von Rittersdorf. "I know it's hard to break the bad news with the good. Maybe the review board will take pity on me."

"But, we won a major victory," said the other officer, her eyes narrowing. "Why would you have to go before a review board?"

"Price of command," said the Captain. "Win, lose or draw, they have to look into it and satisfy themselves. You'll learn that as soon as you get your own command."

"Hell of a thing," said Katherine. "Anything else I can do for you, Captain?"

"Not a thing, exec. I'm going to catch some sleep. You keep an eye on things and don't let everything go to hell."

"In the middle of a heavily defended system," laughed Schuler. "Only if we accidentally run into something."

"It's happened," said the Captain. "Always some idiot who couldn't control a ground car in command of a high c fraction spacecraft."

"Good night, Captain," said the exec. "I'll make sure that we keep any idiots at long range until we get near to the planet."

Von Rittersdorf closed his comp panel and sauntered off to his sleeping compartment. Sleep came hard, and the images of his dead intruded onto his thoughts as they had ever since the battle. *If only*, he thought. If only what would have saved their lives?

The hours went by as *Johann Peterson* accelerated toward the planet at a hundred gravities, well below her maximum, but all she needed for a quick transit. The time came for vector turnover and decel, and the grabbers pulled at space, glowing white hot as they converted inertia to heat. Lasardo looked at his tactical display as the ship slowed at one hundred and fifty gravities, bleeding off almost one and a half KPS of velocity every second.

Other ships glowed like small stars on the infrared sensors. A carrier task force; a fleet carrier, a cruiser and five destroyers; moved up the ecliptic. A pair of battle cruisers moved through the opposite side of the system. A quintet of medium freighters and their two escorting frigates came in from galactic north. And of course the superfreighters that had followed the destroyer into the system were coasting slowly behind the *Peterson*. There were dozens of other contacts, patrol vessels, miners and other commercials.

Everything flashing the identification signals mandated in civilized space.

The Captain was finishing his final reports and log entries in his day cabin as the destroyer slowed, moving toward the blue and white marble of Alderzion IV. The planet was on his wall viewer, where normally he kept wildlife scenes from his home world of Nova Brandenburg, with its ice age mammalians.   Two continents were visible on the night side by their settlement and base lights, and the shining of the full moons on the surrounding oceans.

The planet was home to over a million servicemen and women, army divisions, naval support facilities, and ground based space defense artillery.   Six million civilian workers provided for the Fleet and Army's needs, and many had their families with them.   There were also several hundred thousand farmers providing fresh foodstuffs to those tired of the products of food processors.   And several hundred thousand military personnel in orbit or on other space based facilities. The system was growing fast, and in ten years would probably reach fifty million inhabitants.

"Captain to the bridge," called a voice over the intercom. "Captain requested to the bridge."

Von Rittersdorf cursed under his breath and turned off his comp. Though born of the nobility, he was the fourth son of a third son, and though of wealth commanded no real civil power. If he was hung out to dry by the powers that be he would be able to survive in comfort.   But he loved the Fleet, and wanted to continue moving up the ranks.   And now the continuance of his career would be determined by a board of his peers, who might find fault in his decisions.

Nothing I can do about it this moment, he thought, as he got up from his desk and walked to the access hatch to the bridge. He keyed the unlock sequence and moved forward as the hatch slid silently into its recess.

"We're on final approach to the planet," said the helm as the Captain slid into his command couch. "We've received permission for docking at the repair facility."

The front screen showed a schematic of the planet, with cities and towns marked in green, military installations in flashing red. There were hundreds of the red dots, indicating sensor stations, landing fields, ground force barracks and shore batteries. Of particular interest to a warship, the dots of the batteries blinked a different pattern than the other symbols. Small figures blinked under the dots, spelling out their identity and function. Some were short ranged torpedo batteries, holding fifty to a hundred hypervelocity fusion warhead missiles. There were also kinetic cannon. The largest were the capital ship class laser batteries, protected by hundreds of meters of plasticrete and carbon armors, as well as gigawatts of electromag field projectors.

In the surrounding space of the display blinked the ring of orbital defense satellites, with their laser or particle beam projectors and missile batteries. Others dots blinked in blue, indicating warehouses and depots orbiting the planet. Orange dots were vital weapons and engineering supply depots, as well as a trio of large space docks.

"Focus on symbol sixty-four," ordered the Captain, pointing to the large red blinker seventy-five degrees to the west of their approach. That object was showing the destroyer a lot of interest, painting them with radar and lidar. It sprung to life on the viewer, a large saucer shaped object with a domed top and bottom.

"Class I fort," said Ensign Lasardo, looking over his board. "Four and a half kilometers in diameter. Two hundred megatons mass. It's capable of maneuvers at one gee in order to get out of the path of long range kinetics."

"Be a hard damned nut to crack," said the exec, walking onto the bridge. She smiled over at the Captain as she took an empty couch to his right. "Glad they're our friends."

"This is part of the logistics train for the entire fleet in this sector," said von Rittersdorf, looking at the massive defensive structure. "One of four in this sector. It's supposed to be a hard nut to crack. Especially if the fleet is out doing what it does best."

"Killing sentients and breaking things," said the tactical officer with a smile.

"Transmission coming in," called out the com tech.

"Put it on the screen," ordered the Captain. The space fort disappeared, replaced by the image of a middle aged woman in fleet uniform, the single star insignia of a Commodore on her collar.

"Welcome to Alderzion IV, *Peterson*," said the woman in a high soprano, white teeth shining from her golden skinned face. "I'm Commodore Eunice Mihn, commanding the Fleet Repair and Supply Facility here."

"Lt. Commander von Rittersdorf here, ma'am," said the Captain. "We've got most of the major repairs done. We need some armor, spares and missiles."

"We have what you need, Captain," said the woman. "You are cleared to dock at spacedock Alpha

291D. Upon dock you are relieved of command, von Rittersdorf, and are to report to Vice Admiral van Lytle on the planet's surface. Your exec will assume temporary command and see to your repairs."

The Captain felt his face fall. He had known it was coming. And why else have a flag officer greet a mere destroyer coming into port. But it still caught him off guard.

"I'm sure you will be pleasantly surprised, Commander," said the woman, her smile widening. "So don't let the formalities be too much of a burden."

"Yes ma'am," said the Captain, nodding his head as he swallowed. *What in the hell does she mean? The formalities. Relieved of command. They normally wait until the board renders a decision to take command away.*

"Your berth awaits, *Peterson,"* said the small woman. "Mihn out."

"Spacedock Alpha 291D transmitting," said the com tech. "Requesting that we turn the helm over to her."

"Turn the helm over," ordered the Captain, looking up at the screen which had switched to the view of the spacedock.

"Aye, sir," called the helmsman. "Helm given to the dock."

Von Rittersdorf sat in silent thought for the minutes that the dock grew in the viewer. His thoughts were on the unknown future and what it might bring to him. Still he allowed himself to look up at the approaching dock as his ship was lined up for insertion. The six kilometer wide, nine and a quarter kilometer tall bell shape was impressive. It massed a hundred and ten megatons, making it much less dense than the fort they had just viewed. But then it was mostly empty space on the inside.

The two kilometer wide hatch slid open as they approached, revealing the emptiness within. The hatch locked into position and the destroyer slowly made its way through, now barely creeping forward. The kilometer wide central umbilical was two and a half kilometers ahead. The locking plates of the berth were opened on either side of the docking space. *Johann Peterson* moved into the docking area, her velocity a mere couple of meters a second and slowing. The docking area came closer as the ship slowed.

"This is where mistakes happen," said the exec, her face tight as the nose of the destroyer slid toward the berth.

"That's why they bring us in by computer control," said the helm, relaxing at his station.

"Damned computers are what I don't trust," said the exec under her breath.

Von Rittersdorf looked at her with a slight smile. She also hailed from Nova Brandenburg. And it was common there for mothers to scare their children into good behavior with stories about how the machines had risen against their creators four centuries before. About how mankind had fought them in a dozen systems, and scorched the surfaces of a dozen planets to destroy the scourge. And how people thought some of the machines had escaped into the night of interstellar space; building up their strength and waiting to return.

The destroyer slid into its berth perfectly, the nose barely bumping the cuff with a slight vibration. The cuff closed tight on the nose. Then the two sides of the berth slid in and made contact with the sides of the ship, access ways and power couplings sealing into place.

"We have station power coming through," called the chief engineer over the com.

"Power down the reactors, engineer," ordered the Captain. "Set ship to station status."

"Station status aye," came the voice of the engineer. Within seconds the MAM reactors were shut down and the ship absorbed energy from the station.

"Will you look at that," said the exec, motioning to one of the smaller viewers that was set to the port side of the ship. Another destroyer sat in a berthing space. Several access hatches were open and the long, lean shapes of missiles were being hoisted aboard by station robots and space suited humans. The ship, with her berth as a reference, looked to be slightly larger than the *Peterson*. And the hyper translators were almost twice the size of the pair their destroyer carried.

"She's a beauty, alright," said Lasardo from his station. He glanced down at his board for a second before looking back up. "DDF 63587. The *Dot McArthur*. Hyper VII capable."

"Four times our relative interstellar," said the helmsman with a whistle. "Thirty gravities more acceleration." The ship was capable of reaching and operating in the seventh dimension of hyperspace, where the correspondence with normal space was a fourth that of the dimension that a hyper VI ship could reach.

"Two hundred and fifty k-tons," continued Lasardo. "Twenty-five percent larger than *Peterson*. But with a third fewer missiles in her loadout because of the extra mass her translators require. Larger MAM reactors to power her into VII. And slightly more powerful lasers to take advantage of that extra power."

"I would sure love to have that ship as my first

command," said Katherine Schuler, a faraway look on her face.

I would be happy to just keep the Peterson, thought von Rittersdorf, getting up from his chair.

"You have command of the ship, Lieutenant Schuler," he announced as he walked from the bridge. "If I don't come back be as faithful to your new commander as you have been for me."

The Captain exited the bridge as the officers and crew looked around with shocked expressions on their faces.

It didn't take long to catch a lift from the central core to the nearest shuttle bay. His comp implant registered with the station as soon as he stepped on board, and station schematics and directions flashed into his visual centers. The shuttle pilot, a young ensign with short red hair, greeted him as he walked toward the open hatch.

The shuttle dropped out of the station and headed toward the planet, grabbers pulling it effortlessly through the entry and shrugging off the turbulence that would have been felt on most civilian craft using fusion engines to propel them. Within minutes he was on the hard surface of a landing field, exiting the shuttle that was radiating waves of heat while he walked quickly away to a waiting air-car. The gravity felt light to him, though the air smelled sweet and the sound of the planet's analogue to birds was pleasant to his ears. Or would have, if he wasn't so worried about how quickly he had been summoned to meet the lord and master of the system.

Another ensign; this one a large, swarthy skinned man; greeted him and made sure the officer was strapped in. The air-car lifted on whirling fans and headed off the field in the direction of a complex of buildings. One of the buildings seemed to grow as the car headed directly toward it. Soon the air-car was over that building. The fans revved as the car hovered, then lowered itself onto the landing pad on top of the structure.

His comp implant linked into the building as soon as he left the air-car and headed for the pad elevator. The door opened as he approached, and closed behind him as he entered. It automatically headed down, moving several floors and coming to a stop. The door opened to reveal yet another ensign, waiting to escort him to the Admiral's office.

A chain of junior officers taking me to my doom, thought Maurice as he returned the salute of the ensign. They walked down the busy hallway, dodging around some personnel who seemed to be lollygagging around. Von Rittersdorf returned the salutes of several junior officers and saluted a couple of seniors. Then they were at the door marked with the three stars of a vice admiral, and the ensign knocked.

"Come in," called a voice, and the door slid open. A large blond woman with the looks of Valhalla sat behind the desk, the tabs of a chief petty officer on her shoulder boards.

"Lt. Commander von Rittersdorf reporting to the Admiral's office," said the Commander as he returned the salute of the NCO.

"The Admiral is expecting you, Commander," said the NCO in return, motioning toward the door to her left rear.

Von Rittersdorf nodded and moved toward that door, which opened at his approach. He took two paces into the room and stopped as the door closed behind him.   Coming to attention he faced the man behind the desk and snapped off a crisp salute.

"Lt. Commander von Rittersdorf reporting as ordered, sir."

The Admiral, a big, beefy man in his mid one hundreds, stood up and smiled at the officer.   He returned the salute and came around his desk, offering his large hand.

"Welcome   Commander,"   said   the   Admiral, clasping the officer's hand in his and grunting in satisfaction at the strength of the return grip.

"Thank you, sir," replied von Rittersdorf. "May I ask why the Admiral requested my presence so soon into docking?"

"Kind of unusual that, wasn't it?" said the large man, gesturing for the younger officer to take a seat. "Would you like a drink, Commander?"

"I am on duty sir," said the officer, taking the seat and keeping his back stiff. "Unless the board of inquiry is going to relieve me of that duty."

"Oh," said the Admiral, pouring himself a small glass of bourbon. "I think the board can be dispensed with.   I have gone over your transmitted reports and the ship's databanks of the battle.   I have determined that you acted in the highest standards of the service. You fought a superior enemy force on your own and defeated them in detail, bringing your ship and crew back."

"Most of the crew, sir," said the younger officer, his throat catching. He looked down for a moment. "I think I will take a drink, sir." He started to get up and the Admiral waved him back into his seat.

"My pleasure," said the officer, taking another glass from the cabinet over the bar and pouring three fingers of bourbon into the container. The Admiral brought the glass over to the Commander, then headed back to his desk, taking a seat on the surface and looking at the officer.

"Feel responsible for the loss of your men?" said the Admiral, looking into von Rittersdorf's eyes. "Feeling that if you had made better decisions you might have brought them all back?"

Von Rittersdorf nodded and looked down.

"Well that is bullshit, young man," said the Admiral loudly. "You did a fine job out there. As well as could be expected of any officer. And now you get the punishment."

"Punishment, sir," said von Rittersdorf, not sure if he had heard correctly.

"Yes," said the Admiral with a smile, reaching into a pocket and pulling out a box. He opened it and held it in front of von Rittersdorf.

"The Imperial Star, second class," gasped the officer, his eyes widening. "But that's for..."

"Bravery under fire, in the face of the enemy," said the Admiral. "And well deserved if I say so myself. Of course there will be an official ceremony later on, so you don't get to actually wear the medal. But I can give you something to put on right now."

The Admiral reached into another pocket and pulled out another small box. The top flipped open to reveal a set of silver oak leaves.

"Congratulations, Commander," said the Admiral, holding the box out to the young officer. Von Rittersdorf took the box with a smile on his face.

"So you see, young man," said the Admiral, grinning, "you have been punished for your attention to duty. Unfortunately, in this fleet initiative often leads to greater responsibility."

"I don't know what to say, sir," said the Commander, looking at the new rank insignia. "But, what about my command? Do I return to the *Peterson?*

"That's the third surprise, son," said the Admiral. "And maybe the best of all. You don't get the *Peterson* back, because we are giving you a new ship."

"The *Dot McArthur*," said the Commander, his eyes open wide. "That's why she was sitting in the next berth."

"Perceptive, young man," said the Admiral, smiling again. "Just what we are looking for in senior destroyer captains. Now get your butt on a three day R and R leave, and then you can repair to your new ship."

"What about my old crew?" said von Rittersdorf, pulling the new rank insignia from the box. "Do I get commander's prerogative?"

"If you mean do you get to take an officer with you to your new command, the answer is yes."

"Then I want Katherine Schuler on the *McArthur*."

"Can't do that, Commander," said the Admiral. Von Rittersdorf's face fell. "Don't look so glum, son. I'm sure you wouldn't want to deprive that young woman of her punishment."

"Punishment?"

"Of course," said the Admiral with a laugh. "Her punishment for a job well done is command of the *Peterson*. A fitting punishment I would think."

"Then I request Ensign Lasardo, my tac officer," said the Commander. "If you can find a proper berth for the current tac officer of *McArthur*."

"Lieutenant JG Lasardo will be waiting for you on your ship when you report in three days," said the Admiral. "We can find an assignment for the current tac officer of *McArthur*. Maybe the *Peterson* could do with one.

"Now we need to prepare you for a medal ceremony, young man," said the Admiral. "There is a dress uniform your size and a set of decorations of your set waiting for you down the hall. We can't keep the reporters waiting all day. The last part of your punishment, you see."

Von Rittersdorf rose from his chair and snapped a salute to the Admiral, who put an arm around the young officer and led him to the door.

"I knew your grandfather, Maurice," said the Admiral, stopping for a moment. "And your uncle. They were both very brave men, and competent officers."

Von Rittersdorf felt himself tighten for a moment.

"Don't worry, young man," said the Admiral. "There was no favoritism in this sequence of punishments. You are so like your elder relatives. Wanting to rise up the ranks on your own merit. And that is why you have moved up, young man. And if you fail in your duties you will be moved down or moved out. Believe me when I say that, Commander."

"Yes sir," said von Rittersdorf as the door opened. "I wouldn't have it any other way."

And then the time for talking was over as the Admiral ushered him down the hall and into his future.

Chapter 7

It had long since come to my attention that people of accomplishment rarely sat back and let things happen to them. They went out and happened to things.

Leonardo da Vinci

Chief Petty Officer First Class Jana Gorbachev smiled as the young man cursed yet again. *He's kind of cute, in a regal sort of way.* The Lieutenant was tall and muscular, with the same build as his more famous father. Ice blue eyes with an Asian cast peered out of a face that had more than a bit of all the races of humanity in it. Mahogany brown skin, high cheekbones, crowned by reddish brown curly hair.

If I were an officer, she thought. *Or even a noblewoman. Which sort of accounts for the same thing. Since when did you ever see a noble who wasn't an officer?*

"Who the hell did he think he was talking to," shouted the officer while he paced back and forth through the B Ring section office.

"One of his officers, sir," said the CPO, sitting behind her desk and looking at the requisition forms for a new emitter. "In this human's Fleet that makes you just another of the mortals, subject to his godlike will."

"I know that he's the captain of this ship," said Sean, his voice breaking high in his emotion. His voice caught for a moment as he shook his head.

"That's correct, your royal highness," said Gorbachev, looking up at the young man as he stopped walking and rubbed the back of his neck.

"But I am the son of the Emperor," he said through clenched teeth. "I may not be in immediate line for the throne. But I am the son of the Emperor. How dare he talk to me like that?"

He needs to calm down before he storms up to the bridge and tells the old man what he thinks, thought Gorbachev. *Not that he has anything to worry about. The most they can do to him is let him out of the Navy. With an honorable discharge at that. But he will have to carry that release within him for the rest of his life.*

"The low born son-of-a-bitch," growled the Prince, resuming his walk. "As if it was my fault that the nanobots were from a flawed lot that couldn't fix the Captain's ass, much less reconfigure the circuitry of the laser emitter. Why is that my fault?"

"Because you are responsible for the B ring of the *Sergiov*'s laser armament," said Gorbachev, rising from her desk and walking around to get in the Prince's way. She looked up into his eyes with an angry glare. "Because he trusts that as part of your responsibility the ring will work as it is supposed to work when it is needed. When it is needed to save our ship."

"I understand that," said the Prince, looking down at her with a sneer on his lip.

"I don't think you do, your highness," she snapped back. "If this ship is lost in combat because of your mistake. Your mistake, mind you. It is his responsibility. If you are lost with this ship. It is his responsibility. He was willing to take you aboard his ship. To accept your transfer in. Because he is a loyal subject of the Empire. Even if he is a low born son-of-a-bitch, as you called him."

"What do you mean, take me aboard," blurted the

Prince, glaring down at the CPO. "He had no choice. Personnel assigned me to this ship. He had no choice."

"With all due respect, your highness," said the CPO, returning the glare, "shut up. And grow up. He did not have to take you. He could have refused to take the responsibility for your royal ass."

"But..."

"I said shut up, your princeness," growled the NCO, backing him up as she moved toward him. "You can put me up on charges later. Or charge me with disrespect of a noble. Or whatever. But you will listen to me.

"Your line likes to feel that it serves the Empire," she said, turning and walking to the other side of the room. "Good sentiments, that. All of your line serves in some fashion, most in the military. That's great. It gives you some appreciation for the forces you may one day be called on to command. But you are also a liability to those you serve with. Not because of any lack of ability on your part. Not because you are any worse than any other young officer who has been through one of the military schools. In fact, you're better than most. But because they have the additional worry of being the commanding officer of a member of the Imperial Family."

"We don't ask for any kind of special treatment."

"From that low born SOB who dared to speak to you the way he did," said Gorbachev, waving away the argument with a gesture. "I admit that most of the time you bend over backwards to just be one of the boys. Even though you have been raised to be a member of the Imperial Family, and that goes deep. Commanders are told not to give you any special treatment. While at the same time getting the unspoken order to protect your ass from any of the many things that can kill serving officers. And knowing that if anything happens to any of you they will be held responsible."

"But that's insane," said Sean, shaking his head. "How could he be held responsible for something that occurred because of my actions?"

"Because you are important to the Empire in a way in which the Captain is not. In which this whole damned trillion Imperial ship is not. They choose your captain for his special abilities in bringing his officers and crew back from whatever hell he has been through. And they station the ship in a quiet sector."

"But..."

"They don't want you dead, your highness," she continued, speaking over him. "They want you to serve your time, get your experience, and get on with your life. That doesn't mean that you won't be put at risk if this ship does have to go into battle. There is always the possibility, even in a quiet sector, of that happening. And if a total war breaks out, all bets are off. But mostly they want you to come off of your time in service as a live prince with an appreciation for the Fleet."

"I didn't even realize," said the Prince, shrugging his shoulders. "I couldn't have dreamed."

"You weren't supposed to know," said the CPO. "It will mean my career if they realize that I told you this. But you needed to know before you made a total ass of yourself, and destroyed the careers of those around you in a tantrum."

"I won't tell anyone what you told me," he said, shaking his head. "And I'll try to not act like a spoiled brat, Chief Gorbachev. Just try not to hold my recent actions against me."

"I won't, your highness," she said with a laugh, opening her arms and giving him a hug. "I was assigned to be your mother, after all. And I think you are a fine officer. And one day you may make a fine Emperor."

"May that day never come," said Sean, making the sign of the cross taught him in his Reformed Catholic upbringing, while thinking unmotherly thoughts about the CPO.

"Amen to that, your highness," agreed the CPO, thinking back to her own Orthodox childhood. "Amen to..."

"Battle stations, battle stations. This is not a drill," came the call over the intercom along with a Klaxon, at the same instant that the implants in both crewmen buzzed a warning and information came over the link.

"Let's go," said the Prince, running from the office with the CPO on his heels.

The tactical situation came over the link into the officer's brain. Unknown vessel detected that did not respond to hails. In hyper VI. The ship had run as the squadron came into visual, jumping up into hyper VII. While the warships could not give chase in VII, they carried weapons that could. The two closest battleships, which did not include the *Sergiov,* had sent hyper VII capable torpedoes chasing after the unknown. Torpedoes had detonated, as tracked by the grav waves they had generated. If they had been close enough to the target and worked as advertised they should have dropped the unknown ship back into normal space.

"So much for a quiet sector," said the Prince as they hit the lift. The doors closed behind them and the lift slid out, from the forward central capsule to the control center of Laser B.

"In space you never know what you'll run into," agreed the CPO as the lift accelerated.

Sean looked over the sensor information through his link as they moved forward. The ship was estimated to be in the two million ton range, a little larger than an Imperial heavy cruiser. Energy emissions of an unknown resonance, but much stronger than an Imperial HC was capable of generating. Closer to that of a battle cruiser. Obviously too large for a spy ship or other stealth vessel, but it had been much more stealthy than anything that size had a right to be.

The lift door opened and the pair ran out into a scene of disciplined chaos, while the rest of the weapons team put on battle armor or started punching up interface codes into control panels. The Prince nodded to the CPO and ran to his locker, which opened at his approach. Pulling off his overall and stripping to the skin tight underalls that would protect him from light radiation and other hazards, the Prince threw the outer uniform into the bottom of the locker. His armor opened up on a link command and he backed into the suit. As his back touched the padded armor the front section swung closed and locked into place. Seals on chest, arm and leg sections shut as nanolinks formed a seamless closure. He felt a bit of discomfort as the sanitary units of the suit attached. Then the suit was linked to his neural system and moved at his commands like an extension of his body. But much stronger, with much greater capabilities.

Sean walked from the locker and turned, pushing his hands into the gloves that were held out to him by the locker. Again nanolinks made the gloves a seamless part of the armor. Lastly he pulled the helmet from its rack and placed it over his head. It sealed in place, visor still up, and he quickly went down the suit checklist. Everything was in the green, full up power, oxygen and consumables.

CPO Gorbachev smiled under her visorless helm and gave Sean the thumbs up. She ran to the door that opened as she approached, Sean on her heels. Into the central command and control room for the battery. Other crew had already locked themselves into seats before control boards. Sean sat at his station and punched his codes into the panel, giving him control of the B ring.

"Report," he called, while his link went over the system to verify the verbal information.

"All crystal matrixes at full load," yelled one of the techs, at the same time that the Lieutenant looked over the power bars in his mind's eye. Topped off green, enough to power the ring for a full ten seconds without incoming energy.

"Emitters at full draw," called another tech.

Sean acknowledged over the link, while checking the system for himself. To his satisfaction the eight emitter units were drawing energy from the main conduits at maximum rate, and were feeding photons into the ring.

"B ring linked into central fire control," called out the Ensign who was second in command of the battery, sitting in a redundant control room on the opposite side of the ship's central umbilical.

"B ring reporting all nominal," called the Prince over the com circuit while simultaneously sending the information over the link. The link supplied information in return, showing that the other laser rings were coming online (and giving him a momentary rush of pride that his was first up). Missile rooms were manned and the first load outs were entering the tubes. Within less than two minutes the fifteen megaton warship was ready for combat.

"Prepare for translation to normal space," came the voice on the intercom. The link indicated that *HIMS Duke Roger Sergiov II* and her two squadron mates were opening holes in the fabric of space and moving through. They were moving in opposite vectors, fifty thousand kilometers apart. They would enter normal space at over two hundred million kilometers separation due to the correspondence of Hyper VI and the universe known to man. The ships would be at over eleven minutes one way communication range, essentially on their own until they made contact and called their consorts to their aid.

The Prince felt his stomach turn as the ship entered its portal and appeared in normal space. Looking through the ship's sensors, like all of the other linked crew, he could see no trace of the unknown vessel. Which didn't mean much as information traveled at light speed in normal space, and they were at least light minutes from an object that had only translated back into N-space seconds before. Still the passive sensors, especially the infrareds, searched the heavens.

Sean looked through the eyes of the ship with one part of his mind while he paid attention to his responsibility, the B ring, with the rest. *Sergiov* and her squadron mates were a long way from any star, the nearest being three and a half light years. The heavens blazed with points of light. The ship's computers located, analyzed and matched each one against its internal cartography bank. Each was eliminated as a target while the ship continued to search.

Moments after entering N-space the ship's nanofabric outer skin reconfigured itself into an active sensor surface. Energies pumped into the skin and were released as multi-frequency radio waves in all directions. The laser rings reconfigured their surfaces and pumped coherent light into the globe surrounding the ship. The radio waves would have fried any living thing within thousands of meters of the skin, while the coherent light would have vaporized the same object. Power fell off with the square of distance, so that the energies were tolerable a hundred thousand kilometers away. The ship pulsed energies a half dozen times, sending the waves of radar and lidar out into the cosmos. After that would come the minutes of waiting to see if something reflected some of the radiation back to the vessel's outer skin.

Sean waited along with the rest of the crew as they dealt with the paradox of space warfare. They could cover distances at a velocity unimagined by the planet bound forces of their past. They could unleash energies that were still considered stupendous. But they were confined by the speed of light and the great distances of space. Like an ancient sailing ship they were cut off from command while on patrol. And they were not able to communicate in real time with their squadron mates other than through the limited bandwidth of grav waves while separated enough to effectively patrol a relatively small volume of space.

"Infrared's picked something out," said CPO Gorbachev from her station, at the same time as the Prince's implant gave him a look to their stern. A bright object had appeared there, and the computer analyzed it as the heat signature of a MAM reactor at high power.

"Three point four one light minutes," said Sean as he read the incoming data. Over sixty million kilometers to her stern. The bridge sent the signal to the other ships while she turned her bow to the unknown.

"Laser ring firing," called a tech as the boards showed the energy drain.

The Prince knew that C and D rings had been firing a multiple spread of bursts as the ship was turning, joined by A and B as they came to bear. They probably wouldn't hit anything at this distance, certainly not if it were moving. But there was always the chance.

Duke Roger Sergiov II started accelerating toward the unknown, her reactors feeding energy into the grabber units while it sent signals to its consorts. Signals they would receive in about eleven minutes. It pulsed its H-space translators a few times, sending out a warning signal that they would receive instantaneously, but one that conveyed little information other than they had spotted something and their basic heading. As the ship pointed toward its target the grabbers pulled a hundred gees acceleration, building up to two hundred and beyond. Its passive sensors focused on the object, gaining visual resolution.

"You ever seen anything like that, sir?" asked the CPO as the object tightened into focus. It was a stubby cylinder with a thin fringe like a circular wing around the center. The image magnified and they could read the symbols on the vessel, which looked like nothing they had ever seen before.

"No, chief," he replied as his heart beat faster. "And from the chatter on the net no one else has either."

The object appeared to be sitting there doing nothing. Which could mean it was too damaged to do anything. Or that it had already started to move away minutes before, but they were still seeing the image of it sitting there doing nothing from three minutes ago.

There was a burst of noise on the net that signified that two objects had translated out of N-space into the other dimensions. The two battleships further following standard procedure in an op like this. One would translate out and right back in, hoping to drop closer to the target. The other would enter H-space and stay there, hoping to catch the prey if they moved into hyper and attempted to get clear.

"She's moving," said the CPO, as the image started to crawl away from them. It started to dwindle, and it seemed to be pulling more gees than their battleship was capable of. The visuals pulled it closer as they refocused.

"A and B rings continuing to fire," said one of the techs. They were firing with as much energy as the reactors could give them after supplying power to grabbers and sensors. The crystal matrix batteries were left untouched, so that they would be fully powered if they did in fact face battle.

"Sensor return," called the Prince as the first pings of radar and lidar returned from the target. Information began pouring in as the computers analyzed the signals and made interpretations of their resonances. "Computer can't identify it."

"We have missile lock," called the Lt. Commander who was manning central weapons control over the net.

The Prince watched as a pair of missiles flew from their tubes, accelerated at ten thousand gees by the magnetic rails. On leaving the ship their own engines kicked in and accelerated them at five thousand gravities toward the alien vessel, far beyond the capabilities of manned warships and the fragile cargo they carried.

"I don't think he's going to outrun them," said Gorbachev, following the action over the ship's net. "If he can we're in big trouble."

The noise of a translation hit then, the energies released through the opening of an H-space hole. It was of a different resonance than theirs, and of a higher energy than a Hyper VI translation.

"She's gone to Hyper VII," said the voice of the Captain over the net. "We're just chasing her light speed image. But she's gone."

Sergiov continued toward the alien until its image disappeared from visual and active sensors. The missiles were ordered back and retrieved as her companion battleships warped back to N-space. The alien had fled and was not to be found.

"Well, that was exciting," said CPO Gorbachev, stripping out of her armor.

"Means that this part of space is no longer quiet," said the Prince, unlocking his own armor back into the storage locker, where it would be serviced and replenished. "There's someone out here we've never seen before, operating within the borders of the Empire."

"Kind of worrisome, huh," said the CPO.

"I would say," said the Prince. "Something to add to dad's worries, if not ours."

*   *   *

Cornelius Walborski cursed under his breath when the doctor pulled the bones in his left forearm into place. Not that they hurt that much, not after the doc had played a neural inhibitor over the arm and shut off the pain nerves.

"Does it still hurt?" asked the physician, Dr. Jennifer Conway, looking over his vitals on her system scanner.

"No ma'am," said Walborski, looking at the red haired beauty that was working on his arm. "I'm just cursing my stupidity at letting a Tigeron catching me off guard."

"Those are the big predators that prey on those mid-sized herbivores?" she said in a lilting accent, her blue eyes looking into his. "The ones that look like a brownish cross of a bear and a tiger."

"Those would be the ones," he agreed while her gentle fingers moved bones into place. Her eyes were like pools of deep water that looked like they could drown a man. "I was trying to chase one of those big herbivores out of my field," he continued after taking a breath. "And the son-of-a-bitch came out of the tree line and knocked me over going after something more to his liking."

"Lucky you weren't to his liking," she said, placing an inflatable cast over the arm. "And I hope he removed the herbivores from your field."

"Yes ma'am," he said, watching as she made sure the cast was properly in place. "I just wish he had missed me, though. I have work to do, and a broken arm is not to my liking."

"Better than being eaten," she replied, double checking his DNA before tapping her panel.

"I would have poisoned the bugger," said Cornelius, shaking his head. "He couldn't have tolerated my proteins, even if I could have handled his."

"So you would have been his last meal," she said with a smile. "But you still would have been a meal."

"Point taken," he said with a laugh. "I guess I am lucky at that. So, what's the verdict?"

"You'll have to ask a lawyer about that," she said, the corners of her mouth crinkling with her smile. "But in my medical opinion you should be good as new by this time tomorrow. I've got the nanos programmed to your DNA and instructed on what to do."

She pulled an air syringe from a compartment of the medical panel and placed it over the antebracheal part of his forearm. She pushed the button on the syringe and it hissed as it pushed its contents into his skin.

"So they'll knit the bone by morning?" he asked. She nodded her head with a smile. "Why can't we carry bone repair nanos around inside us all the time? Like they do in the military?"

"Because military grade nanos will fix tissue damage, including bleeding," she replied, gently pulling his arm into an apparatus that closed easily around the cast. "But even they can't set a bone. So your arm would be mended, but at a weird angle. I don't think you would like that."

"No ma'am," he said, shaking his head. She made some adjustments to her panel and he could feel a tingling in his arm. Energizing the nanos, he knew, so they could do their job. "And the anti-infective and antibiotic nanos we do have in that are in the system only have to hunt down and destroy things that shouldn't be in us. Not repair complicated damage."

"You got it," she said, pulling the apparatus apart and freeing his arm. She checked his vitals one last time, nodding her head.

"Tell me a little bit about this wildlife you have to deal with," she said, smiling. "I just got here from New Scanbria. And I'm originally from Nova Scotia. Since we've been settled for almost five hundred years they've pretty much tamed the wildlife there."

"Well," he said, feeling the numbness in his forearm deepen, "you don't want to travel in the Backcountry by yourself. And you always want to be armed. The animals here are very big mammalians. Much bigger than Pleistocene animals on old Earth were. Closer to dinosaur size."

"Doesn't sound pleasant," she said, frowning, though he got the impression that she was humoring him with her listening. "So why did you come out here?"

"For the land and the freedom," he said, trying to move his fingers and failing. "You came from a core world, though I'm not so sure about this New Scandria place, or how big it is. And I don't know about Nova Scotia, but New Detroit was overcrowded. There was no way up. No land to own. Too many nobles to bow to."

He looked at her for a second, thinking that she was an educated woman. One who could make her way on any planet. And the community she settled in would be glad to have her. And he would be more than happy to share a bed with her. He decided to take a chance.

"And it's beautiful here," he continued. "The untamed wilderness stretching for thousands of kilometers in every direction. As beautiful as you are, Jennifer Conway. I would be glad to show you this world."

"And what would your wife say to you showing me

this world?" she asked, frowning.

"She probably wouldn't like it," he agreed.

"Well, neither would my fiance'," she replied, shaking her head. "In fact, I don't think he would like you for making the offer."

"I don't think I should be too afraid of some intellectual," said Walborski, smiling and puffing out his chest. "I'm in the militia, you know."

"I don't think Glen would be too worried about that," she said, looking him straight in the eye. "He's a captain in the Imperial Marines. Stationed with the local naval base's battalion."

"Oh," said Cornelius, imagining a marine in full battle armor tearing him apart. Not that the marine would need the battle armor.

"He's a very nice fellow," she continued. "I don't think you have much to worry about him. As long as you maintain a proper patient to doctor relationship."

"Yes ma'am," agreed the farmer with a nod of his head. "Nothing to worry about there."

"Good," she said, tapping him gently on the casted arm. "You should feel normal by the morning. If full feeling doesn't return by then, call my office. And come back in the afternoon and we'll take that cast off, and make sure that everything is OK."

"Yes, ma'am," he said, getting up from his chair. She held out her right hand and he took it in his, after which she shook his hand gently.

"One last thing, ma'am?" he asked as he was turning to leave.

"Of course," she said. "No emergencies at this moment. And doctors really aren't needed for much else these days."

"Has your boyfriend said anything about the

military status of Sestius VI? I mean, there's been some talk about this becoming a naval logistics base."

"Not anything I've heard," she said. "He mentioned something about Zephira getting a bunch of military hardware. I think that might be where the logistics base is going to be. Why? Is it important?"

"No ma'am," he said, shaking his head. "It would have been nice to have a couple of major forts in orbit, maybe some more picket ships, and some real troops planet side."

"I see," said the doctor with a smile. "The best of both worlds, huh. Free land, not many to bow down to. And the best defense the Empire can provide."

"We are out here on the fringe, ma'am," he replied, nodding his head. "And there are some frightening things out here. Real and imagined."

Real and imagined, he thought as he left the office and called a cab on his com link. No riding a cycle today, until he had both arms to use. *And when does the imagined come out of the darkness to become the real?*

Chapter 8

Firstly you must always implicitly obey orders, without attempting to form any opinion of your own regarding their propriety. Secondly, you must consider every man your enemy who speaks ill of your king; and thirdly you must hate a Frenchman as you hate the devil.

Horatio Nelson.

Captain Dame Mye Lei cursed again under her breath as she left the Admiral's office. After the long trip out here to the frontier command of the Fourth Naval District, the bordering district of, nothing. The backwater that faced Galactic North. The backwater that didn't front directly on any of the alien polities that were of concern to the Empire.

Not even the Klang or New Moscow fronts this space, she thought, going over the map of the Empire in her mind. *They're both hundreds of light years from the border. So normally the only thing we'll be looking at will be the odd pirate. But at least we would get to scout the frontier and look for the unknown.*

And the unknown had visited this space, recently. The planet was abuzz with the news brought in by a battleship squadron (one that happened to have an Imperial Prince serving on it) of an unknown craft that got away through Hyper VII. And the poor capital ships couldn't catch it. This was the perfect prey for her command. *Joan de Arc* could cruise in Hyper VII for months at a time, looking for signs of this intruder and making sure that it wasn't able to spy on Imperial space with impunity.

The pilot of her air-car saluted as she came onto the landing deck. She returned the salute with an abbreviated one of her own and climbed in the car. The young rating closed the door behind the Captain, then climbed into the front of the car and started up the engines. The Captain looked out of the window of the car as it jumped into the air and turned toward the landing field. The small city stretched out to the horizon, home to a couple of hundred thousand people.

A metropolis out here, she thought, her mind traveling back to her home world of Xuanchu. Her hometown was not even in the top one hundred cities of that core world, and still it would swallow this frontier city without noticing the increase. She thought for a moment more, then hooked into her com link.

"Jackson here," came the voice in her head as she sent out the summons. "What's going on, ma'am? Are we going to get in on the hunt?"

"Dammit, no," she subvocalized over the link, projecting her anger. "Seems that every ship in the sector fleet is out trolling the dark looking for demons. Which leaves them shorthanded when it comes to escort vessels."

"You're not saying?"

"Yes, Commander," she growled, shaking her head while she looked at the low rise city passing below. "We get the shit detail. Our beautiful Hyper VII battle cruiser is detailed to escort a bunch of Hyper V freighters to a logistics base."

"They must want what those freighters are carrying at that base pretty badly," he said, his mellow voice having a calming effect on her.

"It's a new base," she replied, feeling some of the tension drain from her. "It will be over a year before all the permanent defenses are built and manned. And they want some temporary units stationed there to take up the slack."

"So it may not be what we are really suited for," he replied, as the air-car dropped down to the tarmac of the landing field to the side of a shuttle marked with the name of her ship. "But something that really needs doing. Especially with something unknown running around in this sector."

"There is that," she said, climbing out of the air-car after the rating pulled open the door, and striding toward the shuttle. She gave the crew chief a quick salute and followed him through the open hatch. "I don't like it that our first duty is convoying some slow ships to their destination. But I guess I can see that the Admiralty wants them there for a damned good reason. Thanks, exec."

"For what ma'am," he said, as the crew chief made sure she was buckled in and then strapped himself in toward the forward section of the compartment.

"For calming me down while I was going off like a damned fool," she replied, the lifting of the shuttle pushing her gently back into her seat. "I'll see you on the bridge in about ten minutes. Lei out."

The small Captain lay back in her seat and tried to enjoy the short trip up to where her ship orbited the planet. She thought that at least one of the other ships of her new and temporary command would also resent the fact that it was tied to slow freighters and a couple of troop transports. But it had been unlucky enough to come into the system at the same time, redeployed from Third Fleet sector.

And its new captain has seen combat, she thought, *at least in his old ship. Might be a good idea to grill him for what he can teach, while he's my subordinate.*

After docking in the port stern bay she rode the lift up to the bridge. As the bridge door opened the crew jumped to their feet when the first officer to see her shouted "Captain on the bridge."

"As you were," she ordered, walking to her command chair and sitting down. Commander Jackson was at her elbow in an instant, holding a comp sheet in his hands.

"The convoy is already gathering out at geosynch," he rumbled in his basso voice. "Four freighters and five troop transports, three of them armor carriers. About thirty-six megatons of shipping."

"And what the hell are we carrying in those things," she said, pointing at the armor carriers on his sheet while running through her own ship's readiness indicators on her link, and finding nothing amiss. Not that she had expected to with Commander Jackson running the show.

"A brigade of heavy armor, a mixed armor brigade and a brigade of mobile shore defense artillery," he rumbled, looking at his comp sheet. She knew he had most of it in his head, but it didn't hurt to make sure that the records matched what he remembered.

Captain Lei whistled. "That's over a million tons of heavy equipment. And over nine thousand personnel. What's on the other transports?"

"Two brigades of light infantry," he said, looking up from the comp sheet. "And about five thousand naval personnel. Freighters are carrying hardware for docks and orbital defenses."

"No wonder they wanted the heaviest ship they

could get their hands on to lead the convoy," she said. "That would be a hell of a target for someone."

"Yes, ma'am," he agreed.

She looked at the viewer, which showed their ship pulling away from the planet and moving on an intercept with the convoy.

"And the escorts?" she asked, looking at the tactical display on her internal link.

"One Hyper VI light cruiser," he replied. "Along with a quartet of Hyper VI destroyers. And a newly arrived Hyper VII destroyer. The *Dot McArthur*. DDF 63587. Commander Maurice von Rittersdorf commanding."

"How long before we are underway as a convoy?" she asked her exec.

"About an hour ma'am," said the officer, looking back at his comp sheet. "We should arrive at the Massadara system, which is approximately two hundred and seventy-four light years, in about fifty-four days."

"Or a little over four days on our own," she said with a sigh. "Even less than fourteen with the Hyper VI's."

"Might as well wish the *Donut* were spinning out ship gates," he said with a smile. "Then we could just go in one end of the rabbit hole and arrive at our destination."

"Amen to that," she said, nodding her head. "But I don't think we're going to have a network of those things anytime soon. So it's just rip our own hole in the dimensions and plod on to wherever we're going?"

"I doubt our illustrious ancestors would have called this plodding," said Commander Jackson, shaking his head, "cruising through subspace on the *Exodus*. They would have taken about twenty seven years to go the distance we can cover in four days."

"Point taken," said Captain Lei, nodding her head. "No matter how fast we go we still complain that it takes too long.

"Com," she ordered, turning her chair and looking over at the communications officer at his station behind her. "Request the presence of all the ship's captains and execs at dinner. Ask them to arrive about twenty-two hundred hours Galactic standard."

"Yes ma'am," said the officer, starting to work on his board.

"That gives them about three hours," she said to the air.

"Kind of nice though, isn't it," said Xavier Jackson. She gave him a questioning look.

"Normally we would be running to our cabins to get out our best dress uniforms," he explained. "Then we would hurry to the shuttle to repair aboard the Commodore's ship, to meet with someone we had never met before. Someone our lives would be in the hands of for the length of the mission."

"I see your point," she said with a smile. "I am the godlike being they will entrust their paltry lives to."

"Poor suckers," said Jackson with a laugh. "They don't know how their lives have gotten unmanageable."

"It's good to be king," she said with a smile. "Now you peasants get this convoy arranged and on its way. While I go to the royal quarters and relax for an hour or two, so I might look my regal best for my new subjects."

Captain Dame Mei Lei sprang from her seat and hurried from the bridge. She felt herself relaxing, sure that her exec would handle everything. She knew the tension would return in a couple of hours, when she was in front of the gathered captains of the convoy. When she felt they were sizing her up and judging her. Just as she had sized up and judged every officer she had found herself under throughout her career.

When the Captain entered her living room Satin jumped down from his perch on the bookshelves and ran over to her. She picked up the big smoke and silver Himalayan cat and ran her hand through his soft fur. The cat meowed, then started purring deeply in his chest.

"Miss me," she said to the cat, sure that her steward had made sure the animal was fed and pampered. "You visit any of the other kitties?" There were other cats on the ship, felines considered one of the few types of animals compatible with spaceships. She knew of other captains who had large dogs on their ships, though there were only a couple of small canines on *Jean de Arc*.

Lei carried the cat into her study through the automatic door and placed him on the top of the desk, then settled in to do some of the unending paperwork that was the lot of a captain. The cat lay there on the desk, happy to simply be in her presence. The idea that something was happy with her because of just being her was a thought that brought another smile to her lips. Then she was into the data systems, looking over reports that had been approved by other trusted officers and affixing her electronic signature to them. Time seemed to go by too quickly, and her internal alarm let her know that it was now time to get ready for dinner.

"You be good, stinker," she said to Satin, giving his head a quick rub. She shooed him from the desk and headed for her bedroom to get ready for the meal.

Soon she was sizing up those other officers, while being sized up by them in return. *Joan de Arc*, like all capital ships, had been designed as a possible flagship, and so had an admiral's quarters, including a dining hall. Normally a captain would not use those facilities, as there would be no need for them on a cruise. But with the captain and execs from seven warships and the nine auxiliaries, they would have felt cramped even in the captain's normally spacious dining hall.

Captain Mei Lei looked over the officers while they sat and chatted for a moment. At least she wasn't dealing with civilian ship masters here. The troop transports were naval vessels, crewed by active duty naval personnel. The freighters were contract auxiliaries, crewed by naval reserve personnel. While not capable keeping up with fleet units like navy fast freighters, they at least weren't the dragging anchors that most commercial cargo ships or tramps would have been.

I wonder why they didn't send fleet freighters, she thought again. That would have allowed them to get to the destination system in fourteen days. But then again there was a lot of movement going on in what had been a quiet sector, and there might not have been enough hulls.

"Gentlemen and ladies," she said over the low rumble of conversation. The gathered officers stopped their talk and looked to the head of the table. She picked up her wine glass and raised it.

"Normally the junior most officer would give the opening toast," she said, looking around the room and seeing the varied faces of the human race looking back at her. "Since I am not really sure who that is at this gathering, I will give the toast."

"To the Emperor," she said, holding up her glass, "may he rule long and wisely."

"To the Emperor," echoed the officers, raising their glasses and clinking them together over the table.

After the toast the officers resumed their conversations and addressed the meal that had been laid out before them.

"This is very good, Captain Lei," said a slightly overweight Asian man wearing the uniform of a contract officer. He gestured at the remains of the Beef Wellington on his plate. "You will have to share the recipe with me, so I can give it to my chief cook."

"I will see to it that the mess chief sends it to your ship, Captain Wu," said Mei Lei with a smile.

"You have a beautiful ship, ma'am," said a young Lieutenant SG sitting to the right of the freighter's Captain.

"Thank you, Lieutenant Andropolis," she replied. "I just took command of her right out of the yards. She's one of the most advanced vessels in the fleet."

"And you find yourself playing sheepdog to a bunch of auxies," said one of the troop transport captains with a laugh.

"We do as we are ordered in the service of the Emperor," she replied, frowning.

"A consummate diplomat, Captain," said Commander von Rittersdorf, speaking from down the table. "I for one know what it is like to have to run herd dog, when I want to play wolf."

"Yes," she said, giving the young Commander a smile. "But it is important to get these cargoes and passengers to the Massadara system intact."

"Could you tell me why it's so important for us to have this heavy an escort, ma'am," said a junior officer in a contract freighter uniform.

"Lieutenant?"

"Vasilev, ma'am," replied the officer. "I mean, we would normally have a pair of destroyers along to scare the odd pirate. Last I heard the Empire was at peace, so we really shouldn't have any other worries. Not that I mind having the extra protection."

"Well, son," said the Captain, choosing her words with care. "Let us just say that there are some strange things going on in this sector right now. I'm sure you've heard the rumor of the sighting of an unknown ship just a hundred light years toward the border."

The heads of the assemblage nodded, and a few whispered among themselves.

"We don't have any reason to think it was hostile, whatever it was," she continued. "And we also have no reason to think that it isn't. So until we know different we are going to assume that there is something new out here that might not have the best of intentions towards the Empire."

"And we do have a very valuable cargo," said Commander Verazoni of the troop transport *Gallipoli*.

"Especially the personnel," agreed Lei, nodding toward the ship captain. "I know we are carrying a lot of expensive hardware, but the hardware can be replaced. Human life cannot."

"They already shipped a brigade of heavy armor and a brigade of mobile planet defense to Massadara," said a tall, black skinned woman. "We just got back from that run, which took us a lot less time than this one will."

"I guess the sector Marshal decided they needed more," said Lei. "But not that quickly. Or they need the hardware for the orbital defenses more. I'm not really sure why they put such disparate vessels together. I just know that I have been given command of this convoy as it is constituted. And so we sail with what we have been given.

"Which brings me to the reason for this gathering," she said. The voices of side conversations died as officers looked up the table at her. "I wanted to meet with you all in person so I could put names with faces, and have some real life contact."

"Have you ever commanded more than one vessel, ma'am?" asked another contract skipper. *Captain van Dupfers*, she thought, remembering what she had read of the man before dinner. *Brought up on charges while with the Fleet for repeatedly disobeying orders. Had a protector that got him into reserve duty.*

"I have commanded a destroyer team in the past," she replied tightly. "When I made Commander. Besides that, no Captain Dupfers. Why do you ask?"

"I was just wondering how qualified you were to command this convoy," he said, frowning. "Meaning no disrespect."

"My qualifications are that the Admiralty has put me in charge of this convoy," she said, glaring at the Captain. "That is good enough for me. Is it good enough for you, Captain Dupfers?"

"Yes ma'am," said the Captain with a smirk, returning the stare.

"Good," she said, looking around the table. "Make no mistake, people. I am the ranking officer in this convoy. And I have the largest ship. So I will expect every officer to obey my orders without question. Is that understood?"

Heads nodded and officers mouthed assent as she looked around the table.

"Now as to the sailing order. We are proceeding out system at one hundred gees. The speed of our slowest vessel, I might add." She returned a glare to Dupfers. "Total transit time to hyper limit will be about thirty-two hours, including deceleration to point one c, the limit of our freighters translation velocity.

"Once in hyper V we will accelerate up to point nine c and move from here to the hyper limit of Massadara.   Total estimated transit time fifty-four days."

"What about the sailing order, ma'am?" asked von Rittersdorf, his blue eyes looking intently into hers.

"Light Cruiser *Athens*, Captain Nina Bennett, will lead the convoy," she said, looking at the blond haired officer. Bennett nodded her understanding.

"Destroyer *Artemis*, Lt. Commander Jussin Gourupthinkal, you will be the tail end Charlie, making sure no one is following, and that no one falls behind."

"Destroyers *Garrett Clay*, *Greyhound*, and *Yuri Tomorav* will form the outer cordon of the convoy. Lt. Commander Nora Lafayette of the *Tomorov* will command the destroyer squadron. *Joan de Arc* will stay in the center of the convoy where she can respond to any attacks."

"What about me and the *McArthur*, ma'am?" asked von Rittersdorf.

"Normally you would be in command of the destroyer squadron, given your rank," she said, steepling her fingers and looking over them. "But you have my fastest ship.   And you are the most experienced combat commander in the convoy. So you are going to be my scout. I want your ship to range out six hours ahead of the convoy.   Look out for ambuscades or any other signs of danger.

"You all have the data chips that were handed to you by my com officer when you came on board," she continued. "On the chips are com codes, frequencies and contingencies for this mission. I expect that the sailing will go smoothly, and we will reach Massadara after an uneventful passage."

Lei sat for a moment, waiting for any last minute questions. None came, and she rose to dismiss the conference.

"One last thing," she said while the officers looked at personnel comps and made sure they hadn't forgotten anything. "While we are in transit we will have limited face to face contact. But remember, *Joan* and *Athens* have hyper capable shuttles on board. So we can bring people between the ships while we are in hyperspace. But only as necessary."

Captain Mei Lei turned to leave the room, her exec following her out as the other officers filed out another exit.

"Well," said Jackson from her side as they walked toward the lift. "That wasn't a total disaster."

"If not for that asshole, Dupfers," she growled as they boarded the lift. "What are your qualifications for leading this convoy? Only that I have the rank and the ship. And he better not give me any trouble for the rest of the voyage."

"I'm sure you will handle it if he does," said Jackson as the lift carried them up and over to the bridge.

"I hope so," she said as the door opened and they walked out. "If not, then you have my permission to shoot me and put me out of my misery."

*   *   *

"Now this is what I was talking about," said Dr.

Lucille Yu, looking at the figures in her mind on the link. Production of negative matter was up by three hundred percent. Still less than had been expected when the units had entered production. But a magnitude greater than what they had been getting.

"I'm happy to be the bearer of good news," said Dr. Rafael Gomez after a moment's delay. "Seems a few of the younger minds were able to wrap around the problem. A little bit of fine tuning was able to damp out most of the gravity swirl energy. But I'm afraid that is about as good as it gets."

Lucille looked up on the office viewer, which had been set to watch a generator unit being lowered into place. It didn't look like much on the screen until she remembered that each of the lowering tugs was four kilometers long. They were a mass of grabber units, with the vector shifting power of a dozen battleships. And five of them were lowering the twenty-five kilometer long generator into its berth on the ribbon of the station.

"The Emperor and his family will be here for their visit in thirty-seven days," she told the other scientist. "I would be happy to tell him we will be able to open a ship gate in the near future."

"I'm sure we will have enough in about a month to do just that," he said, grinning. "With the increased production and the new units farmed out in the system, we should be able to make at least four ship gates within the next year."

The greatest engineering project in the history of the human race, she thought. *Over two centuries of work from conception. And it will be completed within the next twenty years. Completed. I think the Empire can be a little more patient with us.*

"I guess he'll have to be satisfied with that," she replied, nodding her head. "I'll let Dr. Baxter know that you and your team have done everything humanly possible."

After a moment's delay the man on the link nodded his head and smiled.

"And how is the passenger gate to central docks holding up?" asked Gomez, relaxing in his chair.

"The gate is open for business," she replied, linking to the gate room where the shimmering wormhole mouth was locked into place between negative matter squares held by magnetic fields, encased in hard metal. "We've sent dozens of people through to the docks and returned about the same number. And so far there haven't been any fatalities."

"Makes it easier to transfer personnel," said the other scientist, "and maybe go on vacations to see family, without having to climb the thirty-five light hours out of the gravity well in N-Space."

"Whole idea of the station," said Lucille, thinking of getting some time on a real world herself. It would be good to feel wind and sun on her skin. "This is going to turn into some busy property in a little while, when this finally becomes the transportation hub of the Empire."

"It's already getting a little busy around here," said Gomez. "I almost tripped over Imperial Marines this morning, running the corridors for exercise. And I hope those warships don't do something stupid like fall into the hole."

"Just getting the security in place for the Emperor's visit," said Yu. "He can walk through the rabbit hole and be here instantaneously. But his security task force can't."

"I don't know why he needs all that security out here anyway," said Gomez. "We are about the most secure location in the Empire. Anybody coming at us has to go through normal space. And it's a long trip in."

"His security chiefs are professional paranoids," said Lucille, shrugging her shoulders. "They make the same preparations when he visits a military planet. Even though all of the soldiers and spacemen are sworn to protect him."

"Just as long as they don't fall into the hole and create some kind of stink," said Gomez. "I don't think too many of those skippers have been around anything like this hole. They aren't survey or explorer captains after all."

"As long as the Emperor doesn't fall in the hole I think we'll be OK," said Lucille. "And I don't see that happening."

"Pray not," said Gomez, crossing himself like the good Orthodox Catholic he was. "Pray not."

"And how goes the quantum teleportation experiments?" asked Lucille, more out of courtesy than anything else. Mankind had been working on quantum teleportation for almost a thousand years, and it was the only theoretically possible means of moving matter, quantum tunneling an object from one place to another. Unfortunately theory didn't quite interface with reality. And Gomez had a laboratory on the station for just such trials of the theory, a major interest of his.

"We teleported a ham yesterday," said Gomez with a chuckle. "Half of it actually tunneled out. Almost a tenth of it actually showed up where we wanted it. And of that almost a third was still made up of edible protein."

"So the prospects of teleporting a marine to the surface of a planet are not good," said Lucille after a short laugh of her own.

"Not if they want him to do anything when he gets there," said Gomez with a frown. "Not really good for much at all is it?"

"We'll just have to keep relying on ships and gates then," said Lucille, her own mind toying with some ideas that might just be useful for quantum teleportation after all.

"I guess we will," said the other scientist. "At least in our lifetimes."

Yes, thought Lucille, a shiver passing down her spine as she looked at the other man. *At least in our lifetimes.*

Chapter 9

Don't ever become a pessimist... a pessimist is correct oftener than an optimist, but an optimist has more fun, and neither can stop the march of events.

Robert A Heinlein.

"I know how to shoot a gun," said Dr. Jennifer Conway as she sighted the small mag pistol down range. They were in the Marine range at the landing field, Glen having used his position to get her space to familiarize herself with weapons.

"I'm sure you do," said Captain McKinnon, his hands on her shoulders, holding her in a steady position. "I know your history, after all."

"So why are you holding me in position like a novice?"

"Because I like holding you," said Glen with a smile.

Jennifer stuck her tongue out at him and he laughed, a sound she enjoyed hearing from the big man.

"Just fire the clip into the target," said Glen, taking his hands off her and pointing at the target seventy-five meters down the range.

Jennifer nodded and took a good sight picture with the pistol. She squeezed the trigger and sent a round downrange, focusing her eyes on the target and watching the small hole appear in the human silhouette about the same time the gun bucked a bit in her hand.

"Not bad," said Glen, pointing to the head of the target, where the round had penetrated about mouth level. "Probably a kill. Now send the rest down after it."

Jennifer set her feet and squeezed off round after round, sending them into a tight group around the first strike.

"Let off the last ten on rapid fire," said Glen after she had put thirty holes in the target.

Jennifer squeezed the rounds off rapidly, sending all ten down in less than five seconds. The groups were still fairly tight, into the chest region this time, but nowhere near as close as the aimed fire.

"Ok," said Glen, smiling at his Fiancé. "That was good, and might even be useful against an intruder in your house. But it's not going to do squat to something in the Backcountry here. So let's try this one."

Glen picked up a sleek looking pistol, checked the charge, then aimed it down range. The weapon buzzed a bit when he pulled the trigger, and there were sparks coming off the target as a hole appeared near the throat. The sparks continued on the back stop beyond the target.

"That's a laser," said Jennifer in an excited tone. "I've used the surgical variety."

"Right," said Glen, setting the target to retract, while another rotated into place. "Now you try it."

Jennifer took the weapon, which was just a little heavier than the mag pistol. She took a good sight picture at the target and squeezed the trigger. The weapon buzzed, and she was surprised by the lack of recoil. *It's a laser, dumb ass*, she thought while watching the pistol burn an instantaneous hole in the target.

"Now with this one you can sweep it through the target like an infinite sword," said Glen, settling his arms around her again and taking a gentle grip on her wrists. He moved her hands and the pistol while she continued to press the trigger, cutting out to the right, then back in and across the neck. The head of the target fell to the floor.

"This would be much more effective out in the brush," said Glen, taking the pistol back and safing it. "But I think this next one will be much better."

Glen picked up a large pistol, much bigger than the laser or mag weapons. He checked the bottom of the pistol, then the battery read. "This is a particle beam pistol," he explained, pulling the boxy magazine from the bottom. "This is the proton storage chamber." He slapped the magazine back into place, then pulled another section off the pistol. "And this is the crystalline matrix battery pack."

"What kind of protons?" asked Jennifer, looking with fascination at the weapon she had only heard about. A restricted weapon on most worlds, though not on frontier planets like Sestius.

"Just regular run of the mill protons," said Glen, shrugging his shoulders. "In space, for long range, we might strip the charges from them and send neutrons out the end of the barrel. So the charge wouldn't split the beam so far apart. In atmosphere and close range we don't bother. And we definitely wouldn't use anti-protons in an atmospheric beam, not for civilian use."

Thank God, thought Jennifer, knowing that she would want to use any kind of weapon that sent a beam out that exploded when it touched matter.

"Here's how you hold this weapon," said Glen, making sure he had a two handed grip and arms extended. "You turn it on here," he said, pushing two separated buttons at the same time. The pistol emitted a whirring sound that built up over a couple of seconds. "That's the particle accelerator whipping the protons up to speed." He took aim and pulled the trigger. The pistol bucked back some as it let out a dark red beam with the sound of a swarm of angry bees.

The target exploded the instant the pistol fired. Jennifer knew it wasn't really instantaneous. The beam traveled much slower than light. But it seemed to be at the same time.

"The beam is very energetic," said the Marine Captain, handing the pistol to the woman. "It strikes with kinetic energy and built up heat the protons gain from the air. First blast is kinetic, but then the beam also creates more heat in the target. A powerful enough beam essentially vaporizes the target."

"Sounds deadly," said Jennifer, pointing the pistol at the target.

"Very," said Glen after a short chuckle. "Please make sure the target is more than twenty-five meters away, or the superheated steam coming off it can be deadly to you as well."

Jennifer pressed the trigger, and let out a yell as the pistol seemed to want to come out of her hands and hit her face. But she held it steady, and the new target exploded under the impact, most of it converted to vapor.

"That will let you take care of most anything you will run into out in the brush," said Glen with a smile.

"Hell yeah," cried Jennifer, aiming the pistol at the next target to come up and blasting it out of existence. "I want one of these."

"Then it's yours," said Glen, smiling. "But we need to make sure you are proficient with it."

They spent the next hour on the range firing. And then Glen fitted her with a holster. *Hell yeah*, thought Jennifer as they left the range. *Let a damned mammalian dinosaur come near me now, and we'll have steaks for dinner.*

* * *

"And now we start the invasion," said Grand Field Marshal Mishori Yamakuri, the Imperial Army Chief of Staff.

Augustine stood on the flag bridge of the fast troop transport *Kursk*, his eyes riveted to the wrap around 3D screen that occupied half the area of the large chamber. Being an invasion ship this was the flag bridge of the Army invasion force, and most of the officers and crew on this bridge were from that service, with a smattering of Naval liaison personnel.

Centered on the viewer was the planet Hydra, a small, lifeless rock sitting outside the life zone of Home, the Imperial capital star. Hydra had an atmosphere, a fairly thick layer of methane-ammonia. This made it a good candidate for training in the planetary assault of inhabited planets.

On the screen were shown the mass of invasion ships involved in the exercise. A dozen of the troop transports, all launching missiles and kinetic weapons at the planet. Among them were a quartet of assault carriers, a smaller version of the fleet and light carriers of the Navy, carrying atmospheric fighters and sting ships. They were constantly launching and landing these small craft to carry out missions on the planet. Behind them, some visible on the viewer, were the warships that were conducting planetary bombardment. Kinetic rounds showed as streaks on the screens, and the normal invisible laser beams were highlighted for the observers.

"Of course most of that ordnance you see out there is simulated," said the General, following the eyes of the Emperor. "We're launching real kinetic weapons, so the troops can get used to the feel of the ground rumbling under foot. But it's just too hazardous to do a training operation with real light amp and particle weapons."

The big ship started to shudder underneath them, and the viewer highlighted the assault capsules launching from the vessel on a trajectory into the atmosphere. Small vector arrows and numbers appeared beneath each of the small capsules that contained one heavy infantry trooper. Within moments there were hundreds of the capsules heading into the atmosphere, and within a minute that number had risen to several thousand.

"These are the assault battalions," said the Lt. General in charge of the corps, Murdock according to his name plate. "They will grab the ground and hold it for the follow up forces."

"And what's the casualty rate among this first wave?" asked the Emperor, noting that some of the capsules were turning the red that indicated they were destroyed, though he knew that was only a simulation as well.

"In this exercise, your majesty?" said the General, looking at a flat screen he was holding. "Probably about thirty percent. Simulated of course, though there is always the chance of a couple of real casualties, though not many among these heavily armored troopers. In the real thing it would depend on the opposition. We've had as little as less than a percent, and as many as seventy."

That many, thought the Emperor, watching as thousands more capsules flooded the screen with their vector arrows and numbers. He turned away for a moment and looked back at the sixty or so soldiers and spacers who manned consoles, all with fingers flying over boards while they talked into mics, controlling the operation as much as possible from their stations. He nodded, then looked back at the screen, which was now a mass of objects, more turning red as he watched.

"We send two decoy capsules for every real trooper," said the General, looking at the Emperor. "We are also jamming constantly, messing with the sensory platforms of the enemy, and striking back at any weapons system that opens up on the capsules."

"And there are still such heavy casualties?" said the Emperor, looking down at the floor.

"This is the most dangerous operation in ground warfare," said the COS, nodding at the screen. "We have to open up a landing zone against a resistant opponent. These training exercises are invaluable to our units, teaching them to perform in an environment of total chaos."

The Emperor nodded his head, knowing what the man was trying to communicate, and also remembering that when they went to war, he would be ordering young people into this chaos. And many would not return.

"This might interest you, your majesty," said the corps commander, pointing to a group of capsules that was leaving a nearby ship. "This is a battalion made up entirely of Phlistarins."

"They don't look any different from the other capsules," said Augustine, looking closely at the rounded shapes. Maybe a little more oblong."

"The troopers look like this," said the General, pointing to a screen that popped up in the main viewer. The trooper did look formidable in his heavy battle armor, his centauroid body making him look like a metal encased horse. "They are really a sight to see in action."

"Not very good at getting low, are they?" asked the Emperor.

"No, your majesty. They're not. But they carry a heavy weapons suite better than humans."

"Landing zones have been secured, sir," called out a Colonel who stood behind a bank of manned consoles.

"Proceed to phase two," ordered the corps commander. "Now watch this, your majesty."

Augustine watched as a hundred assault shuttles left the ships, and some other large objects that lacked the aerodynamic shape of the landing craft. He recognized them as heavy tanks, over a thousand tons of armored vehicle, with grabber units attacked to turn them into their own landing craft. All sped toward the planet, the tanks turned so that the heat shield they rode on would hit the atmosphere first.

"We're linking in to an atmospheric fighter that is following one of the shuttles down," said the COS, pointing to another slaved screen that appeared in the viewer. The shuttle in the view juked and dodged simulated weapons as it dropped. It lost acceleration quickly as it neared the ground, and a dozen ports tossed armored troopers out, where they floated to the ground under their own grabber units.

"Would you like to tour the field, your Majesty?" asked the corps commander.

"Yes," agreed Augustine. "I would."

It took just a little time to get the Emperor ready to go down to the surface. First he had to don his own medium armor suit. He stepped into the cubby which had been brought aboard and let the suit configure itself to his body, the nanites turning the halves of the armor into a unified whole. When he stepped out of the cubby his bodyguard was similarly prepared. The Emperor looked at the dozen men in suits that were just as capable as the larger heavy armor suits of the divisions on exercise. His suit cost as much as a squad of heavy armor, and those of his guard nearly as much. They were too expensive to provide masses of infantry with, and were only issued to special elite units. His own suit was capable of keeping him alive through almost any imaginable attack. Almost any. He felt a bit of guilt that he would have such protection when his troops didn't. But it was part of the dynastic game, and he played along.

The surface of the planet was definitely someone's definition of Hell. It was too cold to even be terraformed, but had almost one gravity, making it the perfect training ground for planetary assault. Which meant that the planet was battered several times a year so Imperial soldiers could get realistic training. Just like another dozen useless planets across the Empire.

"This way, your majesty," said the corps commander, accompanied by the COS and a man with the rank of a division commander.

The Emperor followed him through the cloudy atmosphere, over a couple of hills, surrounded by the body guard detail. *That is so silly*, thought Augustine, following the officers while conversing about the capabilities of heavy infantry. *These are my own troops here. I don't know why I need a body guard among men sworn to my service.*

Augustine smiled as they walked around another hill and came to a flat area. There, arrayed before him, were a mass of troopers in full armor drawn up in company formations.   He counted three of the rectangles, and a smaller one to its front, all made up of centaur shaped troopers. Phlistarins, alien subjects of his, assimilated three centuries before, and now serving in his Empire.

Augustine returned the salutes of the officers in the headquarters unit, speaking with a lt. Colonel who commanded perfect Anglo. The being towered over him, at least two and a half meters from front heel to helmeted crown. He had to stretch over three meters from front to rear, and mass at least three hundred kilos. Of course in heavy armor he would mass more than two tons, and the weapons mounts on his shoulders showed that he used the strength of suit to carry more than a human could.

Next followed a review of the troops. There was no spit and polish here. The suits had dirt on them from the drop, and the camo covering made them blend colors with the near soil. But the Emperor could see that all the soldiers were squared away, suits fully functional and all equipment ready to deploy.

"You have good soldiers, Colonel," he told the battalion commander after the review, before heading back to his shuttle. "I'm sure you are proud of them. Know that your Empire is."

"Thank you, your majesty," said the Phlistarin in his unaccented English. "I'm sure the men will be proud to hear that."

Augustine nodded his helmeted head, in his mind comparing the Phlistarin to the Ca'cadassians they might be pitted against in the near future. And in his mind, the four armed horned monsters were found wanting in the balance.

*   *   *

The Prime Minister Count Mejoris Jeraviki looked out the window of his luxurious air-car, watching the traffic go by. There were thousands of other vehicles in sight, moving along the various levels that separated the traffic pattern. Below them was the mass of the great city that was the capital of Empire. Most of the people of that city could not afford air-cars of their own, though they were in no way destitute. Taxes and fees drove the price of operating an aerial vehicle up, and kept most of the people using the high speed monorails or the public air buses. That was a regulation he approved of.

"It's very beautiful," said Baroness Tabitha Romanov, looking past him through the window.

The Prime Minister looked into the face of the woman and thought the same. "You're beautiful, my dear," he told the Lady Seatholder, a distant cousin of the Emperor.

The woman's face dimpled into a smile, her nanite spa treatments hiding her age and making her seem like a little girl. "Flatterer," she said with a laugh. "Is that why you got me up into this air-car, without a driver?"

I got you into the air-car without a driver for the same reason I don't use one whenever I discuss business, thought the Prime Minister, looking at the other member of the Lords. *I would like to fuck you into next week, but I can't risk the possible alienation, at this time.*

"I got you up here, my dear Baroness, to discuss business," said the Count, reaching into the cooler and pulling out a bottle of wine, following with some glasses. "We can discuss pleasure at a later time."

The Baroness laughed, then pouted out her lip while reaching for a glass, making sure that her wedding ring was prominently displayed.

While everyone knows you have slept with half of the Lords, thought the Count, forcing a smile to stay on his face. *But you have some pull with your faction, so I must make you think I might be interested.* He poured her a glass of wine that cost more per bottle than a factory worker made in a year. *Our just reward,* he thought, as he put the cork back in the bottle and the bottle back into the cooler.

"To the elite," he said, touching his glass to hers.

"To the elite," she agreed, taking a sip of her wine and smacking her lips in appreciation.

The car started into a gentle bank, following the autopilot that would keep it circling over the huge city as long as its owner wanted it to do so. The Count had been taught this method by his mentor in the Lords, those decades ago when he was a new Seatholder, inheriting the position from his father. If the car was swept for listening devices, and employed its own security procedures, it offered an untapable moving office. The Count looked out the window once again, at the familiar row of megascrapers to the north, then turned back to his guest.

"So," said the Count with a smile. "How is your faction going to vote on the supplemental military appropriations bill?" *That that damned cousin of yours keeps reintroducing to Parliament, like we're going to change our minds.*

"I thought that was obvious," said the Baroness, the smile leaving her face. "We will side with his majesty."

"But, why?" asked the Count, keeping his expression pleasant. "Of what benefit to you or your constituents does voting more money to expand an already bloated Fleet?"

"It protects us from those who would harm us," said the Baroness, glaring at the Count over her wine glass. "Why else do you think we need the Fleet, and the Army?"

"To defend our interests," said the Count, poking himself in the sternum with his thumb. "To defend those of us who really count. The core worlds, and then the developing worlds."

"And what about the frontier worlds?" asked the Baroness, her eyes narrowing. "What about those who find themselves in out of the way science or mining outposts? What about those, Prime Minister? Do they deserve less protection?"

"They deserve what we give them," said the Count, waving the thought away with his hand. "They are not important. The only important ones are those of the gentry, and the commoners wealthy enough to donate to our cause."

The Baroness stared at him for a moment, her eyes narrowed like a predator just waiting for the right moment to leap.

"Come on," said the Count, putting his empty glass into a holder. "You live on a core world. The worlds we depend upon to prop up our state, and give us the life style we enjoy. The rest of the worlds are useless to us. I admit that the developing worlds may someday actually pay for themselves, but right now they're just a drain on resources. And don't get me started on the frontier worlds."

"My brother is the Archduke of one of those frontier worlds," said the Baroness in an icy voice. "He risks much to give them stable government."

"And he is a fool," said the Count with a laugh. "Only an idiot would put his life at risk on the frontier, when the safety and luxuries of the core worlds await."

"Yes," said the Baroness, looking down at the

floor as if in thought. "You might be right." She looked back into the eyes of the Count. "You might be right. And what about all of these people we serve here in the heart of the Empire?"

"They are ants," said the Count with a smile. "The labor that builds this great society that we, the elite, benefit from. Nothing more, nothing less."

"And the rich ants, like Alfred Krupp? Or Yuri Chekov?"

"They are bigger ants, and of more benefit to us, but still ants."

"And we want them to be ants because?"

"They benefit their betters," said the Count in the tone one uses to explain something to a child. "And they benefit from our beneficence."

"You really are an asshole," said the Baroness with a short laugh, the mirth not extending to her eyes. "And you think I and my faction would go along with you."

"But you stand to benefit as much as the rest of us," said the Count, his eyes widening in surprise. "How could you turn your back on your own class?"

"I don't give a shit for my own class," said the Baroness, her gaze turning into a stare, then a glare. "I only give a shit for the human race. All of them. Just because of some fortune in my birth, that does not mean I am not one of them. In my family we are taught that with our wealth and power comes a duty to service. I can see that was not true in the pack of rogues you call family."

"How dare you," growled the Count, feeling the red flush come to his face.

"I dare," shouted the Baroness, pushing her face close to his. "I may not be of the same exalted rank as you, but I am of the nobility, and count dukes and archdukes among my close relatives. And if you try to touch me, fat boy, I will hurt you. More than you can imagine."

"Take us home," said the Count to the car, leaning back in his seat. He believed that last remark. This woman had served in the military, in the Marines of all things, and he was sure she would hurt him in a hand to hand fight. He of course had a weapon within reach, but he knew the same of her. It was not worth risking a gunfight, and then police investigation. *I'll take care of you later*, he thought, an evil smile on his face.

"I don't want to sit in the same car as you," said the Baroness with a sneer. "Land this vehicle immediately, so I can escape the stench of you."

"Car," said the nobleman in an angry tone. "Land as the nearest possible zone." He turned his glare on the Baroness. "You will regret those words."

"Not as much as I regret getting in this car for your private meeting," said the woman as the car pulled out of the traffic stream, then lowered itself to the parking roof of an enormous shopping mall. "And you can also be assured that my faction will never side with yours on any vote that goes against the people of this great Empire."

The car bumped down onto the roof and the door raised open. "I'll call my own car to come get me," said the Baroness, who then slipped from the luxurious cab of the air-car and out into the bright sunlight.

I don't care if you call the ferry for Hell, thought the Prime Minister, ordering the car back into the air and sending it back to the House of Lords. *Stupid bitch. We'll see how much you stand on your principles when I'm the power behind the throne.*

Fifteen minutes later the Prime Minister was storming back into his chambers at the Lord's Office Building. The day was bright and beautiful outside, but his mood denied any feelings for it. He looked down from the tall building on the Lord's Meeting Hall, large enough to seat all of the houses of Parliament in joint session, as well as ten thousand press and spectators. *I'll be glad when we can dispense with their attendance*, he thought of those distractions. *And those damned commons and scholars as well. As if any amount of achievement can make them equal their betters.*

"The Duke of Coventry is here to see you, my Lord," came a call over the intercom from the Count's private secretary.

"Send him in," shouted the Count, sitting behind his desk and trying to calm down.

"How did it go?" asked Theo Streeter as soon as he walked into the large office.

The Count looked him in the eye and growled, his hands clenching into fists.

"I thought so," said the Duke with a smirk. "I told you that she held to egalitarian concepts, that one. It was a total waste of time."

"How can she so betray her class," said the Count, standing up and walking to the sidebar. "Drink?" he asked, pulling down a couple of glasses, then a bottle of scotch.

"Of course," said the Duke with a smile, walking over to the bar. "Anything to dull the afternoon. So, she didn't take too kindly to your call for governance by the better class."

"No, damn her," growled the Count, pouring some splashes of alcohol in the glasses, then throwing some ice in for good measure. "How can anyone be so stupid? I offered her the Galaxy, and the power that our class deserves."

"Some don't see it that way," said the Duke, accepting the glass. "Some see it as their duty to make things better for the common folk."

"The commoners already have it pretty damn good," said the Count after taking a sip of his drink. "They are housed, fed, protected, even given an occupation if they wish. What more do they want?"

"Determination of their future," said the Duke. He held up a hand as the Count slammed his glass on the table and took a truculent stance. "I know. It causes pure chaos if everyone goes and does things without direction from those who see the big picture. I agree with you. I just want to point out that some don't agree, even among the nobles."

"Then they are wrong," said the Count, picking up his glass and swirling the liquid in it. "And they must be shown the error of their ways."

Chapter 10

Death may be the greatest of all human blessings.
                                                                    Socrates

"How the hell did he get in so close?" yelled Lt. Commander Kathomas Hubbard, throwing an angry glance at her tactical officer. The HICS (His Imperial Czar's Ship) *Ekaterina* shuddered again as the terawatt lasers of the unknown enemy struck at her hull.

"Increasing electromag shields to port," yelled back the tactical officer, his fingers dancing over his board. "Venting more cold plasma into the shield matrix." The rest of the bridge crew was performing admirably, trying to stay cool under fire, fighting the ship to the best of their abilities.

And it won't be enough, thought the Captain, tapping into her link for a private conversation. *That ship has to be at least three times our mass. And her weapons are hitting too damned hard, even for a ship that size. They have some tech that we don't, and home needs to know about her.*

"How the hell did they get on top of us?" she asked her sensor chief over the link. "They shouldn't have known we were there. Right?"

"I'm not sure, ma'am," said the Senior Chief Petty officer from her room toward the bow. "I'd never seen anything like them before, and was still trying to firm up a reading…"

The ship shuddered again as the alien hit them with another blast. Circuits sparked for a moment, then went silent as the ship shunted them around to undamaged hardware.

"C Ring at fifty percent," yelled the tactical officer.

"Keep the A and B rings on target," said the Captain. The helm nodded his head as he maneuvered the vessel, keeping the functional rings on target as the *Ekaterina* fired everything she had.

"He was in Hyper VII when we picked him up," continued the chief on the private link. "I'd never heard anything like that resonance. The ship didn't have anything in its memory like it either. But I assumed from the power that it was a capital ship, at least a battle cruiser."

And much further off, thought the Captain. *Same as I thought when I looked at the readings.* The ship's computers had nothing to compare the energy signatures too, and thought he was much further off, even if he was coming toward them. And a good tech; and the chief was a good tech; could read things from the resonances that even the ship's computers could miss. But only if they had a frame of reference. So when they thought they were safe and undetectable, they had crept into the range of the enemy's scanners. And said enemy dropped down into Hyper VI and caught them off guard.

"Fire off all of our hyper capable missiles," she ordered, looking at the tactical plot on the screen. Her ship had suffered some superficial damage. But it would start to add up quickly. While she really couldn't tell how much damage the other ship had taken. *Not bloody much*, she thought, looking at the energy signatures. The surface of the enemy ship was blurred under electromag and cold plasma, same as her ship. Both to attenuate the effects of light amp weapons, and to camouflage any surface damage and hide it from enemy eyes.

"All missiles away," called tactical as the quartet of hyper capable missiles left their tubes and headed for the enemy, followed by another four.

"As soon as one of them detonates drop us to N-Space," she ordered the helmsman.

"Why not to another level of Hyper," asked the tactical, sending tasking orders to the weapon systems.

"They'll just follow us down," said the Captain, nodding toward the enemy ship on the tac display. The vector arrows of the hyper capable missiles pointed toward the angry red dot of the enemy, acceleration and velocity numbers underneath. The hyper capable missiles had their own hyper bubble generator that would allow them to survive in this space. But it came at the price of mass, and the missiles were only pulling four thousand gravities as they headed toward their targets.

As she watched one of the missiles exploded, the enemy's defensive lasers tracking and focusing long enough to burn through the defenses of the twisting and turning weapon. Antimatter contacted matter as the containment field ruptured. The brilliant light of detonation blossomed as five hundred megatons of explosive power was released in light and radiation. One of the nearer missiles detonated as it was struck by debris from missile one, sympathetically detonating as well.

As soon as the missiles detonated the helmsman started the translation process. The iris to normal space opened in front of them as the ship went into emergency decel. Hubbard felt as if a giant's hand was pushing her back into her couch as decel went over the limits of the ship's inertial compensators. Her vision blacked out for a moment, then swung back into focus just in time for the nausea of translation to hit her. Then they were through, and she shook her head to clear it, knowing that she didn't have long to get it together and take charge.

"Full military acel," she ordered. "Along the prime vector of velocity."

The giant's hand pushed her back into her chair again as the destroyer pulled as many gees as she was capable without killing the crew. Hubbard felt her brain begin to fade again into blackout, and fought to stay conscious.

"Fire all tubes as soon as we have a target," she ordered. The enemy ship had to be coming through soon, unless they had gotten lucky up in Hyper VI.

"Enemy ship still moving in VI," came the sensor chief over the com. "Still moving. Translation," he called out. The graviton waves made by the energy release of translation from VI to N-space pinpointed the enemy ship well before anything could be seen on sensors. Good enough to send out missiles, setting them to lock on as soon as they actually saw the target.

Ekaterina bucked slightly as the missiles were thrown out of their accelerator tubes, a full spread of six. Cycling time was five seconds, to move new missiles already mated to their warheads into place. Then another six fired out of the tubes and vectored to the stern. Five seconds and another half dozen fired. Followed by another six.

"Cease fire on the missiles," ordered the Captain, fighting the gee forces and hoping that her tactical officer was able to comply. She had just fired over half her complement of N-space missiles. And she would need to shift missiles from the bow mags if she wanted to fire full spreads from six or eight tubes, up to the eighteen left.

Hubbard watched the vector arrows of the missiles as they sped to the stern, moving toward the target. They were actually losing velocity as they fell behind the ship, accelerating at five thousand gravities the other direction. Her own ship was now moving at just above point two c, accelerating at two hundred and sixty two gravities.

Damn, she thought, looking at the vector arrow on the much bigger alien ship. They were moving at about point three three c at a forty degree angle to the port side of her ship. But they were starting to curve around as their vessel pulled over three hundred gravities. At a bit over three million kilometers. *So they can translate through hyper at a fifty percent greater velocity than we can, as well as out accelerate us. We are fucked.* She watched the vector arrow move, every second getting closer to *Ekaterina's* own vector.

Eleven light seconds and closing, she thought, looking at her own ship moving straight as an arrow. Just as she opened her mouth to order evasive the enemy's lasers struck her rear.

"Going to evasive," called out the tactical officer, setting the random program in motion. Nausea returned along with random jerks as the ship put some of its acceleration potential into moving the ship back and forth, up and down, side to side, making it impossible for the enemy to accurately target light amp weapons on her. The lasers still struck, but in quick sweeps that did minimal damage to the target, instead of focused blasts that could vaporize layers of hull.

The enemy ship was still looping around and closing, gaining velocity. The human missiles were bleeding velocity on the forward vector while pulling gees on an angle toward the enemy ship. The missiles were also on evasive, moving in random jinks that protected them from targeting by an enemy that could not read their true position because of the light speed limit. But as they closed on the enemy its targeting solution improved. One of the missiles was hit squarely on one of its forward grabber units. Alloy spurted as the grabber overheated between its own heat production and the energy added by the laser. The missile veered off course for a moment, then corrected, then blew apart as lasers targeted its length.

Three more missiles detonated outside of four light seconds of the target. Countermissiles, larger and faster than those carried by a human vessel, lanced out from the alien and drove hard to contact. Two hit dead center. Seven more detonated on closest approach, which was close enough to take out their targets. Three were clear misses, and the remaining eleven human missiles drove toward the enemy with machine determination.

Jamming systems came on line as the missiles entered three light seconds, sending out waves of electronic static that spoofed the systems of the alien's target acquisition. Those systems fought through the jamming better than they should have and launched countermissiles and laser beams that took out seven of the incoming. At one light second the alien opened up with close in projectile weapons, filling space with fast moving particles that swept three missiles from space. Leaving one that looped in, detonating its five hundred megaton warhead two kilometers from the alien ship, filling space with heat, light and radiation. But warships were tough beasts, and the alien proved to be no exception. It drove through the detonation that contained very little blast effect and continued after the human ship.

"Damn," cried Kathomas Hubbard as she watched the last of her missiles drop from the plot along with the bright ball of light that blossomed near the enemy vessel. The vessel did not deviate from her vector by one iota, but drove toward the human ship like a predator after prey.

"Prepare all message probes for launch," she ordered. "Everything on them that we have on this bitch. Keep feeding them instantaneous updates until we launch. Hyper one in different directions, then creep out of here till they're out of detection range."

And good luck finding them, you bastard, she thought. At one hundred tons the probes would give out very small detection signals in hyper I. And with three to chase the enemy would have to be very lucky to get them all.

"Enemy is firing missiles," called the tactical officer. Four vector arrows appeared on the board, each traveling at eight thousand gravities. Five light seconds separated the ships now, which meant the missiles had been fired five seconds before they appeared on the plot.

"Fire all remaining missiles at the enemy," ordered the Captain. "Target C and D rings on the enemy and fire full spreads."

"Aye ma'am," said the tactical officer, and the ship bucked. Five seconds later she bucked again, then five seconds later yet again. The enemy missile vectors had closed about a third of the distance at that point and were moving in swiftly.

"Remote detonate the last wave of missiles when they are just ahead of the enemy salvo," she ordered.

"Then detonate the second wave five seconds later."

"And the first wave?" asked the tactical, looking intently at his board.

"Let them close with the enemy," she replied, wiping a bead of sweat from her face. "Maybe we'll get lucky. And get ready to launch the probes. Right when the last wave detonates, set to translate in five seconds after launch." *And then hopefully we can do our duty*, she thought, trying to calm the fear that was roiling her guts.

"We're not going to get out of this, are we, Captain?" came the voice of the exec over the private circuit.

"Not likely," she replied, staring at the tac screen. "But if we get the information home we'll have done our job for Czar and Kingdom." *And I hope that's enough for you.*

The first wave passed the incoming alien weapons. The second wave passed. The outbound missiles of the third wave detonated when they were more or less even with the alien missiles, setting up a wall of radiation between the two vessels. And by luck frying the acquisition system of one of the incoming, sending it arrowing straight ahead, to miss the *Ekaterina.*

At that moment the destroyer bucked back again, a sign that the message probes had left the ship. Moving away they decelerated at five thousand gravities. When they dropped to safe velocity they opened gates into hyper I and disappeared from N-Space. And just as they translated the second wave of missiles detonated, forming another sensor shield in space. As soon as the probes hit Hyper I they accelerated in different directions at five thousand gravities, carrying the information the *Ekaterina* was fighting to bring back.

The three remaining enemy missiles came screaming in, accelerating the entire way. Counter missiles took out one, close in projectile weapons the second at about fifty thousand kilometers. The third came in under the rapid fire weapons, detonating a hundred meters to the starboard stern of the destroyer.

That section of the ship buckled inward, superhard alloys and ultra-tough carbon fibers collapsing under the flood of heat and radiation. The starboard MAM reactor core cracked, venting coolant into space. And the fuel containment vessels buckled and broke through the wall of the reactor, emergency field circuits cutting in to keep antimatter from breaching into the ship.

On the bridge it felt like someone had hit the walls with a ten ton hammer. The alloy and carbon fibers actually rang, and the three hundred megaton blast shoved the ship away. Inertial compensators switched from carrying full military load to dampening the impact of the massive warhead. And the acceleration dropped in an instant as safety mechanisms took the grabbers off line. Still the crew was flung around in their acceleration couches, while armored battle suits stiffened and sprayed life sustaining gels into their interiors.

Hubbard tried to clear her head while emergency lights flickered, then came on, followed quickly by backup power that brought the bridge systems back online. She tried to link with the ship but ran into a wall. The net was out, and she was sure the ship was out of action with it. Something was speaking to her through ears that were almost deaf, and she concentrated to catch what it was saying.

"Reactor breach imminent," said the words over the intercom. "Reactor breach imminent."

"Engineering," she called over the com. Getting no answer she looked at the readouts on the ship's schematic. There were no life signs from engineering. And from the damage projections there was no reason to expect any.

"Jettison the reactor section," she ordered, typing her code into the panel in front of her couch. A part of the display turned red, then green. She punched the display and felt the ship buck.

"Reactor section jettisoned," came the voice from the com system. "Reactor section jettisoned."

She looked at the display that showed the twin chambered reactor, along with most of the antimatter fuel, flying away from the ship. Under the display was a distance readout that was at five hundred kilometers and advancing rapidly as the grabber units on the reactor pulled it away from the ship. Seven hundred. Nine hundred, twelve hundred, fifteen hundred.

The cracked starboard reactor breached, antimatter spilling from the failing containment field and touching the sides of the chamber. Setting off a chain reaction that encompassed the entire reactor and the nearby fuel cells. The hundred gigaton blast dwarfed the explosion that had crippled *Ekaterina*. But the distance also dwarfed the force. There was very little blast effect, though heat and enormous amounts of hard radiation sleeted through space.

Hubbard could feel the radiation sickening her, neutrons mostly, which flew through her body. Nausea pulled at her stomach. She twisted and pushed a panel on the arm of her suit, injecting an army of nanobots into her system to aid those already at work fixing the radiation damage.

"Are you all right, ma'am," croaked the tac officer

from his station. His visor was down and his voice came over her speakers. The Captain reached up to find her visor still in the up position. *Idiot*, she thought. If the hull had been breached down here to the internal capsule she might be sucking vacuum right now. Didn't happen often. But it only had to happen once.

"I'll live," she said, her tongue feeling at the root of a broken tooth. "I don't think the ship will, though. Where are our friends?"

"They're deceling right in behind us," said the tac officer. "Matching velocities."

"Not much we can do about it, is there?" she asked, moving her arms and legs, feeling for what worked and what didn't.

"We still have some charge on A ring," he said, looking at the board. "But we're not oriented properly to bring it to bear."

"Not that it would do us much good," she said. "He would just disable it, and then take the ship."

"Prisoners?"

"The best we can hope for, Lieutenant," she replied, nodding her head. "Don't know how they treat prisoners though, do we? They might see us as valuable sources of information."

"And we can't allow that to happen, can we ma'am?" said the officer, resignation in his face.

"No we can't, Lieutenant," she agreed, punching in a trio of codes on her board. "I've sent the activation to your station. You know what to do."

"Yes, ma'am," he agreed, punching in his own codes. "Maybe someday we can get home, and get our memories back." He said it in a less than hopeful tone, and they both knew that would not happen.

I almost wish I hadn't jettisoned the reactor core, she

thought. But she had grown up loving her life, and did not want to end it or those of her crew without a chance for survival. They didn't know how this enemy treated prisoners. Maybe the same as her Empire and the other human polities did. *And if I believe that, maybe I'll buy some surface area on a Neutron Star.*

The officer hit the final commit panel and lay back in his chair. Commander Hubbard lay back as well, a relaxing sleepy feeling coming over her.

Within seconds the ship's non-catastrophic self-destruct systems came online. Nanobots all over the ship went into overdrive, turning the circuit boards and the inner workings of equipment they normally serviced and protected into piles of dust. Memory cores, from the central computers to every single functioning processor on board, melted to slag. Within less than thirty seconds the ship was a complete nonfunctional unit, only life support, food storage and basic lighting systems still up and running.

The Captain felt the lethargy pull her into a deep sleep as the nanobots in her system took all of the memories from her mind that an enemy might find valuable. She would still remember her home world, growing up, useless facts to someone looking for military intelligence. But she would not remember one iota of militarily or technologically significant information.

*   *   *

"Nothing, my lord," said the officer, standing tall and bringing his hand up to grasp a horn in salute.

"They totally wrecked their data net?" growled the scout ship Captain, staring down his nose at his inferior.

"Completely, lord," said the officer, a twitching eye

showing that he was not the picture of calm under the watch of his superior. "They slagged every piece of useful technology on the ship. We did take a hundred and eleven prisoners though, my lord."

"Medical said they were completely useless to us," growled the Captain. "They wiped their own brains to keep us from getting the information in them. They are nothing more than ignorant sentients who are not worth our time."

"Shall we space them, lord?"

"No," said the officer, giving his head a vigorous shake. "We will bring them back to the fleet. May their biological systems do us some good."

"Sir," came a call over the com.

"What is it now?"

"The pinnaces are back from hyper space."

"And?"

"They found two message probes. They self-destructed when the pinnaces tried to capture them."

"Were those all of them?" asked the Captain, scratching his head.

"We believe so lord," came the answer. "We only tracked two of them through the interference that the enemy missiles created."

And that could have been a clever ruse by a smart foe, thought the Captain. *We will never know. And it would be better to report some success to command. Why risk the displeasure of superiors, when that displeasure can result in nonexistence.*

"Very well," he said. Looking across the bridge he caught the eye of the helm. "Prepare to translate into hyper VII. We will get what information we have back to the fleet."

"Yes lord," replied the helm. "Preparing to

translate into hyper."

Within seconds the six hundred kiloton scout was entering the rip in space that led to the higher dimensions of hyper. The remains of the *Ekatarina* drifted dead in space, light years from the nearest stars. Lost forever in the endless sea of space.

*   *   *

"This is the captain of the small escort that was caught in deep space," said the biologist, leading the Great Admiral to the scanning tube. A naked human floated in the liquid of the tube, a breathing apparatus running from her mouth to the top of the tube providing oxygen.

"Damned ugly things," said Grand Admiral M'tinisasitow, looking over the naked skin of the creature. It only had fur on the top of its head, and a smaller patch between the joining of its lower limbs. From the fleshy notch beneath the hair he could tell that this was a female of the species. That and the discoloration of the nipples tipping its small mammary glands.

"Small and weak too," said the biologist. "At least physically. Mentally they are all that we can handle."

"What does that mean," growled the Admiral, looking down his nose at the smaller scientist. "Are you saying they are smarter than the race? The divine race."

"I know that you don't want to hear it," said the scientist, who was the senior researcher of the conquest fleet, and so had some rank of his own to hide behind. "But I'm here to give you the facts. Not a bunch of pretty stories to lull you to sleep."

I could have your head, and nobody on the fleet would say a word, thought the Admiral, glaring at the scientist. *But you are the best we have, which means pretty damned good. So I can't afford to dispense with your services, and you know it.*

"Go ahead with your facts," said the Admiral. "Maybe you can tell me something useful. Unlike the idiots who have brought me nothing from the ships they took."

"Nothing?"

"The warships completely purged themselves of any useful technology or information," he growled. "We got a basic idea of where they were at militarily by the way the ships fought, and the life support they left intact on their vessels. A couple of freighters we brought in were more or less intact, and give us an idea of where they were twenty years ago in technology and light weapons. And they had library computers that intelligence is still looking at, that will probably give us some good background information on the humans. But not much of military value. And hopefully they still know nothing of our presence here."

"Though you can't guarantee that, I suppose," said the scientist, looking over at the human in the tube, whose eyes were now open and staring widely at the two Ca'cadasans to her front.

"I wish I could," answered the Admiral, baring his fangs at the human and watching her cringe, trying to move away from him and running into the hard plastic of the tube. "But you never know who or what might be watching us out here that we didn't see. Now what about the humans that you have been studying? What are their weaknesses?"

"Comparing their genome to that of the human slaves we studied from their original world," said the scientist, nodding toward the prisoner, "not as many as they once had. They've improved their genome in the intervening millennia. They haven't become a super race. But they're much improved."

"Do you think this holds true for the entire species," grumbled the Admiral, tugging at a horn in thought. "Or just the military portion of it."

"Not just the military," stated the scientist, looking up at the Admiral, "since the merchant spacemen your soldiers brought in had the same genomes, more or less."

"So how improved are they?" asked the Admiral with a frown. They had already known that the humans, though a smaller and weaker race than Ca'cadasans, were more intelligent on average than the so called superior race. They had progressed faster than they had any right to on their own, even if they were still well behind the Ca'cadasans. But they were destined to catch and eventually surpass the larger aliens if given time. Which was another reason the conquerors had wanted them crushed when they found the alarming sophonts. And crushed quickly. Even if they hadn't been responsible for the death of the Emperor's son and heir.

"Speed and reaction time about twenty percent," began the scientist, looking down his list. "Strength about forty percent. They also eliminated all congenital genetic defects, increased healing rate, and more than doubled the natural lifespan."

The Admiral pursed his lips as he thought about those figures. That would increase their durability and effectiveness on the battlefield by a factor of two.

"Mental processing speed and memory increased by twenty-five percent," continued the scientist.

"But not a race of super beings," said the Admiral, digesting those figures. "Just better than they were."

"No," said the scientist, nodding his head. "Not super beings, though they could have been if the enhancements had been taken to their logical conclusion. No telling why they weren't. Their genome is so much more pliable than our own, with the nucleotides they use. And they didn't tamper with some of the more mundane factors, like height, weight, beauty, and skin and eye color."

"Can we develop biologicals that would attack them?" asked the Admiral. "It would be nice if we could seed their planets and watch them fall into the dust. And still have the living worlds for our own."

"Their immune systems are quite strong," said the scientist, giving a negative head nod. "And they all, or at least all of the ones we've studied, have nanobot accessory systems, both biological and mechanical, that will destroy any bacterial or viral infections before they have a chance to take. Also protects them from radiation poisoning. So the dose would have to be quickly life ending or it would do no good. Of course chemical weapons could still be used."

"Or electromagnetic pulse to destroy the nanobots," said the Admiral, looking back at the human and licking his lips at the thought of destroying her kind. "But of course those wouldn't affect the biological nanites. Almost be less trouble to simply scour the surfaces of their planets clean."

"But," stammered the scientist.

"I know," replied the Admiral with a sigh. "It would be sacrilege to destroy hundreds of life bearing planets without using them for the good of the race. So we will just have to destroy their warships, pound their cities into dust from orbit, and land troops to root out and destroy those left."

"Not an easy task," said the scientist. "Especially with war on another front. And those other bastards are sure as hell one tough opponent."

"The Empire is large," said the Admiral, bowing his head for a moment. "The Emperor will give us what we need to do the job here."

He looked once more at the helpless captive in the tube. A captive who didn't have any knowledge that would be of use to them.

"Are her proteins compatible with ours?"

"In that way they are the same as their ancestors. They don't contain complete proteins, but they won't poison us either."

"I'll send my personal cook for this one then," he said. "Since she wiped her mind I might as well get some use out of her. And I have heard that they are tasty."

Chapter 11

What a cruel thing is war: to separate and destroy families and friends, and mar the purest joys and happiness God has granted us in this world; to fill our hearts with hatred instead of love for our neighbors, and to devastate the fair face of this beautiful world.

Robert E. Lee, letter to his wife, 1864

The interplanetary corvette patrolling the outer reaches of the system picked up the message probe as it translated from hyper VII. Normally the probe would have sat there, transmitting a come hither signal for hours until something in the system had picked it up. The corvette was within a couple of million kilometers, sweeping the ether of hyperspace for any signs of the unknown. It had been tracking the incoming probe for over an hour before it translated. The corvette locked onto the probe with a signal and let it know it had been found. The proper code let the probe know it had been found by someone who was supposed to find it.

Probe and patrol ship accelerated toward each other and matched velocities. Along the way the probe transmitted information on tight beam to the patrol ship. The crew looked over the data as it came in, slowing some of it down to take a closer look.

Horrified, the crew sent the information on tight beam as fast as they downloaded it from the probe. The beam went to the system's small orbital fort. As soon as it got the probe on board the corvette accelerated at maximum back into the system. As soon as the fort had all of the information about *Ekaterina's* battle with the alien a fast courier was on its way out of the system, at maximum gee. It hit the hyper barrier decelerated to the maximum safe velocity, and then jumped to Hyper VII, heading for the nearest large base system of the New Moscow Navy.

For all who had seen the images from the doomed destroyer knew. The old enemy had tracked them down, and was on the edge of human space, stalking human ships and probably preparing for invasion.

* * *

Commander Bryce Suttler lay back in his bed and looked up at the glowing ceiling panel. The ship throbbed gently around him with the combined energies of her MAM reactor, hyperdrive projectors and spatial grabbers. He knew they had to be sending out grav waves that could be tracked for ten to twelve light days in normal space.

But we don't have to worry about being tracked here, he thought.

HMIS *Seastag*, moved through hyper VI like a regular ship, up to point nine five c with a velocity relative to normal space of over nine thousand nine hundred times light speed. They were well within Imperial Space, and were broadcasting their IFF signal for all to hear. Anyone in hyper VI, anyone who might pop up to get a look at them, would know right away that they belonged here.

On a forty day redeployment, he thought, looking over at the pictures of his parents on the holoboard built into the wall. *Boring as hell, when we could be doing good work on the Lasharan border. Or even home on leave.*

But the powers that be had decided that they needed as many recon assets as they could get in Sector Four. All because someone had seen a ship they couldn't identify which had gotten away from them. Nobody knew if that ship or what it represented was a threat or not. While the Lasharan sector was heating up and was probably going to blow in the near future.

And we'll miss out on all the action, thought the Commander, swinging his feet up from the bed to the floor and sitting up. *We could be in on the kills of a couple of capital ships. It would do all of us good to claim twenty or thirty megatons of shipping. But instead we're going to chase shadows in the definition of a quiet sector.*

"Captain," came the voice of the duty officer over the tac circuit. "We're tracking a ship coming up from behind in Hyper VII. Looks like a mail courier."

"Are you running a tracking and attack exercise on him, Ensign," replied the Captain, pulling up the tactical display on his link.

"No sir," said the Ensign, projecting the nervousness over the link.

"You know you are supposed to treat every contact like this as an opportunity to train up," said the Captain, projecting his ire with the mental contact.

"But sir…"

"But sir nothing," said the Captain, jumping to his feet and leaving the cabin. "I'm coming up to the bridge. And when I get there I expect to see the command crew working their asses off plotting that contact and figuring up an attack solution. Do you hear me, Ensign?"

"Yes, sir,' said the officer with a mental gulp. "Will do sir."

"Captain out," said Suttler, and he headed for the lift.

The thought struck him when the doors opened in front of him. They were carrying a wormhole in engineering. The one that they used to suck up the heat and other energy they produced that might allow an enemy to track them. It was not being used now, as the ship was fully capable of getting rid of its own waste heat when it wasn't trying to hide. But it was still there, stretching back to the home system to the other opening of the hole, which was floating in a heat dissipation station in empty space. What was that connection really like, in the space that the wormhole traversed, the Planck Dimension. And how did it interact with all the dimension the hyper VI ship was jumping in and out of?

Are we looping it into knots in that infinitesimal space? He shook his head at the thought. If the physicists really couldn't come up with an answer, how could he? He did know that there was an ensign up on the bridge whose stomach was tying in knots thinking about a visit from an angry Captain. That thought brought a grin to his face, remembering his own bouts of terror when a superior officer took notice of his shortcomings. Now he was the superior. His face broke out into a smile as the lift doors opened onto the bridge deck. Yes, it was better to give than to receive.

*   *   *

Major Samuel Baggett groaned for a second as the alarm went off. He forced an eye open, then another, a smile growing on his face as he saw the interior of his shipboard cabin. He was off that hellhole of a Lasharan world. That part was not a dream. Somebody else might be back there catching hell. But it wasn't the men he was responsible for. It wasn't his ass on the line this time.

Pulling off the covers the Major sat up in bed and stretched. The lights in the cabin came up, and he looked around the room that had been his for the past eight days. It was almost as large as his quarters planet side. There was a large desk with chair, several sets of dressers, and an easy chair. Beyond the lace like partitions was a sitting room with couch and coffee table.

We really lucked out getting a contract liner, he thought, contemplating what he would order for breakfast. The ship would normally be hauling civilians, but the Empire had needed to move troops, lots of troops, over long distances quickly. So the First Brigade of the 988th Infantry Division had gotten luxury quarters compared to what they would have received on an Imperial Navy Troop Transport. Even the lower ranking NCOs would have their own state rooms, though nowhere near as spacious as his.

"I'll have a cheese and bacon omelet," he said out loud, knowing that the service program would catch the order and his food would be delivered to his room in moments. Meanwhile, he stripped and got into the hot shower, relishing the unlimited water while he shaved in the stall.

Leaving the shower, grabbing a towel to dry off, he took in the smell of his breakfast sitting on the coffee table, along with a mug of that beverage and a large carafe of refill. *I could get used to this*, he thought. The Army chow wasn't bad, and they gave their hard charging combat soldiers plenty, but it was hard to relax when you knew you would be patrolling streets whose residents wanted nothing more than to see you dead.

The rest of the division should be loading up in about a week, he thought. They had stayed behind to orient the incoming unit as to the lay of the land, who to trust and not, and how to make it through their tour without shipping too many body bags to their home planet.

His brigade, including the 789th Light Infantry Regiment, Brigade Headquarters, the support battalion, attached artillery battalion and light armored recon company, had been the first tasked to go. He had come as the acting battalion commander, since the light colonel in charge had opted to stay on their assigned planet, his wife being a missionary there. And Baggett was hopeful that, Imperial Army policy being to promote from within the regiment, he would get his silver oak leaves soon after arriving at the frontier world to which they had been assigned.

"Major Baggett," came a call over his Divisional com link. "Report to the Brigade staff room ASAP."

Baggett cursed under his breath and acknowledged the call, wondering what it was that couldn't wait. But he was not in charge, and he started shoveling food in his mouth, grabbed a couple of sips of coffee, and took the plate and cup with him to his closet. He took down a garrison coverall and pulled it on, grabbing another bite and another swallow of hot liquid as he climbed into the suit. He sealed his polished boots (another perk of being an officer, someone else had to do that for him) and stood up. He walked out of the cabin while sending his ETA to HQ.

Some junior officers were jogging down the corridor as he walked to the lift. They threw him salutes as they trotted down the hall in their gym clothes. Baggett returned the salutes crisply, keeping his face stern as he laughed inside. He didn't have to get up early in the morning for PT, though he did have to work a little harder to stay fit, internal nanites notwithstanding. And he knew that the enlisted men would have already been gently awakened by their

NCOs and would be going through that dreaded PT in the ship's gyms, before going through the motions of what training could be accomplished on a ship without weapons ranges and realism decks. The large hanger deck and VR goggles would have to make do.

The lift brought him up to two decks to where brigade and regimental HQ's were located for this trip. As the lift door opened Baggett found himself giving a higher ranking officer a salute, to the Lt. Colonel commanding another battalion who was walking hurriedly down the corridor.

"Do you know what this is about, sir?" said the Major, falling in beside the officer.

"Not a clue, Sam," said the Lt. Colonel, giving Baggett a look. "I guess we'll all find out together."

The soldiers on guard nodded to the men, their helmets flashing them recognition codes as the officers approached. The doors slid open and the men walked into the room that was buzzing with conversation. Seats had been reserved for the officers, who saw the empty chairs around the holo tank. Baggett could see his name blinking red over the chair through his link. To his left and right were the chairs of the acting executive officer and the senior company commander. The other three company commanders were sitting in chairs behind that trio. The other battalions were laid out in a similar manner. At the head of the table were seated the Colonel in charge of the regiment and his exec, with an empty chair between them.

"Attention," yelled a lieutenant, the only one in the room, standing near another entrance to the room. Everyone jumped to their feet at the position of attention. The Brigadier General came through the door, a thick cigar curling smoke into the air. Baggett saw that several cigarettes were sitting in ashtrays putting out smoke. He thought it a disgusting habit, even though nanotechnology had taken the adverse effects out of it. But if the commanding officer practiced it, what could a lowly major say?

"At ease," growled the commanding officer of the brigade, marching to his seat. Brigadier General Alphonso Marquett was a bear of a man; well over two meters tall and built like a weight lifter. His black hair was cut short in a manner that only the Imperial Marines favored, and his skin was an ebony sheen under the lights of the room. He fell heavily into his chair and swept the room with a predatory glare.

"I'm sure you are all curious about why you were called here," he said, the cigar moving on the side of his mouth while he spoke. "We received information from a courier that changes things in our area of operations."

The officers in the room looked around at each other, making eye contact with questioning looks. The holo tank that the table was built around came to life, showing a swarm of stars, with the borders of the Empire wrapped around them. The view zoomed in to Sector Four; the stars still a cloud but a little less of one. Several stars blinked. They could recognize the F5 of Sector Headquarters, but the other two were just two other stars among many in the sector.

"Major Nguno will now give his briefing," continued the General, nodding toward an officer sitting behind him. That man came to his feet, his mahogany skin dry as his blue eyes took in the table. Everyone in the room was familiar with the brigade intelligence officer.

"Thank you, General," the Major said in a high pitched voice that did not go with his rugged features.

"The two stars you see blinking, close to the actual border of the Empire, are Massadara and Sestius. "Massadara," he continued, as the G star started to blink, "is one of the new logistics bases being established at the frontier of the Empire, in anticipation of expansion in that area. It is being heavily fortified as we speak, with a system of orbital and planetary defenses. Most of our division will be going there, to help to garrison the surface. But not us."

There were gasps and mutterings around the table. Baggett looked at the star that was to be their new home, with all of the comforts of a major base at their beck and call. Then he looked at the blinking F2 that was to the right of Massadara on the display.

"And this is Sestius," said the intel officer, looking at his personal comp. "Planet four is a frontier colony. A farming world, and all that implies. It is the home to less than three hundred thousand humans. Current defenses include a Marine battalion, a couple of batteries of planetary defense artillery, and one class III orbital fort. Oh, and a brigade of militia, including a regiment of infantry, some light armor, and some aviation assets. There is also a trio of interplanetary patrol corvettes."

"Not much of a fortress is it?" chimed in Colonel Janakowski, the 789th's regimental commander.

"No sir," said the intel officer, nodding his head. "It is not."

"What we have received, gentlemen," said the General, his gravelly voice getting everyone's attention, "are orders from our new sector command to divert our force to Sestius IV. It seems that all of the commotion in the sector that we have heard about makes someone very high up nervous," he raised his eyebrows for emphasis. "That very high up wants the frontier worlds defended with everything we can get out here. Now, with the Lasharans always on a short leash there is not a lot that can be released from Sector Three. We were already up for redeployment to a rear area, so we drew one of the lucky straws. And we are going to Sestius."

"Are there any facilities for us, sir?" asked one of the other battalion commanders.

"There may be a few prefabricated structures," answered the intel officer for the General. "But not much else. We may have to build our own quarters. And dig in ourselves as far as fortifications go. But we will not be lonesome in that regard."

"No we won't, gentlemen," said the General, looking around the table. "Every planet in the sector is going to get something, if command can come up with it. Even units diverted from the core worlds. Which may cause some shouting and crying in Parliament. But they'll get over it. We will be getting, or have already gotten, a battalion of mobile planetary defense artillery, a battalion of mixed armor, heavy and medium; and an aviation brigade, both transport and air superiority. The orbital defenses will be beefed up with about five dozen defense platforms. And what about the Fleet presence, Major?"

"There will be a delivery of another three corvettes, as well as a couple of IP Destroyers," said the intel officer. "And an instel patrol squadron may come calling on us periodically."

"Doesn't sound like much to stop an invasion, sir?" said Baggett after going over the figures quickly. "We'll be lucky if we can hold a small continent with what we have."

"That may be true, Major," growled the General, giving him a carnivore smile. "But we have what we have. And the whole of Fourth Fleet will be operating in this area as well. So we can count on them to be there for us."

I know how that goes, thought Baggett, nodding back at the General. *Fleet will be concerned with the high population systems. And the ones that contribute to their ability to operate, like the major bases. And if they have anything left over they might come to our aid.*

"But no matter what we have or don't have," said the General, again sweeping the table with his gaze, "we will do our best to defend the citizens and property of the Empire. Or we will die trying. Do I make myself clear?"

The assembled officers shouted their acquiescence. *What else can we do,* thought Baggett. The General smiled in approval, though he had to know that there were many doubts flying around the room.

"Very well," he said, putting the cigar out in the ashtray and reaching into his coverall pocket for another. "Continue with the briefing, Nguno. Pay attention gentlemen. Because this is the part about what we can do to hold the fort."

The holo zoomed in very close, flying through the stars, then into the system, and the blue and white globe grew to a planet with recognizable continents. Points on those continents started to blink, showing the cities, landing strips and defensive positions of the globe. And the professionals paid attention, putting their whole minds into figuring out the best way to properly defend that globe against any contingency.

*   *   *

Ensign Mark O'Brien woke screaming from the

dream that had been tormenting him for the last couple of nights. The word NO was on his lips as he watched the Imperial shuttle go screaming into atmosphere to burn up on reentry. There was nothing he could do about it, except exact revenge on the ship that had shot the Emperor's transport out of space. He had failed in his duty, and the Emperor's Protection Detail never failed.

He brought the nose of his ship in line with the enemy, his targeting computer giving him a zoomed image of the imperial fighter that had done the deed. And his breath sucked in as he saw that the transponder numbers matched that of his fighter. And realized that he was the enemy.

How can that be? he thought, running the last dream images over in his mind. The Ensign sat up in his bed, the lights coming on as the room sensed his activity. *Those can't be my thoughts and motivations at work. Just fear of failure.*

O'Brien stood up and walked over to the small bathroom that opened off his sleeping chamber on the *Heraklion*, the heavy cruiser that his fighter was attached to. After relieving himself he thought of going out to the living area to see if his suite mate, another copilot in the fighter flight, might be up and willing to talk, but what could he say? That he was having dreams of harming the Emperor, something he would never contemplate in his waking time.

I was just tested, he thought, his mind going back to the recent memories of sitting in a deep scan chamber, being checked for any hidden thoughts or programing that might compromise his trustworthiness. He had been found to be totally clean, just like all the other times he been checked. So the dream had to be just his mind worrying about his charge, and his duty. Like it was supposed to.

It was just a dream, he thought one more time, climbing back into his bed and calming his mind. The room was totally silent, like all sleeping rooms on Imperial warships, insulated from the noise and vibrations of a working ship. Within moments he was back asleep, and the dream was forgotten.

Chapter 12

A doctor must work eighteen hours a day and seven days a week. If you cannot console yourself to this, get out of the profession.

Martin H. Fischer

Dr. Jennifer Conway climbed out of the air-car while the turbines powered down with a whine. She could feel the smile stretching across her face as she thought of the triplets she had left behind at the farmhouse. It gave her a warm feeling to be there at a birth that might not have gone so well without her presence.

Even with all the enhancements, there can still be difficulties, she thought, running a hand through her shoulder length red hair. Babies still moved in the womb, and breach births could still be a problem. Especially in a freehold located hours away from any medical facilities.

Conway pulled her med bag from the passenger seat of the car, adjusted the strap over her shoulder, and headed for the stairs. *What an interesting world,* she thought, *with cities, towns, villages, just like any core world. But surrounded by endless wilderness, with the freeholds set down among it.* The freeholds were something that they didn't see on the core worlds. A minor noble or wealthy commoner would take from twenty to a hundred family members or followers and carve out a farming stead in the wilderness. They would also take advantage of any mineral resources in the area, engage in light manufacturing, and do anything else that might turn a profit and allow the freehold to grow. And they were a municipality on their own, looking after themselves and asking for help from none. Unless they needed medical help, since most freeholds didn't have the resources to hire a physician. They might have an autodoc, or a medic or two. But not a real doctor. Those had to be called in by air if needed.

Good thing I don't need to take a shuttle out every time, she thought, looking up at the sound of one of those large craft coming down from orbit. She could tell from its lines that is was a military heavy lifter. It fell slowly toward the nearby military field. She turned from the entrance to the stairs and sauntered over to the rooftop wall. Planting her elbows on the top of the wall, she followed the shuttle with her eyes.

It came to a gentle stop on the tarmac, heat rising from its surface from the passage through the atmosphere. As she watched the rear hatch of the enormous shuttle slowly fell open until it hit the hard surface of the tarmac. A rumbling sound came from the field, and a long barrel rolled from the ship, followed by a large tracked vehicle.

"Big, huh," said a deep voice as a large hand came down gently on her shoulder.

"I wish you wouldn't do that," she said, turning her face to look up at the smiling visage of the large man in the undress uniform of an Imperial Marine. His blue eyes smiled into hers from his freckled face.

"Sorry, love," he said, bending down to gently touch his lips to hers. She put her arms around him and leaned into the kiss.

"Why aren't you out terrorizing your men?" she asked with a laugh after breaking the kiss. "I thought that's what captains did in their spare time."

"They're damned tough bastards," replied Captain Glen McKinnon of the Imperial Marine Corps.   "As hard as I try I just don't scare them anymore."

The Captain looked out over the landing field, whistling softly. Jennifer turned in his arms and looked back to the shuttle, her hands over his as he kept his arms around her.

"And that would scare the hell out of any marine," said the Captain, as the thirty-one meter long, ten meter tall heavy tank rolled across the tarmac away from the shuttle. The ground shook under its seventeen hundred ton bulk.

"Nothing short of a nuke, or a heavy kinetic round will take that out," said her lover. "There's a whole company of them coming down here, along with two companies of mediums and a company of lights."

The doctor took a second to digest that. She had already seen a battalion of heavy mobile planetary artillery come down earlier this week, their vehicles almost as large as the heavy tank moving away at what had to be seventy kilometers an hour. Idling speed she knew, remembering that the heavies could move at over two hundred kilometers an hour when they needed to.

"What's going on, Glen?" she said, turning and pulling out of his arms. "I mean, I like the idea of as much of a defensive presence on the planet I happen to be sitting on as possible. But isn't it unusual to build up a frontier world like this. It's not like we have anything really worth defending."

"We have you," said the Captain, smiling. Jennifer frowned up at him and shook her head.

"Sorry," he said.   "I would love to tell you everything. You know that. But some of what I know is classified secret. All I can tell you is there is a new threat materializing in this sector. And Imperial High Command is doing everything it can to defend the planets we have feet on."

"New threat," she said, looking down at her feet and thinking about the political situation in this sector. *What new threat?* she thought. *Can the new threat be the oldest threat of all?*

"The Ca'cadasans?" she said, looking up into his eyes. "I know you can't tell me. But it has to be them. I know it."

She looked back over the landing field at another shuttle coming in for a landing. She looked back up at her fiancé and grabbed his arms.

"Can we beat them?" she asked. "If they have found us, can we finally beat them?"

"Well," he said, frowning. "Since I'm can't really say that I know what you're talking about, I don't really know how to answer that question. But I will say that whoever the bastards are, they will have to get through me and mine to threaten you."

"I'll have to take that as a maybe," she said, giving him a quick smile.

"Well then, Doctor Conway," said the marine, pulling her back into his arms. "If you don't have any looming medical emergencies, I don't have any current invasions to defeat. So do you want to go to your place or mine?"

"I think mine might be better," she said with a smile. "Much as I like the marines, I don't want to join them. At least not until I have to."

*   *   *

"What the hell is that?" groaned Katlyn, scratching her head while she sat up in bed.

Cornelius opened an eye to look at the bedside

clock, groaning himself at a new kink in his back.   It was 3:35 in the morning, local time, and he was supposed to be up and working his fields for the coming harvest in just a couple of hours. Which meant Katlyn had to be up even earlier to get his breakfast ready in the long held tradition of farming families.

"Whatever it is," he groaned in a good imitation of hers, feeling the rumbling of the earth through the mattress, "it's not going to help me get through the next day."

Walborski pulled himself into a sitting position, pushing the large mongrel dog off of his feet where it slept at night.

"Why aren't you out there investigating?" he asked the dog, which turned intelligent eyes toward him as it snuffled a woof.

"Well, I don't want to get out of bed either," he said, waving a finger at the dog. "But since you're too lazy, I guess I have to."

Putting his feet on the floor he could feel the vibrations that the water mattress had dampened. And could hear the sound of the dishware and glasses in the kitchen shaking. He pulled on a robe against the early morning cold and walked from the bedroom into the living room.   At least they were in their permanent dwelling now, which was almost finished. If whatever it was out there didn't bring it down. Whatever that was. Standing at the door and thinking twice about it, he grabbed a heavy sporting rifle from its rack by the entrance. This was, after all, a planet teeming with dinosaur sized mammalians. And something that could make the ground shake like that might not be something he wanted to come face to face with unarmed.

The early morning air was cool, about ten degrees centigrade. The local bird analogues were quiet in the darkness. Cornelius could hear the sounds of metal squealing on metal as he searched the night. A couple of large floods speared the night beyond his fields, out there in the wilderness. About where the sounds were coming from.

Suddenly the sounds stopped, replaced by a low rumbling vibration that he thought had to be a large engine idling. The floods went out. Seconds later a ring of light sprung into existence, illuminating a large boxy object with a rounded bubble on top. The farmer tried to make out details, but from the distance, with no sense of scale, he couldn't tell what it was.

Obviously not a stampede of beasts, he thought, walking back into the house and closing the door behind him. *And probably not an invasion. Just some sort of industrial machine parking its ass near my farm. Maybe they're going to terraform the land out from mine.*

That would be a happy event, he thought as he crawled back into bed. Katlyn was already back in the land of the dead, snoring away on her side of the bed. She had been getting tired recently as she entered her second trimester.

Be nice to have someone else's fence line fronting on the wilderness, he thought, giving her a gentle kiss on the forehead. He pulled the covers back over himself and felt the dog jump up onto the mattress and lay on his feet. Within seconds he knew nothing more as blackness closed over him.

Morning came too quickly as the alarm went off in his link, giving him no option to ignore it. Cornelius groaned again, his hands reaching over to the other side of the bed and finding it empty. The dog was gone as well. The smell of food came to him as the door to the bedroom opened and Katlyn looked in.

"What was that thing last night?" she asked as the light came up in the room. The dog ran in, his long tail banging against the side of the bed while he ran over to his master, looking for attention. Cornelius gave the mongrel a couple of pats on the head and struggled out of bed.

"Some kind of industrial machinery," he answered as he stumbled to the bathroom. "Maybe we're about to get some new neighbors. Someone else who will have to worry about broken fences for a change."

"That would be a relief," she said, setting a cup of steaming liquid down on the counter while he threw water in his face. "Come and have breakfast. I know you have a long day ahead of you."

"Don't remind me," he said with a scowl, taking a sip of the coffee. "I would like nothing better than to crawl back into bed right now. But if I call it a day nothing will get done in the fields."

"Not like working a job in the core worlds," she said with a smile. "Here, if we skip a day the whole thing might come unraveled."

He nodded his head, thinking that it might have been better to stay on the core world they had called home before here. At least there they wouldn't have to work so damned hard. But they also wouldn't have the promise of their own land, and the status that came from being among the earliest settlers to a new world. The status their children and grandchildren would have for generations.

After eating breakfast and taping into the planetary net for a look at news and weather, Cornelius thought he was ready to hit the fields and get the robots to work. Dressed and ready, the bright globe of the F class star poking over the horizon, he opened the door to greet the world. The dog ran outside, barking at the small animals that were getting back to their burrows to wait out the day. The other dogs came running out of the barn/storage shed, barking and sniffing and getting reacquainted with their compatriot who had spent the night inside. A couple of cats came running up too, looking for the breakfast Katlyn would bring for them as well.

The farmer looked over at the object he had spotted the night before, curious to get a good view. His jaw dropped at what the morning light revealed. A couple of crewmen were working on the deck, giving scale to the ten meter tall machine. The large dome on the top resolved into a turret, with a pair of long barrels sticking from it.

"Katlyn," he called, staring at the thousand ton plus war machine. "Katlyn. Get out here."

The door to the house opened and his wife came running to his side, grabbing his arm.

"What is it?" she asked, her eyes wide. The crew men on the top deck were spraying the machine with something that formed a rough covering of the surface. Camouflage that would make it more difficult to pick up from space.

"Mobile planetary defense artillery," he answered, his voice quivering. "A hell of a thing to have as a neighbor."

"What's wrong, Cornelius?" she asked, hearing the tone of his voice and looking up into his face. "Isn't that a good thing? Aren't they here to defend this world from attack?"

"Overall it's a good thing," he said in a hollow

tone, disbelief growing in his mind. "It is here to defend the planet alright. And it will make it more expensive for anyone trying to land here."

"So what's the problem, honey?"

"Because it will also become a target to whatever it is shooting at. It can take quite a bit of punishment itself, up to a near miss by a nuke or AM warhead."

"So it should come out OK," she said, looking back at the machine. "And it will help defend us and our farm."

"Except that our farm can't take the same kind of punishment that it can," he said in a flat tone. "And anything that misses the wrong side of it will flatten us."

Katlyn put her hands in front of her mouth and stared at the MPDA in horror.

"Oh yeah," said Cornelius, shaking his head and he headed for the barn and the robots. "This is just going to be a wonderful fucking day."

*   *   *

Around the fires the warriors bellowed, waving ancient melee weapons to the sky while red eyes looked from fellow to fellow. Only the senior members of the clan were invited to this gathering. The rank and file of the Klang would be gathered around other fires, drinking fermented beverages and eating their fill of grains, fibers and tendered vegetables.

"My brethren," roared the clan chief as he surmounted the dais to the front of the warriors. He held up both four digit hands to wave for silence. The light of the flames shone off the ceremonial chain he wore. One eye was clouded, the result of a fight for dominance when he was a youngster who had to prove his worth by strength alone. Now grown to an elder, though still strong, he was respected for his knowledge and cunning.

"My brethren," he said again to the gathering of raider captains and their senior officers. "Tonight we meet to launch our people on a great crusade to take back that which was stolen from us."

The gathered herd animals roared again, swinging their heavy horned heads back and forth. Drinking vessels were held up, then brought down and drained. Servants, both lesser Klang and slave species, wandered through the gathering, refilling empty vessels. In several places Klang who bumped each other looked with reddened eyes down growling snouts. Nothing came of those interactions among the prickly pride of the sentients. All knew that to fight on the night a raiding fleet was to sail meant death to both parties. The fleet could not sustain casualties from among their leaders before even leaving the home system.

"Always before the humans have beaten us back," said the clan chief in his loud voice that carried through the crowd. "Always we have had to give up the worlds that we bled to take. The slaves that we had fought to bond to us. The resources we needed to become a great people."

The crowd roared, waving their bladed weapons to the sky. The Patriarch, Morgadendra, swung his head around, his circling horns acknowledging his agreement with the cheers. He again raised his hands to quiet the assemblage. There were hundreds of them out there, the captains and senior officers of almost a hundred raiders. The raiders that would form up around his larger clan ship, and swarm the worlds of the hated foe.

"Always before we fought alone against the humans," he continued, his voice filled with sorrow.

"Always before we fell to their superior technology. Not to superior courage or skill, but to the superiority of their machines. We have watched as generations of warriors were scattered across space from their shattered vessels. As hordes of ground troops were mowed down to fertilize the grazing lands of our enemies."

There was a loud lowing sound, as the warriors released their own sorrow at the loss of so many fine companions. The sires of many of those here this day.

"Not this time, my fine warriors," roared the clan chief, raising both hands into the air. Hands that now contained the curving blades of the short swords favored by his people for close combat. "This time we sail with powerful allies who have the measure of the humans. Allies who will shatter the fleets of the hated enemy, and spill their warriors into the airless void between the worlds. Allies who will allow our own fleets, the ships of many clans, to swarm the defenses of the human worlds. Allow our warriors to walk the surface of the planets and root out the defending humans. The cowardly scum who must use their machines to fight for them. Rather than meet their opponent face to face, blade to blade. And when we meet the humans on our terms, we will know victory. There will be fine grazing lands for many new clans. The people will prosper, and in their prosperity grow even stronger. This I pledge to you, my people. Or may my own head adorn the trophy rooms of our enemies."

The crowd went wild with bellowing, roaring and shouting. The clan chief knew that he had his warriors to a fever pitch, ready to take on the great evil one himself to follow him. *To death or glory*, he thought, looking out at the snouted faces staring up at him. *May it be death to our enemies. And glory to us.*

Chapter 13

I always turn to the sports section first. The sports page records people's accomplishments; the front page has nothing but man's failures.

Earl Warren

The golden globe of the G0 star shone down on the playing field. A gentle breeze stirred the pennants around the edge of the stadium as the pitcher wound up his arm. A swing forward and he launched the ball toward the tall, muscular man standing at home plate. The batter swung almost as soon as the pitcher released the ball. With perfect timing he struck the ball as it was on near approach to the plate. With a crack the ball rocketed into the air. The eyes of the fielding team followed it as it arched over two hundred meters, over the reach of the leaping outfielder and into the stands.

The crowd roared its approval as the batter, first baseman Nogio Natashi of the Capitulum Central Barracudas, ran lazily around the bases, waving. Five hundred thousand throats screamed in the sold out stadium, as the planetary champions went ahead of their hated rivals from the northern sector of the city. The batter reached home plate and stood for a second, his eyes looking at the Imperial Box and his hand raised in salute.

Emperor Augustine Ogden Lee Romanov I raised a thumb up at the batter. In his team shirt and hat he did not look like the Emperor of mankind. The box and his surrounding guards put that mark on him. He wished he could feel the breeze along with the rest of the crowd, but the transparent armor dome over the box cut him off from the environment.

"Wish you could give a thumbs down to the opposing team?" asked his guest for the afternoon's game, Prime Minister Count Mejoris Jeraviki, sipping from his expensive wine. The Emperor picked up the beer that went more with the current festivities as he looked over at his political opponent. The Prime Minister was also in a Barracudas shirt and hat, just like the majority of the fans in the stadium.

I wish I could be like Caligula and throw the members of my Senate to their deaths, thought the Emperor, looking at the overweight man sitting beside him. *Unfortunately I have to follow the rules of law.*

"Actually they gave a thumbs up when they wanted somebody dead, Prime Minister," said the Emperor with a forced smile. "A thumb to the side meant life."

"Interesting," said the Prime Minister, giving one of his patented false smiles in return. "Where did you learn that piece of trivia?"

"Despotic Rule 101," said the Emperor, looking back over the field where another batter was getting ready in the box. His eyes drifted above the outfield wall, to the upper deck of the stadium. The tall spires of the Imperial Cathedral shone under the sun. To their right was the clock tower of the House of Lords; a reminder of the power of the man who sat in the box of the most powerful man in the empire.

Limited power, thought the Emperor, a small smile on his face, *even if great. As it should be. No one man or woman should have total power over the destiny of a trillion beings. Not me. And especially not someone such as this worm who controls the premier legislative house of the Empire.*

"You are no despot, your majesty," said the Prime

Minister, watching as the batter swung and missed at the first pitch. "I can claim no misuse of power from you. I don't always agree with you, but you operate totally above board."

I don't know if I can say the same about you, thought Augustine, nodding at the Lord. *But I guess I have to say something to that effect.*

"And you have been an honored opponent in the Lords, my lord," returned the Emperor, flashing another practiced smile. "And now is the time to work more closely together."

"I could wish nothing more sincerely," said the minister. "There is much that we could accomplish if we put out collective minds to it."

"Then about military appropriations," began Augustine, looking straight into the man's eyes. The frown that appeared on the minister's lips did not bode well for the argument he was about to present. But he felt he must present it, to the best of his ability. Otherwise he failed his people.

"Not that again, your majesty," said the minister, cutting the Emperor off, then realizing that he had committed an error with his social superior. "You know my stand on this, sire. But pray go ahead and present yours again."

"OK," said Augustine, keeping his temper under control. "You know that Special Branch has noted some alarming signs that something is operating outside of Fourth Sector, around New Moscow, and in proximity to the Klang."

"We've heard something about it," said the Prime Minister. "The Imperial Intelligence Agency has noticed that something is going on there as well. But they attribute it to Crakasta, or possibly Fenri."

"That well could be," stated the Emperor. "And I don't have conclusive evidence to the contrary. Though we have been picking up intruders in that space that do not match the energy emissions or resonances of either of those powers. But whatever the cause, someone is running through Imperial Space in Hyper VII capable ships, spying on us. Whoever it is, it probably is not in our best interests for them to do so."

"Agreed," said the Prime Minister, watching as the last batter struck out and the teams changed sides. "But who is to say they are the boogie men of the past. For all we know the Ca'cadasans are no more than a fallen empire that now lacks the ability to harm us. We have very real enemies surrounding us. And some very strong allies."

"So you agree that there is a threat from those we can see," said the Emperor. "If not from what we cannot."

"Of course," said the minister after a gulp of wine. "The Lasharans are probably going to launch another ill-timed and ill-advised attack on us in the near future. The Klang may as well. I think our Fleet, along with that of our allies, will defeat them yet again, and we will have more unfriendly territory to govern. But do we need to expand the fleet to cover those eventualities? I think not."

"What about Sector Four?" asked the Emperor, staring at his opponent, wishing he could force the man to change his mind, and knowing that he could not. "What about the so called quiet sector that is not so quiet after all?"

"Go ahead and move your chess pieces if that is what allays your fears, my Lord," said the Prime Minister. "I know you have plenty that you can move from other sectors without weakening them too much. Move some squadrons of battleships, a couple of corps of troops, but do not weaken our defenses where they need to be strong. On the borders with Lasahara, Crakasta and Fenri. If I see too much being pulled from those areas into an area that I don't see a threat developing in, I will go before the Lords and advocate our direct intervention into the deployment of the Imperial Military."

"But that is the province of the Emperor," said Augustine, raising his voice and jumping to his feet. The security men jerked to an even greater level of alertness, hands on weapons, looking from face to face of the two men. "You dare not poke your nose into affairs which do not meet with your mandate." He leaned over the smaller man, trying to intimidate him into acquiescence.

"Look to the constitution, my Lord," said the Prime Minister, not showing a bit of fear or anxiety at his monarch towering over him. "We have control of the purse strings of the military during time of peace. You become commander and chief of said military in all matters. In time of war. We are currently not in a time of war."

"And if I were to bring you incontrovertible proof that we are about to be attacked by an enemy unknown and powerful?" pleaded Augustine, sitting back in his seat and looking back out over the field.

"If you bring me such proof I will present it to the Lords, my Lord," said the minister. "I have the interests of the Empire at heart, and will do what I feel must be done to protect her. Bring me that proof and I will be your man in the Lords. And do you have that proof?"

"No," said Augustine, slouching in his chair and grabbing a new beer from a servant. "Damn you, you know I don't."

"Or you would be showing it to me now," said the minister, smiling like a shark. "Now what say you we enjoy the last couple of innings of this game. And leave the politicking to other times."

An hour later Augustine was back at the Imperial Palace. A quick elevator hop brought him to the Imperial Sanctuary four kilometers below the palace. The people he had asked to meet him were already there, having come across horizontally from the Hexagon's underground complex.

"So you see my dilemma, gentlemen," he said to the three military commanders who sat with him in the secure conference room, "and lady. I feel we must give Sector Four all of the reinforcements we can give her. And we must augment the bordering sectors as well, because they might also be hit in an initial assault. I know you have already moved as much around as Parliament is willing to ignore. But we need more."

"You know the Prime Minister will have his people keeping a close watch on redeployments, your Majesty," said Grand High Admiral Lenkowski, the Chief of Naval Operations.

"I know, Len," said the Emperor. "That's why we have to do this on the sly. Is there any way we can send a unit here or there into Four? Maybe put them down as requiring repairs or overhaul, then ship them to where they will do the most good."

"I can do that, your Majesty," agreed the CNO. "For a time. But eventually the game will be made, and the Lords will come down on us."

"I know, Len. And I wouldn't ask you to do this if

I didn't think it was important. If the shit hits it, it won't matter what the Lords find out later. And if it doesn't, then I will take as much of the flak as I can. But that still doesn't mean that you won't lose your position. So it's your call."

"I swore an oath to you, your Majesty," said the tall Admiral, speaking around a smoking pipe. "I wouldn't be much of a man if I didn't adhere to that oath. So ask of me what you will."

"Thanks Len. What about you other gentleman and lady?"

"I think the Marines can come along with the Navy, your Majesty," said Field Marshal Betty Parker, Commandant of the Imperial Marine Corps. "We can probably bait and switch to the same degree as the ships as far as the Fleet Marines go. But it's going to be a bit more difficult to move assault divisions around like that. We still might be able to get a few of them out there without too much notice, though."

"A few is a few more than I have now," said the Emperor, giving her a smile. "Thanks Betty. And you, Mishori?"

"Same as the Fleet pukes said," growled Grand Marshal Mishori Yamakuri, giving the Emperor a slight smile. "It's going to be hard to spirit away armored brigades from core worlds without someone noticing."

"Can you ship out some of their equipment," said Lenkowski. "Maybe depot it from units with older equipment, making it look like the units have new equipment coming down the pipeline any minute. Then officially give leave to as many personnel as possible. Leave to, let's say, a frontier world where the equipment just happens to be."

"I find myself having fallen in with thieves and

liars," said the Marshal, giving his compatriot a large grin. "It is a delight to find myself among such. I will get my staff to work on the smoke and mirrors as soon as we return to the Hexagon."

"I appreciate all that you can do, gentlemen and lady," said Augustine with a genuine smile stretching his face. "As I said, I will try my damndest to run interference for you if it comes down on the military. But…"

"No need to say it again, your Majesty," said Lenkowski. "I'm ten years from mandatory retirement age for my position anyway. And I know this old warhorse isn't far behind," he said gesturing toward the Marine. "If I have to retire early to my estates and write my memoirs I won't be too sad. After all, I never expected to rise this high when I got out of the academy back in the days of sailing ships. I don't know about this old ground pounder though."

"I concur with my less philosophically minded colleagues," said the smaller officer. "I am here to serve my Emperor. Not to safeguard my career or reputation. And if my Emperor believes that there is a threat to take seriously looming on the horizon, I must take pains to do whatever I can to meet that threat."

"Thank you Len, Betty and Mishori," said the Emperor with a catch in his voice. He felt the tears brimming at the edge of his eyes and he shook each of their hands in turn. *It's good to work with such people,* he thought. *It reminds me of why I serve. And that my own life is not that important, compared to the lives of the citizens of the Empire.*

"Now remember," he cautioned as they stood up to leave the room. "Don't get caught with your hands in the cookie jar. At least not until we have moved enough cookies around to make a difference."

*   *   *

The Prime Minister lay on the padded table, luxuriating in the feel of strong fingers kneading the tension from his back. He took a sip of the wine from the glass on the table to his front, then placed it back as the strong hands continued to work. The sweet natural body scent of the Malticon woman came to his nostrils as she moved her small, humanoid form around his front, the overhead lights shining from her hairless pate, picking up the highlights of her light purple skin.

The Malticons were the third most numerous aliens in the Empire, fifty-six billion full citizens. And as the most humanlike of the aliens they fit smoothly into human society. Filling such positions as cooks, maids, body servants, and technicians, they were much prized among human kind. The Prime Minister knew that Jannalee was talented even among her kind, and was the perfect salve to a stress filled life.

And it helps that she can't get pregnant from a human, he thought, glancing over at the tiny humanoid and her small firm breasts. Not that he couldn't take care of that as well, but the tabloids were always looking for a scandal to sell subscriptions.

"Prime Minister," said a voice coming from the doorway of the relaxation room. "We need to speak."

"Can't it wait for a few more moments?" he said, a whine in his voice even as he tried to control the catch in his throat. "We're almost done here."

"You can fuck the wench some other time," said the voice, chuckling. "I need to talk to you now, in private."

"Very well," said the Prime Minister, again wishing that he had not ever made this deal with the devil.

Even if it brought eventual ultimate power. Through a figurehead, sure. But still he would be the hands controlling the figurehead. If he could ever get rid of those who now controlled him. "You may go, Jannalee. Wait for me in my quarters, if you would."

The Prime Minister rolled over on the table, pulling his robe around him, and the tall man walked into the room. Jeraviki forced himself to look into the man's eyes, frightening as they were. It had started out as a business deal. A little cash for his influence in the Lords. Some support from other members of Parliament for his pet projects. But he had dirtied his hands on a few of the deals, and they had gotten their hold on him.

I should have realized it would happen, he thought, dropping his eyes to the floor for a moment. *Make a deal with the devil and it is always a bad deal.*

"My employers would like to know how your part of the plan is moving forward?" asked the man in a soft voice. "They want to know when they can expect to see the fulfillment of the contract."

"Tell your employers that everything is going according to plan," said the Prime Minister, feeling the sweat flowing from the pores of his forehead. "Soon the Emperor will be dead, and his heirs with him. And you will have a friendlier hand holding the reins of government."

"My employers will be happy to hear that," said the man who had never given his name to the minister.

"I still don't understand what they expect to gain from this," said the Prime Minister, giving the man a hooded glance. "The Lasharans may gain a few of their planets back. But even the seated Emperor cannot order the Fleet to not fight a war against an invading power."

"Let that be the concern of my employers," said the man, those eyes burning into his. "I will relay your words to them. And your concern for their ultimate plans."

The man left as quickly and quietly as he had appeared. As he had always appeared in the secure residence of the Prime Minister. Bypassing all of the guards and the security systems on the way in and out.

The Prime Minister held his face in his hands for a moment, thinking about the deal he had made. And the possible cost. A smile slid across his lips as he thought about the Malticon woman waiting in his private chambers. There was another reason that the Malticon species were so sought after in human society. Their small, exquisite, childlike bodies were matched by the tight smoothness of their sexual organs. With a thrill of anticipated pleasure the Prime Minister stood up from the table and walked from the room.

*   *   *

The unnamed man stood in the shadows, watching the Prime Minister walk down the hall. *Fool,* he thought, watching the overweight man waddle. *You have no idea who you are working for. You cannot see the evidence in front of your face. And have no idea the crime you commit against your own species. You are pathetic, like all of your kind. One day we will rule your space and make you slaves, just as you enslave those you feel are inferior to you.*

He watched the short man waddle up the stairs and thought about how much he would enjoy closing those blind eyes forever. He almost shivered with the pleasure he felt at that thought, and hoped it would come soon. With a smile the man slid back into the shadows and disappeared, going back the way he had come.

*   *   *

The small carrier came out of hyperspace a couple of light minutes from the hyper limit. No larger than a light cruiser, it was in fact built on the general hull of that class of warship. It took a quick scan of the local space, sensors taking track of anything that might pose an immediate threat.

Hanger doors slid open, exposing their interiors to vacuum. A flight of four recon fighters flew from the one of the hangers, oriented themselves to the local star, and accelerated at four hundred gravities toward the hyper limit. Sixty-two meters from heavy laser nose mount to tail, the six hundred ton craft piled on accel while glowing with the heat of their fusion plants. They sniffed the local space with passive sensors and visual arrays, transmitting their findings back to the launching vessel.

Two squadrons of fighters followed on the heels of the recon ships, accelerating at three hundred and eighty gravities, allowing the recon ships to open the distance. The thirty-two ships were about the same size as the recon fighters, carrying weapons in lieu of extra sensors. A moment later a squadron of fourteen attack fighters left the carrier in the wake of the space superiority craft. Eighty meters long, the thousand ton craft formed into two seven craft wedges.

The carrier closed its hanger doors and turned away from the system, accelerating away at two hundred gravities. Within minutes its MAM reactors had built enough power to open a hyper portal. With a burst of energy that could be detected for one hundred and sixty light days the craft left the universe.

The Group Commander, sitting in his command

chair in the cockpit of one of the attack craft, looked over the data flowing into the ship from the rest of the group.   The target information had not changed appreciably from that downloaded during the voyage to this star.   The way appeared open.   He glanced at the pilot and copilot to his front, then looked over his right shoulder at the sensor tech.   His link to the vessel indicated that the engines were working perfectly.   The group engineer or his assistant back in their compartment would have alerted him if anything was amiss.

"Group Commander to all ships," he called over the group circuit, checking the data once again. "Accelerate on attack vector.   Primary target."

The recon flight accelerated to maximum.   One thousand gravities, the greatest acceleration of any human built craft.   They glowed like destroyers with their infrared emissions, their cooling systems working on overdrive to shunt heat into surrounding space. Radiation would not have done the job.   Only the high tech crystalline matrix heat sump, storing the excess energy, then flinging it into space, allowed the ships to operate without cooking their crews.

Behind the recon flight the fighters accelerated up to a little over nine hundred gravities, allowing the recon birds to pull ahead even further and act as forward security.   The attack birds accelerated up to their own maximum of nine hundred gravities.

The Commander thought over the attack plan once again in the momentary downtime.   Later there might be too much going on to think.   There might be time to only react.

Standard attack pattern, he thought, his mind linking to a holo globe projection.   *We accelerate up to point nine c, and blow through the system, firing on the target at closest approach. Then out of the system, decelerate down, and get out of here.*

"The recon birds are picking up a squadron of fast attack craft," said the sensor tech. "At two hundred twenty-five million kilometers. About twelve point five light minutes."

"Have they made us yet?" said the Commander, his holo globe of the system updating with the new information.

"Unknown, sir," said the tech. "They are still too distant for our electromag emissions to have reached them. But it won't be long."

"Hopefully we can get out of their engagement window before they see us," he said aloud. The ten thousand ton fast attack craft were similar to the ubiquitous couriers that were familiar all across the Empire. They could accelerate at five hundred gravities, not in the same class as the smaller fighters. But they carried a quartet of destroyer class antiship missiles that could catch the fighters if deployed properly.

"Corvettes directly in our path," called the sensor tech, shunting the information into the group net. "Two, accelerating toward us at three hundred gees."

"Dammit," cried the Commander, looking over the system schematic. "Only two ways to do it then. We can either keep on going and take out the corvettes. We should still come through with most of the group. Or we can vector the hell out of here."

"Your choice, Commander," called the pilot over his shoulder. "But I think the chaps will be highly pissed off to not get to their new base in time to get a bite to eat."

"You're right, Sheila," said the Commander, laughing. "Send a signal to rest of the group. As soon as the system security tags us send them our IFF codes, and then head for Sestius IV the normal way."

All these new orders, he thought. *Take advantage of any situation to train, and to test the training of other Imperial forces.*

"Let's head for our new home," he said softly to himself. Not the fleet or light carrier he had envisioned when he took command of the group. Not even a space fortress, since the one here already had its full complement of space fighters. Instead a dirt side landing field on a frontier world. It almost made him wish he had commissioned into the army instead.

Chapter 14

Man is the only animal that deals in that atrocity of atrocities, War. He is the only one that gathers his brethren about him and goes forth in cold blood and calm pulse to exterminate his kind. He is the only animal that for sordid wages will march out... and help to slaughter strangers of his own species who have done him no harm and with whom he has no quarrel.... And in the intervals between campaigns he washes the blood off his hands and works for "the universal brotherhood of man" - with his mouth.

Mark Twain

The sky above the city was blood red, with crimson tinged clouds flying under a black moon. The lights of the megalopolis shown from the many buildings, but were swallowed up by the surrounding night. Only the nearby buildings were clear to sight, the further fading into distortion. The city of three billion people and three hundred and seventy-five thousand square kilometers was a blur, over which the veil of evil lay.

The sky was suddenly alive with bright red streaks that contrasted with the darker red of the sky, falling like meteors until they hit the ground below. Where they touched the ground bright flashes shot through the night. Clouds of debris rose from the forming craters. Clouds that assumed a mushroom shape as they rose into the sky, taking on the blood red tinged streak with the brighter flashes of fire. Buildings fell as the shock waves struck, thousand meter skyscrapers toppling like trees. Larger archologies and megascrapers resisted the shock waves with the shattering of glass-steel. Only to fall instants later as kinetic projectiles struck them in turn.

Soon the entire urban area was clouded with dust and smoke, and fires raged through the hundreds of thousands of kilometers of city. The screams of the injured and the dying rose through the rumbling of still collapsing buildings. As a palpable evil pressed down through the night.

"No," yelled Augustine as he sat up in bed, the horror of the dream fading into the background. A soft hand grabbed his arm. He turned to look into the concerned face of his wife as he felt the sweat rolling from his body.

"No," he whispered as he felt the knowledge of the dream in the back of his mind.

"Is everything OK, your majesty," called a voice over the intercom.

"We're fine," said the Empress, looking over at the Emperor. "It was a bad dream."

Augustine knew that though their privacy was important to the staff, so was their safety. And they would be monitoring the voices of the Imperial family to assure themselves that their charges were not under duress.

"I am fine," said Augustine, calming himself with a few deep breathes. "As the Empress said, it was just a dream."

"Very well, sir," said the voice of security. "Have a good night."

"It was more than just a dream, wasn't it?" said Anastasia Romanov, her hands rubbing the shoulders of her beloved husband. "It was a prophecy, wasn't it?"

"I don't know," said the Emperor, shaking his head. "It does not seem to be as strong in me as it was in some of my ancestors. I'm sure that Titus II or James III would have known exactly what this dream meant."

"You have a general idea, don't you?" she asked. "Was it the destruction of the city again?"

"But this time it was several times more detailed," said the Emperor. "The vision was clearer. It is closer."

"How sure are you that it will happen?" asked the Empress, her voice quivering with fright.

I hate causing her fear, thought Augustine, looking into her eyes. *But she is my closest confidant. And the one least likely to call me crazy.*

"I don't know how likely they are to happen," said the Emperor, putting his head in his hands. "I don't think the family curse is that strong in me. Or at least I didn't until recently. But I do know that Igor the Great was able to use the knowledge of his dreams to stop his prophecy from happening. So they can't be looks into a definite future. But more like a glimpse into a possible future. A warning of what might happen if we don't take action."

"And you think it has something to do with our long lost friends?"

"I don't know who else might be a threat to penetrate the defenses of the Empire and attack its heart," he said, looking over at his wife.

"Did you see anything happening to you?" she asked, worry in her voice. "To us?"

"I don't ever see anything directly impacting me or mine," he answered. "Only the Empire as a whole."

The Emperor looked at the ceiling for a moment,

rubbing his temples.

"Maybe you should talk to Sean about this," said Anastasia, continuing to rub at his tense shoulders. "You remember how he used to dream as a child. The nightmares he had. And how so many of them came true."

"The curse seemed to be strong in him," agreed the Emperor. "It always worried me that he would have so much of the curse. And that his older brothers had so little."

"Because the curse normally only manifested in the future ruler of the Empire," said the Empress. "That always worried me as well. Not for him, but for his elder siblings. Since something would have to happen to them for him to become ruler."

"And so far that hasn't happened," said the Emperor, his eyes opening wide. "Which is not the pattern of the curse. Maybe I should talk to Sean. Maybe I need to know what he has seen in his sleep.

"I will send him a message tomorrow," said the Emperor, laying back down and placing his head on his pillow. "It should only take about a week to get to him where his ship is currently stationed. I'll be glad when we have instantaneous communication out of the *Donut* project."

"You and the rest of the Empire," agreed the Empress, laying back on the bed. She rolled over for a second and placed her lips on her husband's. She held the kiss for a moment. Anastasia released as she felt her husband's breathing become soft and regular. She smiled down at her sleeping husband and rolled over herself. Within moments she too was asleep.

*   *   *

"The Lord Ambassador is here to see you, High

Lord," said the Brakakak servant, opening the door to the study. The avian lord sat on a chair made specifically to accommodate his tail plumage and his long slender legs, working on an official document on his computer pad.

"Show him in," said the High Lord Granakakak, his species' equivalent of a sigh escaping from his flexible beak like apparatus. The sigh had double meaning; exasperation at not being able to finish this report to his Empire's governing body, and relief at being able to get away from said report.

"Horatio," he called out in English as the door opened again and the white haired human entered the office. "It is good to see you again." The High Lord jumped out of his chair and came around the desk, a delicate hand held out to the human. Alexanderopolis grasped the hand gently while showing his teeth in a smile. *It is still alarming to see the teeth of such strong creatures*, thought the High Lord. *Even an aged member of his race exudes physical and mental strength*. There were stronger species than humans. There were quicker species. No one could say there were more intelligent species, especially when it came to science and the science of warfare. They were well balanced as a species and intimidating as hell, especially in numbers.

"Good to see you, Granakakak, my friend," said the ambassador, looking around the exquisitely furnished office of the most powerful single being in the Elysium Empire. "I hear you have news for me."

"Would you like a drink, my friend?" said the High Lord in almost unaccented English. "I have your favorite on hand."

"Yes, thank you," said the Ambassador, again showing his teeth. "Just one though. It's a little early to let good alcohol go to my head."

The High Lord nodded to a servant that he knew did not understand any of the human languages, the better to not hear what he wasn't supposed to. He rattled off some of the servant's native language and the small, stocky humanoid made his way to the bar and started making their drinks.

"Is that a Rankakara?" asked Horatio, moving over to a table on which sat an exquisite carving of one of the avians, highlighted with holographic projections that made it come alive.

"Yes it is," said the High Lord with pleasure in his voice.   "An original, just completed by the artist. Perhaps I could have one commissioned for you as well."

"I would love to have another of his works," said the ambassador, marveling over the sculpture. "I have one already, but it is an early piece, before the artist found the depths of his talent."

The High Lord gave a tight beaked rendition of his race's smile. He knew that a good diplomat sometimes had to pretend to enjoy things that he didn't while being diplomatic to his charges. He also knew that Horatio Alexandropolis truly enjoyed the culture of the Brakakak people. It heartened and sorrowed him at the same time. Because he had to remember that the extraordinary human was not always working in the interest of the people that he admired.

"Have a seat, ambassador," said the High Lord, gesturing to a couch that was configuring itself for the human anatomy. He moved over to a facing couch that was already set for his particular body. As he gracefully placed himself in the chair the servant brought a drink in a glass with ice, then brought the human a match for the one he had given the High Lord.

"I am glad you could accept my invitation," said the High Lord, glancing at the human with his sapphire eyes.

"I wouldn't have missed it for anything," said the ambassador. "Even if you didn't have any tidbits of information to offer. I enjoy the company of your kind. Must be why I was given this post. And been able to retain it for the last twenty of our years."

"You are good at it," said the High Lord, nodding his head in a human gesture. "You have come to understand some of us, both my species and others, in ways that would seem impossible for one not born of certain genetics. And that is one of the reasons your species still confuses many of us. And scares some of us."

"And why is that, my lord?" asked the human after taking a sip of the good, human made liquor.

"Because you are, using your own term, such a jack of all trades species," said the High Lord. "And you are also the masters of many. Diplomacy, trade, science, warfare. If you ever had someone in power who truly wished to conquer the galaxy, I am sure you could do so."

"Then we can both thank the stars that we don't have such a one in power," said the ambassador. "We do not want to walk down the same path as those who sent us into exile. Generation after generation of conquest, until the entire society is nothing by a war machine."

"And there are still rumors coming from your Empire," said the High Lord, careful not to say that the rumors came from operatives of his Empire, though both beings knew it. "Some of your people think that this ancient enemy may have finally reached the shores of our spiral arm."

"I don't know for sure if they have or not," said the ambassador. "I think the only way we will truly know is if they burst into our presence and attack our worlds. And hopefully our friends will come to our aid, so that they don't experience the same on their worlds."

"If that day comes," said Granakakak, sipping from his bourbon, "we will stand by our human brothers. If this one is still in charge.

"Now," he said, reaching for a small comp unit by his chair, "it is time to leave the world of speculation. At least speculation without evidence."

"This concerns Lasharan space?" asked the ambassador, leaning forward in his chair and looking over steepled fingers.

"Only what our operatives have brought us," said the High Lord, staring down at the comp screen. "A week to get out by courier, then five and a half of your days by hyperwave relay from the Margravian frontier."

"And what do they show?"

"Lashara has amassed a fleet along the borders," said the High Lord, looking up at the ambassador. "A motley collection by civilized standards. But still a threat. At least eight hundred modern capital ships, two thousand cruiser class, and five thousand escort class."

"Not very many to mount a major offensive against our forces in the area," said the ambassador, pulling out a pocket comp and linking into the High Lord's model. "They might take back their lost worlds, and maybe a couple of dozen other systems, before we swat them back into their own space."

"They are just the covering force for the main

invasion," said the avian. "They will have more than ten thousand tramp steamers and other merchant class vessels following close behind the assault fleet. These will carry twelve million fanatical warriors into your space, as well as a massive arsenal for their compatriots on the worlds you already hold."

"Again," said the ambassador, looking into his nearly empty glass, "something of concern. But not anything we can't handle. The Imperial Army and Marines will have little trouble routing them on the ground."

"They don't intend to fight you in a stand up battle," said the High Lord. "According to the people we have infiltrated into the movement they know they cannot stand up to you in a conventional fight. Even their leaders acknowledge, finally, that it is hopeless to try and beat you at your own game."

The avian took a last swallow of his drink and motioned for the servant to come over. He glanced at the human, who nodded his head and held out his glass for the servant to take and refill.

"They hope to reinforce each of the worlds you have taken from them with a million or so fighters willing to give their lives for the cause. They hope to reequip the people they already have on the ground with more weapons, and recruit more of the populace into bleeding you planet side. Even if they temporarily kick you off those planets they expect you to be back. And then they will bleed you as much as they can."

The servant brought the glasses back, and the man and avian took them gratefully. After taking a swallow the High Lord looked back at the ambassador.

"They will also land large contingents on any of your worlds that they can reach," continued the avian.

"A hundred thousand here, four hundred thousand there. Dig into your cities and towns, take hostages, and prepare for the bloodbath."

"We should still be able to handle them," said the human, his face turning a little green at the thought of what the High Lord was telling him.

"Again," said the avian, the plumage on his head rising with emotion. "They expect you to. But they will make a blood bath of it on every world where they can gain a foothold. And they will bombard from space any world they can get within range of, if they are unable to land a force there. If they can cost you a couple of hundred million sentients. Maybe even a billion. They will consider this attack a success. And when you roll into their empire, seeking to take more of their worlds away from them, there will be dedicated cadres of millions on each planet. Armed and equipped for the long struggle against you. They think that they can make you pay such a price that you will give up and sue for peace."

"And what if we go in and start wiping worlds clean of life," said the ambassador, fire in his eyes.

"They don't believe their god will allow that," said the High Lord quietly. "They don't believe the human race capable of such savagery."

"And you?" asked the ambassador, looking at the floor, then up into the eyes of his alien friend. "What do you believe?"

"I believe that it would pain your race to destroy another sentient species entirely," said the High Lord, his sorrowful eyes looking back into the human's. "I also believe that you would destroy them without a moment's hesitation if they hurt you so badly. I would not want to see your race have to live with that. I would not want to see your reputation so damaged."

"So what can we do about it?"

"I would suggest you take advantage of our communications with Margrave to alert your allies to what is to happen. If they sweep in behind the enemy battle fleet, while your own forces attack the warships, they should be able to destroy most of the auxiliaries before they get to their targets."

"And when is this attack to begin?" said Horatio, sending a signal to his embassy to start the ball rolling.

"No more than a month from now. Most probably within two weeks. We of course will not lend any combatants to you in this war. It would mean my seat on the council if we were to get involved fighting those fanatics. But all of our intelligence resources are at your disposal."

"And very good resources they are," said the ambassador, raising his glass. "Much better than we have in that area."

"We have been prowling the darkest pathways of this area for thousands of years longer than humanity," said the avian with a smile. "We should be good at it."

"Then I guess I had better get back to the embassy and prepare my communiques," said the ambassador, putting his empty glass on the side table and rising to his feet.

"One question I would ask of you?" said the High Lord, looking up from his seat.

"If I can answer it."

"I hope you can," said Granakakak, a thoughtful look on his face. "And please answer truthfully, for much rides on this question."

"Again," said the ambassador straight faced, "if I can."

"This wormhole generating project of yours. Are you experimenting with time travel via wormholes?"

"I don't think that anyone in the Empire knows how to do such a thing," said the ambassador slowly, deep in thought. "I know there are some theories. I know there are a bunch of damned theories, and that no one theorist agrees with any of the others. Why do you ask?"

"You know that you are not the first civilization to build a wormhole generator around that black hole," said the High Lord, his manner serious. "The ancient Elysians did the same, thousands of years ago, at the height of the Empire of which ours is a tiny remnant."

"The ancients were rumored to do a lot of things," answered the ambassador. "Some of them hard to believe."

"They did do this thing," said the avian, looking into the eyes of his human friend. "And they experimented with time travel. At first only observational expeditions into the recent past. But eventually their altruism got the best of them and they started to make small changes. For the good of the Empire and all sentients."

"So what happened?" asked the ambassador out of politeness, though he knew the story by heart.

"They disappeared as a race," said the High Lord, a faraway look on his face. "Some of their ships blew up when containment fields failed. Things fell apart. Eventually the entire race was gone, as if the universe wiped them clean. Though they of course left many of their artifacts and ancient cities behind."

"And you know why that happened?"

"We do not," said the avian. "But whatever the reason, it effectively ended their sojourn into time travel. Which is something your species would do well to remember."

"I can tell you that the Emperor is against any such experiments," said the ambassador.

"You are a freedom loving people," answered the avian with a smile. "He does not have total control over all of his subjects. There is a concern that someone in your Empire with access to the wormhole generating complex might try to experiment on their own."

"And why would anyone with any kind of sense do that?" asked the ambassador, looking around the room. "We don't want to commit suicide."

"And what did you do with the robots?" said the High Lord, his voice rising high in exasperation, then calming as he exerted the control of a consummate statesman. "Four centuries ago, despite what you had learned from other species that had done the same, you build the battle robots. The most advanced war machines ever seen in the known Galaxy."

"A mistake we will never make again," retorted the ambassador. "The man in the loop law makes that impossible."

"But only after you learned the hard lesson yourselves," said the High Lord. "Despite what other species told you, you built the autonomous war machines yourselves, and learned that autonomous war machines are not to be trusted. Scorched worlds and over a billion deaths later you learned your lesson."

"Agreed," said the ambassador. "It was an expensive lesson to learn."

"Your species listens to what others say not to do, and then goes off and does it anyway. Because you feel that nothing is beyond you. That given enough intelligence, work and willpower anything is possible. Even if sometimes the possible should not become the real.   I just hope that you do not make another expensive mistake here.   Because this portion of the Galaxy would be a much poorer place without you."

"If I have anything to say about it," said the ambassador, rising from his seat again and holding out a hand, "it will not happen.   And I am sure the Emperor would not do anything to endanger the race. Beyond that, I can promise nothing."

"Be careful, my friend," said the High Lord, grasping the offered hand. "There are others in your race that are not so wise. As there are in my race.

"If I receive any other information of interest I will let you know," said the High Lord, as another servant came to escort the human from his office.   "Please think of what else I have told you."

"I will, Lord Granakakak," said the human. "Now let me get to the embassy and get this information to my government. And thank you again."

An hour later, after arriving at the Terran Empire Embassy, the ambassador composed his message to the home office as well as a warning message to the embassy in Margrave. He sent the encrypted messages out over the carrier transmitters the humans rented from the Elysians, where they were sent at light speed to a thirty thousand ton nodal station beyond the hyper limit.

The station, a node in the so called hyperwave relay system, processed the signals and routed them to a pair of transmitters.   Each transmitter antennae maintained a small portal into hyper VIII, and punched a laser signal into the higher dimension. The beams traveled a little over forty-five million kilometers through the dimension, exiting through another maintained portal to a relay station. The stations were about point eight light years apart in normal space, corresponding to the forty-five million kilometer distance in hyper VIII. The signal was gathered, boosted by the four thousand ton relay station, and fired back into hyper VIII for the trip to the next node. After ten trips through ten relays the signal arrived at the next larger, manned, nodal station, where it was sent on up the line.

A human invention, the system linked all of the human core worlds and important stations of the developing worlds and frontier worlds, using over twenty eight thousand relays and almost four thousand nodal stations. The system allowed for information to be transmitted much faster than even the swiftest couriers. And the system was imitated by many of the alien polities, linking the human empire with the New Terran Republic and allies and friends.

Including the light speed trip from the planets situated in gravity wells the message took a little over five days to reach the capital of the Empire. And a little under four days to reach the capital of their ally, the Margravians.

Chapter 15

Some might ask why expend the energy to Terraform planets in an era when almost limitless planets stretch before us in space. What does that mean, almost limitless? It means that there is a limit, eventually. There may come a time when the only way to gain more living space is to take it from other races. Or to make it for ourselves. Humanity must expand. There is no question to that. In this Galaxy it is expand the population and the resources, or fall to another race. And humans prefer to live on the surfaces of planets. So I ask the question, why not? Why not bring life to worlds that seem to be in the perfect orbit, or near enough as to make no difference? That possess the perfect gravity, or near enough. Why not, when we possess the energy to make it possible, and the limitless resources of a solar system? Why not, when we can make lifeless rocks habitats teeming with life? Energy is cheap. Life is not. So we make worlds into habitats, and serve the race and the Empire.

Speech of Prime Minister Gwendolyn Travinski before the Lords, year 284 of Empire.

The day of the investiture of the Archduke was fair and clear. Which on Sestius meant the bright sun beat down from the sky and the temperatures rose quickly through the morning. Willoughby, the capital, normally held about twenty thousand inhabitants, or a little under a tenth of the population of the frontier world. On this day the population must have swelled to over a hundred thousand, and the streets were filled with people, swarming the overworked vendors trying to supply them with food and drink.

"Do you think our things will be safe?" asked Katlyn, while Cornelius put the finishing touches on their small campsite, in among hundreds of other tents in a field on the outskirts of the unimaginatively named city.

"They'll be fine," said Cornelius, placing his thumb to the tent security panel, then standing up and brushing off his pants. They had arrived the night before by airbus from their village. Having no family on the planet, and no friends in the capital city, they had been forced to bring camping gear, like twenty thousand others, and find a place to squat for the celebration. Since it was an important day for the colony restrictions had been relaxed, and the campsite had grown quickly into a small community of its own. "Let's see what trouble we can get into before the official festivities spoil all the fun."

Katlyn laughed and put her hand on his offered arm. Cornelius smiled back, feeling the hallucinogens he had taken moments before begin to enter his system. "You took your nanite boost, I hope?" he asked her, putting a hand on her swelling stomach.

"Of course," she replied with a laugh, walking beside him on the path leading out to the road that led into the center of the city. "Wouldn't want the little guy's brain getting fogged by everything we're doing."

When they reached the road they started toward the city until they found a prime space to watch. Cornelius set up their chairs, setting the pads of memory plastic on the ground and activating the expansion. Within seconds a pair of white chairs sat on the ground. Moments later the two adults sat on the chairs, whose luxurious comfort belayed their hard appearance. Katlyn reached into the small cooler she had slung over her shoulder and pulled out two bottles, handing one to Cornelius. He took the beer and clanked his glass against hers, then took a large swig, relishing the cold liquid on the hot morning.

"Look," said Katlyn, pointing to the sky where dark forms swirled and exploded, seemingly in midair.

Walborski laughed at the holographic display, wondering how much his own brain cells were adding to the effect under the action of the hallucinogen. He glanced up and down the roadway, wondering how many others were also under the influence, and decided it had to be the majority, as the drug had been circulating around for the last couple of weeks.

"Here they come," said Katlyn with an excited squeal, tugging at his arm.

Walborski looked up the road and saw the beginning of the celebratory parade coming their way, an honor guard of marching militia, the Flags of Empire and all the services swaying in the small breeze as they marched. Behind them floated an air-car with speakers blaring a marching tune that was old when Earth still existed as the home of humanity. Looking at the car, Cornelius thought of his robots, which brought up the connection that nothing was being done on his farm while he was here at the big party.

Wish I could have set the robots to keep working without me, he thought. But that was a risky proposition at best. If it were discovered that he had left his robots active while there was no human on the property, he would have been guilty of violating the Man In The Loop Law. He would have lost his land and his robots, and faced possible time in a work camp, maybe even personality restructuring. It just wasn't worth the risk.

"Is anyone marching from your unit?" asked Katlyn, as the honor guard passed, along with the robotic air-car, and a company of militia followed.

Not me, he thought, grimacing at the dressing down he still smarted from. "There's a few," he said, hastily pasting a smile he didn't feel on his face. "They had some of the veterans form a marching unit, and let the rest of us enjoy the celebration."

Katlyn nodded, her eyes already locked on the next part of the procession, another marching unit. Then came a police patrol mounted on Hassardics, a one ton omnivore that was trained as riding beasts. Cornelius wondered how much work the patrol actually did on the beasts, since air-cars were so much more practical. He determined they must be a ceremonial unit only, as they made their beasts rear and dance and pivot around each other as they walked.

A trumpeting sound caught the attention of the spectators over the marching music, and the couple looked up the road to where a set of heads on long necks bobbed along. The clubs and schools that marched before the beasts were more or less ignored before the majesty of the creatures that followed behind. And then they were there, a quartet of massive beasts walking down the road, each step causing a small tremor. They were Jassanic Beasts, the largest of the herbivores on the planet, eighty tons each. Cornelius felt his own eyes grow wider as he looked at the massive mammalians, glad that he had never encountered such in his own fields. The ones he had to deal with were less than half the size of these monsters, and he cringed to think of what they might do if they panicked, though he had heard that these particular beasts were controlled by implants.

"I wouldn't want to get stepped on by one of those," he said to Katlyn after taking a last swig of beer.

"I wouldn't want to get caught in a stampede of those things," she replied.

And in his hallucinogenic besotted mind he saw that herd, bearing down on him across a field that shook with their running tread. *Whoa*, he thought, his mind taking control of the drug and throttling back a bit. He didn't want to make imagination a reality by running onto the roadway in panic.

"That's what you need to be in," said Katlyn, breaking him out of his thoughts of being trampled by alien beasts.

Walborski looked up to see that the next formation was made up of Imperial Marines, what looked like a company of them, floating along just off the ground in heavy battle armor. Their one ton suits, which had to be almost three meters from crown to heel, were colored in the Imperial Crimson of the Corps. That was part of the display, and he knew they could change colors at any time to blend in with their surroundings.

"That would be great," said Cornelius, his vision of the suits assuming the gleaming gold of ancient knights. "It ain't going to happen. But it would be great if it did."

"It'd be a lot better than that pitiful equipment you're always complaining about," said his wife, her tone petulant.

"And it probably costs over ten million imperials a suit," countered Cornelius, pointing a finger at one of the ogrish looking warriors floating by. "Even the Imperial Army doesn't outfit all its infantry in such hardware. So I don't see why the militia would. We're supposed to be cheap infantry, just enough to slow something down with our bodies. Then those boys come in to be the hero of the day."

"Ten million imperials," said Katlyn with a whistle. "That's enough to buy a space yacht."

At least an interplanetary one, thought Cornelius as he nodded his agreement.

"Not that we really have to worry about anything happening here," she said, pulling another beer out of the cooler. "It's not like we're in a sector facing the Lasharans, or any of those other assholes."

"No," said Cornelius, accepting a beer and twisting off the top. *But there seems to be a tension in the air as far as the military is concerned. And rumors of old enemies coming out of the stars beyond the frontier.*

"That must be the new archduke," said Katlyn, her voice rising in excitement.

There were four air-cars coming up, and people started to cheer and wave Imperial flags. The first car had a number of grim faced men and women in them. The second had the Honorable Jerry Hathaway, the Imperial Governor, the man who actually answered to the Sector Council for the running of the planet. He looked like a retired military man, a brigadier in the Imperial Army, with his close cut hair and ramrod back. His pretty wife, a lean woman with flowing red hair, sat next to him in the back seat and waved along with her husband.

The third car carried the new Archduke, who looked to be a middle aged businessman of indistinct features. An adolescent boy and a young girl sat on either side of him, the girl waving enthusiastically, the boy looking bored. Cornelius didn't think the Archduke looked very noble, but then again he had seen a lot that didn't. He had read that the man was the younger son of a core world duke, and had been rewarded with this position for service to the Empire. Again, you couldn't tell from the looks, but it must have been something grand to get overlordship of an entire planet, even a sparsely populated frontier world, which would not remain such forever.

"I wonder if there will be a wedding in the near future?" asked Katlyn, looking at the children. "Children need a momma."

"He can afford to buy them all the mothering they can stand," said Cornelius, wincing as his wife elbowed him in the side. "Well, he's rich as hell. And I hear he's going to build a heavy equipment plant right here on Sestius. That will bootstrap the planet if anything will."

"Archduke Yuri Yakamura," said Katlyn in a low voice. "I like the sound of that."

"And don't you be getting any ideas," said Cornelius in mock anger.

"I'm already married to a future count," she said in a dreamy voice, grabbing onto his arm and pulling him close. "Or is that a duke."

"Squire will be good enough for me," he said with a smile as he shook his head. "No way I'll make it to count, or even baron. And I'm sure not going to get knighted, not if I can help it. No way I'm going to do something foolish enough for that to happen."

"Country squire it is then," said Katlyn, squeezing his arm close.

That's at least realistic, thought Walborski, watching the last air-car slide by with its security personnel. *And I'm not sure I want to live a life that requires bodyguards who are mostly just good enough to kill the assassin after they do their job. Even if the people love you, it only takes one disaffected idiot to get lucky to end it all.*

And then the procession was past, with only a half dozen more groups to pass in review.

Cornelius couldn't remember a whole lot of the afternoon, just one endless brain numb. He had to kick his nanites in several times to process intoxicants so he could sober up enough to keep partying. He remembered standing in the crowd as the new Archduke gave an uninspiring speech that still drew hearty cheers. This was a big day, to actually be invested with a figurehead of nobility. It didn't mean they were no longer a frontier world. Just that they were well on their way to becoming a developing world. Another nine million eight hundred thousand colonists and they would be past the ten million level, and officially there.

Fireworks were on the schedule that weekend, but the Walborskis, Mr. and Mrs., were in bed long before the explosives cracked through the night. The next day it was sober pills, and back on the air bus to their own village. Cornelius dreamed on the entire trip back about his own property, growing into a ranch or estate employing later colonists. And his rise to a country squire. That dream was shattered when they came roaring up to his farm on his cycle, to see some native beasts he had yet to behold trampling through his fields.

* * *

"Welcome, your Majesty," said the executive, Jurgen Klevik of Klevik Terraforming, bowing, then holding out a hand for the Emperor to grasp.

"Thank you," said Augustine, griping the man's paw with a firm hand. "I am so happy to be here on the day we open a new world."

The man smiled and gestured the way out of the landing bay where the Emperor's shuttle sat. They walked through the wide halls of the station toward an observation deck where the reception was being held, military personnel snapping to attention while civilians gave a curt bow to the sovereign. Augustine held the hand of his wife, while well aware of the entourage following, including the massive security contingent that went everywhere with him.

The station sat in orbit around the world, a new living planet in the New Han Chou core system. The primary planet, New Han Chou, had been colonized for over eight hundred years, and had a population in the billions. It had also had an airless globe of the proper size and position to be a terrestrial world. And the Empire did not let such worlds go to waste, especially in the developed center of the Imperium. Those planets were turned into living worlds, as this one had been.

Augustine looked out over the blue and white globe revealed by the thirty meter by thirty meter window of the observation room. His breath caught in his throat as he looked down on cloud studded oceans and orange continents.

"It only took us seventy-three years to get it done," said Klevik, motioning a server to bring over a tray of drinks. "The construction crews are down there now taking apart the last of the atmosphere plants so they can be shipped to the next project. The biologists will be fine tuning for another decade or so."

We constantly hunger for new worlds, thought the Emperor. *Even though there are thousands of worlds with less than a million inhabitants, and thousands more with no more than survey and research teams. We still hunger for worlds, so that our population can grow us into a power that even the ancient enemy can't challenge.*

"Have you decided on a name yet, dear?" asked the Empress, accepting a glass of champagne at the same time as her husband.

"I'm still not completely sure," said the ruler of human space, his eyes riveted to the world. "That's Tau Ceti vegetation down there, isn't it?"

"Yes, majesty," said the executive whose company gave him almost as much wealth as the Emperor, but not the social position. "It was decided years ago to set that planet's biome as the pattern for this one, since New Han Chou uses the same and they will be sister worlds."

Meaning the inhabitants can go back and forth and eat each other's food without nanobot boosts, thought Augustine. *Good thinking that. And a Tau Ceti world reminds us of what we lost besides the Earth all those many centuries ago.*

Augustine stood at the window for a couple of minutes, sipping champagne and looking down. He watched as a pair of massive shuttles came up into orbit, probably hauling pieces of the huge atmosphere plants that were being taken away, having done their last bit of work months before. He noted the large barren areas that would someday be farmlands. Most of the world had been seeded with vegetation in what looked like random patterns determined by computer, but it was not thought efficient to do so to lands that would be inhabited by humans. They would put their own marks on the land. Still, over seventy five percent was covered in one kind of vegetation or another, well above the Imperial minimum of sixty percent wilderness lands.

"I think we will name this world New Manchuria,"

said the Emperor, nodding at the terraformer. "I think that will fit in with the system."

"Then that will be the official name," said Klevik, giving a hand gesture toward an underling who input it into a hand comp. In a couple of hours New Han Chou would know the name of its sister world, so far only inhabited by ten thousand or so biotechs finishing up the last touches.

A band started playing from a stand at the end of the room, and the party was on, with employees of Klevik Terraforming blending in with Imperial staff. A young man with the ribbons of a Count asked the Empress to dance, leaving the Emperor alone with his thoughts for a moment. He spent that time looking down on the newest inhabitable world of the Empire, sure to grow through frontier and developing status quickly due to its proximity to many densely populated planets.

A strobe caught Augustine's attention, low on the horizon. He focused his eyes and the form of an Imperial battleship leapt into his visual field. He wasn't sure from this distance if it was one of the three in his escort force, or one that was assigned to the system defense force and had been requisitioned for security, as if the thirty warships that protected his yacht weren't enough. Or maybe it had just been passing through the system, and whoever monitored its movements wanted it in on the event.

His curiosity piqued, the Emperor linked through the station to his yacht and queried about the vessel. *HIMS Black Duke,* he thought as the information came up. *One of the system fleet, at least for another three months, before she rotates to the frontier to take her chances.* He smiled as he thought about his own time on an Imperial warship, also a battleship. Really the only ships that Imperial heirs and spares would be allowed to serve on. The smile grew wider as he thought of Sean, serving with the fleet, wondering what kind of eye opener it had been for the lad. *Do him good to learn some humility, though he was never the most arrogant of our family. And he probably never has to worry about the throne, bless him. He can have a fairly normal life as a planetary or regional governor, or maybe an ambassador.*

Something else flashed by closer, moving across his field of vision, and he focused in. He smiled again as he watched the trio of space fighters moving along, wondering what it would be like to be in charge of the smallest of Imperial warships. At six hundred tons they were not much more than large shuttles. With a crew of five they were a very closed knit society. And they were the dream of many junior officers for a first command. *And I would chuck this crown in a heartbeat to command one, if I could.*

And then people were around him again, and he slipped back into his persona of leader of human space. A persona that took more of the real him away every day.

"Are you ready, your majesty?" asked Klevik as Augustine was answering a question from a young reporter who had adoration in her eyes.

Not that Anastasia has anything to worry about, he thought, glancing over to where his wife was also fielding questions. *And not just because of a scandal. I've found what I wanted.* He looked back at the executive and nodded his head. "Let's get our boots on the ground."

They of course took the Emperor's shuttle down to planet side, to the site where the temporary capital would be located. Augustine sipped another champagne on the way down, directing his nanosystems to metabolize what he had already consumed so he would appear steady and sober before the trivee cameras. He reached over and clasped the hand of his wife, and she looked over from the window with a smile on her face.

The shuttle moved smoothly through entry on its grabbers, its artificial gravity and inertial compensators making for a smooth ride, almost like they were sitting in a room upon some tower. He compared the ride to an assault shuttle he had ridden as a serving officer, blasting its way through atmosphere on fusion engines. It also had artificial gravity and inertial compensators. But the pilot had flown the bird beyond the limits of those devices, and the ride had been rough enough to cause some vomiting among the passengers. Thankfully not in Ensign Ogden Lee Romanov, thank God. But then his genetics had almost guaranteed that nothing motion related would cause that kind of embarrassing incident.

The shuttle touched down smoothly on the tarmac, and within moments everyone was filing out of the bird. Trivee cameras were everywhere, as this event was recorded for posterity and the current news channels. Augustine stepped away from the heat radiating from the shuttle, looking up at the cloud flecked blue sky, taking in deep breaths of air that was a mixture of crystal cleanliness and hot materials. He took a look around the field at the terminal building and hangers, ready for the influx of colonists. A small city was rising on the north side of the field, though no construction was going on at the moment. Those crews were too busy crowding the edge of the field and cheering for the Imperial couple. Augustine gave them a raised fist and their cheers rose in volume. He knew his people loved him, and tried to do his best in return for them. That thought brought to mind the struggle he was having in the Lords to protect them, and anger flashed at that image.

The call of something in the sky broke that spell and created another. The Emperor looked up to see what looked like a hundred or more birds flying over the field. He focused in on one, and a smile creased his face as he recognized a Cetian Morning Loon, its multicolored quartet of wings stroking the air, hooting its pleasure at just being alive. He followed the birds for a moment, then looked over at the smiling executive who was also following the flock.

"Yes, your majesty," said the man as he noted the Emperor's gaze.

"I think the colonists are really going to like this place," said the Emperor Augustine Ogden Lee Romanov. "I know I would. Good job, Mr. Klevik. Good job indeed. How would you like a peerage?"

*   *   *

Ensign Mark O'Brien sat in the copilot's chair of the space fighter, his eyes scanning the instruments to his front while his implant sent information directly into his brain. *Probably the most scrutinized part of human space at this moment*, he thought, glancing over at the commander, Lt. Commander Phoenix, who also had almost his total concentration on a space in which nothing was really happening.

The pilot, Warrant Three Jurviscious, had the ship well in hand. The ship could really fly itself, but when safeguarding the Emperor the pilot was always expected to keep hands on.

"Sure is a beautiful planet," said Sensor Tech Petty

Officer First Flounce from the back of the control room. The Ensign shot her a glance, thinking that she was a really beautiful woman, and untouchable to him as a subordinate in the same chain of command.

"Port bow grabber is heating up a bit, skipper," called the engineer over the com from his post in the power room of the small interplanetary ship.

"How bad?" asked the pilot, looking over his own instruments while O'Brien checked over his.

Nothing wrong that I can see, thought the young officer, seeing maybe a small temperature increase over the indicated unit.

"Just a ten to twenty degree spike and fluctuation," said the tech who was the ship's engineer.

"You're too much of a perfectionist, chief," said the pilot with a laugh. "Just keep an eye on it and have the hanger dogs check it out when we get back." With that the pilot's attention was back on the mission of providing close in watchdogs to the Imperial couple.

"Control reports the shuttle is about to launch," said Flounce, who was also the com tech. "Our flight is to form top cover."

"Acknowledged," said the pilot, maneuvering the small ship around and coming back over the large station.

As they assumed station the Imperial shuttle came accelerating out of the bay, heading toward the planet on a looping course. The pilot pushed the controls and set the fighter in motion after the shuttle. They were on the left side of the flight leader, the other craft on the right. Another trio was covering the bottom, while other flights flew ahead and behind, essentially forming a box around the shuttle, ready to intercept anyone that might try for the life of the Emperor. Even if interception meant their own destruction.

And we wouldn't have it any other way, thought Ensign O'Brien, keeping a close watch on his instruments. *That's why we volunteered for this job, to make sure the head of government is not decapitated. And it won't happen on my watch.* Of that the young officer was sure, and he could see no other way to think or feel.

Well into the atmosphere some planetary fighters joined them, interrogated thoroughly through the security systems to make sure they were the ones that were supposed to be met. The atmospheric craft, which had limited orbital and space capabilities, slotted in on the final approach to the field. O'Brien looked over the craft on his instruments. They were much smaller than the space fighters, much more nimble within an envelope of air, without near the armaments. He wondered what it would be like to fly one of them, but you had to be Army or Marines to do that.

The shuttle headed down to the field, and the space fighters pulled up and headed to a zone twenty kilometers over the ground, providing top cover while the planetary aircraft provided lower cover against a threat that was unlikely to appear. The planet only housed working crews who were already both cleared and watched. But the Emperor's military security detail took its work seriously, and were proud that no Emperor had been assassinated in the history of the group. *And we're not about to let it happen now*, thought the Ensign. *Or in the future, for that matter.*

*   *   *

"This is so beautiful," said Dr. Jennifer Conway, stepping out of the air-car onto the grass of the miniature plateau. Over the edge of the escarpment, about a hundred meters down, was a large open area, grasslands. A sluggish river flowed on the far side of those grasslands, separating the open area from what looked to be a dense forest of needle leaf trees. There were clusters of flowers over many of the trees, that in itself showing this was not terrestrial vegetation.

Several species of herbivore occupied the grassland, from a herd of two score Jassanic Beasts, the largest matriarchs up to eighty tons, to a couple of hundred one ton Klison's Bison, looking tiny compared to the monsters of the veldt. The bison, who did resemble those Terran creatures in a superficial way, were warily looking toward the forest across the river, while the larger beasts only seemed concerned about their young, they being too large to suffer predation, or so it would seem.

"Beautiful and dangerous," said Captain Glen McKinnon, reaching into the car to pull a couple of packs from the rear seat. "You make sure that pistol is on you at all times."

"At all times?" asked Jennifer, smiling and arching an eyebrow at her lover, her hand patting the particle beam pistol that Glen had gifted her with. The weapon was against the law for civilians on most worlds, but here on the frontier anything that could defeat the dominate native life was considered fair game.

Glen laughed for a moment. "I'll let you know when you can take it off," he replied with a smile.

It was a short hike up the mountain to another shelf that contained a small lake fed by water falling down the cliff above. There was an opening in the rock on one side of the pool. Glen stopped for a moment and looked back into the valley, then pointed at something and called Jennifer's name.

"Oh my," said the doctor after she turned to see a

predator come charging up the valley, heading straight for the bison like herbivores. She noticed four more moving with it, pack hunters that must have weighed two tons each, running on four legs and fanning out into a semicircle. The larger beasts were also moving, forming groups that defended the young from the predators. Even the mighty Jassanics formed a circle with the five to ten ton calves in the center.

But the predators ignored the larger beasts and went toward the Klison's with blinding speed. The Klison had almost formed a perimeter, long horns facing out, when one of the predators grabbed a half grown calf by the hind leg and pulled its bleating form away. The adults finished forming their circle, and stood there pawing the earth as the youngster was pulled further away and the pack pounced on it.

"Why don't they do something?" asked Jennifer, holding her hands up to her face and looking on in horror.

"They're just dumb beasts," said Glen, putting his arm over her shoulders. "They do what they do by instinct. And instinct tells them to not risk themselves in battles that are already lost."

The pack made its kill quickly and efficiently. As they settled down to their already decided on pecking order to feed, the rest of the bison moved their circle away, getting a hundred meters or so, then breaking up and walking with swift steps to another feeding area.

"I'm glad you saw that babe," said Glen, pulling her closer. "Especially since you insist on flying around in the back country to the freeholds. That's why you need to keep that weapon with you at all times out here. And make sure it's functioning. I'll show you what to do there as well. And you're always welcome to come see me to check it out."

"They can't eat us, though, right," said Jennifer, still feeling some shock at seeing the kill.

"They can't digest you," said Glen, shaking his head. "But they're too stupid to know that. They can still eat you just fine. And not being digestible is not going to help you one bit."

The Marine captain turned her around and walked with an arm around her to the pool. She looked into the clear water, laughing as she saw the fish analogues that were clustered in the center. Some were quite large, a couple of kilos at least.

"Now these guys won't eat you, and you can eat them just fine," said Glen, picking up a small stone and tossing it into the water, making the fish dart this way and that. "In fact, I think we'll try some fish later, after we use the water to refresh ourselves. But first, for the next surprise."

Glen led her into the opening in the rocks, just barely big enough for them to enter standing up and side by side. The entrance widened some as they passed inside, then through a long tunnel that glowed with some kind of luminescence, and then into a large chamber that was enchantment.

Jennifer drew in her breath as she looked over the thirty meter squared room, with stalactites and stalagmites meeting to form columns. Water dripped down one rippled limestone wall to feed another small pool, and the room glowed with an Eldritch light.

"We put in the lighting with a phosphorescent paint," said Glen, gesturing toward the walls. "Otherwise it would be dark as the pit down here."

"We?"

"Me and some of the men," answered the officer.

"We thought this might make a good refuge if something happened on the planet."

"And this place would protect you?"

"Not against anything heavy from space," said the officer, shrugging his broad shoulders. "Probably not even against a small nuke. But if no one knew you were here, it would probably be safe enough. And we're going to put a heavy blast door in the entrance here. Now let me show you around."

"There's more?" she asked as he took her hand and led her around the pool.

"Much more," he said with a chuckle. He led her through another short tunnel to another large chamber. This with several alloy doors set in the walls.

"We have food and weapons stored down here behind those locked doors. And those three over there open up into semiprivate quarters."

"What about that dark opening down there?"

"That goes much further back into the complex," said Glen, pulling out a minispot and shining it into the dark portal. "We're not really sure how big this complex is, but some deep radar soundings show it going down kilometers and stretching throughout this range."

Glen led her toward one of the doors, which swung open as he pushed a button on his key fob.

"Why all of this?" asked Jennifer, stopping and looking into his eyes. "What is going on out here? Are the rumors true?"

"I don't really known, babe," said the Captain, taking her arms in his hands. "But I'm not going to take chances if I don't have to. This is a place of refuge if worse comes to worse. And I want you to remember that this place is here. Now let's take a look at the quarters."

The room was of Spartan furnishings, with a queen sized bed, a dresser, and a large wardrobe. Glen closed the door after he activated the ceiling fixture. He walked to the bed and started to pull his shirt out of his belt, then over his head. "Babe," he said, turning a smiling face toward her. "Remember what I said about that weapon?" He pulled his shirt over his head, exposing the taunt musculature of his torso.

"Yeah," she said in a hushed voice, feeling her heart beat faster.

He unbuckled his belt and lowered his pants to the floor, then threw pants, holster and pistol over the dresser. "Well," he said, his own voice hushed as he came to her. "Now would be the time to take off that weapon. And everything else as well."

Chapter 16

No one knows why the dimension of hyper I is so much different than the other known hyper dimensions. It corresponds 9.8 to 1 to normal space, while all the other dimensions are one fourth the distance of the ones below it. The highest practical velocity in any dimension of hyper is .95 c, though .9 is more the norm for routine transits, or .8 for many civilian uses. This gives a range of pseudo speed of 7.84 to 9.31 times light speed. The other dimensions nest into each other in increments of four, each taking a little over five times the amount of energy to enter or maintain than the one below. Until recently hyper VI was the limit, at velocity .95 giving a maximum pseudo speed of 9,533 times the speed of light. Now we have access to hyper VII, with a maximum pseudo speed of 38,144 times the speed of light. This sounds impressive, until one realizes it still takes over 38 days to go from one end of the Empire to another at this speed, or over two and a half years to go from one end of the Galaxy to another, assuming a ship could carry enough antimatter for such a non-stop voyage. There is still the possibility of hyper VIII, which so far has resisted all effort to traverse with matter. Is there anything beyond? We do not know. It does not look promising. But it had not looked promising in the past.

Lecture at Imperial Naval Academy, Peal Island, Jewel, Year 930.

"We're picking up something in hyper VII," came the voice of the crewman over the link.

"Must be Fleet," said Captain Horatio Goldenstein, looking up at the screen that showed the bridge crew at work. "Can't think of anyone else up there in that dimension."

"You are doubtless correct, Captain," said the exec, looking up from the captain's chair where she stood her watch. "But I have a bad feeling nonetheless."

The Captain snorted as he stood up from his office chair, where he had been relaxing on the otherwise uneventful run of the *Faded Glory*. His was not a big ship, no more than two million tons, with a two million ton cargo capacity. He was a bit shorthanded on this run to several frontier worlds, missing a few from his full complement of seventy-four. But this was considered a milk run, out here on the edge of sector four. *Not like we have the damned Lasharans in this sector, or the Crakista. And the neutral zone keeps the Klang in their place.*

He headed up to the bridge anyway. Kathleen Chu's hunches had almost always been good, and he would feel better looking at the data himself.

"Captain's here," said the com tech when Goldenstein walked onto the small bridge. There were only stations for five here, and most times three were enough for a watch.

Nothing at all like a Fleet ship, thought the Captain, glad that it wasn't. He still remembered jumping to his feet whenever the captain or a senior officer entered a room, back when he was an able spacer, long before he decided the merchant fleet was the place for him.

"What do we have?" he asked, walking over to the captain's chair. Chu stood up and made way for him, standing at his side and pointing at the main viewer, which was set for tactical.

"Something big, moving through hyper VII," said the exec, pointing at the probable path on the viewer. "It sounds like its decelerating."

"You think they know we're here?" asked the Captain, feeling foolish as soon as the words left his mouth. *Of course they know we're here. They're a warship, with better sensors and operators than we could ever have.*

"They know," said the exec, looking at the Captain. She looked back across at the com tech, who was also the sensory specialist. He also had some military time, but was by no means the kind of expert a capital ship would carry. "I wish we had a better suite."

"They give us enough to get from point A to B, and not run into someone on the way," said the Captain, watching the computer generated track of the unknown. It was definitely slowing down, and its vector was slowly changing to track theirs.

"It's got to be military," said the com tech, looking up from his screen and pulling his headphones off. "Who else could it be? They just want to take a look."

"Not that they'll find anything," said the exec, walking over to the com station and picking up the discarded headphones. "Or at least nothing that will get us into any kind of real trouble." She picked up the headphones and slid them on, reaching forward to punch in some information on the board.

The Captain thought about their cargo for a moment. Mostly machinery, vehicles and commodities for the frontier worlds that were on their route. Even the narcotics they carried were legal. There might be some illegal commodities on board, brought by individual crewmen to line their own pockets. Probably nothing very bad, and if found it would be the responsibility of the crew who brought it aboard. He still didn't like being boarded. It made all ships' captains nervous. But a bad case of nerves would be the only result.

"This doesn't sound right," said Chu, looking up with the headphones on, a frown on her face.

"What do you mean?" asked Goldenstein, his heart in his throat.

"I've never heard resonances quite like these," said the woman, pushing some more on the surface of the board.

"Can we send them a hyperwave transmission?" asked the Captain, looking over at the com tech.

"We can send it," said the tech, nodding his head. "Standard ID and all."

"Then go ahead and do it," said the Captain, looking at the track on the screen as if it would give up its information. Minutes went by, and the com tech looked over and shook his head.

"We have a translation," said Chu, pulling off the earphones. "Close, and like nothing I've ever heard before."

"To what level?" asked the Captain, feeling a chill come over him.

"Our level," said the exe, giving the Captain a wide eyed look. "Hyper VI."

* * *

The hyperwave message had finally made it down the relay from New Moscow, completing the seven day trip through hyper VIII to the Sector Four Headquarters. The top secret header of the Human Alliance prevented the com technicians at the hyper limit station from opening and decrypting the message. The urgent symbol attached to the header caused them to send the message inward by laser as it was in the process of arriving at the station, instead of waiting for the entire message to arrive and sending it in a burst to the inner system.   Meanwhile, the message was forwarded toward the naval bases of the Core Worlds, and on to the capital itself.

Three and a half hours after arrival at the outer com station the initial part of the signal was downloaded and decrypted at the station orbiting Conundrum III. Within minutes it was on the desk of the commanding officer of the sector, Grand Fleet Admiral Duke Taelis Mgonda.   The dark skinned Admiral was woken from a deep sleep after his staff was alerted to the urgent header. As commander of the naval district and all naval assets within it, it was his job to deal with urgents.

Admiral Mgonda pulled his robe around him tighter and picked up the cup of coffee that an aide had brought to his desk. He was still relatively young at one hundred and thirty-seven, in fact very young for his rank. But the nights seemed to be colder when he was woken early in his sleep cycle. He took a small gulp of the coffee, with sugar and cream, and opened the report on his viewer.

Mgondo read for a few minutes, his disbelief growing as he went through paragraph after paragraph, then switched to the raw data downloaded by a destroyer that hadn't survived its encounter with the unknown. He cursed under his breath for a moment. *I thought all of this was hysteria on the Emperor's part,* he thought. He had still done everything in his sector to strengthen the defenses and dispose of his ships to the best of his abilities, thank the gods. But that had been because he was a professional who took his responsibilities seriously. Not because of any belief in the boogie man.

Well, here the boogie man was. And he was just as frightening as had been imagined. He hit the com override switch that put him in touch with all of the important departments on the station.

"This is Mgondo. All staff members are to meet in the briefing room in one half hour."

He hit another button on the com, linking him to the stations com section.

"Alert Field Marshal Maxwell that we have a situation. Please ask him to repair to the station at his earliest convenience. We have a situation orange."

That takes care of the Army, he thought, *letting them know we have an invasion imminent situation.*

"Send hyperwave to all systems in the sector that are in the link. Situation orange. Execute local defensive plans. Prepare ground reserves for call up. All fleet auxiliaries and reserve vessels are to be prepped for immediate duty and to stand by with minimal crews on board. Send out all couriers on hand to the other systems in a sequence that covers them all. Also, order the militarization of all mail packets. We're going to need the couriers.

"Lastly," he said as he peeled off the robe and started to put on a functional duty coverall he kept in the office, "send my actions and responses up the line to Fleet HQ in the home system. Send actions to the New Terran Republic Fleet HQ and to the Neutral Zone."

Surely the New Muscovites will have sent this information over the link to New Terra, he thought as he walked down the station's corridor to the conference room. *But no use taking chances. Same with the Neutral Zone*, he thought of the seven scattered military bases that the Human Alliance used to keep watch on the Klang. *They might get hit early, since they are closer to the enemy that we are. Or the Klang might make use of the situation to attack there.*

The marines were already at the door to the conference room, in full light armor, weapons at ready arms. They snapped to attention and present arms as the Grand Fleet Admiral came into sight. *How like them,* he thought with pride in his own ground troops. *Ready for battle before us navy pukes could get ready for a meeting.* He returned the salute and walked through the opening doors.

The room was only half full, a dozen officers and a half dozen enlisted secretaries seated and looking at their flat comps. Another half dozen stewards bustled around the room, setting up coffee services and snack trays. A young petty officer spied the Admiral first and came to her feet.

"Admiral on deck," she announced, and the rest of the assemblage jumped to their feet at the position of attention.

"Take your seats, ladies and gentlemen," he ordered as he headed for his own at the top of the long table. He fell into the chair and touched his hand to the flat comp on the table to his front, linking to it and making it his own.

"We'll wait a couple of moments for the rest to get here," he ordered, accepting a cup of sweet whitened coffee from a steward. He looked around the room, noting that his intelligence officer had not yet arrived, nor had Fleet Supply or Base Engineering.

Soon the intelligence officer, a female captain with brownish skin and a Pacific Islander's features came through the door, followed by the large pale form of the Fleet Supply Officer, running at a jog. The Admiral called the meeting to order.

"I would like to first show you the synopsis of the attack on the HICS *Ekaterina* by a vessel of an unknown power and origin," said the Admiral as a holo sprung to life above the table. Dozens of pairs of eyes followed the edited battle as the human vessel fought and lost to an alien ship. After a few minutes the holo terminated.

"Those of you interested can watch the full battle at a later time," said the Admiral, looking around the room. "Our colleagues at the New Moscow Admiralty also provided these following shots, though we could have brought them out of our own library."

The holo sprang to life once again. This time the view was of some archaic vessels that they only recognized from their history courses at the various colleges and academies they had attended. Ancient earth vessels, from a time before the exodus, attacking an alien vessel that was larger than all of them put together. A vessel that was destroying an earth ship with every blast of its domed laser weaponry.

The holo switched to a view of the modern version of the ship next to the ancient version. Both were cylinders, with a saucer like skirt along the length, and a number of domes along the side. There were some minor differences, as were to be expected over two thousand years of time. But not what would have been seen in human vessels over that same time span.

"Ca'cadasans," whispered the intelligence officer.

"So it would seem, Captain," said the Grand Fleet Admiral. "So it would seem. They have found us. Whether this presages an immediate attack is a question I don't have the answer to. Can I afford to take that chance? I don't think I can. So we are going to full mobilization alert. Code Orange."

"Not red alert, sir?" asked a Commander with a Fleet Logistics patch on his jumper.

"Would you want every reserve trooper on every planet in the sector standing by at his base with weapons ready?" he asked the younger man. "This will of course be a decision for Field Marshal Maxwell, who will be up here soon. But it will do no good to have everyone manning defense systems that might not be needed for weeks, if not months or years. After all, anyone coming out of hyper will be at least three light hours from inhabited worlds. Say four hours or more to hit them with anything, and probably more than twelve hours to close on the planet. And that's even if they are a lot more advanced than we believe they are.

"What I need from you, ladies and gentlemen, are your best assessments of the threat and our best responses to any contingency," he said, sweeping the room with his glance. "We have a lot of military power gathered here in this system. And through the rest of the sector. The question is whether it is gathered where it needs to be to meet the threat as we understand it. Meet with your staffs and come up with some preliminary reports by, let us say, ten AM station time."

The Admiral got to his feet, the staff jumping to attention as he prepared to leave the room. He turned back to them for a moment as he set his coffee mug on the table.

"I know there is not a lot of information on the actual threat," he said. "Study the data that we do have, especially the scenes of that fight by New Moscow. If you have any ideas on how to even the odds in ship to ship combat, bring them up at the next meeting. No matter how crazy they might seem. That's all ladies and gentlemen.   I'm sorry for interrupting your beauty sleep, but I think most of us will not be getting enough in the near future."

The Admiral walked out of the briefing room to the buzz of conversation.   Moments later his com buzzed with the news that the ground forces Commander for the sector was on his way up from the planet.

*   *   *

Sean didn't think that Massadara III would ever grow to rival the fleshpots of the Core Worlds.   That said, it beat being stuck in the relatively spacious confines of the ship.   It at least had new and different faces and places to spend his hard earned pay on.   Not that he really had to worry about that, either, as his family was the wealthiest in the Empire.

No, he thought, looking at the many humans and some nonhumans who crowded the walkways on a busy landing field street, *the really difficult part was convincing the Captain to let me come down to the surface of the planet and walk the streets with my fellow officers.*   His hide was considered too valuable to risk.   And being a frontier world, there were a lot of armed civilians planet side.

His wearing a sidearm had been part of the provision of his being allowed to roam the wilds of the frontier world capital.   The other half dozen young officers with him were also so equipped.   The other part were the three marines who were his body guards for the evening.   One walked about ten meters to the front of the officers, his eyes continually scanning, searching for threats.   The other two walked ten meters behind, in constant communication with their point man, trying to look in every direction at once.

Except for being big, strong members of their race, and wearing the dress uniforms of Imperial Marines, they didn't look too imposing. But their hands stayed near their sidearms, and underneath their uniforms they wore a nanoweave body armor. Their hats and dark glasses were made out of the same material that could stop most civilian class weapons cold.

"It's so nice to actually feel the air on my face," said the red haired Ensign to the Prince's right, her pert nosed face looking up into his. Sean could feel the adoration in her gaze, something he wished he wouldn't get from females, especially other naval officers. It was great that he didn't need to come down to planet-side bars to get laid. It had always been easy for him to get all the sex he wanted. But what he wanted was for someone to treat him as a human. Even if they were slapping his drunken face for a rude comment.

"If you don't mind being crowded in among a throng of people," said Lieutenant Coxswell Baxter from the other side of cute Ensign Polakowski. "Though I like some of the alien motifs."

The city did seem to have more of the resident aliens of the empire walking the streets than most frontier worlds. But this one had been selected to become one of the centers of the frontier bureaucracy, which attracted many of the alien races that lived alongside humanity.

"This place seems tiny to me," said the Prince, his eye following a large centauroid Phlistarin as it pushed through the crowd accompanied by two small, felanoid Abatalars. The large alien looked as if it was going to force them to move aside, then angled to the other side of the street as it noticed the marine escort.

"Growing up in the largest city of the Empire might cause one to feel that way," said tiny Lieutenant JG Rejardo, her eyes roaming the shops and restaurants they were passing. "I grew up on a developing world. One that had been classed as frontier only a century before. And the largest regional city was not much larger than this one. Maybe four hundred thousand."

"And this city, Port Massadara," said Lt. Commander Bryson Popodopolous, the ranking member of the shore leave party, "is about three hundred and fifty thousand. But I'm sure it is going to explode now that's it's been designated a military hub. There'll be hyper wave brought in, and people will flock here to get land on a frontier world that will boast a real defensive structure."

The Prince looked up at the sky as the other officer spoke, watching the reflected light of the now hidden sun shining off the class two fort in geosynch above the city. He remembered the two class one forts, each over twelve times the mass of a battleship, he had seen under construction up there on the shuttle ride in. Not really anything to compare to a Core World, but still significant defensive firepower.

"What about there," said Rejardo, pointing to the open double doorway under a flashing sign that said the establishment was called the *Recumbent Griffon*, complete with the figure of said beast looking very intoxicated from its lying position.

"Looks good to me," said Popodopolis, flashing the young Lieutenant a smile and offering her his arm. The rest of the party followed the pair as the point marine jogged to their front to make sure he entered the bar ahead of them.

"They're going in the *Griffin*," called the police

sniper on the roof of a nearby building. Acknowledgements came back over the police circuit from the undercover men on the streets and the air-cars overhead. Several other people made their way toward the entrance to the bar/restaurant, the sniper tracking their progress as he noted the lack of energy signals indicative of weaponry on their persons.

The Prince glanced around the establishment as his group entered. It was a lively place, with groups of officers and ratings mingling with locals. There were a few aliens in the main room, mostly small humanoid Malticons carrying drinks and food orders to tables. The bar's air purification system fought a losing battle with the smoke that was generated from many people partaking in a variety of combustibles.

Patrons took a quick glance toward the group, their eyes mostly on the marines who took positions near the walls and looked actively around the barroom. Conversations resumed, though a few tables sat and stared at the Prince as he tried to blend in with the group.

Should have worn a holo mask, he thought, watching the tables that were looking at him and whispering among themselves. His face was just too damned recognizable. Especially since the whole Empire knew that one Prince Sean Lee Ogden Romanov was wearing the Imperial uniform.

The stares soon abated as people went back to their own business, with still a few surreptitious looks his way. And one or two who continued to stare at him with cold eyes.

Not everyone likes us, he thought, figuring they were disgruntled frontiersmen who would cause no trouble. Especially with armed marines and a large contingent of spacemen looking on.

"Over there," said Ensign Polakowski, pointing to a table at the back of the room that a Malticon woman was wiping with a wet rag, a tray of glasses sitting on a pulled out chair. A group of grumbling naval officers, including a full Commander, were moving away from the table to the bar.

"Dammit," cursed Sean under his breath.

"Come along, your highness," said Popodopolis, putting his arm around the Prince's shoulder. "Sometimes it's good to be king."

"You know I hate that kind of treatment, sir," said the young prince, walking toward the table.

"Don't worry, Sean," said Lt. Rejardo, giving him a smile. "You'll always be just another fuck up to the rest of your shipmates."

"Thanks a lot," said Sean with a grimace. "It's so nice to be among friends."

The other officers laughed as the Malticon woman took their orders and headed for the bar. Sean tried to keep himself in the moment, even though he wanted to jump up from his chair and shout for everyone to just treat him like a regular person. He knew that was a pipe dream. He was too well known, too famous, to be treated like an average citizen.

He relaxed a bit when the drinks arrived and he could get his hand around a glass. He relaxed a bit more when he was able to get himself around some of the Scotch. A second drink and some conversation had him feeling like a regular human being again. He was beginning to really relax and enjoy himself, and was thinking of asking Polakowski to dance when he felt that something was not right. He looked around the room, his eyes scanning those standing within sight.

Until they alighted on a small man of middle age leaning against the bar, his cold eyes staring into Sean's.

Like a striking viper the man moved, the arm at his side coming up in a blur, a small handgun held in his paw. The man turned his body slightly while aiming the gun at the Prince.

Augmented human, thought Sean in an instant, wondering where the man had received the retro-genetic engineering that turned humans into superhumans. And which also shortened their lives. Which was why it was outlawed. As this thought went through his head he fell toward Ensign Polakowski, his own reflexes taking hold. His were a result of modifications done generations before to his line. Modifications that made his nervous system faster than normal, including his cerebral cortex.

He heard a boom followed by a crack as he pulled the female officer to the floor. He knew that the second noise was something traveling faster than sound moving over his body. And then the room was full of noise, coming too fast and furious to track.

The assassin fired his carbon fiber chemically propelled pistol at the Prince after lining up the sight. He grunted in surprise as the target moved faster than he could follow, his first round missing the Prince by centimeters. The assassin wished that he could have brought a light amp weapon with him for this mission. But that would have triggered all manner of scanners that were guarding the Prince.

Adjusting his aim the assassin fired a couple of rounds into the table, hoping that he might get penetration and a hit. Movement from the left of the table caught his attention. The tall Lt. Commander was raising his sidearm, moving the pistol into line for a shot at the assassin. A quick shift brought his pistol into line with the officer, as a squeeze of the trigger sent an eight millimeter round into the man's chest. Blood spurted into the air as the round impacted and the officer fell back into his chair, tipping it over to fall to the floor.

The assassin spun back toward the primary target, moving to the right so he could bring the Prince back into sight. Two narrow laser beams intersected the assassin at that moment, one to the chest, the other to his right shoulder. Clothing burned and tissue flared into steam as the marine guards fired their millisecond bursts of invisible energy. The assassin dropped to his knees and his gun fell from nerveless fingers. The third marine guard kept his pistol pointed at the head of the assassin as the other two moved from their positions, walking toward the man who looked at them with pain in his eyes.

That was the moment the other two assassins made their moves. One opened fire on the marine guard who was covering his wounded companion. The round entered the marine's cheek, crunching through bone and teeth and spraying the broken mass from the other side. The wounded marine went down. The assassin fired at another marine. This marine staggered as the round hit her in the chest, the energy absorbed by her body armor. She returned fire with a long burst of laser energy, cutting into his chest. A patron cried out as part of the beam cut into her hand, dropping two fingers to the floor.

The remaining marine took careful aim and fired a shot at the assassin's head. The invisible beam burned through the skin and skull of the forehead. Entering the cranium the beam transfered its megawatts of energy into the tissue of the brain. The brain transformed to steam, and the skull blew apart and splattered those nearby with its bloody contents.

The third assassin waited for the second to draw attention toward himself. She moved toward the Prince, who was struggling to get out from under the weight of the female officer who had pushed herself on top of him. She put a couple of rounds into the female, saw her form jerk and then go slack, and took aim at the Prince, who was lifting the injured officer off of himself.

*   *   *

"Get off of me," Sean yelled at Polakowski as the small officer wrestled him with wiry strength and determination.

"You're staying under cover, your highness," she said with a grimace. "We're responsible for your safety, so keep your damned self down."

The pretty redhead jerked twice as shots boomed, then went slack. Sean grabbed her shoulders and started to push her limp form off of him. He saw the third assassin, moving toward him, holding a gun and bringing it into aim.

The assassin jerked as a number of hypervelocity pellets hit her in the chest and head. Blood spurted from impacts and her head came apart like a struck melon. Her finger pulled off one last shot. The round cracked by the Prince's ear and into the wooden floor, sending splinters into the air. One splinter hit the Prince on the cheek, opening a small wound that bled down the side of his face.

Strong hands pulled the Lieutenant from the top of the Prince. Her sightless eyes looked up at the ceiling as they gently laid her down and reached for the Prince.

"Get the meds here," called a voice. "The Prince is injured."

"Damn me," said Sean, pulling away from an arm that was trying to restrain him. "Get her help."

A pair of medics ran up to the Prince, hands reaching for his slight wound.

"Help them," he yelled at the medics, pushing one of them toward Polakowski.

That man looked over at the Lieutenant and pulled out a scanner from his belt.

"All life signs have ceased," he called out, taking another device from his belt and pressing it to her skin. "She's in biostasis now," he said to the Prince, looking over his shoulder. "She should be as good as new after we repair her."

"This one is still conscious," said the other medic, working on Lt. Commander Popodopolis. "I'm putting him out for transfer."

The first medic ran over to the wounded marine where the man sat on the floor, hands holding his wounded face. Sean stood up and shook off the hand of the other medic who was trying to get a look at his face.

"I'm alright," he said with a growl, walking over to where the first assassin was still on his knees, covered by the pistols of a marine, two officers and a couple of uniformed police who had responded. He looked down at the man, his own ice blue eyes boring into the assassin's cold eyes.

"At least we got one intact," said one of the police officers. "Those other two don't have enough intact neurons left for any kind of forensic scan."

No sooner had the words left his mouth than the assassin's eyes rolled up in his head and he pitched face first into the floor. One of the medics came running over, scanner out.

"Brain dead," pronounced the medic, frowning down at the scanner.

"Probably had a molecular acid capsule in his brain," said the marine who had been covering him. "Didn't want to give away anything under scan. Alive or dead."

"We need to get you up to the ship," said Ensign Rejardo, putting a hand on Sean's back. "You'll be safe there."

Sean looked down at her for a moment, then over at his two injured friends and the wounded marine, all of whom had a part in saving his life. A tear streaked down his face as he thought of the sacrifices they had made. And at the selfish thoughts that were going through his mind. He couldn't be safe in public. Nor could those he called friends be safe with him in public. His birth restrained him from normal life, no matter how else he would have had it.

Chapter 17

Science has made us gods even before we are worthy of being men. Jean Rostand

Lucille Yu was sitting at her desk, trying to figure out more efficient ways to produce wormholes, when her link chimed in with an alert. *What the hell now*, she thought, mentally connecting with the call.

"We have a problem with the alpha wormhole generator," said the voice of an engineer, Bob Landry, at the same time the schematic of the problem appeared in Yu's visual center.

Shit. The whole damned assembly, thought Yu, looking over the enormous construct that was used to generate one end of a wormhole tunnel.

Thirty kilometers long by twenty wide, the cylindrical structure was similar to those used to generate artificial micro black holes for industrial applications. But where those used a globular array of lasers to create the pressure needed to form a singularity, this used graviton projectors. And gravitons, due to their relative lack of energy per particle, required a much greater source of energy for enough to be generated to form the temporary singularity needed to open the mouth of a hole in space. And one of the graviton generator assemblies had broken off and fallen, more likely flew, into the singularity to be crushed out of existence.

Thank God we don't have anyone working on those assemblies during the creation, thought the scientist. She could think of no more awful way to die, to be crushed from existence, as if you never were. *Would the soul even survive such an event?* They didn't know what happened to the matter that entered such a singularity, since there wasn't even an artifact like a black hole that remained. For all they knew the matter went to another Universe. They knew those existed. She had even, in the past, worked on the Other Universe Project, and had seen holes opened to those other planes of existence. But the *Donut* Project seemed to offer so much more tangible rewards, bridging the gaps in the space they knew. Those other Universes didn't even support matter as they knew it, much less life.

"So what's the damage?" she asked the man on the other end of the link. "How soon before it's up and running again?"

"It will probably take a week to get a new graviton projector installed and calibrated," said the engineer. "We can try to rush it, but that doesn't normally come out well."

"Make sure it's done right," said Lucille, looking over the schematic again. "We'll just have to make do with the other two production pairs while we get that one back to working order." *Not that we can't make the same number of wormholes, since the energy production is the limiting factor. But it's still nice to be able to rotate the units.* "And find out what happened. There's no reason that thing should have fallen in like it did. I don't want the same thing to happen on the other assemblies."

"I'll get right on it," said the engineer. The link terminated and Lucille was left alone with her thoughts.

There has to be a more efficient way to make wormholes, she thought, pulling up schematics on her wall holo and zooming in on details. In the Other Universe Project they had been able to open portals to other dimensions just about anywhere, using graviton projectors of similar construction as they were using here. But it took much less energy to open the dimensional portals, and they could be opened in the designated chamber or even in open space. That last had not been the recommended procedure, and was really more of an accident than anything.

A horrible accident, she recalled, though memory of the event had made her wonder if it hadn't been controlled somehow from the other side. Because the Universe revealed had seemed to be inhabited by an enormous entity, if the space itself wasn't the thing. And it was hungry. She still shook at the memory, one of the reasons she had moved on to another project.

I guess as time goes on we will find a way to make the equipment smaller and more efficient, she thought. It was a wonder that they had made them at all, considering the energies involved.

Lucille worked the rest of the afternoon before she received another call from Landry. "We know what happened," said the project engineer, a frown on his face.

"Enlighten me," said Lucille, propping her head up on her desk as she communicated through the link.

"Seems that the maintenance nanites had most all been pulled off of that section by the singularity," said the engineer with a mental shrug. "There weren't enough to repair structural damage from multiple hole mouth formations."

"Only on that one section?" asked Lucille, narrowing her eyes. "How is that possible?"

"It may have happened to some other sections as well," said the engineer. "In fact, it did happen on one other section, but the structural strain had not reached failure at that time."

"So what can we do about it?" asked the sub-director in charge of wormhole production for the project, wondering what else could go wrong.

"I guess we need to monitor the density of nanites on each section after each formation," said the engineer, his voice coming across the link as tired.

As tired as I feel, thought Lucille, closing her eyes for a moment.

"And I recommend a reapplication of nanites to the entire rig after each formation," continued the engineer.

"Do it," said Lucille, sending a confirmation through the system that doubled as her electronic signature. "Nanites are a lot cheaper than new graviton projector assemblies."

"Yes ma'am," said the engineer. "We'll get right on it."

Lucille went back to work, checking and signing off on the thousands of mundane tasks that were her purview. An hour later her link chimed again, indicating that another emergency was occurring, this time with one of the massive tugs that had been in the process of lowering an electron beam generator into place on the *Donut*.

*   *   *

"Not good news to be receiving at this time," said the Emperor, looking at the face of the Chief of Naval Operations on the viewer. He was still going over the information on his link within his mind, and thinking of all the trouble this new development would cause his efforts to reinforce Sector Four. But Sector Three needed all that it could get as well if they were to avoid a bloodbath.

"I didn't think so either, your majesty," said the lanky Admiral, the ever present pipe smoking from the corner of his mouth. "It kind of complicates our plans at that."

"What can we do, Len?" asked the Emperor, his eyes pleading. "I had another dream. It scared the hell out of me. We need to defend Sector Four from the hammer that's going to fall there."

Admiral Lenkoswki sat for a moment, taking a couple of puffs on his pipe. The Emperor knew that the smoking correlated with thinking. He gave his naval commander the moments he needed to come up with something they could use.

"Well," he said with a drawl, pulling the pipe from his mouth. "We probably need to suspend any transfers not already in the pipe, so we can keep a strong presence along the border. Margrave and Klashak need to mobilize their reserves and be ready to come in behind the leading wave of regulars and take out the transports. And I would recommend sending any available fleet and light carriers, and even the transport carriers, to the frontier. We could station a carrier and a few escorts in each of the inhabited systems that we don't have much else in. That way we would have a large fighter presence in those systems to take out any transports that come there. And maybe hit any warships they might have with them."

"Could you detach them from Home Fleet and the sectors bordering Elysium," said the Emperor, looking over the dispositions in his own head. "And what about some squadrons of battleships from home fleet."

"The Parliament will raise holy hell if we detach anything from home fleet," said Grand High Admiral Lenkowski, putting the pipe back in his mouth. "We would be reducing the protection of their precious Core Systems."

"The Core Systems are not at risk here," growled the Emperor. "At least not yet. Anything the Lasharans get that far into the Empire will be broken by the static defenses of those systems. The casualties are going to come from the brave souls on the frontier worlds."

"I understand that, your majesty," said the Admiral. "I'm on your side. I'm just saying that they will demand explanations."

"Then pass the blame on to me," said Augustine. "I'll take the heat. And station some of those battleships far enough back to form a sector wide reserve. That way they can also form a reaction force for Sector Four if it comes down there."

"Yes, your majesty," said the Admiral. "Your wish is my command."

"I have one more favor to ask, Admiral," said Augustine, looking into his long time friend's eyes. "It's not one I ask lightly. But it is something I need done and done quickly."

"What can I do for my sovereign," said the white haired man.

"I want Sean back in the capital, on the quickest courier you can get him on," said the Emperor. "I need to talk with him, face to face."

The Admiral's face dropped and his mouth opened, his eyes staring at the Emperor's.

"That's highly irregular, your majesty. Sean is a serving officer in an active duty command. I'm not sure how he would take a command that removed him from that vessel."

"I need to talk to him," said Augustine in a firm

voice. "Personally. And it is not expedient that I go to where he is. So he must come here. That is my command."

"Very well, your majesty," said the Admiral, swallowing. "I will dispatch a message to Sector Four HQ by hyperwave. The system that the Prince's ship is based at is not on the hyperwave circuit, so we will have to send a courier from there. It will take about a week to get the message to him."

"And about two weeks to get him back," said the Emperor, "since we can't send him by laser beam through the hyperwave system. I understand, Admiral. And I appreciate it.

"Now," he said, looking at some displays on his desk, "I have to get ready. The Imperial family is going to the *Donut* in the morning to tour the project."

"They're really coming through with those energy sink wormholes for the navy," said the Admiral, a smile crossing his face.

"I wish I could say the same with the gate wormholes," said Augustine, frowning. "It would be a lot easier just bringing the Prince home in an instant. Then he could go back to his command. Or I could take a short walk out to his base and talk with him there."

"Well at least you won't have to spend a week in N-space getting to the *Donut*," said the Admiral.

"There's that," said the Emperor. "We can look at the place tomorrow and be back at the palace in the evening. I'll let you get back to your work, Admiral. And thank you again."

"My pleasure, your majesty," said the Admiral. "Out here."

The viewer went blank as the Emperor looked

around his office for a few moments. *So much to do*, he thought, *even with the help of my wife and heir. So much to do, and so much more crashing down on me.*

He shook his head for a moment before getting up from his chair and heading for the lift to his private quarters. He didn't really notice anything on the way there, his mind too preoccupied with all of the multiple crises that seemed too much for the resources on hand.

* * *

The Neutral Zone was neither a zone nor neutral. It was more of an imaginary wall in space, five hundred twenty light years wide by four hundred light years high and sixty light years deep. And it was in no way neutral. The ships of the human powers were allowed to travel unhindered through the space. They constantly patrolled the zone. Put simply, the Klang were not allowed to enter. There was still trade between the Klang and the humans, through routes that went around the wall. But nothing was allowed through on the direct path to New Moscow and the unaffiliated worlds behind the wall.

Seven fortified systems made up the strength of the zone. One was manned by the forces of New Moscow. Two were manned by the New Terran Republic, and three by the Terran Empire. The largest, the central base, was manned by all the forces of the alliance. The mobile units constantly patrolled the area, backed up by strong task forces.

The Klang raiding parties came through the wall in force. A hundred clan battleships, a thousand raiders, they swept onto the fortified systems while hundreds of other raiders moved through the zone and into the space beyond. The Klang attacked in their savagery, with faith in the promises of their new allies. They fought with all of the skills of a warrior people. They fought with the same lack of cohesion and strategy that had ever been their downfall in the past.

Humans used fire and maneuver, long range missiles and quick strike fighters to destroy enemy ships well out of laser range. They destroyed the Klang fleet in detail, taking their own casualties and reforming. In the end the Klang faired as they always had. A few dozen vessels made it back to their Empire. The humans had beaten them again despite the promises of their new allies.

The survivors of the human fleets repaired to their bases, out of missiles and having sustained various amounts of damage. Many ships had been destroyed, and many more were not capable of further operations. There had been some damage to the infrastructure as well. Hyperwave relays had been destroyed, enough that the spares in the systems could not replace the damaged lines immediately. Fastest communications with any of the home polities were out for at least the weeks it would take new units to be put into place. And many of the hyperdrive monitoring buoys had also been taken out. But they had been victorious against the barbarians.

It came as a total surprise when the unknown alien ships approached all of the fortified worlds. In five of the systems only the sensors of ships well within the gravity well picked up the intruders. The resonances matched those of the new hostiles that New Moscow had warned about. The systems prepared for an attack in the hours the track gave them. It was not enough with what they had left.

Within less than two days all of the mobile units of the human fleets had been destroyed. On day three the troops landed and the hard battle for the planets began. Two couriers escaped, one headed for New Moscow, one for the Republic. They warned every ship they came across on the way. But it would still take twelve days to reach New Moscow, twenty-five to reach the Republic.

*   *   *

Great Admiral Miierrowanasa M'tinisasitow looked out over the assembled task group commanders and fleet admirals as they stood at attention in the gathering chamber. There was elation in the atmosphere, and gleaming eyes in the faces of the Ca'cadasans crowding the large room. The enemy had been met, and they had tasted victory against the hated humans.

"We will go with the Omega plan," he said, his voice amplified across the huge room. "The human kingdom known as New Moscow will garner the attention of task groups one through twenty. Groups one through five will strike directly at the capital system, while the rest of the groups move through the inhabited systems according to plan. We will take the minor player out of the equation."

"Great Admiral," said a large male with the platinum horns of an Admiral.

"Yes Admiral Mirramanadon," growled the Great Admiral, readying himself for his subordinate's protest.

"Great Admiral," said the Admiral, crossing his hands over his chest in a sign of respect. "I believe it would be better to strike with all of our strength at the primary kingdom. With they in disarray we could then take the two smaller kingdoms at our leisure."

"And by then his majesty would have heard of our discovery," said the Grand Admiral, "and will have dispatched reinforcements to our fleet. I know the argument, Admiral. I acknowledge that it has its merits. But it is not the plan that I favor. We have the measure of the enemy. They fight hard, with great skill. But we are their superior."

"Not by much," said Admiral Mirramanadon. "My analysts have estimated that in the time the humans have been in this space they have narrowed the technological gap between them and us by almost three thousand years. In less than a thousand. We are barely ahead of them as it is. During a protracted conflict they will most probably pull ahead of us."

"I object, Admiral," called another large male, crossing his arms over his chest.

"Admiral Lorraterdon," said the Grand Admiral. "You may speak."

"Thank you Grand Admiral," said the new speaker. "I wish to acknowledge that my esteemed colleague, while correct in his analysis of the technical capabilities of the humans, present and future, forgets the relative sizes of our Empires. We are fifty times their size in area and population. In any long term conflict we will overwhelm them with sheer size. Because of that I am not so sure that they will surpass us in technology before we can bring them to their knees."

"I have decided already," said the Grand Admiral, holding up his hand and silencing the chief of intelligence. "We will go ahead with plan Omega. Task forces twenty-one through forty-five will attack the fringes of this New Terran Republic, while task forces forty-six through seventy will attack the largest kingdom. Task forces seventy-one through eighty will form the reserve."

"Can we at least destroy their inhabited planets?" said another large male with the flashes of ground forces on his tunic.

"Sacrilege," called several of the fleet priests simultaneously. The most impressively robed of those worthies waved an arm to get the Grand Admiral's attention.

"In a moment, High Priest," said the Grand Admiral, motioning for the General to continue.

"Thank you, my lord," said the General, glancing at the high priest. "I just wanted to raise the point that we had a very difficult time rooting the humans out of their fortified systems. We lost as many ground force soldiers as they did. And we controlled the space above the planets."

"They also were dug into the planets," said another ground force commander. "We had to land into the teeth of their defensive fire."

"That is correct," said the General, nodding at his subordinate. "And their land warfare machines are fearsome. Better than what we carry with our fleet."

"High Priest?" said the Grand Admiral, looking over at the robed Ca'cadasan.

"It is forbidden to destroy life bearing planets," said the Ca'cada cleric. "God forbids such, as they are the rarest of gems in the Universe."

"Seems to me there are so many of the damned gems we don't know what to do with them all," growled the General, glaring at the high priest.

"Sacrilege," hissed the high priest, glaring back at the General. "Look to your soul, General, lest it not bask in the Glory of Emperors past."

The General started to open his mouth in reply, but was silenced by a look and gesture from the Grand Admiral.

"That answers the question, General," said the

Grand Admiral at the frowning ground forcer. "We can pound them from orbit. But we cannot purposefully do irreversible damage to the ecosystem of any of their worlds.

"So everyone has their instructions," said the Grand Admiral, finality in his voice. "Repair to your vessels immediately and carry out your orders. And may God be with you. And may his avatar, the Emperor, be with you in spirit."

*   *   *

"I'm not going to lose this one," growled Dr. Jennifer Conway, running her med pad over the body of the eight year old boy that lay on the impromptu surgery that had been a kitchen table.

"Will he be OK, doc?" asked the frantic looking father, while the mother stood with him, tears rolling down her cheeks.

"He will be if I have anything to do with it," she said, looking at the results from the med pad and shunting the results up through the net to the local medical computer. *Damn*, she thought, looking at the results on the pad, then zooming in on infected area. *I've never seen anything like this. And I didn't think anything native could infect us like this.*

What she saw on the screen were cells like nothing she had ever seen. They were eating the child's cells and replicating themselves, spreading up his leg veins. *He's going to die if I don't do something, fast.*

Jennifer took a syringe out of her med bag and slotted it into her pad, sending the instructions to the nanites within the tube. When she was satisfied they had been told what she wanted, she pulled the syringe out and injected it into the left thigh of the child. She looked back at her screen and saw from the composite picture that the nanites were flooding the tissue and attacking the new cells. Killing them, but not fast enough in her opinion.

"Can't you just put him in cryo and get him to the hospital?" asked the dad, his eyes barely holding back the tears.

"The ambulance will be here any minute," said Jennifer, giving him a quick glance. *And I'm really not sure what cryo will do to these things. It might kill them. Or they might thrive in the cold, and we could find some biomass converted to whatever the hell this is, instead of a child.*

Alarms started to sound on the med pad, and Jennifer reached quickly into her bag, pulling out a plasma bag. She pushed the ultra-sharp needle into the arm, hitting the vein perfectly. "Here, hold this up," she said to the father, motioning him over. "He needs blood." *And the artificial blood cells will give his system the oxygen it needs, and hopefully avoid carrying the contagion with them.*

"Good," said Jennifer, looking at the pad and seeing that the vital signs were coming up. She focused on the contagion again and let out a yelp of pleasure. The nanites seemed to have stopped it in place. She pulled out another syringe, programmed it in the pad, and injected it into the child's neck, sending more search and destroy micro robots into his system.

"I think we got it licked," said Jennifer, a smile on her face. Then the contagion pulled a major trick on her. Something that looked like a cross between a twig and a snake erupted from the child's thigh and went over the nanite block, pushing through the skin of the thigh and spreading through the muscle.

"Shit," said Jennifer, moving her gloved hand off the thigh and looking at the nanoweave, hoping nothing had pushed through to her flesh. She sighed in relief, then focused on the child. "I'm going to have to amputate the leg."

"No," said the mom. "My poor Timmy."

"He can grow a new leg," said Jennifer, reaching into her bag for the old fashioned surgical kit she always carried. "If that thing gets into his core I think we will lose him."

"Do what you need to do, doc," said the father, holding his crying wife.

Jennifer slapped another pain patch on the child's neck, then pulled out a nano saw, looking at the blade to make sure it was new. She didn't worry about being sterile at this time. The nanites in the child's system would kill any normal infection. But the one attacking the leg was a horror she wasn't sure they could deal with.

"Here goes," she said, putting her off hand on the leg just below where she had decided to make the cut. She placed the nanosaw on the leg and pushed, feeling only slight resistance as the monomolecular blade sliced through skin, muscle and bone. In an instant the leg was off, and blood was spurting from the truncated thigh which ended a couple of centimeters below the hip. That was one reason she had decided on the saw and not a laser. It could be beneficial for the child's system to flush some of the blood out of the body, sweeping out any contamination that might have made it past the nanites.

Jennifer grabbed a wound patch from her bag and put it on the stump. The patch expanded, covering the area of the stump and stretching over a couple centimeters of skin on the truncated limb. It set in place, closing off all the open veins, arteries and nerve sheaths now leading to nowhere.

The doctor gave the child another injection of nanites just above the amputation, then grabbed the discarded limb with forceps and placed it in a cryo bag, sealing it and triggering the liquid nitrogen freezing pack. *Hope that holds it*, she thought, moving the bag aside, then picked up the nanosaw and made sure the blade guard was in place. Doctors had been known to perform unintended self-amputations with the ultimately sharp instrument, something she wanted to avoid if possible.

She checked the vitals of the child and breathed a sigh of relief. "I think he'll make it now," she said to the parents. "We'll get him to the hospital and start the leg regrowth, and he'll be good as new."

"Thank you, Dr. Conway," said the father, holding the mother tight as she cried into his shoulder.

The door opened and a couple of medics came running in, unfolding a gurney while they looked at the child.

"Get him to the hospital ASAP," said Jennifer to the senior of the medics, a woman known as Gracie. "And get that limb to the lab. Extreme caution with it."

"Yes, ma'am," said Gracie, reaching into her voluminous bag and pulling out a metal cylinder of the proper size. The medic grabbed the cryo bag and shoved it into the cylinder, then shut the cylinder and twisted the top. The seams of the cylinder closed up and formed a secure unit that no living organism was going to get out of. The medic placed the cylinder in her bag, then helped her partner to get the child on the gurney and hook up the diagnostic instruments.

"I will check on him as soon as I get back to the

city," said Jennifer to the parents, handing the dad a flat disk. "I will update you as soon as I can, and you can contact me on my personal com through this."

"Dammit, but that was one strange mother," said one of a pair of men who entered just as the medics were taking the child out to the ambulance.

"We found whatever it was that attacked Timmy," said the other younger man, who must have just become an official adult.

"Have you destroyed it yet?" asked Jennifer, hoping for a negative.

"Hell no, doc," said the older man, looking at her with a surprised expression. "I don't have any weapons other than a hunting rifle. I was thinking we might burn it."

"Let me have a look at it first," said Conway, walking outside with the men in tow. She watched the ambulance jump to the air and accelerate away, taking her patient to the hospital. As soon as it was out of sight she went to her car and removed an isolation suit, wishing she had worn it during the surgery. But there hadn't been time, and she just hoped that her nanites would keep her clear of contagion. *I'll check myself and everyone else here before I leave*, she thought, pulling on the suit, then belting her pistol on over it.

It was short walk through the forest to find the thing they were looking for. It looked like some kind of fungus mass to the doctor, who was not a botanist by any means. It was growing out of the carcass of some big herbivore, and from the nearby broken trees that animal had not been in good shape when it walked here. She surmised that it must have become infected with the fungus in some other place, got sick as the organism started to ravage its system, then fell at this spot. The fungus converted most of its body to its own mass and was spreading over the trees. Even as she watched a bird landed on it and was swiftly caught. She wondered if there was anything here to stop it, when some different birds landed on a covered branch and started to attack it, tearing off hunks and eating it.

My botanist and zoologist friends will be fascinated by this, she thought, looking back at one of the homesteaders. "I need to get a sample of this," she said to Timmy's father. "Can you get one of your robots to help me out?"

The humanoid construction robot walked up to the mass of the organism and started to snip pieces off and place them in a sample container. The organism went wild, sprouting tentacle like extrusions and hitting the robot about its body. The mechanism ignored the strikes, gathering samples and then walking away.

"Move everyone back," said Jennifer, making sure her suit was sealed, then pulling out her pistol. "I don't want anyone breathing any part of this thing in." The people moved away and she readied her weapon, setting it for maximum. *You aren't hurting any more children, you bastard,* she thought as she carefully aimed the particle beam at her target, the center mass of the thing.

The air buzzed as the red proton beam, visible from the heat it generated as it ripped through the atmosphere, hit the mass of the strange organism. Where it struck the biomass turned to vapor, while the living tissue on the edges shriveled and died. Jessica played the beam over the thing, back and forth. She stopped for a few moments, then went to burst mode, firing the beam for a couple of seconds, then letting it rest. The creature flailed about with tentacles that had nothing to strike. It has not evolved to face such an attack. Nothing that the doctor had ever heard of had.

The pistol beeped and a light blinked a moment after the beam stopped coming. Jessica gingerly handled the pistol, making sure to not touch the barrel, while she inserted a new power pack and proton store back in the weapon. Then it was back to the job of destruction, until there was nothing left of the organism, and the trees it had enveloped were reduced to smoking stumps.

"That should take care of it," said Jessica, holding the empty pistol in a firm grip while she walked away, letting the overheated weapon cool.

"Keep a lookout for any more of these things," she told the holders, while they looked around her at the area of the forest she had blasted out of existence.

They all nodded their heads, and she headed back to her air-car, hoping this world had no other surprises such as this, and sure that it had.

*   *   *

"We have more reports, sir," said Commander Ricardo Scott, walking up to the Grand Admiral's table in the cafeteria.

"How many?" asked Grand Fleet Admiral Duke Taelis Mgonda, overall naval commander for Sector Four. *And I thought this was going to be a quiet assignment*, he thought while he looked at the younger officer. *No such luck.*

"Four freighters and a liner," said the officer, his face assuming a strained look. "All were on individual routes with the exception of a couple of freighters that were traveling as a pair."

"And how many on the liner?"

"Passenger manifest of six hundred and fifty, all colonists on their way to a frontier world. And a crew of eighty-three."

Over seven hundred souls, thought the Admiral, making the sign of the cross and saying a quick prayer. *Plus over three hundred more for the freighters.*

"Do we have any idea what has happened?" asked the Admiral, leveling an intense stare onto his subordinate.

"No sir," said the Commander, looking down for a moment, then back up to the eyes of the Admiral. "They simply didn't show up in the systems as scheduled. We've sent search and rescue ships back up their routes with no sign. And two of the S and R ships have disappeared as well."

"Crap," said the Admiral, closing his eyes. *More lives lost.* He looked back at the Commander. "So what does your brain trust think?"

"Could be pirates, sir," said the man, his own expression showing that he didn't agree.

"Pirates don't normally attack Imperial Navy vessels," said the Admiral, waving off that suggestion. "There's no profit in taking on even a frigate. So what does that leave?"

"The Cacas are snatching up ships to gain information about this sector," said the younger officer. "At least that's my take on it."

"And I think it's the right take, young man," said the Admiral, pushing his tray away and standing up. "Now we need to do something about it before we lose more ships for no gain." He pulled his flat comp from his belt and expanded it. "I want patrols increased on all the shipping routes. And I want there to be more than single ships in the patrols, at least two cruisers and more ships if we're talking escorts. It doesn't do us any good to send out ships that are going to disappear before they bring the information back."

"What about the merchant ships, Admiral?" asked the Commander. "Do you have any orders for them?"

"I can't give them orders, son," said the Admiral with a scowl. "At least not in peace time. And even with an Orange Alert in effect it is still peace time, at least for the time being. But I suggest that they only travel in convoys, and that we assign escorts to those groupings. If they have any sense they will listen. If not, then they don't have any sense, and they can deal with whatever happens to them."

"Yes sir," said the Commander, pulling out his own flat comp and accepting the written orders from the sector commander.

"And keep me informed of any new developments," said the Admiral, turning and walking away, signaling to his strategic staff that he wanted to meet with them.

This is looking worse all the time, he thought, pondering the losses the sector had already suffered. *Over thirty merchant vessels and a half dozen military ships in a month. When we normally don't have near that many in a several year period. Our friends are near to striking. They have to be. To be this active in our space. And here I was hoping they would stay out by New Moscow for a while longer. Or maybe strike at the Republic.* He dismissed that thought as soon as it came. New Moscow and the New Terran Republic were allies. And even if they weren't they were human. And when the Cacas hit it would be all humans together, or none were likely to come out of this alive.

The Grand Admiral dictated a report as he headed for the conference room, sending it to the communications section for transmission up the hyper relay chain. The hexagon would have the information within a couple of days, and maybe he would get the reinforcements he was promised. *They have to keep sending them, after getting that report from New Moscow. The Emperor was proven right, and now they will have to give him what he wants. And maybe a declaration of war, so I can ride herd on these civilians who insist on getting themselves killed.*

It was still two days before the hyperwave message from New Moscow would make it to the capital.

*   *   *

Cornelius Walborski looked out over his farm through the quiet night air. One of the small moons was in the sky, not more than a coin sized circle of shining silver. The other was due up in another couple of hours. Due to the high albedo of the body it shone with considerable light, illuminating the field in a fairy glow.

One of the dogs barked, and the dog that was lying at the farmer's feet perked up her ears, then jumped to her feet and took off into the night. Walborski tapped into the system of cameras he had set by the fence line, a precaution he had taken after the last big herbivore had broken into the fields. He focused in on the section where stood the pack of dogs, barking into the night. The camera panned to the outside, showing an infrared image of a large beast. It was not doing anything to be alarmed about. In fact, it was shuffling away from the farm under the noisy attentions of the dogs. *They were a good investment*, thought the farmer of his mongrels. *And I'm not restricted as to how many I can own. Not like the robots.*

Cornelius frowned at that last thought. On New Detroit there had been billions of robots, in every facet of society. And that didn't include the uncounted nanites that were the basis of the system's manufacturing. But there were also billions of citizens on the planet, and the robots were the basis of their employment, most of them. But here on the frontier the man in the loop law was a recipe for disaster for the small property holder, like himself.

If I had two more work robots I could do so much more, he thought. He glanced back at his house for a moment, then back into the fields. *If only Katlyn could get approved as a robot supervisor.* But his wife had never worked with industrial robots like he had. She did not have the certification. He guessed that she could get it, by taking a part time job here on Sestius. After all, there were so many construction projects going on they had to have need of more workers. Even pregnant it was a job she could handle. But she didn't seem all that interested in being off their farm and her home for any length of time.

The door closed behind him, and he could feel his wife's light tread on the porch floor boards behind him. "It's beautiful out here," she said, putting her arms around him and leaning her gravid belly into his back.

"It sure is," he said, turning in her arms so he was facing her, putting his own around her neck and shoulders, then kissing her. "You are really beautiful too," he said, leaning back a little onto the porch railing.

"What got the dogs going?" she asked, and Cornelius was again aware of their barking in the distance.

He gave the cameras a quick check and was satisfied that nothing was going on. "Just some stupid plant eater wandering around outside the fields." Walborski looked up for a minute at the moon, then back at her face. "Tell me the truth. Do you miss our home world?"

"A little bit," she said, nodding her head. "But I really like having my own house, and not living in an Archology apartment." She patted her belly with a hand. "And I like the idea of having children. As many as I want."

Cornelius nodded his head and put a hand on her belly, sucking in a breath as he felt the baby stirring. *That part is nice. We might have been able to have one on New Detroit. If we were very lucky.* The planet had already reached the legal population limit that had been established by the Imperium for a planet that size. No one wanted to live on an overcrowded world, and there was no need to with all the planets opening up in the Empire. Child bearing licenses were hard to come by, when the only births were replacements for those who died or emigrated, and people lived a long time in this day and age. For a couple like Cornelius and Katlyn the possibility of having children was remote, and they would probably have to wait decades for the chance, if it came.

"Not that New Detroit was awful," said Katlyn, a little bit of homesickness in her expression.

No, thought Cornelius, nodding his head. *New Detroit was not a crowded slum. There were plenty of green spaces in the cities, and a lot of parkland outside of them.*

"But I so glad that we came here," she said, a smile stretching her face that had that motherly glow on it. "To make a new start for our children."

"Then I'm glad we came here too," said Cornelius, pulling her in and holding her tight. "I…"

The barking of the dogs picked up in tempo, and Walborksi looked back to the camera and cursed. Something big had backed into the fence, while something smaller darted around it. He let go of

Katlyn and ran back into the house, grabbing his rifle and cursing again this damned planet he had brought them to.

Chapter 18

In some ways naval operations are much like those in the pre-radio wet water navies of old Earth. We have no way of communicating with ships on patrol other than by courier. A crisis can occur within the Empire, and ships may not receive the news from days to weeks after it happens, sometimes months. Strikes may be launched that occur after peace has already been declared. Which is shy it is so important that commanders have the ability to think for themselves, and still know that there are consequences for failure.

Lecture at the Imperial Naval Command College,
Year 812.

"Sir, we're picking up traces in hyper VII," said the tactical officer, looking back at the captain's station.

"ID?" asked Captain Horace La Blanc, leaning forward in his command chair, wondering who would have hyper VII ships out here in the middle of nowhere. *Definitely not ours,* he thought, running through what he knew about local naval dispositions in his mind. *All of ours would be on the other side of the kingdom, and the Imperials and Republicans most probably wouldn't have anything this far out of their space.*

"Can't confirm ID, sir," said the tactical, a frown on his face. "They resonate like nothing I've ever seen. And there are four of them, sitting there in hyper VII like they're lying in wait."

But for what? thought the Captain of HICS (His Imperial Czar's Ship) *Majestic. It couldn't be us, could it?* *Majestic* had been escorting this convoy for over two weeks, and the Captain wondered what might be going on that he didn't know about.

Pirates were always a very real danger out here in the wilderness that existed between New Moscow and the rest of the *civilized* star nations. But pirates would usually operate ships in the frigate to destroyer range, and hyper VII was really beyond their means. He didn't think pirates would challenge his convoy, not with an escort of a heavy cruiser and three destroyers. That left the possibility of the Klang, who had been known to attack heavily escorted convoys with their *Raider* class ships, which were peers of the human heavy cruisers. But VII was beyond them as well, unless some fool had gone and sold them the technology.

"They're translating," called out the tactical officer, his eyes widening. "Down to VI. They've dropped off the plot."

The Captain let out a sigh of relief. Off the plot meant that they were still some distance away. If he had a purely military formation he might be able to evade them before they came back into detection range. But with merchies and liners to guard he didn't really have a hope of that. And their own velocity was point eight c, about as much as he could push the civilian ships, unless he wanted radiation breakthrough of their electromag shields.

"Keep a close watch, Lieutenant," he told the tactical officer, transcribing a message for the com to send to the convoy. He had to hope that the unknowns would go away, or would prove to be no match for his own firepower if they closed. *And what are the odds of that?* he thought.

*   *   *

"Maximum acceleration toward the last contact,"

ordered the Ca'cadasan pod leader, Llillissarada'ing, turning a baleful glare on his helmsman.

"Yes, my lord," said the crewman, pushing claws into control holes on his board. The four million ton warship leapt forward as her grabber units gripped the fabric of space, building up acceleration until she topped three hundred gravities, killing her velocity on the old vector and curving her onto a new course. Her three consorts followed suit, and within a half hour the four vessels were on a straight line vector toward the prizes. *First glory goes to me*, thought the pod leader, his mind on the loot and intelligence that would be his to bring back to the fleet commander.

*   *   *

"We have movement," called out the tactical flag officer of the HICS *Champion*, sitting in normal space several light hours from the developing pursuit.

"What do you have?" asked Commodore Stephan Gunther, sitting in his commander's chair overlooking the battle cruiser's flag bridge.

"We were already tracking that convoy coming in from the Republic," said the tactical officer, looking back at the flag officer. "And then something came along in hyper VII. Within moments it dropped down into VI and we lost it."

"But you figure they're heading for the convoy in VI?"

"Yes, sir," said the officer, nodding his head.

"Any ID on the unknowns?"

"No sir," said the officer, giving a head shake. "They were like nothing I've ever seen."

The Commodore nodded and looked over at his navigation officer. "Give me a least time intercept that allows us the closest approach without giving ourselves away."

The navigator worked for a few moments, then looked back at the flag officer. "I can get us in front of them in IV," said the officer. "And they won't know we're there until we jump into VI."

"Do it," said the Commodore. "Send order to the captains of both of our consorts as to our intentions and their part."

The com officer nodded from his position on the flag bridge. Moments later the three battle cruisers of the patrol jumped up into hyper IV, their translation signals too distant to travel to any of the concerned parties. And twenty-four million tons of hyper VI warships made ready to get into the game.

* * *

"They're back," yelled the tactical officer.

Captain Horace La Blanc looked up from a flat screen he had been reading, catching up on his paperwork, the knot of fear in his stomach loosening now that the inevitable was happening. "Our friends?"

"Looks like them, sir," said the tactical officer. "Same resonance and all. I'm trying to get a fix on their acceleration."

Which could take several attempts in a trial and error solution, thought the Captain. *But they have to be hauling ass to have gotten into our observation range in less than half a day.* So much routine had happened in that time that some of the crew might have forgotten about the unknowns. But they had been on the Captain's mind the whole time.

"Initial estimates are three hundred gravities," called out the tac officer. "Velocity point nine two c."

"Crap," swore the officer. Both of those figures were outside of his operating range. His own warships might be able to get to point nine five c, but the merchies would never approach it. And the acceleration was well outside the limits of his warships. "What the hell are they?"

"Still unknown, sir," said the tac. "Like nothing in any of the databases."

"Com," said the Captain, looking at the tech manning that station. "Make sure that all of our charges are aware of what's happening."

"Aye, Captain," said the tech, getting to work on his board.

La Blanc followed the approaching vector arrows on the tactical board, trying mentally to force them to give up their secrets. They continued to maddeningly close without telling him what they were.

"Clarence is asking if we should scatter?" said the tech, looking back at the Captain.

"Hell no," said La Blanc, glaring at the man. "What the hell does that liner think he's going to do? The enemy will snatch him up in no time."

The Captain continued to look at the plot, calling up figures from the ship's computer in his mind. *They won't be in practical laser range for another eight hours, and extreme missile range in six. And extreme missile range really won't be that effective, now will it. Even if they get up to point nine five light, they will only be closing at point one five light. Definitely within our maximum engagement envelope.*

"Order all escorts to drop behind the convoy and form up as a screen," ordered the Captain. "Everyone to set ECM to maximum. No use letting them get free information about us." *And maybe we can spook them a bit if they don't know exactly what we are.* The Captain continued to stare at the plot, taking what hope he could out of whatever he could manufacture.

*   *   *

"We're within maximum missile engagement range, my lord," called out the tactical officer.

The pod leader grunted, running the figures over at his own station. There really was no such thing as a maximum range on the missiles in normal space. Only a maximum number of G minutes that they could boost, which could be used for acceleration, deceleration, and course change. The missiles could travel forever if they didn't hit anything, though it was always useful to have a terminal boost near the target to compensate for any evasive maneuvers. And of course as the missiles got closer to light speed the boost would start reaching the diminishing returns due to relativity. In hyper the limit was the power supply of the missile, and how long it could power the hyperdrive to keep it in the strange dimensions.

"What is the probable makeup of that group?" asked the pod leader, looking at his screen and all the noise of jamming that his own sensors were trying to fight through.

"There appear to be fourteen vessels," said the tactical officer, looking at his screen. "Ten in the two million ton and up range, one slightly smaller, and three much smaller."

"Ten cargo transport ships and four escorts?" asked the Captain, looking at the officer's figures on his own screen.

"That's my guess as well, pod leader," said the officer, tipping his head in agreement.

"Fire a volley," ordered the pod leader. "Let's see if we can stir things up a bit."

Each ship released twenty of the hundred ton missiles from its tubes, pushing them out at high acceleration through a magnetic system. As soon as they cleared the vessels they boosted with their own eight thousand gravities of acceleration, and eighty missiles were on their way toward the convoy.

*   *   *

"We have missiles on the plot," yelled out the tactical officer at the same moment the red vector arrows appeared on the tactical screen.

"Why the hell would they fire them from so far?" asked the Captain, looking at the arrows and trying to get them to give up their information. These missiles had to carry their own hyperdrive to move through this kind of foreign space. His ship only carried a couple dozen of those kind of missiles, while the destroyers carried ten each. And here this enemy was wasting what? Fifty or sixty missiles? More? And they were still a couple of light hours distant. If they were depending on radar or lider to pick up those projectiles they would still be waiting for almost two hours to get a return. Not that those energy beams would be able to travel that far in hyperspace. But the missiles were putting out their own gravity waves, which traveled through the hyper VIII band and could be picked up by other hyperdrive systems like those on his ships.

"Computer estimates eighty missiles," yelled out the tactical officer. "Accelerating at eight thousand gravities."

So they have better acceleration than ours, and a greater energy storage capacity, making them what? Thirty years our superior? Better? And then the thought struck him that they might be facing someone they had hoped to never face again.

*   *   *

"We are picking up the intruders again, sir," said

the tactical flag officer, while the vector arrows appeared in the holo tank.

The entire area across multiple dimensions was portrayed in the tank for all the flag staff to look upon. The flag bridge was designed slightly differently from that of the Terran Empire ships that the battle cruiser was modeled on. But it still incorporated the same technology. Maybe a year behind the state of most Imperial vessels, but no more than that. And *Champion* had the best tech in the Fleet.

"Any identification on them?"

"No sir," said the tactical officer, fingers flying across his board while he shook his head. "They're moving at a good clip. And from our information that they were using hyper VII I don't think they are any kind of pirate."

"Navigation," said the Gunther, looking over at that officer. "How long till we need to jump."

"One hour, fifteen minutes," said the officer. "Up to VI and full acceleration will get us to the convoy in about seven hours. Of course the intruders are going to know where we're at as soon as we go up to VI."

"That can't be helped," said the Commodore, taking a pull on the pipe he had been holding. "With luck they won't be able to change vectors fast enough to avoid us. And they damned sure won't be able to get back into VII at their velocity." *And if they can we're in real trouble.*

*   *   *

"Missiles incoming," shouted the tactical officer.

La Blanc nodded his head and followed the plot of the missiles. They were tearing in a point nine light, but with a differential of only point one. The three destroyers were cycling their hyper-countermissiles out, taking the enemy birds at maximum range. He had dropped *Majestic* back behind the rest of the convoy, backing up the tin cans while hoping that nothing invisible came at them through hyper. Theoretically impossible, but something that wouldn't surprise him too much on this day.

Majestic bucked as she sent five of her own hyperdrive missiles back at the enemy. Essentially these missiles were decelerating, losing velocity so they could fall back toward their targets. They would have very little closing speed when they approached, and would probably prove to be easy targets. But they might give him a little more information on the enemy capabilities.

"Enemy appears to be four large cruisers in the four million ton range," yelled the tactical officer. "Velocity now at point nine five light and holding steady. They will be in effective laser range in about two hours."

The Captain thought about what he had heard, wracking his brains for a way out. Any way that might get his command out of what looked like a hopeless situation. With sixteen million tons of warships gaining on him, and he had a bit over two million tons of lower tech vessels to oppose them. It might sound good to die in battle, to go down upholding the finest traditions of humanity and the fleet. It was another thing to actually fight in a situation that would see the death of his command and the civilians they were tasked at safely moving from points A to B. Instead they would die at point Hell.

"We have translations ahead," said the tactical officer, his shoulders slumping as he looked wide eyed back at the Captain.

"What are they?" asked the Captain, feeling

hopelessness come over him as well. *As if we aren't outnumbered badly enough already.*

"Computer is still firming up their ID, sir," said the officer, his tone telling that he didn't expect good news. The officer then surprised everyone by whooping and yelling, thrusting both hands into the air. He turned back toward the Captain, a smile on his face. "Three Kingdom battle cruisers," announced the officer in an exultant voice. "Three Goddam eight million ton battle cruisers."

"And when will they get to us?" asked the Captain, his mind grasping at the possibility of salvation and trying not to reject it as a bad joke.

"We will intersect in three and a half hours," said the navigation officer, her face downfallen.

And we will be wreckage by that time, he thought, looking around the bridge, from face to crestfallen face. *So they can avenge us. Still not what I want to hear.*

"Listen," he said to the bridge crew, squaring his shoulders. "We're going to drop back and engage the enemy. I know we aren't in the same weight class, but if we don't do something those ships will catch the merchies before they can be covered by those battle cruisers."

The Captain could see the fear on the faces of the crew, and he hated that he had increased that fear. But it had to be done, or they would all die. There was no way he could leave the merchies and make a run for it, so that left two options. "Com. Contact the destroyers and let them know of my intentions. I would appreciate if they would stay close and guard us while *Majestic* attempts to take out the enemy flag."

"Aye sir," said the com tech, working at his board.

"And tell the merchies to run like hell, and to keep

on running."

*   *   *

"We are picking up translations to VI," said the tactical officer to the pod leader. "Three ships."

"And what are they," said the Ca'cadasan leader with a toothy grin.

"They appear to be in the eight million ton range," said the officer. "Similar resonances to the warships in the convoy. They are accelerating toward us at two hundred and sixty gravities."

"Primitives," said the pod leader in a scornful tone.

"That is a lot of tonnage, my lord," said the tactical officer, lowering his eyes to the floor in an attitude of humility to a superior.

"And we have a surprise for them, do we not?" roared the pod leader, standing from his seat and taking a couple of steps toward the viewer. He stood there staring for a moment, bottom hands clasped behind his back, top hands on his hips. The bridge crew was silent, knowing better to disturb the lord and master of the vessel when he was in an attitude of thought.

"My lord," said the tactical officer, risking interruption. "Some of the enemy vessels are decelerating?"

"Why would they do that?" asked the pod leader, giving the officer an intense look. "Which ships?"

"The warships, my lord," said the tactical officer, staring at his screen. "I have no idea why they would do such a thing."

"He must be planning to engage us, my lord," said the helm, earning a glare from the tactical officer. "That way the other ships can get to the newcomers and possibly gain protection."

"And why would he sacrifice his military vessels to

save some commercial ships?" asked the tactical officer. "Surely they can't be an altruistic race. Not to have survived this long."

"Perhaps there is something of great importance on one of the commercial ships," suggested the helm. "That would explain his actions, would it not?   I suggest that we blow past his warships and take the commercial ships."

But if I do that I will be engaged in combat with the newcomers, and have the convoy warships coming up my tail, thought the pod leader. "I want us to match velocities with those warships dropping back. We will take the information they have by force, and let the other group worry about the commercial vessels and the larger warships."

"As you command, my lord," said the helm, setting his board, while the com officer relayed the command to the other three ships in the pod.

The tactical officer grinned as he glared at the helm. The pod leader saw this and grinned himself. As long as there were rivalries on the bridge, no one would think to challenge for his position. He checked the tactical plot one more time and gave a satisfied head shake. The newcomers would be out of the fight for quite some time, and he would take those warships for his glory and the glory of the race.

*   *   *

"The *Majestic* and her destroyers are decelerating toward the enemy," called out the flag tactical officer, looking back at the Commodore.

"Good boy, La Blanc," said Commodore Stephan Gunter under his breath, looking at the holo tank, then out over the large flag bridge of the *Champion*. *He's doing what he's supposed to, even at the cost of his command. I just wish we could get there sooner, but the laws of physics don't allow it.*

"When will we be in missile range?" he asked the tactical, checking the figures over his own implant.

"In approximately two hours, twenty-one minutes," said the tactical officer, his face a mask of concentration.

Crap, and crap again, thought the Commodore, shaking his head. If it had been normal space he could fire at much further range and hope that he got a hit. But in hyper he had to worry about the ability of the missile to generate the field that would allow it to stay in hyper. Otherwise it would fall back to normal space before it got to the target.

"As soon as we have the range and a solution fire," said the Admiral to the tactical officer. "Relay that order to the Captain and the other commanders of the squadron."

"Aye, sir," said the officer, his fingers hitting his board as he sent out the command on the squadron tactical net.

Gunter continued to look at the holo that showed the green arrows of the merchies heading his way, and the vector arrows of their escort heading away. Right at the angry red arrows of the enemy.

*   *   *

"We have missiles on the way," yelled out the tactical officer of *Majestic*.

La Blanc cursed under his breath as he watched the red vector arrows appear on the holo. At first there were only a few, and the sensory suite had difficulty picking them out as they clustered together. In a few moments the weapons had separated enough for the system to get a good estimate, and the arrows multiplied until there were eighty of them heading his way.

"ETA fifteen minutes," said the tactical officer. He glanced back at his board as klaxons went off through the bridge. "We have light amp energy coming in. *Smithers* just took a major hit to the stern."

The captain looked over his link and concentrated on the two hundred thousand ton escort, watching as hull metal bubbled away and atmosphere gushed out. The destroyer slanted away for a moment, pushed by the jet of gas, before she righted herself.

"All ships," yelled the Captain, even as laser light hit the stern of his vessel. "Reorient and place all power to forward shields. Evasive maneuvers."

The acknowledgements came quickly over the com circuit, and the ships spun in place to put their more heavily armed bows toward the enemy, all the while shifting back and forth in space to present the most difficult target to ships that could only see them ten minutes in the past.

"All ships," yelled the Captain again. "Flush all hyper missiles at the enemy. Let's get them out while we still have them."

Again acknowledgements came over the link, and green arrows sprouted on the holo.

Majestic fired the last fifteen of her hyperdrive missiles, while the three destroyers each fired all six of theirs. Thirty-three missiles came out of tubes, flipping on their own hyperdrive generators prior to leaving the fields of the vessels firing them. They oriented for just a second, locking onto their targets, then accelerating away at five thousand gravities.

The sweating bridge crew waited for the enemy missiles to arrive, watching as their own moved closer to the enemy.   At long range the countermissiles launched, what remained of those with their own hyperdrive fields.   In a few seconds all of those were gone, and the seventy-five surviving enemy missiles came through.   There were no short range hyperdrive counters, they didn't exist, and none of the projectile weapons were of any use knocking missiles out of hyperspace.   As soon as the projectiles left the field of the firing ship they were gone as if they never existed, dropped back to normal space.

Lasers cycled now, reaching out and spearing at the enemy missiles. About thirty fell off the plot, destroyed by light amp weapons or knocked out of hyper by damage to their systems.   The rest came in.   One destroyer caught a direct hit that blasted her from space.   The other nine targeted on that ship lost lock and tried to acquire another target. All failed, and sailed on through space, to eventually drop out as they ran out of energy.   Another destroyer suffered devastating damage when four missiles went off close enough for proximity kills.   The hyperdrive failed and the ship translated catastrophically back into normal space, a total loss of ship and crew.   The third destroyer came through the barrage alive, but in no shape to fight.   She retained enough generating capacity to stay in hyper, and that was all.

Majestic was able to take out most of the fifteen missiles heading her way.   Three lost lock and missed entirely, while four went off within close range, damaging the outer systems of the ship with floods of heat and radiation.

Le Blanc cursed as the holo died.   He waited for several minutes before it came back online, just in time to show his missiles dying on the defenses of the enemy. Two went off close to enemy ships, but if there was any damage, he couldn't tell at this range.

"Light amp hitting us and *Stogans*," called out the tactical officer. "Shields are down on the section being hit. Rotating ship to bring working plasma shields in line."

And that will only delay the inevitable, thought the Captain, watching the tactical display as his ship traded gigawatt laser blasts with four ships, each of which out massed his by more than double. And showed no degrading of their light amp capabilities.

*   *   *

"They're taking a pounding," called out the flag tactical officer, watching the holo that was showing what had happened over an hour ago, but seemed like the here and now to the crew.

The Commodore shook his head as he chewed on his lip. There really wasn't anything he could do about it. But he cursed the Universe and the laws of physics that there wasn't. *But when you get within our laser range you'll eat death, you faceless suckers.*

"We're in missile range," yelled out the tactical officer. "All ships are launching a volley of hyper capable missiles."

Champion shuddered slightly underfoot as the ship let loose a volley of ten of the larger hyper capable missiles. A half minute went by and the ship shuddered again, releasing another volley of ten missiles. The green arrows started to separate from the battle cruisers, sixty missiles moving toward the enemy. It would take them a little over two hours to get to the enemy, and the Commodore was sure the game between them and *Majestic* would be done by then.

*   *   *

"She's helpless, my lord," said the tactical officer, looking back at the pod leader.

The larger of the alien vessels was centered in the viewer. Her hull was a wreck, holes and gashes all through her. There were several deep punctures where lasers had eaten deep into the vessel.

"As far as we can tell the ship has no operational weapons on her hull," continued tactical.

Maybe I should send you across on the first shuttle so you could make sure, thought the pod leader. He gave his head a negative shake. That would be a waste of ability. The officer wouldn't be where he was if he wasn't competent at his position.

"What about the smaller vessel?" asked the pod leader, switching the view to the destroyer, which floated on the screen in even worse condition.

"I don't think it has anything of value," said the tactical officer, pointing a clawed upper hand at the wreck. "It…"

With a flash the destroyer was gone, catastrophically translating back into normal space. Now there would surely be nothing of value on the vessel, which would only exist as small bits of rubble in a swirling cloud of atoms and molecules.

"Send the assault force to the last enemy vessel," said the pod leader, glad that he hadn't had men aboard that other ship. "Immediately."

"It shall be done, pod leader," said the shaken looking tactical officer. "It shall be done."

The pod leader smiled and looked back at the holo plot, watching as the green arrows of assault shuttles appeared. *I don't blame him for being shaken*, thought the pod leader. Unintentional translation was a seldom seen hazard of traveling in hyper. Unless there was combat involved, in which case it became very common.

*   *   *

"We have assault shuttles approaching, sir," said the tactical officer, looking with bleeding face at the Captain.

"Thank you, Mr. Suarez," replied La Blanc, looking through the faceplate of his battle armor. The bridge looked like that of an intact ship, being as it was in the relative protection of the forward central capsule. Everyone was still armored up, that being the regs for combat. The tactical officer and some other bridge crew were injured when a missile almost hit the ship and rocked it beyond the capacity of the inertial compensators to take up all the force.

"Prepare to repel boarders," said the Captain over the intercom. "All crew, prepare to repel boarders." He knew the small company of marines aboard was already equipped for that task. They were assigned damage control during combat, but would carry their assault weapons in case the enemy tried something like they were doing now. The rest of the crew would now be heading for weapons lockers, supplementing their standard side arms with something a little heavier.

"All bridge crew to the defenses," said the Captain, looking around the compartment at the men and women he was so used to working with. "Mr. Suarez," he said to the tactical officer. "Ms. Doblas," he said, looking at the helm. "The two of you draw assault rifles and come back to the bridge. I will need you here."

The two frightened looking officers nodded their heads and turned to leave. *I know how they feel,* thought the Captain. *But we have our parts to play, and the show must go on. All the way to the final curtain.*

*   *   *

"The humans fight hard, my lord," came the voice of the marine Sub-commander though the link, while the pod leader looked at the video feed. There were several armored Ca'cadasan forms lying on the floor of a large chamber, and a couple of smaller four limbed creatures in what looked to be a heavier armor. "The ones that must be their marines of course fight much better than the spacemen. And they have a much higher quality combat armor. In fact, all of them have better armor than do we."

The pod leader gave a head nod of ascension before realizing that the officer on the other end wouldn't see it. He felt a bit of anger at the assertion that marines were better at close in combat than spacers, before laughing at the feeling. It was true. Marines were better trained for that kind of combat.

"How many casualties have you sustained thus far?" he asked the officer, watching as the feed moved, showing a scene of battle on the far end of a corridor.

"I have fifty-one killed," came the voice of the Sub-commander, emotion overlaying the words. "Another one hundred and twelve wounded."

"I'm ordering another company sent over," said the pod leader, making a head motion toward his marine liaison to carry out the command. "You must take that ship as soon as you can. And any prisoners you can gather."

"Prisoners are hard to come by," said the Sub-commander. "We are fighting in vacuum most of the way, and our sonic stunners are not operational in such conditions. And their armor is too good for any other nonlethal methods to be effective."

"Do your best, Sub-commander," said the pod leader, wishing that what the man was saying was not true, but knowing that it was.

The pod leader switched his view to that of one of the troopers. It was as if he was riding on the shoulder of the man, watching from the point of view of the crouching marine as he moved through the too low corridors. *Why can't we find other races on a scale with ourselves*, thought the pod leader, letting out a frustrated breath. *It's nice to be physically superior to most. It's not so nice to always have to be crouching and crawling on ships we take.* But there was really no help for it, unless they trained other species to fight for them. And the Ca'cadasan Empire did not trust any of their subordinate races enough to train and equip them to be soldiers.

A trooper to the front went down, a line of holes showing through his armor, dead eyes behind a spawled face plate looking up at eternity. A line of bright pinpoint explosions moved across the far end of the corridor, the Ca'cadasan marines firing back with micro-grenades. A larger explosion blotted out the transmission for a second. When the video came back a wall of the corridor was shown to have blown out. The view changed as the trooper moved forward, then changed again as he landed on his belly to return the fire of the indistinct figures that appeared ahead.

"We have missile launch from the newcomers," called out the tactical officer. "ETA fifty-four minutes."

"Time to laser range?" asked the pod leader, delinking from the trooper.

"Twenty-eight minutes, my lord."

The pod leader slammed his fist on the arm of his chair. They needed to take that damned ship and strip her of information quickly. Damned quickly, or the opportunity would be lost.

*   *   *

"Captain," came the call over the com link. "They're right outside the bridge. I don't think we'll be able to stop them."

"Very well," said La Blanc, giving the other two officers on the bridge a hopeless look. "Do your best. We'll get the final response ready."

He looked at the tactical officer and helm and gave them a tight smile. "Time to do it, boys and girls."

The two nodded and turned back to their boards, while the Captain called up his. He could see his officers' presence on his board, and knew when they had accomplished what they needed to do when their symbols went from green to red. He keyed in his own codes and received acknowledgement from the computer.

"It has been a real privilege serving with officers such as you," he told the two, his finger poised over his board. The door to the bridge blew inward. A couple of seconds later a huge six limbed figure in battle armor came through that door in a crouch, rifle held in his lower arms, what looked like a grenade launcher in his upper pair. *It is them*, thought the Captain, staring at the creature and watching that large rifle start to track on him. He pushed the button and killed them all.

The ship of course had a self-destruct system, which depended on the matter-antimatter engines blowing. That system had been damaged to the point of being inoperable. But in hyper there was another way of almost insuring the same thing. There was a statistical chance that a ship could survive a catastrophic translation back to normal space. About five percent. And even that would get the *Majestic* away from the ships that were trying to capture her. They would have to slow down to translate down to her, and then boost back, which could take days. All this went through the Captain's mind in his last few seconds of life.

*   *   *

"They're translating back to normal," called out the disbelieving voice of the tactical officer.

The pod leader cursed as he watched the human ship on the viewer. It was blurring along the edges as its matter interacted with space that abhorred that matter, the sign that the hyperdrive field had been deactivated. And then with a flash the ship was gone, no longer in this dimension. And with it the over four hundred marines that had gone aboard her.

The pod leader slammed his hand back on the arm of his chair and screamed. *So close.* They had been trying for some time to capture a human military ship and get intelligence on their tech. And so far they had come up short every time. The humans had well developed policies to keep that from happening, and had so far the Ca'cadasans had not been able to get enough surprise on their side to take one of the enemy vessels. *Well, maybe we can get one of the newcomers,* he thought, dismissing that notion as soon as it came.

*   *   *

"Majestic is gone," said the flag tactical officer in a low voice.

Commodore Stephan Gunter looked up at the viewer as soon as those words registered. The plot showed the enemy ships, four big red arrows centered in the tank. And not a trace of green. "At least we can avenge you," said the Commodore, thinking of the people he had known on those ships, particularly the Captain of the *Majestic*.

"We have translations," came the voice of the tactical officer through the Commodore's thoughts.

"What are they?" he asked, his heart racing.

"Same resonances as the enemy," said the tactical officer, his voice breaking a bit. "Three of them. And they're big. Over twenty million tons each."

"Heading?"

"Toward us," said the white face officer. "At three hundred gravities acceleration."

And Commodore Stephan Gunter realized that avenging the other ships would have to wait, till he saw if he could get his own ships out of the trap they were in.

Epilogue

"Your majesty," came the voice of his personal secretary over his com link. "High Grand Admiral Lenkowski requests permission to speak to you."

Such high sounding titles, thought the head of the New Terran Empire, chuckling softly. But they had seven flag ranks in each of the two services, and six in the Imperial Marines. Admiral and Field Marshal just didn't cover everything.

"Put him through," said Augustine, sitting at his desk and waiting for the link. The holo came to life on his desk, and he found himself looking at the aging but still vigorous man that was his Chief of Naval Operations, as high a rank as was to be had in the Fleet.

"Len," he said, studying the troubled face of the officer. "What do you have?"

"Nothing good, your majesty," said the soft spoken officer in his New Texas drawl.

"The Lasharans?"

"Them and some others," said the officer, taking the pipe from his mouth and blowing out some smoke with each word. "We have a lot of movement along the frontier with Lashara, which is never a good thing. The units there are on orange alert, and we're calling up reserves in ordered stages. I think the attack is soon to materialize."

"And the other news?" asked the emperor, knowing that the frontier in question would always be a problem he wished he had never inherited.

"More ships have disappeared in Sector Four," said the Admiral, his intense eyes gazing out of the holo. "And not just merchies either."

"So what do you have?" asked Augustine with a sinking feeling.

"We had several ships around the frontier disappear, never reaching their scheduled stops, same as before."

"Crap," said the emperor. "Any chance of making them convoy."

"Not without a declaration of war," said the Admiral. "You know how thick headed those merchie captains can get. And that's not the worst of it," said the Admiral, grimacing. "We're also missing a scout team. That's a light cruiser and three destroyers, and almost fifteen hundred naval personnel."

"Double crap," said the emperor, slamming his hand on his desk, and hoping the secret service didn't take alarm like they always seemed to. "Any chance they just found something and continued to go looking?"

"There's always a chance of that, your majesty," said the CNO, nodding, then taking a puff on his pipe. "Remote, as they had orders to be at Conundrum HQ a week before this report was sent, but always a chance."

"So you think something is going on in the sector we should be alarmed about?" said Augustine, disturbed that something might have happened to members of his Fleet, satisfied that the evidence was beginning to arrive to support his speculations.

"Just as you thought, your majesty," said the older man, clamping the pipe in his teeth. "I think our old friends are scouting us out. There have been more reports coming in from squadrons catching contacts with ships in VII. I think we could use some more VII ships in the sector, but they're still pretty rare in the Fleet."

"Well, you have my permission to move as many in as you can get away with," said the Admiral, nodding. "And keep moving those reinforcements into the sector. I'll handle any flak from Parliament. They can't fire me, after all."

"No, sir," said the Admiral with a smile. "They surely can't do that.

"Thanks, Len," said the emperor with a smile. "I need men like you. Remember that. And my heirs will need men like you, if something happens to me."

"Anything I should know about?" asked the CNO, his brows narrowing.

"No," said Augustine, not wanting to burden the man any more with his dreams. "Nothing. Just know that I depend on you, and want you to carry out my wishes to the best of your abilities. Just as you always have. I'll see you in my office tomorrow evening for our weekly meeting, after we get back from the *Donut*. Augustine out."

The emperor stared at the dead holo pad for a moment after breaking the connection, wondering what the information from Sector Four meant. It could be the threat he was dreading. It could be something else. But he thought it prudent to bet on the worst case and be pleasantly surprised if it didn't materialize.

Later that evening he took in the star fields that always brightened the skies of even a well-lit megalopolis like Capitulum. The Supersystem sat near to many brilliant nebulas, the remains of stars that had been blasted out of existence by supernovas. Scientists still could not explain how some of those stars had exploded, they being too light to go out that way. But they had, explanations or not, and some found that troubling as well.

Anastasia came out onto the veranda, walking up to Augustine and sliding onto his lap. He put his arms around her, enjoying the soft feel of his wife and Empress. She looked into his face with a frown on hers.

"You look like you have the weight of the Universe on your shoulders," she said, running a finger across his lips.

"Only the Galaxy," said the emperor with a smile. "Nothing so weighty as the entire Cosmos."

She leaned into him and kissed him on the lips, looked him in the eyes, then kissed him again. "You will make it through this. And when we are old and gray we will look back and laugh about how it seemed like such a hopeless time, while we look upon Dimetre as he prepares to take your place."

Augustine felt a chill run down his spine at those words. He did not think it was going to happen. Any of it. Not his seeing old age. Not his eldest son becoming emperor after him.

"You look like you could use some distraction," said the Empress, stroking her hand across his face.

"I could at that," he said with a smile. "What do you have in mind?"

She leaned in and whispered into his ear, and his smile widened. He stood up from his chair, easily lifting her with him and walking back into the palace.

Above the cold stars looked down upon the empty veranda. Including those that looked through the improbably nebulas that had once been the home stars of the Empire of the Ancients, the original Elysium Empire. They looked down in warning about what happened to another people who dared to fool with powers beyond their comprehension. They looked down on a new people, who had no idea what that warning was.

The End

Excerpt from Exodus: Empires at War: Book 2

"Ring is at full power," called out a Petty Officer from his station in the control chamber. "Matrix is fully charged and there is ninety-nine percent feed from the couplings."

"Check, sir," said Gorbochav from her station. "All systems within parameters."

"Are all ratings at stations?" asked Lt. SG Romanov from his post.

"Yes sir," called back the chief. "All armored and ready to go. Repair robots ready as well."

"Missile impact in eight minutes," called a voice over the link.

The Prince allowed himself to meld into the ship for a moment, looking at the now unblocked tactical display. A hundred red arrows moved toward them, while dozens of green arrows reached out to them.

"Lieutenant Romanov," came a voice he didn't recognize from behind. Turning in his couch, the Prince found himself looking at two battle armored marines. One had gunnery sergeant's stripes on his helmet and armored chest. The other had corporal stripes and carried a shipboard assault rifle.

"What can I do for you, gunny?" he asked, a sinking feeling in his stomach.

"Captain's orders," said the NCO. "You are to accompany us to the bridge."

The damned bridge, he thought, looking in disbelief at the man. The Captain was going to save him no matter what, and not allow him to comport himself like an officer of the Fleet.

"Now, sir," said the gunny, his hand on the butt of a sonic stunner that was holstered at his side.

"We'll take care of it sir," said CPO Gorbachev, giving him a tight smile. "We'll make you proud."

Sean nodded his head and ordered the couch to release his suit with a thought. The Corporal moved aside as he came up to the Sergeant, who led him from the chamber as the Corporal fell in behind.

They entered the lift and Sean turned toward the doors as they closed. He stared ahead without a word. The Captain's word was law on the ship. And the marine professionals were bound to obey that word, no matter the protests of a junior officer. No matter his family. So he would not accomplish anything by protesting to them. Threatening them. Attempting to bribe them.

"Missile impact in six minutes," came the voice over the net with infuriating projected calm. The Prince called the tactical plot up in his mind as the lift moved downward fifty meters, reoriented, and sped away along the central conduit of the ship.

In his mind he was watching the red arrows moving closer. And the green arrows reaching out to them. The first dozen of those arrows were within fifteen seconds of the incoming war birds when they showered space with a cascade of energy. Blinding the incoming missiles on all frequencies, throwing off their targeting systems. The red arrows bored on ahead, toward the target that they could no longer see, but which was entrenched in their inertial systems.

As the enemy missiles passed the jammers they reacquired the battleship and plunged ahead. That was when the first wave of offensive missiles reached them and detonated in space. Not interceptors, they had still been targeted on the incoming missiles and had done their best to find them and kill them. They turned to bright expanding dots on the display, and four of the red arrows disappeared. A second wave of missiles, these from the destroyer, detonated two light seconds behind them and took another three missiles off the board.

The lift came to a stop in the center of the mid-ship central capsule and the doors opened. The hallways were completely empty of crew, everyone gone to their duty stations. The Gunnery Sergeant gestured toward a door set into the bulkhead across from the lift. There were a pair of marine guards stationed outside the door, sitting in acceleration couches within recesses and holding shipboard rifles in their armor gloved hands. The gunny stopped in front of them and gave them a code word.

"In you go, Lieutenant," said the marine as the heavy doors to the bridge opened.

Sean gave him an angry look that seemed to slide off the man, not a bit of concern showing in the marine NCO's eyes. *With a hundred missiles coming in I'm probably the last thing he needs to be concerned about,* thought the Prince as he walked in the door.

"Missile impact in five minutes," came the calm voice over the net.

All of the bridge stations were manned with space armored officers and crew. Despite the environmental control most of them were sweating, and Sean could feel the fear in the room. The same fear that was twisting at his guts as the enemy missiles bore in. But everyone was going about their duties efficiently, training taking charge in the stress of the moment.

The Captain gestured the Prince over and waved at one of the two empty acceleration couches on either side of his chair. The extra chairs for the XO and a visitor. He was the visitor to the bridge, and the XO would be down in the Combat Information Center (CIC) in another capsule of the ship. Both the heads of the ship, primary and auxiliary, in the most protected portions of the heavy vessel.

Sean fell back in the seat and felt the latches attach to his armor, holding him in place. The Captain was subvocalizing orders and did not look like he would brook a disturbance at this time, so Sean held his tongue and looked around the large chamber.

"Prepare for emergency military boost," came a calm voice over the com. "Emergency boost in ten seconds."

The marines had already scrambled from the room, heading for their emergency stations. Their armor would move them through the increased gravity of the boost even if they felt like they were about to fall. It was still safer to be in a couch.

Sean looked up at the ceiling overhead, the meter thick chunk of alloy containing wire runs and pipes that fed the bridge. He thought of the outer skin of the ship, ten meters of ceramic, carbon fiber and hard alloy armor, with a meter thick layer of nanoliquid between the two sections. The nanoliquid would fill and seal any holes punched through that strong mass. Then there were tanks of liquid, stores, and two hundred meters of whatever else the ship might have before the five meter thick armored skin of the central capsule. Then hundreds of meters of ship before the bridge, located in almost the exact center of the capsule, just above the central umbilical. A lot to punch through to get to this protected spot. And something that was all too likely to happen if they were pounded by those following missiles.

Just then all thoughts fled as a giant hand seemed to push him back into his couch. The ship went to two hundred and sixty gees, five above the capacity of the inertial compensators, and the crew felt as if they were on the surface of a superheavy planet. Sean forced his lungs to work, as his armor pulled outward with his breaths to increase the force that his poor muscles were trying to exert. He gritted his teeth as his vision started to blur. Then his implanted systems came online and forced the blood flow through his veins, feeding his brain the needed oxygen.

"It's a pure bitch," came the voice of the Captain through his com circuit on a one on one link. "I hate it. But every little bit of accel might make the difference."

Sean tried to nod his head but it wouldn't move. He looked at the tactical in his mind's eye again, seeing the ninety three remaining missiles meeting the first wave of interceptors. On one view arrow met arrow and seven of the red arrows disappeared. In real space view seven bright points blossomed as fast moving matter met fast moving matter, and antimatter containment breached. And eighty-six red arrows continued to gain on them.

More objects appeared on the plot as decoys were released that would attempt to mimic the signals and sensor profile of the battleship. Each boosted away at the same accel as the battleship and tried to lure missiles toward them. Some succeeded for a while, pulling a couple of dozen missiles off the kill track. Of those about ten lost lock permanently, while the others reacquired after a few moments of continued seeking.

A second wave of interceptors contacted the incoming, taking out eleven of the remaining seventy-four, leaving sixty three coming in at over point five c.

A third wave of interceptors hit six more, leaving fifty-seven screaming in silently through space.

Close range interceptors started cycling from the ships as fast as they could launch, putting multiple hundreds of the small missiles in space. Box cells on the hull released another hundred interceptors. Fifty-seven missiles became forty-eight, then forty-two, then thirty-seven. And then they were within the close range envelope and boring in on the battleship, which had terminated all forward boost and was getting ready for the end game. The ships began to swerve and jerk in random directions as they released another wave of decoys. Everything from large terawatt lasers to fifty millimeter cannon filled the space behind the ships as they attempted to bring the swiftly maneuvering missiles into their firing arcs. A dozen missiles exploded, then five more, two colliding with each other in their maneuvering. Twenty missiles continued in, three more picked off by close in weapons.

Then the destroyer made the ultimate sacrifice, as it was supposed to. Sean felt his mouth form a scream his lungs could not support as the two hundred thousand ton ship pushed at over three hundred gees into the path of several of the missiles. One hit the bow, followed a ten thousandth of a second by one to the stern. The ship vaporized in an instant in a blinding flare, which expanded again as the antimatter breached containment. Six closely following missiles were caught in the expanding cloud of debris and pummeled, their own velocity breaking them apart through the cloud in a series of bright flares.

Nine missiles made it through the thinning barrier, locked onto the battleship. Close in weapons fired a furious cloud of metal, knocking out three more that detonated close enough to put heat and radiation into the outer skin of the ship. Six closed on the ship, four sure to make contact and shatter the capital ship and its precious cargo.

The *Sergiov* jinked in three directions within a millisecond at two hundred and eighty gravities. Sean felt his stomach turn and felt the beginning fuzzy daze of a concussion as his brain rattled around in his skull. But three of the sure hits were thrown off the strike. They detonated at closest approach, two within a hundred meters of the battleship. Sections of the thick hull were breached by heat and radiation, alloys vaporizing and gassing into space. Atmosphere followed the gaseous metals, until the nanoliquid within the hull filled the openings and hardened. The two outliers also went off, adding their radiation from ten and thirty kilometers respectively.

The last missile was hit by several rounds from close in weapons and an ejecting plate of hull metal in the last ditch defensive system. That missile broke up and detonated within milliseconds, sending a wave of material particles into the hull at point five c. Several of the larger particles penetrated the hull and projected deep into the ship, and the vessel shuddered under the impact.

Klaxons sounded as the damage reports came in over the net. One hundred sixty-four killed. Another fifty-two injured. Several grabber units put out of action, as well as many close in weapons and a half dozen counter missile tubes. The most serious was the damage to the port stern missile magazine, which was now jammed beyond immediate repair. The missiles could be shifted to other magazines as space became available. And fortunately none of the warheads had been damaged within their shielded compartment, or that side of the ship might have been a total wreck.

"Nothing else approaching," called the tac officer over the circuit. "We got them all."

"Or they about got us," said Captain Ngano, a slight smile on his face.

Sean saw the smile, thought about the dead crew, and was within an instant of yelling at the man. Then he caught a look at the Captain's eyes and realized that the man was in pain at the loss of crew. And at the loss of the escorting destroyer and all aboard her. And that the smile was the relief that any human might feel at still being alive.

"I am sorry, my Prince," said the man, looking straight into Sean's eyes with an expression of sorrow. Sorrow at something else. "I will explain as soon as we are back to emergency boost.

"Slow the ship to normal acceleration," ordered the Captain. He switched to the all ship circuit and talked into the com. "All crew. Prepare to reenter the tanks. Emergency boost in five minutes.

"Get ready, your majesty," said the Captain as he sat up from his couch. The tanks were in the process of rising up from the floor, and the bridge crew were hurrying to get out of their armor. "I'll jack into your personal circuit once we are boosting. Then I'll explain it to you."

Sean nodded his head as he stood up and moved to an empty cubby. *Explain what to me?* he thought as he let the cubby pull the armor from him. He had a bad feeling. Whatever it was he wasn't going to like it. *And 'your majesty'*, he thought with a grimace. The Captain had always gone out of his way to not put a tag of birth on his young officer. It must be very bad indeed.

About the Author

Doug Dandridge is an ex-professional student with degrees from Florida State University and The University of Alabama, and coursework in Psychology, Biology, Geology, Physics, Chemistry, Anthropology and Nursing. Doug has an interest in all of the fantastic, including science fiction, fantasy and horror, as well as all eras of military history. Doug is a prolific writer, having completed 24 novel length manuscripts. He is still seeking a major publishing contract, but has decided that self- publishing is the way to go at this time. His work can be found on Amazon. Doug lives with his five cats in Tallahassee, Florida, and currently has no social life, as he is too busy writing around his work schedule.

Follow my many characters and settings at http://dougdandridge.net

Contact me at BrotherofCats@gmail.com

Follow my Blog, Doug BrotherofCats Dandridge at http://dougdandridge.com

Made in the USA
Lexington, KY
03 June 2013